Poison in Athens

Also by Margaret Doody

Aristotle Detective
Aristotle and Poetic Justice
Aristotle and the Secrets of Life
Mysteries of Eleusis

MARGARET DOODY

Poison in Athens

arrow books

Published by Arrow Books in 2005

1 3 5 7 9 10 8 6 4 2

Copyright © Margaret Doody 2004

Map designed by Christopher Heim

Margaret Doody has asserted her right under the Copyright, Designs and
Patents Act, 1988 to be identified as the author of this work

First published in the United Kingdom in 2004 by Century

Arrow Books
The Random House Group Limited
20 Vauxhall Bridge Road, London SW1V 2SA

Random House Australia (Pty) Limited
20 Alfred Street, Milsons Point, Sydney
New South Wales 2061, Australia

Random House New Zealand Limited
18 Poland Road, Glenfield
Auckland 10, New Zealand

Random House (Pty) Limited
Endulini, 5a Jubilee Road, Parktown 2193, South Africa

The Random House Group Limited Reg. No. 954009

www.randomhouse.co.uk

A CIP catalogue record for this book
is available from the British Library

Papers used by Random House
are natural, recyclable products made from wood grown in
sustainable forests. The manufacturing processes conform to
the environmental regulations of the country of origin

ISBN 0 099 46833 6

Typeset by Palimpsest Book Production Limited,
Polmont, Stirlingshire
Printed and bound in Great Britain by
Bookmarque Ltd, Croydon, Surrey

In the name of Praxitiles
and all innovators of vision and the visual
this book is dedicated to
my dear nephew Eamon, the artist.

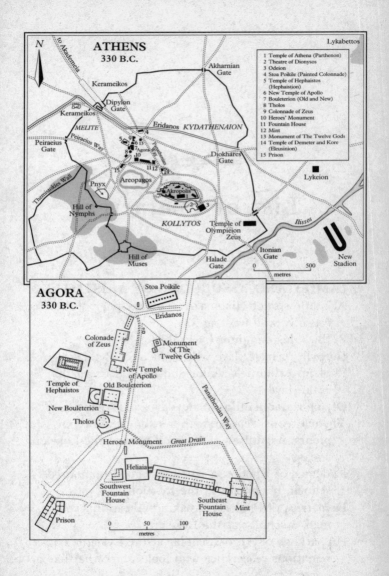

ATHENS
330 B.C.

N

to Akademeia

Kerameikos

Akharnian Gate

Dipylon Gate

Kerameikos

MELITE

Eridanos   KYDATHENAION

Peiraieus Way

Peiraieus Gate

9 13
5 6
8 7 Agora
10
11 12 14

Diokhares Gate

Themistokles Wall

Pnyx

15

Areopagos

Akropolis
1
2
3

Hill of Nymphs

Lykabettos

Lykeion

KOLLYTOS

Temple of Olympieion Zeus

Ilissos

Hill of Muses

Halade Gate

Itonian Gate

New Stadion

0   500
metres

1 Temple of Athena (Parthenon)
2 Theatre of Dionysos
3 Odeion
4 Stoa Poikile (Painted Colonnade)
5 Temple of Hephaistos (Hephaistion)
6 New Temple of Apollo
7 Bouleterion (Old and New)
8 Tholos
9 Colonnade of Zeus
10 Heroes' Monument
11 Fountain House
12 Mint
13 Monument of The Twelve Gods
14 Temple of Demeter and Kore (Eleusinion)
15 Prison

AGORA
330 B.C.

Stoa Poikile

Eridanos

Colonade of Zeus

Monument of The Twelve Gods

New Temple of Apollo

Temple of Hephaistos

Old Bouleterion

Panathenian Way

New Bouleterion

Tholos

Heroes' Monument   Great Drain

Heliaia

Southwest Fountain House

Southeast Fountain House   Mint

Prison

0   50   100
metres

List of Characters

FAMILY AND ASSOCIATES OF ARISTOTLE

Aristotle son of Nikomakhos: philosopher of Athens, recently widowed, age 54

Pythias: his daughter by Pythias, age 6

Herpyllis: female slave who looks after Pythias, age 22

Phokon: Aristotle's senior and most trustworthy male slave

Olympos and Autilos: male slaves of Aristotle

Theophrastos: scholar with a strong interest in plants; Aristotle's right-hand man at the Lykeion, age 40

Eudemos of Rhodos: a witty and good-humoured scholar, important in the Lykeion

Demetrios of Phaleron: strikingly beautiful young man, a scholar at the Lykeion

Hipparkhos of Argos: scholar at the Lykeion, conscientious researcher who looks somewhat like a horse

FAMILY AND ASSOCIATES OF STEPHANOS

Stephanos son of Nikiarkhos: citizen of Athens, nearly 26

Theodoros: Stephanos' younger brother, not quite 10 years old

Eunike daughter of Diogeiton: Stephanos' mother

Smikrenes: irascible farmer of Eleusis area, father of Philomela

Philomela daughter of Smikrenes: intended bride of Stephanos, age 15

Geta: slave of Smikrenes, Philomela's old nurse

Philonike: estrangd wife of Smikrenes, mother of Philomela; a bee-keeper in Hymettos

Philokleia: mother of Philonike, grandmother of Philomela; manager of family farm in Hymettos

Dropides: Philokleia's second husband, a confirmed invalid

Mika: slavewoman at Hymettos farm

Nikeratos: old school friend of Stephanos

FAMILY OF ORTHOBOULOS

Orthoboulos: wealthy citizen of Athens, widower who embarks on a second marriage

Krito son of Orthoboulos: eldest son, age 17

Kleiophon son of Orthoboulos: second son, age 14

Hermia: Orthoboulos' second wife, widow of wealthy Epikhares

Phandemos son of Diyillos: Hermia's uncle; historian and expert in religious observances

Batrakhion: hunchbacked slave of Phanodemos

Kharis daughter of Epikhares: Hermia's only child by her first marriage, age 5

Kyrene: slave from Kyrene in Libya, nurse of Kharis

Marylla: beautiful slave from Sikilia, once shared between Orthoboulos and Ergokles

Butler: aged slave in Orthoboulos' house, formerly in house of Epikhares and Hermia

OTHER CITIZENS AND INHABITANTS OF ATHENS

Philinos son of Philinos of Kephisia: handsome citizen, one of Orthoboulos best friends

Ergokles: snub-nosed citizen who prosecutes Orthoboulos for malicious wounding

Manto: female keeper of a brothel

Meta: Manto's forewoman

Kynara: slave prostitute, *porne* in Manto's brothel

Klisia: long-necked, thin girl, slave *porne* in Manto's brothel

Kybele: girl with large bosom, slave *porne* in Manto's brothel

Tryphaina: keeper of a very expensive brothel

Thisbe of Thebes: flute-girl, slave *porne* attached to Tryphaina's brothel

Kleoboule: witty slave *porne* who works in Tryphaina's brothel

Phryne: high-class hetaira, the most beautiful woman in Athens

Lykaina: a hetaira, daughter of Spartan mother from Kythera

Euboulos: well-born young man who assists at a revel in Tryphaina's brothel

Kalippos of Paiania: young man from the country who attends the revel in Tryphaina's brothel

Aristogeiton: a man of Spartan habits and ideas who wishes to cleanse Athens of its impurities

Hypereides: well-known and popular orator, age 61

Theramenes: agent of Aristogeiton, seeking evidence in prosecution of Phryne

Arkhias: an actor from Italy, also a spy and finder of fugitives under patronage of Antipater

Khryses: goldsmith with artistic pretensions

Hermodoros: citizen with philosophic pretensions

Myrtilos: a young citizen, befriended by Hermodoros

Praxitiles son of Kephisodotos: elderly but enthusiastic sculptor

Timarkhos son of Praxitiles: apprentice sculptor, assistant to his father

Sikon: burly slave with a brand and iron collar, attendant on Lykaina

Ephippos of Lykabettos: charcoal-burner and fuel-seller, with mules for rent

Akharnaian magistrate

CONTENTS

Hear me, O Apollo, lord of light, I pray, and dispel all that is dark and without reason, all that makes for secret death. Let light illumine Athens my city. O sombre Melpomene, Muse of Tragedy, assist me that I may tell in fitting manner this dark tale of secret venom and desperate acts.

Yet let me not omit to raise prayers in thanks and praise to great and glorious Aphrodite, laughter-loving, the golden one, and to call to my aid bright Erato, for whom the lyre sounds the notes of love.

I

Agents and Mechanisms

'There is a trial coming up at the Areopagos,' Aristotle
said. 'I believe you might like to go. A case of malicious wounding – could be interesting. To be sure, at
first glance it is merely the case of a couple of citizens who fought in a brothel over a concubine.'

'This really isn't good enough,' I said – inappropri-
ately. Perhaps I didn't really want to think about
Athens' most ancient and most important court of law,
after my experience of the Areopagos a few years
before. But it was true that this meal warranted an
apology. We were sitting at dinner in my *andron*, the
nicest room of the house; this room reserved to men
served as our dining-room, as is right when one has
guests from outside the family. From a child I had
thought of this space as our 'best room'. Yet now I
could see that my *andron* looked shabby, the paint on
the walls chipped and dulled. There was a little crack
along one wall. Some table-legs were unmistakably

dusty, and there were other little symptoms of a lack of sharp-eyed housekeepers.

Now that I was seriously thinking of getting married, the defects of my housekeeping were more visible – and more vexatious. It occurred to me – too late – that I should not have invited the Master of the Lykeion into my house to dine with me. At this time, the late spring of the year before my strange journey to the East, Aristotle's wife Pythias had not been very well. So it had seemed a kindness to offer him a meal. Aristotle's wife was merely expecting a baby, but matters were not proceeding as well as they might, and Aristotle was slightly worried. It had been my intention to cheer him up. I had also dutifully invited Theophrastos, Aristotle's right-hand man. How fortunate it was that the solemn and fastidious Theophrastos had declined; he was within the city walls, but visiting another former student.

My invitation had been issued on the spur of the moment, without home consultation on my part. I was paying for having forgotten that my mother's absence left an uncaptained kitchen. My mother Eunike daughter of Diogeiton had gone to our farm for a few days, obtaining the benefit of some fresh air (and the opportunity to look into the ways of all the servants and the stores). Mother, a widow for some three years, could be gently agreeable or gently complaining, but she had her formidable side. My father Nikiarkhos, well-born but not of the most wealthy, had managed to spend a great deal of money before he died, relatively young; our family was in a more precarious financial position than I should have wished. Therefore it was a pity that my mother's family were not better off, as well as aristocratically proud of their direct descent from Athens' founder Erektheus. Of course, everyone in Athens – except foreigners like Aristotle – is descended from Erektheus or Theseus or Orestes. But not everyone can trace the lineage exactly as my mother's family claims to do, or inherit the capacity to tame snakes. It was too bad their branch of a distinguished family had omitted to give me any powerful male relatives.

Mother has never (as far as I know) tried to tame snakes, but she could do it if she had to. She is certainly capable of keeping the household servants in order. Yesterday, however, she had taken our two best slaves into the country with her – so I realized belatedly. And I had no turn for housekeeping. Though at this point, as marriage was contemplated, it had crossed my mind that I ought to start taking more interest in our household. Such good thoughts had not borne fruit as yet, at least on this evening. Not only had I forgotten to do any marketing myself, but I had not even really ordered it specifically to be done. We were left to the mercy of what the house had to provide, according to the judgement of the one remaining servant, most inefficient of the slaves.

The offerings for the evening proved to be a very watery and tepid soup, dry bread, three very small dried fish accompanied by a little celery (surprisingly flabby with age); to finish with, there were a few nuts and dried figs. It was spring, just turning into summer, and one could hardly expect the best fruit quite yet, but surely something better could have been offered than these dusty-looking figs and some aged walnuts that had seen much better days. Moreover, even to bring this modest meal to the *andron* took an unconscionable time. If only those two slaves who had gone to the farm for some fresh supplies had returned in time for dinner! Our remaining servant had never found kitchen work his strong point. The wine was served in an old chipped jar, with two cups that did not quite match.

'I will be better off,' I remarked, 'when I have more slaves. We need more household help. How I wish the dinner would cook and serve itself!'

'You are not the first to wish that,' Aristotle remarked. 'You remember what Homer says in the *Iliad*, describing the god Hephaistos at work in his house of bronze. Hephaistos made twenty tripods designed to run about on gold wheels, so they could go in or out of the great hall of the gods by themselves, merely at his wish: "a wonder to see". Homer certainly thought it would be splendid to have objects self-moved, acting spontaneously! That's why he gave that gift to the gods.'

'It would certainly save us a world of trouble,' I remarked.

'Ah, yes – what a different world it would turn out to be. If the shuttles shuttled back and forth at the loom by themselves, or the plektra could play the kithara on their own – why then, masters of crafts would have no need of workmen, and no master would need a slave. Slavery would vanish. The world would be utterly changed.'

'But that won't happen. We all need slaves as our

tools. And after all, in Homer the things are being invented — they aren't quite ready. We don't actually see the magic tripods, just brawny lame Hephaistos, sweating among his anvils and bellows. A poor condition in which to meet the goddess Thetis when she comes to see him!'

'An acute — and polite — observation.'

'Those self-moving tripods,' I continued, 'are not as interesting as the other self-movers that Hephaistos made. The figures of gold in the shape of young girls.'

'Quite so. And here he has reached a high point, as you indicate, for these golden handmaidens have *minds*, as well as being able to move on their own.

"In their minds is understanding and reasoning power, as well as speech and strength."

'To create objects that can think and speak seems more wonderful than to make things that merely move. Really godlike creation. Though these lovely metal maidens are a supplement to his weakness. They support his limping steps by holding him up on each side.'

'Almost sad,' I remarked idly. 'Girls of metal might not be as nice as those of flesh. Perhaps the limping god made them because he lived with golden Aphrodite, who ignored him.'

'How brilliant you are this evening, Stephanos,' Aristotle teased. 'As you say, Homer shows us very vividly the lame god working and sweating. His skill in creating self-moved servants, even these metal slave girls who understand human speech, has not brought him leisure. Nor happiness.'

'But it cannot happen to us – we are not gods. We have to depend on workers and slaves.'

'True enough. Although in all mechanical arts we have improved over time, and invented new instruments, yet we still need tools capable of rudimentary thought. And slaves supply us with that. Useful possessions, living tools not of metal but of flesh and blood, acting out the will of the master. Slaves are the best mechanisms, active and versatile, under another's control. Animals and men are the only real automata, the only things that truly move by themselves, of their own will. By "self-moving", however, we customarily mean beings that move according to choice and will. Slaves are not truly "self-moving" in that sense, as we own them, as we do a hoe or a lamp – or as Hephaistos owns his tripods. Free men alone are truly self-movers.'

'Unless you count things like the little puppets that some folk put on shows with. I used to love those when I was a little boy – I *believed* they could move.'

'I enjoyed them, too. The best ones work on a cunningly wound spring. But few artificial things are lifelike. No one is really deceived by a statue. At least, not since Daidalos, who according to legend made statues so lively they had to be chained to prevent their running away. But things don't move of themselves.'

Just as he said that, my knife fell on the floor. 'Sometimes they seem to do so,' I pointed out.

'Random Chance as a self-mover? An agent without choice,' he mockingly agreed.

We were laughing a little over this, when I heard someone at the front door. My least efficient slave added poor portering to his other acquirements, and I heard him stumbling along the passageway, and then yelling to me.

'It's someone as wants to see Master Aristotle,' he bellowed. 'You want I let her in?'

As it was evident from the sound of brisk sandalled feet coming to the door that he had done so, there seemed little to say. The door was flung open by an unknown attendant carrying a lantern, to serve the person who walked in. A woman. She was veiled, as a lady must be, and covered with a light cloak, so finely woven that it made her appear like a lady of high rank.

'You have come to see Aristotle? Who are you?' I demanded, rising. I felt slightly annoyed by this unexpected visitant – the more as I knew no ladies with well-woven cloaks would come calling here for my sake. This woman's garb was modest and all-concealing, yet there were shining subtle threads at its edging, and the weave was in a wavy pattern difficult to execute. Through all this muffling apparel, it could be seen that the newcomer was a small-boned little woman, very slender, yet not short. Her dress, visible in part under the cloak, had a saffron threading woven into it, a touch of golden light upon the light brown of the soft wool. She seemed so fine and so well-off that her first words came as a shock.

'Oh, please! We have such trouble. Please, good sir – Aristotle – help me.'

'And you are——?'

'Marylla. A woman of Sikilia. The slave of Orthoboulos.' She slowly raised both hands – slim

hands with long fingers – and removed her veil. The
sight was very pleasing. A delicate face, wide at the
temples and coming to a perfect little point at the chin.
This sweet face was set off by the short curls around
it, curls the colour of dark honey. The face's owner
looked at us out of great deep-grey eyes. Her hair was
cut short, indicating her position as a slave, and the
absence of gold jewellery also indicated that she was
not a citizen woman, nor even a freed person. This
lovely creature looked at us beseechingly. These grey
eyes focused on Aristotle, and she knelt to him, and
tried to grasp his knees.

'You – please! You are a great rhetorician and a
cunning man of logic. You can save me from the
torture! And save my master from confusion and loss
– even to the loss of his whole estate!'

'Ah! Marylla. I have heard of you.' Aristotle pulled
her upright. 'The concubine, the bone of contention.
But I do not see clearly what you wish from me—'

'I pray you, come and talk with my master
Orthoboulos. His enemies have pressed and persecuted
him, now Ergokles accuses him of a serious crime.
Some of his best friends have dropped off, a few of his
associates now throw their favour to Ergokles. My
master has saved me and all of our household from
being witnesses – saving us from torture! But
Orthoboulos must endure the trial at the Areopagos
in a short time. His opponent presses him very hard.
He has a favourable witness in his good friend Philinos,
but we don't know how able Philinos will be in actually speaking. Orthoboulos must handle it all himself.
Please come and help him. You have great learning in

argument and persuasion. Discuss his speeches with him—'

'I might be willing to do so. But why does not Orthoboulos ask me himself?'

She flung out a hand with a despairing gesture. 'Because he is proud. He is not the sort of man to ask for help. But we are worried. Philinos' mistress Lykaina has let on to me that she knows Philinos too is worried about how this case will go. Orthoboulos is not vain, but he is well-born, and has pride. Like all gentlemen, he needs to feel he can manage his own affairs. But I heard that you were within the city walls this evening, and have come to plead. I know you would not be rebuffed, if you came. *Please!*'

Aristotle pursed his lips and nodded slightly. 'I think,' he said, 'you could tell Orthoboulos straight away that I am going to drop in on him this evening, on the chance that he might be at home at that time. In short, I will come after I have finished dining.'

It seemed kind of him to give this description to partaking of my wretched dried fish and figs. The woman, with profuse utterances of thanks, sprang to her feet.

'You will help him – help all of us! The gods reward you! I shall take no more of your time. Forgive the intrusion.' She vanished with remarkable celerity, before we were tired of looking at her, in company with her light-bearer.

'What a household!' I commented. 'Where even the slaves have slaves.'

'She is a mistress as well as a slave, I think. Some men insist on bringing their sexual lives into the home scene, which causes difficulties in the household. Though such a weakness is the less censurable in Orthoboulos' case. He is not married, but a widower. This lovely creature commands her master's bed, most probably, and his heart – or at least some of his money. That cloak she wears is of the first quality. That simple tunic is very fine – with saffron-coloured threads cunningly worked into it. "Robes richly and colourfully wrought, the work of Sidonian women." You have brought Homer to my mind and he won't go away.'

'She speaks with an odd accent.'

'Marylla is a Greek-speaking Sikilian. Yet there is about her more than a dash of Karthago. There are many colonists of Karthago along the shores of Sikilia. And in the wars in Sikilia the Greeks have taken Punic captives.'

'A girl of gold – but flesh, not metal. Tell me more about this Orthoboulos who keeps such a pet at home. I think my father knew him, but I do not.'

'Orthoboulos is the defendant in the trial at the Areopagos,' Aristotle said. 'Of an old Athenian family, he has been one of the Athenian patriots, somewhat hostile to Makedonia. He is, however, a patriot in a calm and moderate fashion. He might be won over to support Makedonian rule – in a temperate way. Orthoboulos does everything moderately and temperately, which makes this serious charge against him – assault, malicious wounding – the more surprising. I should like to aid him, now he has deigned to ask for my help. I had already wished to go to the trial to find out if he got fair play. But of course *I* cannot officially attend a trial before the court of the

Areopagos. I am one of the foreigners who has to stop at the barrier. So – I want you to go. I am not a citizen. *You* are.'

'I suppose I should go,' I sighed. 'Since that case of my own, when I had to defend my cousin on a charge of murder, I am not over-fond of the court of the Areopagos. Still, if Orthoboulos was a friend – or something like one – of my father, I ought to show up for his trial.'

Orthoboulos had been an associate of my father – at least, at one point he had lent my father money. That, unhappily, had been true of most of my father's friends, as I had discovered when I tried to disentangle his affairs after his death.

'A good sort of man,' commented Aristotle. 'Orthoboulos might have some claim to be called "a great-souled man". A rich man who is not mean. He has performed liturgies, given benefits to Athens. He would much rather give a favour than take one.'

'A man of importance,' I agreed.

'And Orthoboulos has at least one thing entirely in his favour – he possesses the kind of deep, slow, important voice that does well in a lawcourt. So far in the preliminary hearings he has refused to give way on the point of having his slaves as witnesses.'

'So I suppose his household slaves haven't had to be tortured – not yet, anyway.'

'Exactly. This woman's testimony would be desirable, and it is true his opponents will press him hard. It is something of a degradation for a man to yield on such a point, I grant you. The citizen who can keep his own slaves from getting tortured always looks stronger than the man who gives way. But Ergokles has a case, and I daresay he will make the best of it, even without evidence extracted from Orthoboulos' servants.'

At this point in our conversation Theophrastos arrived, a tall man, oblong in shape and always somewhat stiff. He was ready to walk back to the Lykeion, but I had to invite him in. I always found Theophrastos, so unbending and such a precise speaker, rather a strain to talk to, and on this occasion I was also embarrassed at his seeing the remains of my poor dinner. Theophrastos followed the Pythagorean doctrine, at least as far as not eating flesh of any kind was concerned, but I could not fancy that he would have found pleasure in the flabby celery. As the plate of musty figs and nuts was still with us, I had to offer it to him, for hospitality's sake, but was not surprised when he declined to become involved with these old fruits of another season.

'We were just talking of Orthoboulos' trial,' Aristotle said, kindly diverting Theophrastos' attention.

'Athens has a lot of courts and trials,' I remarked. 'I wonder who thought of them, and why it works that way.'

'That's the kind of thing that my scholars are studying now,' exclaimed Aristotle. 'You should come and discuss it with them. At the Lykeion. It is good to have one place separate from the pressures of the agora, the assembly or the law courts, in which such matters can be fully discussed, bringing knowledge to bear rather than passion or interest.'

'I miss the philosophical conversations,' I admitted.

'What I should like to know, really, is this: what is the happiest life for the individual and for his city? How should a man live and what should laws be?'

'Indeed,' said Theophrastos, 'you ask questions that are not small! These matters certainly concern us at the Lykeion.'

At this point there was a further diversion as my young brother Theodoros took it upon himself to join us. He had been supposed to eat apart in the *gynaikon*. A boy child of only ten years, he was of the age to be kept in the women's quarters – so everyone thought but Theodoros himself. Some men invite their children in to entertain visitors (and attract gifts) after dinner, but I do not approve of this practice, and it was not my intention to introduce Theodoros. He was too young to join in men's talk. But now that we were finished the actual business of eating, he had made bold to enter. He had no qualms about helping himself to one of the questionable figs, nor about joining in the conversation.

'I know what you're talking of,' he said. 'The trial. The big case. Ergokles says Orthoboulos attacked and wounded him. The boys were talking about it at school. Does someone found guilty of attack and wounding have to *die*?'

'No,' said Aristotle slowly. 'But his estate is in question. He could lose everything he has.'

'But not be put to death?' Theodoros sounded almost disappointed. 'People who are sentenced to death – they have to take poison. Up there in the gaol, just at the corner of the Agora. Not far from us. One of the older boys told us about it – his father was one of the Eleven and had charge of the prison once. The gaoler brings hemlock poison to the man who is to die. The man drinks the hemlock. It tastes very nasty! Then he coughs and turns blue and goes stiff.'

'That was how Sokrates died,' Aristotle said sadly. 'I know a great deal about that. Plato, my teacher, who adored Sokrates, was not there at his death. I think he was too upset to go, though he said he was ill. But I have heard about the event from a few people who were there, including the once-beautiful Phaido, who like Plato was so young when Sokrates died that he survived well into my own time.'

'What do you know? Please tell me!' said Theodoros. 'Why was Sokrates killed? And who was Phaido?'

'Sokrates was executed because he was found guilty of impiety – and corrupting the young in his teaching. Phaido was a disciple of Sokrates, a very young one. Plato in his narrative has Phaido give the account. Actually, Phaido lived for many years to tell his story himself, and not just as he is made to speak by Plato.'

'How exactly did Sokrates die?' Theophrastos was curious to hear gruesome details, and Aristotle replied before I could reprove the boy and turn the topic.

'He was in prison. People had tried to get him to consider escape. It was a refutation of the charge of impiety that he accepted his sentence with religious tranquillity and did not let it alter what he thought or believed, even while he sat in a prison cell, in chains and awaiting death. It was very hard for the great philosopher's friends to believe they were really going to put Sokrates to death, but when they came one morning they found it was so. They not only wept, as in Plato's story of the event, but several of them became sick to their stomachs, especially later when the hemlock was brought in. Sokrates, now freed of his fetters, talked of immortality and endeavoured to cheer his friends. Then he had an evacuation of bowels and bladder, and a bath, and put on clean clothing, before saying farewell to the women and to his children. After that, he sat among his friends until the poison came.'

Aristotle sighed, and then smiled.

'Sokrates was very brave, you know. He could have saved himself by running away (his friends had a plan for escape). But he refused. He emphasized that his remaining to accept Athens' sentence was his own will, his own choice. There is an example, Stephanos, of a self-mover!'

'Why didn't he run away? I would! Or if I couldn't, I would throw down the cup when they brought it to me,' said Theodoros with energy.

'The brave man accepts necessity, Theodoros. Sokrates was brave. He did not shrink from the very end. Some condemned persons put off putting the poison cup to their lips, and have feasts or even make love well into the night of their execution, but not Sokrates. The sunlight had not left the tops of the mountains, yet he refused to wait, and drank the poison. He conversed as tranquilly as ever, and walked about, and then lay down, soon unable to move. When the poison reached his heart, he gave a great convulsion and died, as the gaoler had predicted.'

Theophrastos sighed, while Aristotle gazed into the

distance as if he could see that spectacular sad scene.

'You should not dwell on that event,' I said gently. 'It happened before your time, long ago.'

'Time seems different to me, at my age, than it does to yourself, Stephanos. And I find much hope in Sokrates' end. For I believe it must be possible to find a good death.'

Athens' long-ago insult to philosophy in putting to death one of its most brilliant and outspoken citizens was depressing Aristotle's spirit. So I attempted to change the subject, if perhaps not very happily.

'Not everyone is executed in that way,' I explained to my young brother. 'Only Athenian citizens of good standing. It is of a piece with the fact that no Athenian can be flogged or tortured. Citizens do not inflict physical pain on each other, for we Athenians are not slaves. But other malefactors die more unpleasantly – nailed or stapled to a plank of wood.'

'I knew *that*,' said Theodoros, helping himself to a tired walnut left over from this meal of state. 'But I'd like to see the poison. There must be a lot of it in Athens – in the prison, I mean. Could anybody make hemlock poison?'

'The gods forbid! I hope not,' I said.

'I guess the prison *must* have a jar of poison in it,' persisted Theodoros. 'All ready. If the gaoler doesn't want to have to make it. They'd probably make Orthoboulos drink it, if he went about wounding people all the time.'

'Little boys should be thinking about their lessons and not of poisons,' I said repressively. 'Now, go, and ask the slave to see that you get to bed at the right time.'

'Your little brother is almost right,' said Aristotle, as Theodoros made his departure. 'Though the charge against Orthoboulos seems almost ridiculous, considering the circumstances of the alleged crime, the consequences could be serious. Orthoboulos could be banished, losing his citizenship. All his property, land and goods included, would be confiscated. He is evidently concerned, or he would not have sent Marylla in this roundabout way to ask my help. I shall explain later, Theophrastos, but I cannot go home yet.'

He rose and the two men prepared to depart.

'Yes,' said Aristotle, 'I shall call on Orthoboulos this evening, and if he is in the humour to bear it, we will go over his defence. A charge of malicious wounding is not to be trifled with. As the woman indicated, he could lose his whole estate – including the woman Marylla herself. If Ergokles succeeds in putting his case, that pretty Sikilian would at once be taken over by him as the rightful property of Ergokles.'

II

—————◦○◦—————

The Constitution
of Athens

I had dismissed Theodoros' question – 'Could anybody make hemlock poison?' as I realized this line of conversation could scarcely be pleasing to Aristotle. Sokrates' execution was not an old piece of history to the Master of the Lykeion. Yet Theodoros' curious question regarding hemlock remained in my mind, chiefly as I was irritated at not knowing how to answer it. I felt it my job to assure Theodoros that I knew practically everything. The problem returned to my mind some while later when I was at the Lykeion. By the term 'Lykeion', I mean not the general area east of the city walls so named, but Aristotle's own particular academy in that pleasant well-watered region south of the hill of Lykabettos, a flat area green and full of trees. Here boys can do gymnastics and young soldiers perform military exercises. Here Aristotle had established his school, and caused the buildings to be erected or improved; he was always adding to them, and to his book-collection. As a resident foreigner, a *metoikos*, Aristotle could not own house or land in Athens (which is why he could not have inherited Plato's Akademeia, even had Plato wished it). These buildings of his in the Lykeion area formally belonged to the state or to private individuals who 'lent' or rented them to Aristotle.

I was in the Lykeion talking with some of the scholars, enquiring about the best way to get to the island of Rhodes or Kos, since at that time it was evident that I might have to make a journey there. I was already aware of changes in the Lykeion since the days when I had studied there. Now Aristotle's senior scholars were engaged with him in a gigantic project of describing all the animals, sorted into categories.

Eudemos of Rhodos had received me cordially. I liked this handsome and debonair middle-aged man, one of the best talkers and teachers among Aristotle's scholars. Eudemos was accompanied by the extraordinarily handsome Demetrios of Phaleron, a youth of eighteen or nineteen summers. Demetrios, golden-haired and endowed with a perfect straight nose, had the kind of profile one associates with noble art. It was odd to find this beautiful young Athenian man so devoted to the Master and to the analysis of animal life, as well as to other forms of knowledge of interest to Aristotle. Hipparkhos of Argos was much less attractive, a serious young man with a face that always reminded me strongly of a horse.

'You should know,' Eudemos explained, 'that we do not work only on the nature and function of squid and bees. We have in hand a new work, a short treatise on the political nature and function of Athens. This may be the most immediately helpful to others when completed.'

'I thought Aristotle wrote the books, but you say "we". How do you write a book together?'

'Well, this book is largely the work of the scholars themselves,' explained Hipparkhos the horse-faced. 'We discuss it with Aristotle – and of course we are inspired by what he says. Then we collaborate, writing a rough draft, in pieces.'

'Difficult,' I remarked dubiously.

'Not necessarily,' said Eudemos. 'What Hipparkhos means is that individuals supply different material and we then pool our findings. After each section is complete we go over it again, reading aloud to detect errors.'

'There always *are* errors,' Demetrios added.

'Then, when it is good enough, we give it to Aristotle, who reads it himself, and adds his own statements and corrections, which we then incorporate. It is Aristotle's book about Athens – but basically ours, too. We are writing this short treatise in much the same way, you see, as we write the big books on animals.'

'Really?' I felt slightly affronted at Athens being compared to animals. 'I cannot imagine what such a book would say. And most of you are foreigners.'

It was true. Most of these scholars were from elsewhere – not Demetrios, to be sure, but Theophrastos and Eudemos, and even Aristotle himself. It seemed bizarre, the sort of thing foreigners would do, writing about Athens. My annoyance had made me speak impolitely. Eudemos saved the situation.

'Quite true,' he replied genially. 'That is one of the

reasons why we are writing it – so that foreigners may understand Athens and see its political excellence. Even Athenians do not appreciate fully what they have done and what they have constructed.'

'Is it a history?'

'No, not really. Though we do use the discoveries of historians – of whom there are many now. Phanodemos son of Diyillos, for example, is writing a huge book on the history of Attika. He spends much of his money on that, when he isn't sponsoring religious festivals.'

'The first part of our treatise,' explained Hipparkhos, 'supplies a short history, especially concerning the overthrow of the democracy under the Thirty Tyrants, and how it was regained. Aristotle thinks it is important for people to realize the dangers that a state is in without sufficient *balance*. The latter parts explain how the city functions.'

'Aristotle says,' Demetrios explained, 'that a good city-state has a vital function, just like an animal or a man. Its working parts act in harmony and make possible continued existence and activity.'

'Even though the state is an artificial animal,' interjected Theophrastos on entering.

I greeted Aristotle's solemn and square-shouldered henchman, before turning back to the matter under discussion. I wanted to be entirely clear about this book they were writing.

'This thing you call a constitution of a city?' I queried. 'That would mean – how the Ekklesia meets, and how laws are made.'

'Yes. And all the separate functions – the arkhons and the Prytaneion, the committees like the Grain

Guardians. The creation of a system that will not allow monarchy or dictatorship.'

'And also,' Theophrastos added, 'the efforts to keep a balance so that all demes are constantly represented, and to achieve a harmony so that neither the richest citizens nor the poorer ones feel excluded. We will display Athens' emphasis on Justice. A high idea. But it is realized through the plain workaday existence of specific laws, and through the existence of courts to which citizens have access.'

'And Aristotle believes,' remarked Demetrios, 'that we must not ignore the very plain and necessary regulations governing the city. We keep in mind the diurnal and common as well as the grand. For instance, the disposing of dung, human and animal, under the board of Town Regulators.'

'The regulation of the brothels comes under their jurisdiction also,' added Eudemos. 'And Aristotle insists that we include in our book even mundane laws like those concerning prostitution. Such as that no prostitute – including flute-girls and players on the psaltery and kithara – may charge more than two drakhmai for one night's service. And that if two men fall out over a prostitute, the officials will see that lots are cast to decide who has the right to her.'

'Trouble is, men don't call the officials in at such a juncture,' said Demetrios, with a disdainful laugh. 'Otherwise, Orthoboulos and Ergokles would not have come to fisticuffs in Manto's brothel.'

'But such a book as you describe – it's not of too much use, is it?' I wondered. 'For we Athenians already know all this sort of thing.'

'It *is* useful,' insisted Theophrastos, 'for one generation after another to be reminded as to the sources of the city's excellence. And our book on Athens will also be of great utility to other states.'

'Athens interests us *all*,' said Eudemos. 'Take myself, for example, a man of Rhodos. Athens offers Rhodos a powerful example. She has learned by experience what *not* to do — not to make rich men too powerful, for instance. And not to sway the masses by their emotions and short-sighted interests. Greed and short-term emotions — the poison of the good state! Now, in our day, the cities in Asia, newly liberated, are at last free to be totally Greek. They need not go back to governance by local tyrants. If we do a good job in creating this treatise, citizens of many cities can look into our book and see how they ought to establish themselves and make their laws.'

'Yes,' said Aristotle, entering unexpectedly. 'But, Eudemos, should we speak as if a constitution were something easy to *copy*? It is after all the work of men, in time. It is not an eternal and immortal entity, so merely to copy it would be a mistake. Isokrates, now,' continued the Master of the Lykeion, sitting down comfortably among his scholars, 'Isokrates said something exquisitely ridiculous! He said there are so many laws nowadays in all sorts of different states that all the new legislator had to do was to pick out the best ones and make those the laws of his city. Ridiculous! He might as well advocate taking the best points of an ox, a dog and a cockroach and putting them together.'

'We take your point, I think,' said Eudemos. 'Our description of Athens' constitution will be a guide, not a model to follow slavishly. The treatise will also remind Athens of itself, as a kind of mirror.'

'But,' Aristotle added, 'part of the value of our treatise – when it does get written – lies in the truthful account of what went *wrong*. I used not to think of history as very important. Now I do.'

'*I* still don't quite see,' said Demetrios, wrinkling his handsome nose, 'what history has to do with us. Philosophers should deal with first principles, and things like the True and the Beautiful.'

'Ah, that is very well, Demetrios, if one takes no interest in the life of the community as it really is. As soon as you do, you run into very practical considerations. A legislator must not only have a sense of the true and eternal – Justice and the Good – but must also have a practical experience. A knowledge of human behaviour and of this state's own past. It would not be possible to import the constitution of Athens, for example, and set it down exact and entire in one of the cities in Asia. Indeed, that would be most foolish.'

'Because with different peoples you have experiences and expectations, I suppose,' said Eudemos.

'Exactly. Athens' constitution has changed through time; much has resulted from errors – even violent errors – and mistaken experiments. If Athenians understand why and how things have developed as they have done, they will be reluctant either to rush into foolish changes, or to cling blindly to mere tradition. I most admire Solon, who showed that a balance must be kept between the forces of the poorer many and the wealthy few.'

'Never easy,' said Demetrios knowingly.

'No, indeed. He had all debt forgiven, so no Athenians remained in serfdom. But then he did not help the poorer sort to grab the land of the richer men. He says himself he doesn't approve of equal shares for all: "nor that low and noble might divide/In equal share rich soil of fatherland." The very wealthy hoped he would assist them in being the only power, but he did not. He looked to justice and a good balance. As he says:

> "Thus I mixed it well,
> One life and one justice alike, harmonious
> For needy and for wealthy both alike."'

'The search for Justice – undertaken in a practical spirit. That is Athenian,' said Eudemos thoughtfully.

'It entails change,' said Aristotle, 'as people investigate what they mean by Justice. At one time the General Council, the Boulé, had the power to order any Athenian's death. A man named Lysimakhos was once sentenced to death by the Boulé, but then a friend of his argued that it was not possible to put a citizen to death without a lawcourt. Not only did the court of law acquit this Lysimakhos, but the Athenians made a rule from then on that all punishments of citizens must be decided in a court of law.'

'The Athenians love their courts of law,' said Hipparkhos. 'You know what people say of Athenians: "They love a good dinner much better than a good battle, and a good long argument better than either."'

'Not true – most unfair!' I interjected.

'Justice – in real life – is a *search* for Justice, as Eudemos has just said,' Aristotle commented. 'Slow,

cumbersome, but vital. The rule of one man – king or
tyrant – or of a few rich and powerful people, like the
Thirty Tyrants, makes Justice impossible. The Thirty
Tyrants, a group of rich and very well-born men,
wooed the city at first by the promise that they would
make everything better. And then once they had all
the power given them, they didn't bother with law
courts any more, but sent their bravoes to kill anybody
whom they disliked – or whose property would be
worth confiscating.'

'Surely the law was against that!'

'People had been coaxed or coerced into giving up
the law. So in the end a thousand and five hundred citizens – at least – were killed, with who knows how
many others. Here we see the dangers of oligarkhy,
which are closely paralleled by the dangers of democracy. A majority can itself become a tyrant. It was the
democracy of Athens which decided to take away the
rights of other states in their League – who soon
revolted from their alliance. People can easily be swayed
by claptrap and emotion, whether in a court of law or
in a public assembly. We need to find some way to make
it unthinkable and indeed impossible for a majority vote
in the Assembly – or even in the Boulé – to overturn
a basic principle. For example, it should not be possible for an assembly to vote that the rule of law will no
longer apply – or that citizens can now be tortured.'

'Slaves must be tortured, however,' Demetrios
added, 'so as not to encourage them to foment dissen-
sion in the city. It is good for them to dread being
witnesses. If they did not fear all Athenian law cases,
they would have too much power over citizens! And

unlicensed foreigners, too, can be questioned by torture – as a means of control.'

'When we say torture, what do we mean, actually?' I asked. 'If it is for questioning, the questioner is not supposed to take life.'

'Certainly,' said Hipparkhos, 'all states employ torture as a reasonable way of enforcing the public will, and compelling witness and confession. Some forms of torture are quite mild – flogging, or pinching the joints with pincers. Some are more serious. The same inflictions may be used for punishment, or for questioning to find proof of a crime.'

'But Athenian citizens are not questioned by torture – not ever,' declared young Demetrios. 'That is essential to our true freedom. Is that not right, Aristotle?'

'Athens has something like a developing theory. All – all citizens – are to be treated alike—'

'But,' objected Hipparkhos, 'they do *not* treat everyone alike. It isn't just that the wealthier and better educated tend to rise to the top, most often – as they really should. Athenians don't treat foreigners the same as citizens.'

'You might as well add,' Demetrios laughed, 'that Athenians don't treat women and slaves as part of the one life, one rule of law.'

'Well, they do in a sense,' argued Eudemos. 'The women, under the rule of their men, participate insofar as they bring citizens into the world. They have their role – as citizen women. Athenian women, if accused of a crime, must be tried in a law court. As for slaves – *nobody* could argue that slaves could or should be treated the same.'

'Some say,' observed Demetrios, 'that all people in base mechanical trades — and money-grubbing commercial persons too — should also be without franchise and subject to different rules. Only the really well-educated men who have leisure to think and to reason should participate in the life of the state. Why should the ignorant and base create laws?'

'There is an argument for that,' said Aristotle. 'Plato has made it. Athens honours it in part — or did originally — by selecting those who might be elected arkhon only from members of the two top classes But it is too late now in Athens to institute such a drastic change as disenfranchizing all men who work with their hands or in trade. A change which I must admit would itself be in some degree against the whole spirit of Solon. Besides, how are you to prevent some of that sort — sculptors, for example — from becoming rich? Wealth will always have its influence. The aristocrats at first were the only rich men and great landowners, but wealth is no longer founded only in land.'

'Perhaps,' ventured Hipparkhos of Argos, 'the most successful way is the Spartan way. For the citizens do *no* base work of any kind — at least, before Sparta got so weak. Spartan citizens are warriors only. No buying and selling — no servile work. Their women don't even do housework! The Spartans early conquered the lands of Messenia as well as Lakonia, and forced the inhabitants to become helots. These folk were only their tools, and had no higher existence.'

'You forget,' argued Eudemos, 'how greatly Sparta depended on the small towns on their borders for trade and manufacture. And on ports like Kythera.'

'I suppose,' I hazarded, 'that warlike Spartans would have to have swords and shields manufactured in their own territories.'

'It is hard to know what Sparta can do now, after the terrible loss in the great battle, when King Agis was crushed by Makedonian forces,' commented Theophrastos. 'Spartan life will have to change.'

'They had the best, most enviable system, though,' urged Hipparkhos. 'Spartan men are all equal, all plainly dressed. No low traders. No rhetoricians, no money-grubbers. No frivolous display, not even in language – men of Lakonia are truly laconic. That manly system enabled Sparta to conquer even Athens for a while. Only recently did Messenia thrown off this yoke.'

'Yes, all very well – but you see the Spartans' system didn't last,' argued Aristotle. 'For one thing, they regulated the lives of their men, but not of the women. Women who can do as they please become luxury-loving and peremptory.'

'So,' enquired young Demetrios, 'lawgivers, you think, should pay special attention to regulating the manners and decency of the womenfolk?'

'Yes – and the Spartans failed to do so. But in any case Sparta can hardly be a model for a new state now. How difficult it would be now to find an entire population of serfs! Even Alexander in conquering Asia cannot do that. And Sparta lost its grip.'

'The Spartans educated their women, and gave them gymnastic training, just like the boys,' Demetrios remarked with interest. 'Imagine! Discus throwing and running races!'

'Indecent,' sniffed Hipparkhos. 'Other Greek women

are always covered. An Athenian citizen woman would *never* be seen naked – even by her husband. An Athenian husband must not ask to see his wife naked. Even during sexual congress she is not only allowed but enjoined to keep her breasts covered.'

'But these Spartan girls – they were supposed to be the healthiest and most beautiful women in Greece. Helen, whose beauty caused the Trojan war, was the most beautiful woman in the world.'

'Helen of Troy is only a character in a legend or story,' said Aristotle.

'Besides, Helen was an Argive, like me,' said Hipparkhos of Argos proudly. It occurred to me that if Helen had possessed the horse-face of Hipparkhos, there would have been no war at Troy.

'We are getting off the topic,' observed Aristotle. 'You see, Stephanos, why it will take us some time to produce our little treatise! I intend to write separately on Sparta. But here I cannot resist pointing out that in Sparta at least officially there was no prostitution. Of course the towns roundabout produced prostitutes – particularly since coin money had come in after long resistance to it. But at least Spartan cities were not crowded with brothels full of freed and slave *pornai* mingled together.'

'Yet,' said Demetrios, 'Athens' system is more sensible. There is sexual relief to be found in the brothels, but a citizen woman's sphere is strictly the household. Women in Athens rightly cannot own land or houses. And they are not supposed to conduct any business beyond the value of one *medimnos* of barley. Spartan women could be wealthy landowners, and that would cause trouble, besides making females arrogant and unattractive.'

'Yet the men would sneak off from their barracks in order to make love to these Spartan girls –'

'We really *are* wandering,' objected Aristotle. 'Though certainly the originator of the myth coupling Ares and Aphrodite was not unreasonable. All men who like fighting tend to fall heartily in love with either men or women, and to value sexual association. Aphrodite ought to love hard-working Hephaistos, but she always creeps over to Ares.'

'But what I would like to know,' I said, meaning it, 'is what is the best way for a man – a man with natural desires – to live?'

'Scholars, who are not servants of Ares, can give Aphrodite the nod and cross the road,' said Theophrastos, chuckling gently at one of his own rare jokes. 'Aphrodite need not meddle with *us*. Our treatise, as you see, Stephanos, is more difficult to write than we originally thought, as we so often digress. The Master himself is not guiltless,' smiling at Aristotle, 'for he insists on considering the political significance of old drinking songs and ancient ballads. But our book will be a fine and unusual treatise, offering a new and unique description of what a state is.'

'Of course Athens is the best of states, the model for all others,' Demetrios said proudly.

Aristotle smiled. With a nod to Theophrastos, he left the room as swiftly as he had come into it. I believe he went back to his house to see his wife Pythias.

'Theophrastos said a while ago that the state is an artificial animal,' I remarked. 'As if Athens were just a sort of puppet or doll with movable limbs. I am not sure people will like that.'

'Better, perhaps,' argued Theophrastos mildly, 'to be like an artificial being than an organism – a single organism. For all organisms grow cold and die sooner or later.'

'Why not just let Athens alone? People will like the books about animals better.'

'Books about plants too,' said Eudemos. 'You know that Theophrastos is taking all plants to be his province. We call him "Farmer Theophrastos".'

'Of course,' said Demetrios, 'he does have slave help, but he sows things himself, and studies them so intently! In fine weather, like now, it is hard to get him to leave his gardens. And we keep teasing him just to grow fresh lettuces for us!'

'So, Theophrastos,' I asked, 'is it your scheme to make a complete catalogue and account of plants? The way Aristotle – with his scholars – is doing for the animals?'

'Something like that,' said Theophrastos, almost bashfully. Like a boy complimented on his recitation, he blushed slightly and looked down. 'It sounds presumptuous, as there are so many plants in the world. Yet with regular effort and the methods that Aristotle has taught us – if the gods grant me a decent span of life—!'

'Theophrastos already knows a great deal,' said Eudemos.

'Well, then – you, Theophrastos, know what is poison and what isn't. Useful,' I agreed. 'As you know, my little brother was asking whether anybody could make hemlock poison, and I didn't exactly know the answer. I don't even know where the hemlock they use to put men to death comes from.'

'The best hemlock – the stuff used for that purpose you mention – comes from cold, shady and mountainous spots,' said Theophrastos, deliberatively. He settled back in his chair, putting his fingers together and speaking in a regular and thoughtful fashion; we gathered round like good students.

'So Thrasyas of Mantinea found,' Theophrastos continued, happily launched into his subject, and forgetting his shyness. 'The root is found in Mantinea itself, but the island Kyrnos, which is all wild mountains, produces the best. Even the honey from that island is supposed to be poisoned by contamination with the true *koneion*. A poison dose can be made fairly easily by those who know how to do it. With most vegetables, the fruit is stronger than the root, but not so with *koneion*. The best way of preparing it is to extract juice from the root. Take the rind or husk off. Cut up the root, thoroughly bruise the pieces in a mortar, then push it through a sieve. Pour the resulting pulp into some clean water. Juice of the root, especially prepared this way, not just shredded, causes a faster death – even a small dose. Thrasyas found out, and taught others, how to mix *koneion* and poppy juice to make death almost painless.'

'Yet the death of Sokrates – so noble – was not entirely painless,' said Demetrios. 'Aristotle has said so, having heard of it from others who were alive at the time. Even though the executioner, the "public man", made certain to mix a good dose of hemlock and to conduct the case correctly.'

'Essentially – compared to other deaths – it was practically painless,' Eudemos argued. 'Everyone says the account given by Phaido is basically correct.'

'It leaves out who Phaido was, though,' laughed Demetrios. 'People call him "a disciple of Sokrates" — but he was really a male whore plying his trade in a "little house". Eventually, Sokrates was coaxed into buying his freedom.'

'But the account attributed to this person is correct,' Eudemos insisted, reacting to the aristocratic Demetrios' dismissal of Sokrates' friend. 'Phaido himself was a prisoner of war who had become enslaved — not *born* a slave. No ordinary prostitute, no trash of the streets. He spoke so well of philosophy to Sokrates that the philosopher bought his freedom.'

'Once a whore, always a whore!' said Demetrios decidedly. The young man's countenance had assumed the haughty expression of generations of men of noble blood.

'On the contrary!' Eudemos, usually so urbane, was becoming a trifle warm. 'I believe Phaido founded a school of philosophy in Elis. Absurd to say he wasn't a disciple!'

'It is Phaido who tells us,' said Hipparkhos of Argos, 'that Sokrates kept on talking, even though the gaoler warned him that much talk might overheat him, and slow the action of the medicine, so he might have to drink more than one dose, and prolong the ugly process of dying. Speaking was the best thing Sokrates could do for his friends, and he was not afraid of taking the dreadful dose two or three times if necessary.'

'Yes,' said Demetrios. 'I believe *that*, certainly. But the death-day was not as pretty a scene as Plato — who wasn't there — makes out. There was yawning and gagging. Spasms of the limbs and torso. A couple of the young men present actually threw up under the pressure of the event and the horrid smell of the poison.'

'Shame on Athens to kill Sokrates!' exclaimed Theophrastos. 'But as far as the effects of the poison itself are concerned, Plato is essentially right. The arms and legs get colder and colder and more lacking in feeling, until the action of the poison paralyses the vital organs, and the patient dies.'

We were all silent for a moment.

'Of course, making the poison is hazardous in itself,' Theophrastos added. 'If the operator were to get some on his hands, and then eat lunch —! But there may be an antidote,' he added thoughtfully. 'The effect of *koneion* is to make the body extremely cold, driving out vital heat. Hence Sokrates' gaoler was right in believing that increase of heat through animating talk might necessitate more doses. It has been claimed that the long pepper of India, a hot herb, if ground up and digested, can relieve and reverse the symptoms of this poison. Naturally, I have not been able to test this, but the principle seems sound. There's a dried sweet gum that could have the same effect — from an Arabian tree, found only in mountain areas.'

'What a lot you do know about plants!' I admired.

'Theophrastos,' laughed Eudemos, 'reigns a king over the vegetable world. The book he writes all about plants will be gigantic!'

'It will take years,' said Theophrastos, not unhappy at the prospect. 'By the way, Aristotle is not available any longer today, but he very much hopes, Stephanos, that he will see you at the trial of Orthoboulos.'

III

The Trial of Orthoboulos for Malicious Wounding

Of course I went to the trial of Orthoboulos, held before the court of the Areopagos. There is something awe-inspiring about the Areopagos. The jury of the Court of the Areopagos is composed of all the former arkhons who are still alive, so all the chief men of Athens who had been elected to the governing body of the Eleven are members of the court of the Areopagos for life after their year's term of office. This jury is thus very large, and also the most distinguished and rational available to man. Men of this court in general possess the distinction of good birth and education (whereas common juries may be made up of any citizens, high or low). The Areopagos jury is thus also extremely dignified. Some say that the reason Sokrates received such a harsh sentence was that he acted disrespectfully in the court of the Areopagos, trying to joke with the jury.

A case heard by the Areopagos brings important people out in droves. Men who aren't arkhons yet but hope to be elected at some future time naturally flock to the scene. There are numerous law courts in Athens, and everyone gets to be a juror. Some cases are heard in the Odeion, others in the Stoa Poikile, and of course we have the New Courts in the agora. But the Areopagos is the most dignified law court, and the most antique, still meeting on its ancient site on the Akropolis. Only the major cases, regarding the gravest crimes, are heard in this court. Homicide of course is the chief of such crimes. But the Areopagos is also the court of judgement for the destruction of sacred olive trees of Athena, for impiety, for arson, and for intentional wounding of a citizen. This last was the case today. Ergokles, citizen of Athens, charged Orthoboulos, citizen of Athens, with assault upon his person, and malicious wounding with the intention of serious bodily harm.

The crowd having gathered, the Basileus made his ritual proclamation, 'Foreigners away! Let only citizens draw near to hear!' He did this before any of the ceremony began. Sacrifices were offered by the Accuser and Defender at the little temple on top of the rocks of the Hill of Ares. Prosecutor and Defender took their oaths, the man making the charge stationing himself on the historic Stone of Accusation and the Defender (Orthoboulos in this instance) standing on the Stone of the Accused. Such trials are religious and civic occasions, and it is no wonder that citizens only are allowed to participate. Foreign residents are allowed (unofficially) to watch from a remote place beyond the barrier, though oddly some of the best forensic speech-writers in the past have been foreigners.

After the oaths and the charges at the top of the hill, the little group moved down the steep incline to the flat space between the rocks of the Hill of Ares and the higher reaches of the Akropolis. In this flat space there had been placed a narrow platform, the *bema*, upon which pleaders could stand. Around it were grouped officials, including the presiding Basileus and the Chief Arkhon (sitting in good chairs) and the great jury sitting on benches. Near the Basileus were the attendants whose duty it was to keep time by minding the two officially marked water pots which make up the *klepsydra*. Familiar jokes had been exchanged about this.

'Don't drink out of it – give us a full pot this time,' some begged the attendant, while others scoffed : 'Him? He's more likely to piss in it and keep us here all day!' It was unlikely that the attendant would be anything but exact in the performance of his duty, ensuring that the specially designed top pot was full to the marked line and was uncorked just when each speaker began. Since the time it takes for the contents to flow from the slender hole in the upper pot into the lower one is the time allotted for each man's speech, Athenian court cases are not designed to favour the long-winded. The crowd had standing room only. We were shouldering each other to get a good view within the roped-off enclosure for citizens, as we waited for the trial itself to begin. Far behind us and outside the ropes was the uncomfortable space unofficially allowed to foreigners.

The time just before a trial really gets under way is more exciting than the moments just before a new play begins at the Dionysia. It also feels somewhat like a sporting event. Like all athletic shows and competitions, a trial is a contest with rules. Both Prosecutor and Defender have two speeches only; each must be silent whilst the other speaks. Either speaker can discourse only so long as the water-clock indicates. When the *klepsydra* has run out, so perforce must the speech. The Prosecutor begins, then the Defender responds; the Prosecutor picks up his case again, refuting points made by the Defender, and then the Defender has the last word. The jury must decide the case on the basis of the four speeches, but these may include the introduction of witnesses and other pieces of evidence, like documents.

Malicious wounding is a solemn enough charge. But it was soon evident that the circumstances of this particular case – a fight in a brothel – put a different complexion on it. Before the oaths were administered, many lewd jests had been exchanged, even among the arkhons. A number of the spectators were fascinated to watch the dignified Orthoboulos, who usually appeared in public as a benefactor, in this novel position of an accused man, a man threatened with ridicule, shame and loss.

Orthoboulos, a man of just above the middle height, was neither large nor heavy-boned, but he always held himself erect, and walked so gracefully and deliberately that he seemed bigger than he was. He had light brown curling hair, and a soft, well-trimmed brown beard. One of the things one noticed about Orthoboulos was his perfect teeth; he had a very engaging smile. But today there was no smile. He was dressed in a beautiful white khiton, and stood with his usual dignity, at the side, waiting for his opponent to begin the proceedings with an explication of his charge.

On the left side of Orthoboulos stood his eldest son, Krito, his chief supporter, as was proper. On his right stood his friend Philinos. Philinos was an extremely handsome citizen, taller than Orthoboulos. His deep blue eyes, curly dark hair, and long eyelashes had aroused the interest of both men and women; lovers had written ardent poems upon his beauty, at least in his youth which was still in the recent past. His tastes, however, ran on the whole to women. Indeed, Philinos was known to have kept several mistresses. And now he had a new freedwoman mistress called Lykaina, as we had heard from Marylla. Philinos was popular enough; he could lend money without being too stern about getting it returned to him, and he was known for his easy temper as well as good looks. This man Philinos, I thought as I looked at him, had more to him than an easy manner and long eyelashes. I admired him for showing his pith in standing by Orthoboulos. It takes a certain courage to volunteer oneself as a witness for a friend, especially in Athens' most intimidating court.

These two gentlemen, Orthoboulos the moderate and handsome Philinos, stood beside young Krito as the Defender's party. But I noticed in the background a little group of anxious and ill-dressed people guarded by the Skythian archers who serve the order of the state. Obviously, the slaves of Orthoboulos' household, ready to be taken away and put to the question should the request for their testimony at last prevail with the court. The brothel's resident slaves must have been tortured already, but Orthoboulos had so far protected his household. Among this group of slaves I spied the muffled form of the woman I had met. Marylla, the girl with the poignant face and big grey eyes, brought under guard to wait and find out if she must be tortured.

The Basileus again shouted the ritual injunction: 'Foreigners away! Let none but citizens draw near to hear!' The jury of elders settled on their benches, the rest of the citizen audience found what station they could, and all hearers were silent as the first speaker approached. Naturally Ergokles the complainant was to speak first. Ergokles was only a small man, but he increased his height by a copious and bushy head of brown hair, today smoothed into some sort of order. This Accuser had small eyes, lively and always darting to and fro; a jester had once said that these swift-moving eyes were peering about looking for Ergokles' nose which they could never espy, it was so short and snub. Ergokles always possessed a certain confidence; his malicious tongue kept his enemies in check, and even won him some friends. Today, he advanced confidently and rapidly to the platform as if he could hardly wait to open his case. He was sweating a little in the spring sunshine as he stood on the low *bema*, his eyes fixed most earnestly upon the most important of the arkhons. As soon as the cork began to be removed from the *klepsydra*, he spoke up.

SPEECH OF ERGOKLES FOR THE PROSECUTION

'Men of Athens : the charge I bring today, the complaint I lay before you, is simple – and yet terrible. It is by the mercy of the gods that I am alive – and not blind! For Orthoboulos laid in ambush to beat me; he struck me and almost succeeded in depriving me of sight! Only through the mercy of the gods and timely assistance was I saved from this man's reckless power and cruel passion. "How did this come to pass?" you will ask. "What was the cause?" The cause does Orthoboulos no credit. Likewise, the cause reflects no glory upon myself, that I admit – for it was only a quarrel over a woman, a slave-girl at that. Yet, men of Athens, we know that the quarrel between Agamemnon and great Akhilleus, a quarrel that shook the Greeks and imperilled the taking of Troy, was based on nothing more than a dispute about the ownership of a slave-girl. I am in the position of Akhilleus who was injured and oppressed when the cuckold's brother took his woman from him.

'Here are the facts, men of Athens. This man Orthoboulos entered into an agreement with me to purchase a slave-girl as mistress and share her together. The two of us – share and share alike. The receipted bill for this purchase is produced in evidence. I will acknowledge what witnesses could tell you, that I was glad of this original bargain, for I could not at that time afford to buy this particular female, who was costly, on my own. The young slave in question is a Sikilian called Marylla. Nobody disputes that it was she.'

He looked directly at her muffled form, there under the guard of the archers.

'But then – such injustice! Orthoboulos kept her and would not give her back to me, even though *I* had an absolute right to a share of her!'

Ergokles glared fiercely at this point towards the dignified Orthoboulos, where he stood in his beautiful white khiton. Orthoboulos simply stood still, and listened with imperturbable gravity and calm. His accuser glared all the harder.

'I am asking again,' Ergokles announced, 'that the slaves of Orthoboulos and particularly the slave in question, Marylla the Sikilian, be put to the question. For the evidence supplied would make for my case, and it is Orthoboulos' injustice that has prevented me from enjoying this support. I still claim this woman, as I did then. Orthoboulos, now trying to cover his error, will try to persuade you that he was plotted against by us – by me and my friends. It is true that we came to his front door one evening. My friends came with me to aid me in demanding my share of Marylla, and that she leave Orthoboulos' house. *He* will tell you that we tried to break in, and came deliberately intending to cause damage! That is untrue. He will claim that we exchanged fisticuffs with his porter and damaged his entrance, trying to force our way into his house and into the women's quarters. I'm sure Orthoboulos deserved to have his entryway damaged, so brutally he treated us! But if we had wanted to assail his women's quarters we would have used the back entrance; his back entrance is unguarded and it would have been easily damaged and given way.'

There was some stifled laughter in the audience, but Ergokles continued.

'My friends will witness that we made a dignified request that Orthoboulos give the girl to us, but he and his porter treated us with abusive words, and even thumps and kicks. And we also call Orthoboulos' eldest son Krito – even though he had rather appear for the defence.'

Here Ergokles called witnesses, two friends who briefly, if with different degrees of clarity, confirmed that this was what had happened. He then called the most important witness, Orthoboulos' elder son.

THIRD WITNESS FOR THE PROSECUTION:
KRITO SON OF ORTHOBOULOS

'I just remember hearing a noise at the front door, after a lot of humming and banging and shouting – the way a drunken group may sometimes shout. It wasn't until my father called aloud to me that I realized there was serious trouble at the door. I came out to the entry and saw these men. Then I tried to push them back. I hit one in the shoulder and the other in the chest, but I cannot say which man I hit where. Yes, I hit more than one and more than once. They were cursing and shouting and I feared they were going to storm the house.'

ERGOKLES' ACCUSATION CONTINUES

'I repeat – we were given nothing but bad words, kicks and thumps. The eldest son Krito, a well-grown youth as you have seen, soldier-ripe at the age of seventeen years, himself admits – you heard him – that he struck us several times. When plainly asked to restore the girl, Orthoboulos refused to do the decent and legal thing. Though he has been heard to say if he married again he would give up some of his slaves to accommodate those of his wife. He cannot rationally expect to keep all his slaves for ever – why not let the Sikilian girl go? You see, men of Athens, how badly he takes his pleasure. In a good brothel you enjoy and pay, but Orthoboulos, just because he thinks he is somebody, wants to take the woman Marylla and have his pleasure for nothing. She should and must come to me, as I paid part of her price originally. But he would on no account listen to reason when I went to his house to plead with him.

'But that is by no means all. The really terrible assault took place when we met in – in a house that many of you know too, though it isn't often talked about in respectable public gatherings, I grant you that. The house of Manto, the freedwoman, who runs a place of resort for gentlemen. I and my friends went out that evening for a little pleasure. I admit that. We went out to see boys and flute-girls and we had a bit of wine taken – more than a little, perhaps. But *he* – Orthoboulos – also came to that house on that evening. He is a frequenter of brothels. See what a loose liver he is, men of Athens! Not content with the lovely Marylla, the luxurious fellow wished to make free with Manto's store of girls as well. But that evening he had an additional purpose; I believe he had followed me to Manto's for his own malicious ends. Seeing him, I, in all innocence and suspecting no harm, went up to my former friend and addressed him in a dignified manner. I was entitled to speak. Winged words – that's what Homer says. I spoke winged words. I accused him truly of having stolen from me that girl, and said I could take her back any day and use her frequently and vigorously to make up for lost time.

'Well, men of Athens, it slowly became clear to me

that Orthoboulos had obviously planned to come after me in that house. A plot against me! He had been biding his time, hoping to find me in an unguarded moment so he could eliminate me for ever from life – as well as from Marylla's sight. Seeing I was disabled by drink, he jeered at me. When I remonstrated, he punched and hit me – repeatedly struck me! Although he *knew* I am a citizen, and striking me is illegal! Orthoboulos threw me down on the floor. Then as I got up again he took – just imagine this – a deadly weapon! He broke a pot and came at me with the jagged edge of the potsherd.'

Stifled laughter among his auditors. Ergokles glared.

'You think that a little thing? A shard is as good as a dagger, it can cut and even kill a man. This Orthoboulos, brawling in the house of a madam, like a madman struck me a great blow on the head. I fell down – the blood was running over my eye like a red curtain. I could see nothing and thought I should bleed to death. My friends cried out – I heard one say, "You have killed him!" Then Orthoboulos went away in haste, not waiting to find out if his victim – that's me, gentlemen – were alive or dead.

'You see this scar?' Everyone squinted and tried to see what seemed to be a little line above his left eyebrow. 'And my eye? It has healed, thanks to my doctor, but I thought I should lose my sight, and the whole area was fearfully discoloured – for weeks. My doctor will testify. I was so weak I was carried about in a litter for a long time, and could not go about.'

The next witness was a physician, a resident alien, a meek little man frightened of displeasing any

employer, past or future. This doctor testified that
Ergokles had been cut and had a black eye and seemed
shaken. But when asked if he had advised the man to
go in a litter for three weeks, he said, 'No.' Asked if
he had ever advised him to recommence walking, he
said, 'Yes'. Asked if there were permanent lameness,
or damage to the head, he said, 'You never can tell.'

ERGOKLES' ACCUSATION CONTINUES

'By the mercy of the gods and with the help of
Asklepios I have survived. But that does not negate
the crime of this evildoer. Happily for Orthoboulos,
his homicidal plan did not succeed. But his pursuit or
ambush of me was very vile. His malicious assault
upon me was an outrage! Malicious wounding so that
I was in danger of my life and have suffered permanent damage – that is a *crime*. By the laws of Athens.

'And Orthoboulos has committed this crime and
defends this crime with a criminal mind throughout.
This guilt is easily seen from one important fact: that
evidence is being kept from the court. Where is the
girl Marylla? An important witness should be part of
this trial. *Why* is she not brought in to testify, or her
testimony recorded? I will tell you why. As you know,
she is a slave, and slaves cannot give testimony without torture. And Orthoboulos says he won't allow it!
Thus *he* claims to be the sole owner of Marylla – the
very point in our dispute! Claiming – wrongfully – to
be sole owner, he refuses to have her tortured and thus
refuses to allow her to be a witness. You see his
cunning. You must reject his claim. *Make* the girl be
put to the torture. *Force* him to yield her to you, if not

to me. She is our common possession. And I am running a risk too, for I am putting myself at a disadvantage with her. Plainly she is more attached to him than to me. *She* has joined with him in doing me wrong. And she never joined with *me* in doing him wrong.'

[*Auditors put their grave hands over their smiling mouths.*]

'In conclusion, gentlemen, the accused man is guilty of a heinous crime. An outrage against an Athenian citizen! Orthoboulos' property should be forfeit to you – all but the harlot girl, in whom I claim my original share. For the rest of her price, I will pay the Treasury once you have attached all of this man's property. I have already made this offer to the officers of the state, and also to pay – without admitting blame – for the damage to Orthoboulos' entryway. I am sure,' Ergokles concluded with a self-consciously coy glance at his auditors, 'I am sure that some say he is more accustomed than he lets on to having his passage forced. Though if I had really wanted or intended to force a passage I could do so in a passage narrower than his!'

[*Explosions of amusement.*]

With a sulky look of pleasure at his last insult, Ergokles sat down. The presiding Basileus implored us to maintain sobriety, and not to behave like schoolboys. Then it was Orthoboulos' turn to take the centre of the platform. There was much interest in seeing how such a man would conduct himself. It is hardly the thing for dignified citizens to be caught out in brawls over harlot slaves. Orthoboulos kept his calm demeanour. He spoke clearly and well, without his voice rising in the manner of Ergokles' impassioned tones. Yet even his voice, usually so deep and firm, had a slight tremor of anxiety in it.

SPEECH OF ORTHOBOULOS FOR THE DEFENCE

'Men of Athens, it is surprising to me to find myself here, and on so serious a charge. I assure you that I deeply and honestly believe that I am unjustly accused of assault and malicious wounding. It is true that Ergokles and I together bought a slavewoman known as Marylla. It is also true that I paid the larger share — these were *not* equal shares. The bill that has been produced clearly shows this inequality. But what Ergokles has not told you is that we had an earlier conversation *before* the events he has dwelt upon — or his own version of them, rather. For I told him that he abused the slavewoman, and that such abuse was not in our pact. I informed Ergokles that I would buy him out — as I had the larger share of her already. And I said that I proposed ultimately to make this woman a free person. This put Ergokles into an exceeding ill humour, yet my offer was fairly made. I knew that the girl herself wanted no more to do with him because of his gross and unkindly ways. I warned him fairly that he could have the money but not the girl, who was residing in my own house.

'Then one evening, as you have heard, Ergokles and his friends came to my house door and made rough and abusive demands, and many threats. Even their own account makes it clear that they were unruly and outrageous. They tried to force their way in, and my servant, assisted at last by myself as well as by my elder son, pushed them out again — as we were fully entitled to do by Athenian law. If Ergokles and his party got nothing more than thumps and kicks they may frankly account themselves lucky. They deserved worse! And many a schoolboy undergoes as much in the schoolyard without turning a hair or thinking to go crying "Papa!" about it.

'Then this man found me in a place neither truly private (like my own house) nor truly public (like the agora), a place where he thought it safe to assault me. I came to Manto's brothel not knowing he was there, but he found me. It is not a matter of particular pride to me that I was found frequenting a brothel. But I have made no secret of my visit to Manto's house. All the world knows that I am a widower, so this is but a relief to the prompting of nature and not unreasonable. Indeed, this man Ergokles could well have known that I was to be there. Far from *my* ambushing him, as he claims, it seems more reasonable to believe that he laid in wait for me, but got more drunk during the time of waiting than was good for him. Seeing me, he lurched towards me and started to behave abusively. As my witness will confirm.'

FIRST WITNESS FOR THE DEFENCE:
PHILINOS SON OF PHILINOS OF KEPHISIA

'I am Philinos son of Philinos, an Athenian of the deme Kephisia. I have known Orthoboulos a long time; we have many acquaintances in common. Orthoboulos is always even-tempered and benevolent to others, never inciting enmity. I was in Manto's house that night likewise, and I know exactly what happened. Ergokles seemed to have been drinking before we arrived.

Certainly, *he* came up to Orthoboulos – not the other way around. Ergokles uttered many insults – do I have to recite them all again? Some are not very proper in the repetition. I had not really known Ergokles before this time, and was surprised at his behaviour. I told him to stop and go back and sit down. I suggested he eat something to help him to mitigate his visibly drunken condition. Ergokles said something like "I'll eat the ears and privates of Orthoboulos, fried!" Then he raised his hand in a threatening manner, and started the whole fight. There didn't seem to be any danger. Orthoboulos was merely defending himself. I do not believe he did any real damage to Ergokles. I went for assistance, to require the people of the house to put an end to this brawl by taking Ergokles away.'

ORTHOBOULOS' DEFENCE CONTINUES

'There you have it. It is just as Philinos attests. Ergokles saw me and came up to me – whereas I had not sought nor molested him. He began a confused diatribe, calling me many bad words, and then raised his hand against me. Surely I had the right to act to defend myself! I raised my hand against him in turn, and trying to quiet him, pushed him down. In the process he upset the table and broke the jar that was on it. I picked up a potsherd from the broken jar – true. But I did not use that broken piece as a weapon. Ergokles hit his own head on the broken jar when he was down – that is all.

'And surely the last thing I can be accused of is premeditation! Does a man planning a murder or an assault go *unarmed* to the site, trusting to Fortune to supply him with some handy weapon? *No!* That would be ludicrous, gentlemen. A man who premeditates a murder or an affray goes armed to the place where he has planned that the attack must take place. He takes a weapon – a club, a dagger – with him. Nobody plans to commit serious mayhem without weapons. And if I had Ergokles at my mercy, as he claims, by my own plan of ambush as he also claims, then *why* did I not make the moment good and kill him? Having him in my power, why – if my intentions were so evil – should I not do away with the man altogether? His charge is ridiculous, trumped up on the basis of his own incompetent drunken brawling.

'Men of Athens, Ergokles was struck – that is true. I hit him a great box on the ear. That is all. Out of that he has made this song-and-dance – claiming that his black eye is a vicious wound. And why is Ergokles doing all this? Because he has designs upon my property. And because he is jealous in general of my success in life, and in particular of my success with the slave girl Marylla. For there are some men so weak and unsure they must be upset over the preference even of a slave or a dog. His plan is to destroy me – merely to gratify his own pique. Ergokles has portrayed himself more unsparingly than I could do.

'What more need I say? My opponent has represented himself as a sniveller and a coward, and a liar – and a bully. He shows himself as a speaker of vulgar insults, good for a tavern brawl. What cause is there to believe in him? Take logic and reason for your guides. Ask yourselves, most worthy men of Athens, whether it is for such trifles as this that the serious laws of Athens were designed? Is a black eye worthy of the Areopagos? Knowing you as I do, even as I stand here humbly before you, I believe in your justice as well as your power, and I hope that you will not allow injustice and pique to prevail.'

Orthoboulos' speech was well received. It was not really surprising that the jury largely sympathized with him. The second speeches were in effect repetitions with variations of the first ones, and not only the jury but the whole audience was satisfied as to the truth. This Orthoboulos was clever enough to see, so he finished the delivery of his second speech even before the water-clock had run out. The Basileus pointed out that the laws of Athens dictated that in such a case of dispute over a prostitute the two men ought to have appealed to an official mediator. After this, the jury took no time to deliver a verdict. The verdict was decisive, if not unanimous. Fortunately for Ergokles, he received about one quarter of the votes (or at least the tallymen *said* it was one quarter), a fact which saved him from the true humiliation of a penalty for a frivolous suit, a penalty awaiting those who bring a lawsuit before the Areopagos and cannot convince one quarter of the jury. The jury's majority judgement was for Orthoboulos, but it was agreed that Orthoboulos should pay a fine for disturbances of the peace – and this seemed to satisfy most of those who had voted for Ergokles. Orthoboulos would be the owner of the slave-girl as soon as the money to complete the payment for her as well as the sum of the fine was handed to an officer of the court. The court would see to it that the debt to Ergokles was formally cleared. This sum due from Orthoboulos in payment for the slave-girl was to be lessened by the amount of fifteen drakhmai in compensation for damage done to Orthoboulos' hall. Most insultingly, the fine laid upon Orthoboulos was the truly nominal sum of two drakhmai.

Almost more shaming to Ergokles and his party (a party rapidly diminishing), Orthoboulos was able to pay up on the spot, turning over not only the two drakhmai but also the remainder due of the price of Marylla, and a receipt for the transaction was rendered straight away.

'So we see how it goes with this great man,' grumbled one of Ergokles' friends. 'He can walk away from the charge of assault and wounding by paying the price of a dinner – or of a visit to a whore in a brothel!'

'There he goes, with his ill-gotten fancy woman,' said another of Ergokles' witnesses. Ergokles stopped to stare malevolently after the departing enemy. It was true, the little group of household slaves, relieved of their great anxiety, were being led away by Orthoboulos himself. As he turned back to acknowledge the plaudits of friends, Orthoboulos once more displayed his attractive smile. Philinos the beautiful caught up with his friend and this staunch supporter strode along with Krito and Orthoboulos, all three visibly rejoicing.

'I told Ergokles it wouldn't go well,' Ergokles' witness added.

'You said nothing of the sort,' Ergokles growled. 'And I still want what is mine! He has no right to her!'

Ergokles and his witnesses were the only ones dissatisfied. Most arkhons of the Areopagos were pleased at the outcome and had been entertained by the trial. Members of the audience in general were bursting with mirth, and lewd jokes flew back and forth as we walked down the hill.

'Not totally ridiculous, Ergokles' accusation,' Aristotle remarked. 'But it was ridiculous enough. It was unconvincing to the extent that it was comical. It is a point in the art of persuasion not to cause your auditors to laugh in the wrong places. Even when Ergokles thought he was giving an intentional gibe, it sounded as if he could not speak properly, like a decent Athenian citizen.'

'So you heard the trial from way back there,' I commented. 'How much did you contribute to Orthoboulos' defence?'

'I didn't hear everything,' Aristotle said. 'But enough. As for Orthoboulos' defence, I suggested only a couple of touches. He required encouragement and support, but his own ideas were largely the right ones. Certainly he saw he should not try to hide or diminish the fact that he and Ergokles had that encounter in Manto's brothel.'

'I suppose,' I remarked, 'that Orthoboulos can be happy now. He keeps the slave girl, his concubine. And she will feel undying gratitude to him for sparing her the torture. I am glad that I have seen the beauteous Marylla. The jury would have liked to see her, I think—'

'So would everyone else.'

'Isn't it odd – I feel that Orthoboulos has somehow gone up in public estimation, even though he is now discovered to be a brawler in a brothel.'

'His political opponents will remember that,'

Aristotle pointed out. 'It may perhaps be recollected unfavourably in the future. But he was lucky in his opponent today. Nobody really *likes* Ergokles. Perhaps this peccadillo at Manto's brothel, and the fuss over the slave concubine, will work in Orthoboulos' favour. Makes him less stiff – Oh no, there, I'm making bad jokes without intending it. What I mean is, people will like Orthoboulos better when they think he has human weaknesses. We never like what is too perfect. The fate of Aristides. If he had been called Aristides the Indolent instead of Aristides the Just he wouldn't have been ostracized.'

Aristotle seemed to be proved right. Orthoboulos' influence increased. And later that summer – the long summer in which Darius the Great of Persia was in flight from Alexander, only to be murdered by his former supporters – Orthoboulos married. In the sunshiny season, not long after the first crops were gathered in, without waiting for the marriage month of chilly Gamelion, he wed himself to one Hermia, widow of Epikhares. This woman was immensely rich. At this time Aristotle and I were both away, so we heard about this event only in the autumn when we returned to Athens. Everyone said that Orthoboulos had done well in marrying such a wealthy young widow.

'Young enough to give him children,' my mother reported. Once I was settled back in Athens in our house, Mother enjoyed informing me of all that had transpired in Athens over the summer. She particularly liked telling me bits of cheerful news when she was working on my troublesome left shoulder; the spear wound I had received off the coast of Asia still pained me, but Mother worked with balsam and hot cloths, and made shoulder and left arm less inflexible. She kept telling me, however, that I was 'a silly boy' for running into such trouble, and she got cross when I tried to explain the complex situation in which the fight had occurred. Mother desired me to stop travelling ('rushing about the world to no purpose', as she put it, tartly and ungratefully); she wished me to keep my mind on Athens, and to become intimate with important people.

'How lucky Orthoboulos is to get a woman without boy children – just a little girl. So we know she can breed, but there's no male descendant of Epikhares to claim the goods,' Mother went on, rubbing and flexing my upper left arm in a businesslike way. 'Oh, Stephanos, it hurts me to see you in such poor condition! *Why* will you run abroad and neglect us at home? I could weep when I look at you. Well, this woman Hermia is good-looking – such a lot of dark curly hair. Straight as a tree, and her slaves say she has a good shape. She'll soon be breeding, most like. Yes, on the whole I approve of this match.' I laughed inwardly, thinking that neither Orthoboulos nor Hermia's family had bothered to consult the opinion or gain the approval of Eunike daughter of Diogeiton.

'Mind you,' Mother continued, 'she's used to running things herself, that Hermia. That family always wants to shine. You know Hermia's uncle Phanodemos got a golden crown, and spends his own money on religious festivals for Athens. We hear that Hermia managed Epikhares' farm and the other places, even when her husband was not away. A mind of her own, I dare say. All her father's family were fond of bossing people about – not like Orthoboulos' folks, more good-natured and retiring.'

This was the chatter of slaves and women. But all citizens talked of it, if only because Orthoboulos, patriotic and somewhat anti-Makedonian, was marrying the widow of rich Epikhares, who had (at least in recent years) been a supporter of Alexander. This Hermia had benefited from much of her first husband's property. Naturally, Epikhares' second cousin got the family farm and its house, and the rental properties in Athens and Peiraieus. A woman is really not supposed to control money, or engage in any business worth more than a *medimnos* of barley. But women can be left personal goods by the husband's will, and Hermia, we heard, was richly gifted with the kind of things a woman may receive: jewelry, personal slaves, household furnishings of the richest kind, silver pots and pans, great antique vases. And there were chattels of even more substantial value in trust for Epikhares' child, the use of which was given to Hermia: bronze statues, costly jewellery, bags of coins, cattle, horses, mules and slaves. Hermia also received from her father's bequest a silent share in a bronze factory, an income managed by her. Would this rich widow, presumably of her former husband's way of thinking, be able with Epikhares' pro-Makedonian wealth to dazzle and convert the mind of the patriotic Orthoboulos? So some wondered.

Although Epikhares' house in Athens could not be legally Hermia's, as women cannot own real property, relations of Epikhares and Hermia were to combine to sell this town mansion, also for the benefit of Epikhares' surviving child. When I arrived back in Athens at the end of the summer, that house of Epikhares was being readied for sale. As a concession to his new wife (so rumour had it) Orthoboulos was to get rid of his own household slaves and take her familiar servants into his own house. By an agreement quietly made before their nuptials, he would sell his own slaves, as soon as her first husband's house was sold. Then Hermia's slaves would come from Epikhares' house to live with her in her new marital household.

Orthoboulos' sons, Krito and Kleiophon, would have to content themselves with gaining a step-mother. Some said these boys would be anxious about the possibility of future heirs. Others argued that Hermia's contribution would make the family richer – and at once. The boys had expensive tastes – Krito was fond of chariot-racing, and wanted horses and a chariot of his own. Their father would be better able to set his boys up in the world. Orthoboulos himself certainly seemed well pleased with this turn of affairs. He had made a good impression upon his fellow citizens at the trial; now he could advance his career with the assistance of agreeably exchangeable new wealth. When I saw him, on my return in the early autumn, he did look pleased with himself. Perhaps Orthoboulos had been too much favoured by the gods, or some of them.

IV

Poison in Athens

Looking back, I see the unfolding events as pertaining to two times. My dinner party (though in this instance that term is patently a satire) with Aristotle, the conversation about the hemlock, and the trial of Orthoboulos took place in what I tended to think of as 'the good time', before disaster struck. Aristotle's wife died, and the Master of the Lykeion, while in a state of grief, was subjected to surprising insults by Athenian patriots. He felt it would be wiser for him to leave Athens for a while. Events conspired to take the two of us together on a journey to the eastern islands. In fact, we went further east than originally planned, and I actually set foot in Asia for the first time. We returned, after many vicissitudes, in the autumn of that year, the year of the death of Pythias and of Darius, the Great King of the Persians. By the time my journey home was completed, Alexander was headed ever further eastward, towards the chilly mountains of the Caucasus. He was pursuing the enemy Persians, chiefly Bessos the traitor who in the end had conspired against Darius and declared himself the new King of Persia.

After my own difficult journey to the East and back, I was extremely glad to be at home in Athens again. As I have indicated, I had received a wound in the left shoulder, inflicted by a spear in a desperate fight; I was still not quite recovered. But I now was mended sufficiently to pay a visit once more to a brothel. I was grateful for the chance; it had been a long time since I had truly been able to relieve my desires properly, and I felt that I had earned this pleasure. How long I was to regret that I had chosen that particular night and not the night before! For that night was not going to give me as much pleasure as I felt I deserved, while for others it entailed danger, pain and deprivation – including the greatest deprivation of all.

I had chosen – how perverse it seemed later – to go myself to the house of Manto, which had been so well advertised in the trial. Manto's house, as one might guess from the fact that a man of wealth and taste like Orthoboulos frequented it, was one of the better and more expensive houses of pleasure. Not that the law does not regulate the cost of each brothel visit – officially it is two drakhmai, no more. And in some places you can receive entertainment for less, not to mention with the poor draggle-tails who beat the dust of side alleys with their backs, or couple for a hemi-obol or two under the shadows of the city walls. Really good houses of accommodation give you fine bedding to lie on, and offer furnished apartments of entertainment where you can drink good wine and eat little tasty things in company with the partner or partners of your choice – and much good-looking company. It was thus that a peaceful man like Orthoboulos could encounter a pot-valiant trouble-maker like Ergokles. Manto's house is also one of the kind where there is music – sometimes a couple of flute-girls or boys, and whores who play a tambourine or something. For fine linen, tolerable drink, good food and music one is slyly charged extra. So it is not a cheap thing to decide to spend the night in such a good establishment, instead of in one of the modest 'little houses' under the Akropolis. On market days men line up by the row of miniature 'houses', little better than booths with doors, where some poor girl – or boy, like Sokrates' friend Phaido – ekes out a living taking many customers in rapid series on a small bed in a tiny room.

At first all went well as I sampled the pleasures of Manto's abode. The girls were attractively grouped in a semicircle in the main room of the establishment, clothed in the thinnest raiment, each with earrings in her ears. (Custom winks at the jewellery of prosti-tutes, although when they are slaves any trinkets given them belong to their masters.) After a good look, I chose a girl who said her name was Kynara. I had a light supper, accompanied by some good wine only slightly mixed with water, with my partner for the night. Athenian citizens' daughters and wives aren't allowed to drink wine, but prostitutes drink quite a lot of it. We went to her little cubicle upstairs.

Once she was undressed, I took a good long look

at this girl, recollecting that when married I could never look at my wife naked. But just as we were getting to the point of the evening, a loud outcry arose below. So loud that I couldn't ignore it, though I wanted to – the more impossible as my Kynara leaped up like a startled hare. I supposed she feared the madam was being taken into custody, or that a brawl had broken out. But the cries came largely from women: 'Zeus!' 'By Persephone!' 'Oh no!' And 'Help!' So I ran down, hardly clothed, with Kynara tripping before me. I didn't want her to impede. But far from hanging round my neck and bewailing the accident, however, when she got downstairs she made off smartly in the opposite direction and disappeared into the labyrinth of the house.

Everything was confused; in an inadequate light people were milling about, some coming in from a side door. I found this side door opened on a short path leading to the house next door. This house, when I got to it, seemed small – at least a very modest dwelling compared to Manto's. I went into this abode by its side door. And there, in a small bedroom on the ground floor, was a man and a bed.

There was no pretty hetaira lying with this man, and it was easy to see why. He was slumped against the bed rather than lying fully on it. He stank. Towels sopping with vomit lay beside him. 'He's dead!' wailed a woman bending over him with a lamp in her hand. I easily recognized Manto, the mistress of the mansion, twice the age of any of her girls. Manto was right, as I saw when I got a good look at the man. His face was congested, puffy and blue, his lips purple and stiff like a mask, with a kind of distorted grin. From between his teeth his tongue fell out horribly. His body was slightly arched, making a sort of semicircle, as if he wanted to turn a somersault or tumble in a cart-wheel. I could not tell if that meant he had departed in the midst of a convulsion, and was now laughing at that grim fact.

'By Herakles!' I cried, startled. 'It is Orthoboulos! Dead – yes, indeed! How long has he been here?'

'How should I know?' said Manto distractedly. 'Keep all the girls well away, Meta,' addressing her assistant, a kind of forewoman of her business. 'If they see nothing maybe they'll not have to give evidence. Thank the gods I am a freedwoman. But what to do?'

'I think I know someone who might help,' I said. 'But you must send a message to the man's home – to his elder son, Krito. Meanwhile, let us look at the evidence of this case. Bring more lights!' And I walked to and fro, trying to avoid the stinking towels. The scene was most unpleasing, yet I tried to observe closely as Aristotle would do, and to keep a clear head.

'Look,' I said, after pondering. 'The vomit is already drying on these towels. And there is no puke on the floor. That's odd.' Reluctantly, I touched the body. 'The man is cool,' I said. 'He is fairly recently dead, but his death happened much longer ago than just now. His limbs are strangely stiff already – the muscles are like boards! That strong ugly smell, not just ordinary puke, but – what on earth is it?'

'It smells like hemlock. I had a client once who snuffed it in the gaol, by orders. Executed, I mean. No trial – he'd confessed at once. I helped with his laying-out. By the Two Goddesses,' Manto said, sniffing, 'I did for that man what his wife would not do for him. Right to the end.'

'I suppose you're right. Yes.' I caught a whiff of the smell again, and nearly gagged. 'Poisoned – the man was certainly poisoned. Poison in Athens! According to you, it is essence of *koneion*. There is an antidote – Indian pepper.'

'No use wasting any pepper on *that*,' she retorted. '*He* doesn't need any fine flavours – 'cepting for burial.'

'True,' I was forced to agree. 'Orthoboulos is dead – dead as Sokrates. Poisoned by hemlock – like a murderer or an offender sentenced for impiety against the gods! Why, I wonder – why like this? And *where* was he killed? Was this house in use tonight? Were your *pornai* entertaining clients here?'

'No – no. Not until we got so full, suddenly there was an overflow, and I sent three couples out here – one couple to this room. With it – him – in it.' She nodded at the corpse. 'They screeched and alarmed the whole household.'

I was still walking around the corpse, pondering and shining a lamp on it. 'It was meant to look as if he had died here. Taken poison here, and then died? But it probably was not here that he died. Not in this room. He wasn't first taken ill in this room, he must have puked a lot somewhere else. I wonder why he is in a kind of semicircle? Let us look elsewhere in the house, if you can get Meta to watch the corpse. See if any of the other rooms have any signs of his death in them.'

Manto and I went through the other rooms, but

except for some dust and a few rags they were clean. It was a very small house and the search didn't take long.

'What is this house anyway?' I said. 'Is it yours – another part of the business?'

'No. This little house belongs to a freedwoman who has two daughters of her own. Well, it doesn't exactly belong to her of course, she has the use of it as a gift from one of her old keepers. She and her daughters – that whole trio are in our line of business. But when she's away, we are allowed to use the house if there's an overflow, and pay her a little rent. Lucky for her – she is away. That woman has a good regular customer in Megara, and she's packed up her brats and gone off for a while. I wouldn't have had anyone come here at all if we hadn't been short of space. It's been a good night – until now.'

'You say one of your girls and her customer came here and found Orthoboulos like that? Which girl?'

She hesitated. I thought I knew why. She didn't want to compromise one of her slave girls, so she compromised with the truth.

'I didn't speak clearly before. I came in just ahead of the customer – the man – to see if everything were all right before the lovebird came to him. That's how I saw this – this mess! Orthoboulos was just as you see him now, I swear!'

Although I was sure that one of the girls and probably her customer had actually been the first to catch sight of this corpse, I believed Manto when she said Orthoboulos had looked exactly like this when she first saw him. There were no signs of attempts to move the body from its current odd position. I was still puzzling over this unbeautiful corpse, walking about it while struggling with my nausea, when the door was opened again, and another man entered; with a frightened small slave bearing a torch. The flickering glow made the corpse seem to grin and try again to complete his somersault. I knew the man who entered. Krito. The elder son of that Orthoboulos who had been so successful at the Areopagos and so unsuccessful here.

'By the gods!' Krito had a deep, tragic tone, though his voice still young betrayed him by a slight squeak at the end. 'I didn't want to believe it! O ye gods – it is – yes, it is – my father! Orthoboulos is dead!'

'Yes, so it is, Krito. I am very sorry to tell—'

'Dead. Yes, I know. She has done it – she has done it! By the gods – by Zeus father of all the gods, she shall pay for it! I swear it!'

'*I* have done nothing!' cried Manto while I was still saying 'Who? What do you mean?'

'That infernal stepmother of mine. Oh yes, it's easy to see what *she*'s been up to. In order to please her own fancy man! Getting my father's gifts and a rise in the world, and then hoping to run off to her adulterous lover. You will see – this is her doing! Bringing down our house in ruin. Oh, a very Klytaimnestra, the despoiler of our hearth!'

'But this isn't your house,' I said. 'And this is far from being your hearth. It's a brothel. The question is, how did your father get here?'

Krito waved me away. 'We shall find all that out. He was lured here – that's it. Look at his poor blue face! We shall find the poisoned drink, or the poisoned washing oil with which— Oh, the wicked creature! The foul fiend come to torment us!' He shook with rage and grief. 'When my father was safe from that ridiculous attack of Ergokles, I thought we could be happy again. But what must he do but fall prey to that harpy of a widow! How I could – oh, would she were in Hades already, this monstrous Hermia! She has been too much for us! The woman must have an assistant, some cunning adulterer who has helped her. She beguiled him to this empty house and killed him. And didn't she pretend to *dote* on Papa – so he wouldn't listen!'

Krito broke down, sobbing, and had to fling his cloak over his face. His little slave started crying and wailing too, as was right. It was a while before things could be calm enough to make arrangements to have the body of Orthoboulos washed and transported home. I am certain the slaves enjoyed neither of these tasks. Manto meanwhile lamented her lost business and the wretched room which she would have to clean before her friend returned.

I thought that the outburst of Krito, the eldest son, at seeing his father's hapless body might be a temporary relief, a refuge in delusion. I wasn't at all sure at the time how seriously to take his statement. But the whole of Athens had to take it seriously when he made the formal accusation just after the funeral. It had been an impressive funeral, crowded with folk in attendance.

The many slaves of Orthoboulos made a fine ring of grievers, especially the women, who were dressed in black and wept properly in the procession and around the grave in the Kerameikos. I saw poor Marylla with tears coursing down her cheeks. 'That slave weeps now her deliverer and protector is gone,' I pointed out to Aristotle. 'But his wife is veiled, and we cannot know whether she weeps or not.'

'As citizens' wives are supposed to be hidden from view and not to display emotion,' he pointed out, 'we can judge nothing from that.'

Many important citizens were present at this impressive funeral, including of course handsome Philinos, the friend of Orthoboulos who had supported him at the trial, and now supported Krito in his grief. To my surprise, even Ergokles turned up. We were all, I think, startled when Krito, standing over the fresh grave of his parent, took up a spear as custom demanded, and gave tongue:

'I charge my father's wretched second wife Hermia of having plotted and worked to kill and destroy my father Orthoboulos. I, Krito son of Orthoboulos, proclaim to you Hermia, widow of Orthoboulos, that you are a known murderess, and I charge you to keep from all legal and holy things, from holy water, wine and libations, from the agora, from the temples and from all sacred places!'

'No!' cried his younger brother Kleiophon, breaking away from the group and running boldly up to Krito. 'No! It's all wrong, brother! That cannot be true!'

Hermia had fainted. Fallen back, at least, into the arms of Marylla, who grabbed her shoulders and supported her, not letting the widow sink down abjectly under the cruel gaze of this crowd. Meanwhile Kleiophon clung to Krito, clawing at him, until the older boy pushed him off.

'Alas!' said Krito. 'This is but a boy of fourteen, gentlemen, not come to manly years. Poor lamb, he cannot believe that something so dreadful can exist. But this wickedness has polluted our house and all of Athens with the deadly crime of homicide. We are all in danger of the displeasure of the gods, until our city is cleansed and we have driven out the poison that infects it. And I swear to the shade of Orthoboulos my father: *your death will be avenged.* Hermia must be tried for murder. This charge I lay before the Basileus and the city! Hear me, O gods, and defend the right!'

Then of course everyone who had come to the funeral was indeed glad that they had been there for this piece of drama, and the whole of Athens, free and slave, could talk of nothing else that day.

As soon as the charge was formally laid, Hermia was taken away from her home (once Orthoboulos' house, now Krito's) under guard. Fortunately her family was still well-connected and moderately rich, so the authorities didn't put Hermia in the prison. That would have been an utter disgrace and a great danger to a woman. Instead, they gave her into the charge of her uncle Phanodemos and his wife, with strict orders that Hermia was not to go out except on official business and under armed guard. I felt somewhat sorry for Hermia, and even for myself. Krito, who had undoubtedly found me at the scene of the discovery of his father's body, naturally summoned me as a witness. That meant that it was necessary for me to go to the first of the three preliminary hearings. This wasn't so very bad in itself, perhaps, but that fact alone ensured that anyone in Athens who cared to know would realize that I had been found in Manto's establishment. And on a night that was worse than merely rowdy. I was even less happy at the prospect of having eventually to speak up in the Areopagos at the trial. I could imagine what my enemies were saying when my very friends teased me.

'So, Stephanos, who would have thought it?' My old schoolmate Nikeratos pretended to be much shocked. 'You, a brothel-haunter, like poor little Ergokles, a bawdy-house reveller and brawler—'

'There was no brawl,' I insisted, foolishly enough. 'There was an outcry when the body was discovered – but that was in the house next door.'

'I suppose,' replied Nikeratos, with a deep affected sigh, 'that I must believe you. So Papa won't scold. But many won't be so trusting. And what is a bawdy-house story ending in a corpse if not the story of an affray? Jealousy, you know, drunken men fighting over a whore, and all that.'

'That is the kind of story Athenians love,' I complained to Aristotle. 'I am not so well beloved as it is. Now I am nearly as badly off as poor Orthoboulos himself when facing his trial for assault! Men will say I am nightly engaged in lechery and drunken brawling.'

'That sort of thing dies off eventually. Usually,' said Aristotle. 'But the nub of the matter is that you saw the corpse. Nobody was with you save the brothel-house keeper, Manto, standing over the body. Only the two of you – for some while. Some ill-wisher might insist that you were in the room with the man *before* he died.'

It had not, oddly enough, until this moment crossed my mind that I could be in any way tied in with the horrid crime itself.

'I could have nothing to do with it,' I assured Aristotle. 'The evidence of the – the circumstances, as even Krito will agree – the towels and the bed – indicates that Orthoboulos – or somebody – had been sick elsewhere, and the towels brought, but he hadn't thrown up there. That body was already stiff, and was not lying properly in the bed. There is no sign that the room had recently been used for sexual congress, or eating, or anything else. There was nothing in the chamber pot. It is pretty plain to me that the body was brought there. The scene was set up to look *as if* Orthoboulos had died there, but the indications are that he did not.'

'Better to bring that up in your own testimony before the Basileus at the first hearing,' Aristotle advised. 'Don't wait for Krito and his prosecution to ask you. Think carefully. What does Krito most want out of this trial?'

'That's not hard. To see his stepmother found guilty. And executed,' I answered promptly.

'Well. And if that is his burning desire, will he care overmuch who emerges as her confederate – or confederates? As long as he can make the charge hold?'

'Perhaps not.' This was hardly encouraging.

'What will be the final state of Krito if he succeeds in this objective?'

'Well – his stepmother will be dead. And he will be the heir of Orthoboulos – including all the money the man's second wife brought to the marriage. Therefore, I daresay with such prospects he could easily pay witnesses to say whatever he wanted them to say.'

'Exactly. At least you see that. So – make your own case and your role clear. Don't tie yourself in too strongly with the prosecution. A helpful man, a public-spirited witness. That is you. Say only what you clearly know, or what you strongly deduce from exactly what you did see. Do not seem speculative or accusatory. But do not wait too humbly or too long to be asked. Speak up. Your information is important – if the murder did not take place there, in the house where the body was found, that opens up another enquiry.'

V

Sour Words and Honey

The new load on my mind troubled my days and my nights too. I slept worse than usual nowadays anyway, and not just because of my wound. Dreams came, of water and sand and an invisible or only partly visible enemy struggling with me, as well as odd visions such as an octopus rowing a boat, hissing and ready to bite. I felt tired even on awakening. But there was no good putting off an immediate expedition to Eleusis. It was now necessary for me to explain myself to Smikrenes, my future father-in-law.

I had already been to see Smikrenes, almost as soon as I arrived in Athens upon my return from the East. That journey to the islands, however fraught with tribulations, was a modest triumph in terms of family business. I had succeeded in doing precisely what I had set out to do – I had found Philomela's maternal uncle, and had procured an agreement regarding her share of the maternal estate. Even the usually grumbling Smikrenes could not pretend to be dissatisfied. We had immediately gone over our future financial arrangements, and had recently undertaken the *engye*, a public betrothal agreement, registering our engagement and the amount of Philomela's dowry. On that public occasion of the *engye* I realized I was not going to impress the well-born in Athens over-much in producing such a new relative as Smikrenes. Still, Smikrenes was an old Athenian, a citizen, a man with fertile lands in the deme of Eleusis.

On this day, as I tramped once more to Eleusis, I wished earnestly that I were visiting him on another occasion. But I had to see him, now that the world of Athens knew of those memorable, unpleasant and withal mysterious events in Manto's brothel. I needed to inform the ageing farmer in a manly fashion of my involvement in the case. On this very day, the day after the wretched Orthoboulos' funeral and the accusations uttered by Krito, tidings had already had time to take wing from the Kerameikos to Eleusis. And I would not – and could not if I would – hold back from my intended bride's dour father the fact that I would have to be a witness in a trial of the most unpleasant kind.

'Well, here's a pretty mess you've all got into in Athens,' was Smikrenes' greeting to me. I was not mistaken in thinking that Smikrenes might already be in possession of the news. 'Some rich citizen and brothel-haunter has got hisself nicely killed, I hear. Stiff as a dried herring with poison – so they say. And now his son accuses his father's wife! Fine doings in the city!'

'We don't know all the facts of the case yet,' I said

cautiously. My future father-in-law waved caution away.

'I don't know as what I'm doing is right. It worries me at night some. Vexes me. Letting my Philomela marry into a town-dwelling family, with so much bad behaviour going on right around all of you there. Thefts every night, nothing safe. And brothels in every street, I'm told.'

'It's not as bad — I mean, they're not as numerous as that.' I swallowed. 'But indeed, you do need to be apprised of the full facts of the case. I fear I am involved in this trial for poisoning. Can we sit down?'

We sat down on a bench outside his house, where we could take advantage of the sun, had there been any. The autumn day had brought a haze with it, and a little cloud. I shivered. The walk to Eleusis had tired me, as it would not have done in the days before I was wounded. But part of my fatigue, I thought, arose from the task that lay just ahead — of telling Smikrenes about the unpleasantly memorable night at Manto's establishment. I gave a summary as succinctly as I could, but not omitting any important facts. Smikrenes certainly gave me his full attention. And, for a wonder, he did not interrupt. (I don't count little 'phoos' and 'humnphs' as interruptions.)

'Well, I never did!' he exclaimed as I came to the end of my narrative. 'And I never knew,' he said reproachfully. 'So mild as you look — I never knew you was a brothel-frequenter, and a rioter. Paying good money for what you might do for free if you had your wits about you. The *money* those places cost — two drakhmai! It's dreadful to think on. And

I suppose you treat yourself to wine and everything?'

'Well, I did on that night,' I admitted. 'But a man has to have some release. You forget I am not married yet. And I had gone many weeks without enjoyment, since I was wounded. I wanted to celebrate my recovery.'

'Celebrate, my backside,' said Smikrenes elegantly. 'You'll be celebrating in a courtroom, with some accuser snarling after you. If you was in the brothel, why'd you have to go and investigate a corpse? Why didn't you slip out another door and get yourself gone? Seems to me like the bitch you was with had the better sense.'

'I didn't know at first what all the outcry was about,' I explained. 'It seemed to me only right to find out what the trouble was. It is perhaps in part Aristotle's training – to go into problems in the hope of solutions.'

'Philosophy!' Smikrenes spat on the ground. 'Philosophy is just making you more woolly-brained than necessary. That and your cock together are leading you straight into trouble.' He sighed. 'I doubt you're over-young for marriage—'

'No, no!' I said hastily. 'And I do think this is unjust. I have taken care of my family for over three years now, since my father died. I have worked hard to get us out of debt. As you know, I have come back from the eastern islands with a written agreement from your daughter's uncle, Philokles. He gives us a share of the property at Hymettos, and we will soon all be much better off. Once I get the honey business organized.'

'Well, it seems that's so,' said Smikrenes, abating a

little of his contempt. 'And you *are* young still, so I daresay you can't always be held accountable like older and wiser heads. But if I was you, young fellow, I'd stop sticking my poker up all and sundry, like of what you're doing in them brothels. Poking slave-girls you don't know! Why, they service so many customers, they're littered with other men's seed. Not good for the health.'

'But it's not good for the health to go without,' I said, laughing a little. 'And once I am married I will have no need for such recreation.'

'I dunno. A taste for carousal is by no means cured by a wedding.' Smikrenes was determined neither to be cheerful nor to meet my smile with another. 'You think of Alkibiades and all them sort,' he advised. '*They* was married, wasn't they? Yet Alkibiades would pursue anything on two legs. Men and women, boys and girls. And they all had to love him – absolutely *dote* on him – or he'd know the reason why.'

'Alkibiades is long dead,' I remarked soothingly.

'But there's others of that breed alive today. Hypereides, for instance. You wouldn't think it to look at him, would you? Old Jug Face as he is, with those ears sticking out! But he's popular with the women, even now he's so old. Of course, he's always had money. Keeping three women at once – one of them is right here in Eleusis. Phila, her name is. He still visits her regular, but even at sixty he's not going to settle for just one. People say that the beauteous Phryne is one of his girls – or was recently. "The most beautiful woman in Attika": that's what *she*'s said to be. More beautiful than virtuous – it don't need much mind to guess that. Oh, I tell you, my boy, money disappears fast down that drain! Talk about throwing your goods down a well!'

I was the more distressed at the turn this conversation was taking as I thought I had heard the door move. It seemed to have opened, just a crack. Enough for a woman inside to listen a little, without losing modesty. Philomela, my intended bride, might be the listener. Either that or it was her old nurse Geta, who would of course relate everything to her mistress, perhaps with embellishments or commentary I could do without.

'Whatever you may think of the matter, sir,' I said rather stiffly, 'I am not truly accountable to *you*. I simply thought it right, out of courtesy, to explain how things were. And that I am likely to be called as a witness in the trial resulting from the death of this man. I am *not* a suspected person, I shall simply have to give evidence about the finding of the body. No doubt that will be disagreeable, and it may give rise to some transient jests at my expense. But it should not be a serious matter in my life, nor in yours. I do not care to discuss it any further.'

As I expected, this firm statement made him peevish, but he did abate something of his hectoring tone and obscene reference.

'All I can say,' he said loftily, staring into the sky, or perhaps just over his precious fields, 'is that it would be better for people to have real work to do on some real land. As you got yourself hooked into this coming trial for murder, my lad, you can get along on your own, as you say. I can see as you're ashamed of it – *I*

don't want to rub it in, I'm sure. I am sorry about it,
that's all. At least here in Eleusis I won't have to hear
people jabbering about it every day, as I don't go into
town much.'

'You never go anywhere much,' I remarked. 'So you
won't hear much about it, no.'

'Trouble is,' said Smikrenes in a grave and considering tone, 'the *real* trouble is that these homicide trials
drag on for three or four months. You haven't had the
first prodikasia yet. I won't have Philomela marrying
you until it's all over. That's flat. This here trial has
to be settled first. I mean it. That means, if it drags
on into Gamelion, you won't get married in Gamelion.
Philomela's only fifteen. Maybe wait till she's sixteen.
No hurry. It would be bad luck – and bad for my reputation and Philomela's – to mix up your marriage with
you being a witness in such a bad crime. What makes
it worse, the murder of this man is a family case. Like
Klytaimnestra and all those dreadful families in the
plays who are no better than they should be. Killing
their parents, or girls trying to kill their brothers, or
some such. *My* family have always kept theirselves
decent.'

Here was a setback I had not dreamed of. I had
imagined that Smikrenes would scold and look sour.
But it had never occurred to me that the timing of the
homicide trial could affect the time of my marriage.
Since the betrothal had first been spoken of between
Smikrenes and myself, it had always been taken for
granted that we would marry in the following
Gamelion. The marriage month falls in the coldest
and most wintry time, when men keep holiday from

farm work and there is leisure, even in the country, to hold a wedding festival. Gamelion was not far off now – less than three full months. I could not absolutely *make* Smikrenes hand me over his daughter in marriage, when it came to it.

Smikrenes was undoubtedly right in working out the chronological order. There would be three hearings, with a month between them, before the actual trial for murder. At these hearings, facts would be produced, witnesses would appear, and each side would learn what the other had to say while the authorities would consider whether there were an actual case to answer. The first prodikasia had not yet taken place. We would be going from autumn into winter, and almost out of it, before the trial was over. At this rate, I could hardly plan on getting married even in Anthesterion, when the spring starts to stir.

'I cannot agree with you there,' I said, as equably as I could manage. 'It will cause more talk if we postpone the wedding. The *engye* has already taken place. The world knows that you and I have pledged our agreement. I am fully determined on this marriage. Let us talk more about it later, when we see how things come to pass. Turn now to other matters. Am I correct in believing that Philomela will be bringing to my house her servant Geta – her old nurse?'

'What? What's that?' Smikrenes stared at me as if he couldn't believe his senses. He cupped his large and soil-stained hand about one of his ears, as if he felt a defect in his hearing must have distorted my words. 'Geta? You thought *Geta* was going to come to your house – along of Philomela?'

'Well, yes,' I admitted. 'It is customary for the girl, if she's young and it's her first marriage, to bring such an old family servant, her personal nurse, with her—'

'Can't be done,' said Smikrenes decidedly. 'By the gods, this is amazing! Fellow thinks he can steal my servants! No, no, I need Geta much more than Philomela will. After all, when she goes to your house, you have your mother and a female servant. Philomela can do kitchen work on her own. No need to cosset the girl. I cannot do without Geta. Whoever would wash my clothes, do the garden and small truck, and get my meals?'

'Oh. I see.' I brooded a while. 'I think – I know, in fact – that I am understaffed. The farm is presently rented out, but I need to keep a couple of servants there to keep an eye on the place and do the basic work. And my household in Athens really needs a new slave. Either a man or a woman.'

'Get a man slave. More use,' advised Smikrenes. 'You can make him do some of the hard work at the farm, and then he can make and mend at home and run errands around the city for you if you want him there. But don't get a young fellow – they're always after the maids. And you know what they say,' he drolled, looking at me sidewise. 'Like master, like man. He'd be haunting the brothels shortly.'

I recognized in this jest an overture of a kind, and tried to respond with a grudged cordiality. I suggested taking a stroll. We went to the back of the grove, where there were the shrines of Pan and the Nymphs. These were a source of exasperation rather than of pride to Smikrenes, however, as people kept trying to come to perform sacrifices and have picnics on this spot. It was odd to think of the Nymphs having anything to do with Smikrenes – still less the Graces.

Our conversation had left my mind somewhat raw. It appeared I wasn't going to get any new help from Smikrenes' household, and my irascible relative-to-be might insist on the delay of our marriage. I stayed overnight in Eleusis in Smikrenes' house, because I needed to recuperate before walking the many stadia back to Athens. But it was a grim visit. There was no chance of seeing my girl with the grey-green eyes. (For, against all propriety, we had once met and talked, although a man should not see his wife until after the wedding. As we had conversed, I knew of her eyes, and of her hair with its sheen of a ripe acorn.) Philomela remained virtuously invisible, a very subdued Geta served us supper, and I went to bed early in order to avoid any more remarks from Smikrenes.

While walking back to Athens, I realized it was more important than ever for me to get to Hymettos and begin to put my financial affairs (which would include my own and Philomela's future affairs) on a good foot-ing. Financial success might persuade Smikrenes to give over his resistance to the marriage taking place, even during the time of the trial for the murder of Orthoboulos.

I set out for Hymettos as soon as I could. This time I did not go on foot, but took a donkey and cart with me, and rode much of the way, until the slope of

Hymettos became really steep. I envied my former self, the young man I had been in the previous summer, swinging confidently through the hot landscape. Now even in this cool weather, I rode like an older man – or like the invalid that I had recently been.

When I entered the farmhouse on the mountain slope, I was confronted by a man who was certainly as much of an invalid as he had been when I first met him: Dropides, the second husband of my intended bride's grandmother Philokleia. Philokleia, very active for her age, managed the farm and estate, nominally for her son, the absent Philokles. He had gone out to the newly liberated islands, supposedly to be a settler on Rhodos, but I had found him taking his ease with a female friend in Kos. As this woman, Nanno, formerly mistress of a general, had a house of her own in Kos and a share in a sponge fishery in Kalymnos, Philokles was too comfortable to wish to come home. His faithful mother Philokleia went on working for the family, and Dropides had certainly found a comfortable nest. This Dropides was an amazing man – he never seemed to bestir himself, mind or body, at all. He was now sitting, as I walked in, in his great chair, just as I had seen him in the heat of summer. He was still surrounded, as he loved to be, by old and seedy furniture (collected from his former home and stuffed into his new habitation). Now that it was autumn, he was swaddled in more blankets, and covered by two sheepskins instead of one.

'I'm tolerable, thank you,' he responded gloomily in answer to my salutations. 'But these cooling days get to a man. Breezy here, very breezy. Of course, in these uplands—' He sighed.

'There is still some warmth in the sun,' I responded. 'Even though the feast of the seeds is behind us, some good weather usually follows.'

'Many a good blow and sharp rainfall after that,' he said with satisfaction.

'I wish to discuss some business,' I remarked, not caring whether or not I seemed too abrupt. And he said, as I hoped he would, 'Ah! Then you need my wife, Philokleia. Fetch her, Mika.'

The little slavewoman went out into the fields; it was not long before she trotted back with her mistress in tow. As was proper, Mika saw to it that a curtain was pinned up in the inner doorway, and Philokleia spoke through that, ostensibly to her husband.

'I know,' I said, 'that in our earlier talk after I got back from Kos we clarified the arrangement made by Philokles. And you are agreeable to letting me sell the honey and take a share of the proceeds.'

'Good thing you came with a cart,' she said. 'I was going to send for you, to say we could give you some.'

'I am sure I can sell it,' I said. 'With winter coming on, there may be a new demand. Of course we won't get the sea-traffic, but many around Attika will purchase at a fair price. I could get more for the honey – real honey of Hymettos – perhaps if I had a way of getting it to Korinthos, or Megara or somewhere. But I shall need more slaves; a lot of labour's needed in moving things to a market.'

'Certainly is,' interjected Dropides, under the pretence that he was the active member of the discussion.

'We have more we wanted to say, too,' continued Philokleia. 'Ah, here's my daughter Philonike.' And another light step came behind her. Now there were two forms of veiled women behind the curtain, both pairs of eyes watching me. I felt embarrassed. For there was nothing for it – I must really tell this household too of my unfortunate involvement in the upcoming trial.

'Before we get into any more business,' I said firmly, 'I have something to confess – I don't mean that. I mean – something to *say*. To announce. You live so far out of the way here, and see so few, the news does not seem yet to have reached you.'

'News? My Philomela?' Philonike was apprehensive.

'Nothing like that. But I was in a brothel kept by a woman named Manto when a man was found dead, evidently of foul play. As I was among the first to see the body, I am to be called as a witness in the trial.'

'Oh, is that all?' sniffed Philonike.

'A brothel boy, are you?' Dropides cackled. 'I could tell you pretty tales of houses in Athens in my younger days—'

'You'd be hard put to get to them now,' said Philokleia. 'I doubt you could go up their stairs. But Stephanos, will this have serious consequences for you, do you think?'

'I cannot see why it would, in the long run,' I responded honestly. 'The man had been murdered, but I had nothing to do with that. I serve only as a witness to the finding of the body. I shall have to endure a little ridicule about the circumstances – probably nothing more weighty than a few jokes. I am no kin or connection of the murdered man, who certainly

seemed to have been poisoned. His son accuses his
new second wife, and Athens is in an uproar about
that. But I know nothing of who did it. The man was
certainly dead well before I saw him – his corpse,
rather.'

'Oh well, if he was nobody we know,' said Philokleia.

'But,' I added, 'I am additionally vexed because now
Smikrenes says he cannot have Philomela wed me
while the trial is going on – not until after it is over.
And that may delay us for a while. Certainly beyond
Gamelion.'

'Oh, *him*!' Philonike snorted, openly contemptuous
of her husband, the man from whom she had lived
apart for so many years. 'Smikrenes loves to grumble
and drop stones in your path. Can't bear to part with
his daughter, I dare say!'

'All the same,' said Philokleia, more cautiously, 'this
isn't the best thing to have happen. I wouldn't want
my granddaughter Philomela associated with brothel
murders and the like, either.'

'*Nobody* wants it,' I said despondently. 'It is all a
mess, and I am exceedingly sorry that I was in the
brothel that night.'

'It cannot be helped,' said Philokleia resignedly.
'We appreciate your telling us. We are rather out of
the way here, it's true, so you could have let the
matter rest, and maybe we wouldn't have found out
for a long time. I'd be very sorry to have the wedding
delayed – especially since you and Smikrenes are
publicly pledged to it. Once there's an *engye*, any
delay or breaking-off is a serious matter. Creates
talk, and that's bad for Philomela. Smikrenes will

probably come to see that, and stand to his word, however.'

'Best not to say any more to him right now,' advised Dropides with unexpected wisdom.

'What was it you wanted to tell me?' I asked.

'Oh – it would have been such good news on another occasion,' Philonike said impetuously. 'My dowry – we have the dowry land now, free and clear; it was rented out and there was dispute about it. But now it is clear. Smikrenes will allow us to tend this land and give up any other claim to it if we hand over all the income to you and my daughter. It's just a few fields near here, you know. Not very convenient for Smikrenes! We thought we could rent it out anyway, now the ownership is established, and give you and Philomela the proceeds.'

'There's even a house on it – of sorts,' said Dropides.

'More like a hut,' said Philokleia. 'No value at all. But the land yields produce. Good for root vegetables, lettuce and beans. Maybe even some wheat.'

'That will be helpful,' I agreed. 'Once the extra money starts coming in, I can purchase a slave, which I badly need. I think I need a man rather than a woman, though as I thought Philomela's old nurse would be coming with her, it had seemed to me that there would be an extra worker in the family. Now I find that it isn't so. I really should make a purchase before Philomela comes to me.'

'Oh, by Demeter and her Daughter, isn't that just like my husband!' said Philonike unguardedly. 'Of course the woman Geta should come to your house with my daughter, but that's just the sort of thing he'd stick at. He *hates* getting used to anyone or anything new!'

'I think we can help you,' said Philokleia. 'We can give you an advance payment on the honey and on the rental of the dowry lands. Of course, if the marriage does not come off, you will be indebted to us for the amount. But I have every belief that it will, despite Smikrenes' bad humour about the law case.'

'Here, wife, are you sure you want to let money be going out of the house like that?' protested Dropides. But it was easy for the women to override him.

'No better place for it,' said Philokleia briskly. 'We should regard it as an investment. An extra worker would make it easier for Stephanos to build up the business of selling the honey. Stay overnight, Stephanos – I can see that the travelling tires you a little. And tomorrow morning my daughter with my help can arrange the honeycombs for you to take back.'

I was glad of the night's lodging, even if it meant sleeping amid the furniture of the inert Dropides. He was not, however, so completely inert as not to move to his wife's bedroom for the night, so I had the worm-eaten tables and the chairs with shaky legs all to myself. Next morning, the women were as good as their word. Well veiled, they conducted me to the outbuildings, to the cellar in the earth where they stored the honey. The sight of the golden honeycombs was most welcome. I took many neat combs away with me on wooden trays supplied by the Hymettos estab-lishment; everything was fitted nicely into my modest little one-ass cart.

'And here's the money,' said Philokleia. Evidently

not trusting it to Dropides, she went against etiquette so far as to give it directly to me. But she dropped the coins into a pottery jar, and we listened to each clink as she counted them out. 'Two hundred and fifty drakhmai. There!' she said proudly, holding the jar towards me. 'That's more than enough to buy you a slave for your household.'

'Truly, yes,' I said. 'I am more than grateful, I will write out a receipt at once.' And I took a piece of broken potsherd and scratched on it what I owed her.

And so we, the ass and I, trundled slowly and steadily back to Athens with our load of honey, and my load of silver coins. It had been a great relief talking with the Hymettos family, cheering that they had not taken the bad news too hard, nor blamed me. My spirits revived. Now I had something to sell, and some money in hand. To my surprise, I was able to sell a good deal of the honey in the agora of Athens that very afternoon – an unexpected gift of fortune. I had thought of taking the sweet load down to Peiraieus, but getting there would be a long walk. So I went home to store the rest of the honey, and my hoard of new cash. It seemed, at least momentarily, possible to surmount all difficulties.

VI

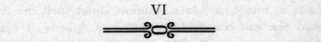

Generous Women

So elated was I that my earlier worries and embarrass-
ment seemed ill-founded. In a sudden access of return-
ing well-being I felt again the prickles of desire. After
all, my future father-in-law was treating me most
unkindly in postponing my marriage – or threatening
to. An old man doesn't understand – he has forgotten.
A young man needs relief. The urges of Eros are sharp
and ever-present. And what need I care for the opinions of elderly gentlemen as unattractive and inactive
as Dropides and Smikrenes? Fortifying myself with
such thoughts, I decided to go to a really good brothel.
I had sense enough to wrap the pot of silver coins in
a bundle of rags and deposit it carefully at home. Athens
had been subjected to so many robberies recently that
even this was something of a worry to me; I wished
to hide the coins even from the rest of the family. Before
I hid the treasure away, I put a number of my new
silver coins into a small leather pouch. Tonight's

entertainment was going to be a high-class affair. I washed before I went, and put on a clean khiton.

The brothel I chose, run by a woman called Tryphaina, was a superior establishment, to which leading men often resorted. Tryphaina had a deal of taste in music; people who know about such things said she had the best musicians in Athens at her parties. Even on ordinary nights you could hear the kithara beautifully played, and the flute-boys and girls never puffed unduly or made false notes. Her rooms were well furnished, and the *pornai* were of the best sort, very attractive indeed. Not only were these girls clean and well dressed, they had their hair done in various attractive ways and wore subtle perfumes and good jewellery. Their garments were clean and nearly transparent, of finest linen or even (in the most expensive cases) of Koan silk, in rainbow dyes.

It was a surprise to the eyes to gaze on such a flock of loveliness. My only disappointment was to find no Egyptian among these birds, for I had been hankering in vain since the spring for an Egyptian girl seen briefly (but not enjoyed) at the port near Delphi. Otherwise there was nothing to complain of at Tryphaina's, and I was treated extraordinarily well. This was as far as you could get from your low-class 'little house' of one-room action. This elegant place was free of the hurried air found in even a good brothel like Manto's. There were fine ornaments in the public room and good chairs, so you felt you were on a pleasant visit. These lovely and well-mannered girls indeed approached as if you were a friend they had been waiting to see. They summoned tastefully dressed – or rather, sweetly undressed – servitors to offer wine, and took a leisurely interest in one's welfare which was quite delightful to experience.

I handed over more of my Hymettos money than I cared later to think about. No gold, but at least the money was all in silver – no lowly pieces of bronze. And I made a pretty speech about buying my chosen girl a wreath of flowers for her hair. My particular young woman, who gave her name as 'Kleoboule,' registered no great elation, but I had evidently offered a sufficient sum. She set about entertaining me in very good style, sitting on my knee and braiding my hair.

'What is your name?' she asked, but I would not give a straight answer; it is not good policy to tell people in a brothel your real name. As I would not be a regular visitor at Tryphaina's, there was no honest use to this girl in her knowing it. Then Kleoboule tried to undress me, pushing at my khiton at the top, and I had to warn her, in a low voice, that I was wounded.

'By the Two Goddesses,' she exclaimed, 'so you are. A soldier – a hero – from the wars?'

'You can say that,' I agreed rather stupidly. 'But I am no hero.'

'But you have fought in the wars? You are a Makedonian soldier?'

'Yes,' I agreed. 'That's what you can call me. Makedonian Soldier.'

She gave me more wine, and played gently with my hair again; then she took up some greenery, saying I must wear a victory garland on my head. The drink was very good. 'Chian wine,' she cooed. The room was warm, even though it was cool outside. This place smelled good, full of sweet scents, like jasmine flowers, like summer returned.

'There! See yourself, Makedonian Soldier!' She showed me the result of her activity in a bronze mirror. I had a few green branches, my victory garland, twined about my flushed brow. The bronze mirror was old and beautiful, with figures of goats and two small images of Eros at the side of the handle. I gave her another silver coin for making the garland. We danced a little to the music of a kithara and a lyre, played by able musicians in delightful dishevelment. I drank a glass of almost neat wine off with a flourish, and we stumbled into the bedroom.

There this delicious Kleoboule did things with me that I cannot repeat, and at times can barely remember. But she gave her money's worth. She was very sympathetic about my wound, and made me feel much better. The bed was very nice too, with new fresh covers. That must cost a lot in laundry, I calculated aloud. She giggled and said I could have a laundry maid if that was my desire. Then she imitated a laundry maid, her skirts up on her knees scrubbing and rubbing, and I took her from the back, just in case we were tired of frontways. 'I will give you honey,' I offered. 'Lots and lots of honey. I am in the honey business.'

She laughed. 'Oh, I am in the honey business too,' she responded. This seemed to me good enough to write down. Some people keep collections of the smart saying of hetairai and *pornai*, and these women often gain the reputation of wits.

The night must have been running out when we left our exhausted bed and returned back to the public area for a change of scene. We had cast some clothes on, and I clapped my now-wilting garland on my head. Some new musicians were playing. Somebody had tidied up the room with lovely painted walls. There were stands with elegant antique pots on them, showing scenes of a kind that would not be displayed in the *andron* of the gravest and most serious citizen. These vases illustrated many scenes of action, not the action of the Trojan War but the activity of Eros. There were scenes of extremely vivacious parties, with here a young man puking into a basin his excess of drink, there a hetaira lifting her skirt while her attendants fingered a bald man bent over. A group of satyrs were at a symposium, where they both ate with and took possession of very curvaceous ladies with elegant ringlets and prominent bosoms. A woman in diaphanous clothing laughingly raised a slipper aloft, threatening the naked buttocks of a young man with instant chastisement.

Everywhere one looked, there seemed to be lively parties, which made one glad to be in one already. There was a buzz of conversation around us, and a kithara rang softly into the lighted night. Fine lamps, neatly trimmed and burning the best oil (the unsmoky kind), were attractively arranged on stands and tables. How different from life at the farm in Eleusis, or in Hymettos, where you turned in to sleep shortly after sundown, and the only sound was the hooting of owls and other nocturnal birds. Here the night was as the day.

'You are nocturnal birds!' I yelled. 'You are the owls of Athena!' The girls hooted and made noises like birds. 'Aha,' said my Kleoboule to me. 'You forget, that was the joke about Sophokles in his old age, and his mistress Arkhippe. Sophokles was very old, all white hair and bleary eyes, but he insisted on Arkhippe staying with him and looking after his wants. And when one of Arkhippe's friends asked one of her former lovers what she was doing these days, he replied, "She's sitting on a tomb like an owl."'

'But I am young!' I protested. I did feel glad to be alive (if wounded) and still young.

'Let us drink,' said Kleoboule. 'We shall pour a libation to Youth and Health.'

I readily drank to that, and then I composed a kind of poem, which fortunately I cannot remember. By this time there were a number of other men around me, talking to the girls, and I was not really surprised to see the rich and excessively handsome Philinos among them. If a man of Philinos' standing wished to go to a brothel, he could obviously choose the best. Then a crowd of new people suddenly came in – I realized they must be the tag-end of a couple of symposia. The tail-end of an expensive and riotous dinner party tends to turn at last into the sort of merrymaking of which sober householders complain: a *komos*, a line of drunken revellers and their whores and servants singing and playing and dancing through the streets, in search of further festivity. This night two parties (of the superior sort) had each turned at the end into a straggling *komos* and gone noisily roaming the streets, simultaneously deciding that Tryphaina's brothel offered the best opportunity for finishing a night of pleasure. Their combined forces made a large party, made larger by a number of musical slaves, one or two boys playing the pan-pipes and many more females the *krotala*, those sticks that make such fascinating rhythmic sounds, or the little *kumbala*, the metal circles placed on the fingertips that clash together in such a pleasing manner. The men seemed all to be very rich. A great deal of money went in short order to Tryphaina, with commands to bring more Chian wine. The room was crowded, and the music, which had been playing softly, grew loud, emphasized by the rhythms of the sticks and *kumbala*. Then suddenly one man called for silence, banging on a wine-jar with a knife.

'Gentlemen – and ladies – from Athens and out of it! Now you are to imagine the trumpets sounding!' He imitated the sound of trumpets, and the flute-boys and girls gallantly followed his lead, making their noise as much like a salpinx as they could.

'Ta-ra-ra-ra!' the youth imitated. 'But the trumpets are sounding not for Alexander – but for something more wonderful. Lo! Phryne is here!'

And he drew back the door, and a veiled figure entered, very dramatically. Then the figure, tall and obviously beautifully shaped even under a cloak, cast off its covering. The veiled presence unveiled itself. And there was simply the most beautiful woman one could ever imagine seeing.

Phryne. Yes, *Phryne* herself. How can I describe her? The most beautiful woman in all Athens. Statues and paintings have been made of her, and poets have written about her, the most famous hetaira of her era. Her face was a perfect shape, a calm oval, with the pure Grecian nose that artists talk about, but which is seldom seen in all its perfection. In a woman too, such a nose can look ugly, too strong, but in her face everything was in proportion, from her beautiful large dark eyes to her finely etched mouth. Waves of golden hair rippled back off her brow. Her eyelashes were long and dark, her eyebrows high-arched, with just a touch of the quizzical or impudent. This nobly shaped head was set upon the most perfect swan-like neck. Her gown, though modest, was drawn tight enough to the body to hint fully that everything Phryne had under her clothes was pleasing to excess.

Even these partygoers and their companions, men and women loud from hard drinking and amorous disport, became quiet. We all stared at this woman, as at some wonder beyond exclamation, beyond praise.

'Well, I never thought it,' said my companion. 'I didn't know she was coming. This is beyond anything great! Phryne is so magnificent. It's as good as a play to watch her. She can keep the room in a roar. We'll have good new games now.' It surprised me, but I could see that the women were as pleased at Phryne's gracing their lodging as the men were. And who could wonder at it? If Aphrodite came among us, the golden laughter-loving goddess, then women and men would all alike be pleased.

'Welcome, Phryne, my girl,' said Tryphaina, bustling up to her. 'Here is your second home.'

'Second, third or fourth – what difference?' Phryne waved a beautiful hand with tapering fingers. 'I have had many homes, Aphrodite knows. Hey-ho. Oh for the ocean waves! Maybe my true home is the foam of the sea.'

'We'll toss you into it,' threatened Philinos, playfully.

He went up to embrace her. 'Come back to sea with me, Phryne,' he entreated.

'Ah, but Philinos, your dwelling is in plain Kephisia, near smoky Akharnai. Good for charcoal, I admit, but not for fish, nor caves of coral.'

'Poor Akharnai – what has it done to you? It is,' suggested Philinos, 'a home of Ares, and you know Ares always attracts Aphrodite.'

'They do make a handsome couple!' exclaimed my Kleoboule. 'You must admit, those who say Philinos is the best-looking man in Athens may not be wrong.'

Philinos continued to stroke Phryne's hair and cheek.

'Would you not come and live with me if I take you to a sea-cave, Phryne? With all the pearls and coral?'

She did not turn him away, but laughingly flicked him under the chin.

'Oh, my dear Philinos! Pearls and coral are lovely, but one can see them better on dry land.' She squeezed his arm affectionately. 'And you and I have made our excursion over the foaming sea, and come home.'

'I hope you will be at home to *me*,' said Philinos. 'My boat has room always for a passenger who enchants the waters.'

'Oh, you have a boat?' said one of the young men. 'Is it a merchant ship? Will you take me for a voyage? I want to go with Phryne for a ride. Please, Phryne, come to sea with *me*.'

'Catch *you* anywhere near the sea, you'd be in danger of being taken for a sprat,' retorted the lovely woman.

'Oh, you are severe tonight, my sharp little toad,' laughed Philinos. 'I think I shall go to my own abode, to elude your cruelty.'

And despite the entreaties of the woman with whom he had come downstairs, Philinos strode off.

'Phryne, come here,' begged one of the men. 'Give me a little kiss – only one.'

'But darling, why should I?'

'Because I must make Phoebe here jealous – that's why. You know how easily women are rendered jealous—'

'Especially whores – especially the slave kind,' laughed another boy.

'Whores *and* wives,' said an older man. 'See how Hermia behaved to her husband. Did for him. Must have been out of jealousy.'

'Begone with all such slanders,' commanded Phryne lightly. 'Athens is full of slanders – I don't believe a word they say against the widow of Orthoboulos.'

'Oh, Hermia – she's no better than she should be. And you should be at mortal odds with such as she – for Hermia the poisonous had the repute of a virtuous wife. Not your sort at all, Phryne, my jewel-eyed toad.'

'Look you,' said Phryne, sitting up tall and straight, 'it is not women who ruin the world by greed and jealousy. It is men. Women are more forgiving, more generous. My friend Lykaina and I – deep thinkers, both of us – have agreed that we hetairai are the most generous of all. Listen, I will tell you a story, if you, my pets, consent to listen.'

'A tale – from Phryne? Telling tales, oh my!' They crowded around her, teasing in the lamplight, but eager.

'Just pretend I'm your old nurse, my little babes,' and she stroked the hair of the young man kneeling at her feet. 'Take care to listen correctly. I will call my story – my *true* story, mind that – "**The Tale of the Generous Women**":

'Once upon a time a Milesian woman of great beauty named Plangon was beloved by a youth of Kolophon. He had a mistress already, a servant of Dionysos named Bakkhis, a woman of Samos. He was living with Bakkhis, but he beheld the overwhelming beauty of Plangon of Miletos and was undone. When he had ardent speech with her and begged her favours, Plangon was puzzled what to do. She herself knew of the beautiful Bakkhis, and hoped to send the lad back to her. So Plangon said to the youth that she would give him the favour that he asked for, but only if he would give her the famous necklace belonging to Bakkhis. This celebrated necklace of gold studded with many valuable gems was very curious and costly, and she knew that Bakkhis would never give it up.

'The doleful youth, however, went to his mistress Bakkhis, who loved him, and told her of his plight. He was so passionately in love with Plangon, he told her, he was sure he would die if his love could not be gratified. He pleaded with his mistress to help him. And Bakkhis' heart was turned with pity, and she gave to him (ungrateful youth) the most valuable thing she owned, her inimitable necklace. Plangon lived up to her agreement, but she sent the necklace back to Bakkhis, with a note expressing her admiration. And then the two girls became firm friends, happy in each other's company, and they shared between them the young man from Kolophon.

'There! Is not that a nice tale! So out of the door with all slanders and ill-speaking about women.'

One of the girls standing near me said fondly, 'Isn't she fun!'

'She's glorious. But why do *you* like her so much?' I enquired.

'Oh, because she is generous and playful. And she makes those who are slaves forget they are slaves, and those who are considered bad as if they were good.'

'Where's little Thisbe of Thebes?' another young man demanded. He grabbed one of the flute-girls as she was eating – or rather drinking – a quick and nourishing supper of gruel from a bowl. 'Do you remember any Theban dances, my poppet? Aren't you one of those enslaved at the taking of Thebes? When Alexander and his men won the siege and stormed the city? You were one of the thirty thousand Thebans captured after the men were killed – sold straight into a brothel in Peiraieus.'

'It was my mother who was captured from Thebes, and sold as a slave, and me with her,' said the young girl sadly. 'I was so little, I hardly remember anything. Except the yelling and the fire. Now they cannot sell Theban slaves in Athens any more.'

'But that,' said a knowledgeable older man, 'only means that they are all shipped off to Asia, even further away, and made to work in the Makedonian's army, answering the needs of a parcel of brutes from Pella. You're better off here.'

'Until they rebuild Thebes,' said Phryne, rising and stretching.

'That's a kindly thought,' said one of the men, 'especially since you are from Boiotian Thespiai, and the men of Thespiai fought against the Thebans in the old days.'

'Yet, Thebes will be rebuilt – someday.'

'Phryne – that's impossible! Alexander left nothing of it standing, save Pindar's house.'

'Forever impossible? Will Thebes never be rebuilt? I'll tell you a secret, boys and girls. I am wealthy, and I intend to be wealthier still. And with my money I will build a city wall around Thebes, if only the Thebans will write upon the wall an inscription – like this:

"What Alexander destroyed, Phryne the Hetaira raised again."'

'You're good at raising things, aren't you?' said an older man, teasingly, lifting a lock of her hair to kiss it. With a butterfly move she lightly slapped his hand away.

'None of that, unless you're *very* good. It costs a mina to do my hair – unless you're my maid.'

'Come, Phryne, what shall we play?' asked one of the eager youths. 'Shall we play at divination? Or dance all together? Would you like to see me dance the *kordax*?'

'What, watch you fling your balls about, Euboulos? No, thank you.'

'Euboulos throws his balls, but nobody catches them,' said one of the other men.

'You behave,' the young man Euboulos said to Phryne, 'or I will kidnap you.'

'You couldn't hold me for a minute – you always let go too soon. I know you!' said Phryne with joking contempt.

'Then I'll kidnap this maiden here!' And the young Euboulos grabbed one of the smaller women, who struggled as he picked her up. 'Why you—' and she lashed out with her nails, scratching his cheek. He gave her a shake.

'Stop fussing, little vixen.' She began to struggle in reality, striking out with her nails, and he twisted her arm behind her, still holding her.

'I will kidnap you, and Phryne will have to ransom you.'

'I can grab her back – she's right there where I can see her.'

'Oh, but I will hide her.' And the young man started to move off, now with the thin girl slung over his shoulders. She kicked and he hit her. 'Do that again, lass, and you'll have a black eye! Yes, Phryne, I can take her, and hide her – hide her from you so you cannot see her.'

'So-o! Is that how the wind blows?! Why then, I shall be a desolate mother.' Phryne straightened her hair and her gown, and stood in the centre of the room:

'I sorrowing Mother, I desolate Demeter seek
Throughout the desolate land, the ravaged land,
    my daughter.

I take the life from spring, the light from summer
All harvests will wither and die, until I am
    satisfied.
Surely –'

Here she turned towards the kidnapped girl and
the violent young man, who now slowly swung the
girl down off his shoulders; the two of them ceased
fighting and stood still before Phryne, both already
partly in awe of this new manifestation:

'Surely I see her, struggling in the grasp of dark
    Hades,
The grip of Hades' dark King. Sleeping not, I eat
nothing—'

One of the girls from the kitchen tossed Phryne a
wreath of entwined wheat stalks, their corn nodding
on them. Phryne put it on her brows.

'I sorrow for day after day, in the grip of despair.
But now—'

and here Phryne seized on the supper of gruel, belonging most properly to the little Theban flute-player—

'Now I eat the *kykeion*, now my soul will be eased
For surely at last my Daughter, my Kore, returns.'

We clapped and yelled as at a play. The young
man who had let go of the girl seemed to forget all
intentions of harm, and applauded too.

'You are good boys and girls,' cried Phryne. 'I am for Isodaites, the god of equal shares, and I shall tell Tryphaina to provide at my expense bread and wine for everybody! Wake up! Why sleep while we can dance and sport all night?'

Much happy laughter followed as many of the company took advantage of this offer. Two men started a tipsy dance, while the lyre was played and the girls took the *krotala* and clicked a lively rhythm in accompaniment.

'Let's do it properly,' Phryne commanded. 'All together, now. Fetch some torches!' And we formed a long line including everybody, a line unsteady and rolling with pleasure, while the pipes played softly and then began to roar, the *krotala* and the little finger cymbals began to click and clash, and the flutes wailed. Torches shone at the front and at the back of the procession, as we went on our way, dancing along, feeling magnificent, like stars in the heavens circling the earth.

Soon we were in one long line of revellers, dancing through the house, upstairs and down, in a drunken *komos*, a revel rout led by Phryne. A little boy with a psaltery played beside her, *krotala* and *kumbala* crashed and rang, and amidst the moving crowd the flute-girls struggled valiantly to blow us to victory. We were not thoughtful people in a thoughtful mood. It was only later that we realized that Phryne's beautiful imitation of the story of Demeter, and her immediately ensuing invitation to the dance, might not have been wise.

VII

The Slave Market

The next day wasn't so pleasant, of course. I say 'next day' rather than 'next morning' because I saw nothing of the morning. Stumbling home at dawn I went straight to bed. Bad dreams pursued me. Yet I slept, in a fitful hot, tossing way, until the sun was high in the sky. Before I was wounded, I would have been able to take a night's carouse better. Or perhaps not. I couldn't say that I had ever been part of such a glorious and wild party before. This, I realized, was the kind of thing the really rich young men did all the time – handsome, wealthy men like Alkibiades and his ilk in times of yore, and young Euboulos now. It was rather gratifying to know about it, though I should have felt more glorious if I hadn't had a strong headache and a tendency to puke.

I got up, washed my head and drank a lot of cold water. As I had no wish to encounter my mother or Theodoros, I carefully arrayed myself, and went out.

I stumbled rather than walked to the agora, then had to go to the Fountain House at once for more cold water to drink, and drank too much of it. As I passed the bread-sellers hunched on the ground over their portable ovens, old crones making gruel and flat bread, and uttering the high-pitched female cry of bread-sellers, '*Sition!*', I felt my gorge rise. Quickly, I found a place in which to puke discreetly. My skin was itchy and hot; my eyes seemed inclined to shirk their task. Yet, I reminded myself, I had important work to do. Must look for a new slave. I had the money, the new Hymettos money (lessened, of course, by what I had spent in the house of Tryphaina the night before), in a leather pouch under my cloak, and I clutched this bag of silver as I wandered about.

With a renewed effort at finding a focus both for my eyes and for my rambling woolly thoughts that strayed and fell down like sick lambs, I told myself that I would go to an auction and see if there were any suitable slaves there. Luckily, I supposed, I found an auction going on. It was the sale of some of the effects from the house of Hermia's first husband, Epikhares. I was surprised to find that this was still taking place, now that her second husband was dead. The association of Hermia with a gruesome murder charge gave an extra interest to the proceedings.

'So, Hypereides, I did not expect to see you here among the gapers,' one of the men attending exclaimed to a tall citizen who walked up with long confident strides.

'No? Why, I am almost surprised there are not more gapers,' Hypereides replied. 'Athenians are like crows and ravens – you find them where the slain are. They love a spectacle and story of misfortune. We pleaders have to gratify them, or we perish in our turn.'

Hypereides was a famous pleader and orator. He was by now over sixty years old, but he moved with the assurance of a much younger man. I did not love him after seeing his treatment of Aristotle last summer. Hypereides had told Aristotle that he could not leave in place the monument to his dead Pythias that the widowed philosopher had erected. Furthermore, this elderly statesman had made sure the philosopher knew his place as a *metoikos*, a mere alien. Yet Hypereides was beloved by many, and genial to all, even to those of the party of Alexander. My father-in-law-to-be had called Hypereides 'Jug Face', a normal soubriquet and appropriate. The orator had a long face, with extremely long ears that went in and out like the handles on a tall old amphora. If all the commentators were correct, Hypereides' looks had never told against him with the women.

Hypereides graced the auction with his presence only briefly, but he was right about the Athenian interest in the spoils of Epikhares and the connection of the auction with Hermia. A number of people came by to look and to comment, although evidently the truly good posses- sions of Epikhares, like the fine furniture, were not being sold today – or, at least, not here. The things being sold at this time were of the most everyday sort:

One lot of chamber pots and basins of common
    pottery, unglazed
Wicker baskets

A cracked portable stove
Set of much-used black tableware, chipped
Sieve, heavy mortar, and pestle
Two braziers, a poker and a stilus
One tarnished bronze bowl, noticeably dented

It was foolish of me to stand and look at such stuff, which had little to do with what I required. But the auctioneer was a witty fellow, and there was a dull kind of entertainment in looking at this procession of tired goods.

'What is the use of this sort of rubbish?' a man near me asked rhetorically. I thought he was addressing myself, but another person, tall and bulky in a red woollen cloak, answered the questioner.

'This is none of the best ware, but eventually they must reach some of the better goods. As for me, I am interested in no household stuff. Not I!' This red-cloaked speaker frowned, severely. He had the kind of broad overhanging forehead that is good at looking severe.

'No,' said a wag nearby, 'for you have been in debt all your life, and your kitchen is cold.'

'Come away,' said this jester's friend. 'You know Aristogeiton, a dog always growling at somebody. He haunts the marketplace, like a snake among the vegetables, looking for something to hiss at.'

This speaker moved away, but his friend the wag remained, and the other speaker, the one who had asked the rhetorical question, engaged himself in drawing out the man in the short red cloak.

'Why come to an auction, then, Aristogeiton?'

'I wished to make sure that matters are proceeding appropriately. Poor Epikhares! I cannot approve his political views, but I can pity him as a man. Little did he know that ungrateful baggage of his wife would marry herself off almost instantly to another – and still less could her unhappy first husband know she was a murderess. Unless she also helped him, unasked, to the shore of the Styx.'

'What a thought is there! I never heard there was anything the least out of the way about Epikhares' death.'

'And we all know how "out of the way" the death of our unfortunate Orthoboulos was.' Aristogeiton gave a dry laugh. 'Now at least the proceeds of this sale will benefit the good Krito. Though his wicked stepmother was trying to pervert her new family to the views of her first husband and her own relatives, Krito is staunch and well-affected. Therefore, I wish the sale to succeed. Let Krito have money enough to prosecute that wicked woman his stepmother, and drive her to her death.'

'Ahh!' The man speaking with him was evidently impressed. He drew back nervously, almost shivered. 'So you don't see just cups and pokers, but revenge, in this miscellaneous heap of objects?'

'Try a pestle, gentlemen – just the thing for the lady at home! Wife or housekeeper, sister or slave – tell them to make fresh flour for your pancakes.' The auctioneer pressed on with his task. 'Fine solid stone, neatly balanced, with mortar to match. In perfect good order. See – it grinds small!' In order to prove his point the vivacious auctioneer placed some grains of barley in the mortar and ground the pestle with a display of wonder and many flourishes, to the amusement of the company assembled.

'Grinding – yes,' said the severe Aristogeiton. 'Grind on. The evil woman – we may hope – will be dispatched to the Styx by the way of the mortar and pestle. Oh, there's a compound worth the grinding and pounding, the hemlock of her everlasting supper.' He gave a flounce of his short red cloak, as if he would walk away and see the deed that would dispatch Hermia immediately performed.

'But what is it to *you?*' his friend asked wonderingly.

'What to *me*? Friend and fellow citizen, have you not seen the disgraceful relaxation of all rule and order in Athens? This monstrous pustule, this woman poisoner, announces that there is a great sickness among us. Lancing that boil is the beginning of our cure. For Athens has let itself go, declining into decadence. Not just in Peiraieus but in sacred Athens itself, wineshops abound full of lazy men, foreigners mixing with citizens. Even in our most sacred agora. Brothels, like mushrooms, spring up in every corner. Manliness drifts away. The young men waste their strength and substance and become effeminated themselves.'

'Well, yes, I suppose so. But isn't it always the case? Did not Aristophanes complain about such things in the old days as well?'

Aristogeiton shook his head. 'It has never been as bad as now. The rule over us of the young man of Makedon, and his deputies, is pernicious. Subjugated, we are sick and weak. We lack good leaders. Take Hypereides! He says he is a patriot. He has charm and is persuasive in the Council. But his solution to our peril was to make the slaves into citizens! All order lost, all good custom and high birth to be thrown away.'

Nobody argued that point. It was not good form to do so. It was well known that Aristogeiton had led the charge against Hypereides for what most citizens thought were ill-considered suggestions regarding making aliens and slaves into citizens and arming them so Athens could defend itself against Makedon. Hypereides had been able to deflect the charge of treason, saying that the shields of the Makedonian phalanxes had dazzled his vision, and that not he but the battle of Khaironeia had made this shocking proposal. Nowadays nobody with an interest in maintaining the daily peace of Athens would wish to irritate Aristogeiton by defending Hypereides in his presence.

'Well, then, what of Lykourgos?' The questioner was not willing to let Aristogeiton off altogether; he was probing, perhaps to see if he could make the moralist speak well of anyone. 'No man could be better-born than the man who keeps the treasure of Athens. One of the best-born, of the clan of the Etioboutadai. Wealthy, yet he lives simply, with but one sheepskin on his bed. Doesn't even wear sandals except in bad weather. Lykourgos studies the good of Athens day and night.'

'I grant you,' Aristogeiton said grudgingly, 'Lykourgos is not self-indulgent. Too fond of money, though – not for himself but for the state. Always wants to be putting his hands into the taxes and the monuments. And that has led him to temporize with Makedon. He'd rather give Athens a Stadion than an effective army.'

'There's always Demosthenes.' The person who made this innocent suggestion was mischievous. For everyone surely knew that Aristogeiton and Demosthenes were at loggerheads since the time twenty years before when Demosthenes was producing a play for the Dionysia and Aristogeiton had struck him – and also, it was alleged, destroyed costumes and props. Though these men were similar in their opposition to the rule of the Makedonian kings, they never had any good words to say of each other.

'Demosthenes,' Aristogeiton said heavily. 'Yes, Demosthenes, who has cheated the city into giving him at last his golden crown. Far from bringing us a celebrated victory, Demosthenes talked us into war – and into a first-class defeat, he himself running away from the battlefield as fast as his little legs would carry him! This braggart loves gold.'

'True,' said the wag, who had enjoyed listening to these characterizations. 'Some say Demosthenes is fond of taverns, and loves parties at which he dresses in women's clothes—'

'Mere slander,' interjected a grey-haired man who spoke with authority. 'Demosthenes was a drinker in his youth, but he sips only water these days.'

'Yet,' said Aristogeiton, 'you must admit, this hero is not above subjugation to meretricious charms. Demosthenes has a foreign female on whom he dotes. A black-haired hussy from Sikilia, named Lais.'

'You are too severe,' protested his acquaintance.

'Though I know that nowadays you affect the Spartan style, Aristogeiton – hence your red cloak—'

'I emulate only the Spartan virtues. The Spartans are our ancient enemies, but they fought the Makedonians like men, while Athens has cowered. Athenian spirit has been worn out by letting into our midst low persons, of no blood. Sparta in her greatness had no prostitutes, *no* foreigners, and no mean luxury. Manliness. That true *men* value above sweet words and shiny gold. True honour. Manliness exists no more when men become subject to prostitutes – including some rich whores who go in very fine apparel, bought by the proceeds of their crimes.'

'Aristogeiton,' protested his friend, 'you must make allowance for youth – a little harmless fun—'

'Harmless! Is it not harmless to divert the ephebes from war and the young men from their serious work as citizens?'

'Are they to have no relief for the passions and pressures of youth?'

'It is true,' said Aristogeiton seriously, 'that there is a desire for pleasure in youth. Let men of good birth hold dinner parties, inviting the virtuous young men of their choice, and let them there read poetry and discourse of philosophy – sending the flute-girls and other riff-raff away, as did Sokrates and Agathon. This is the Athenian tradition.'

'But I was talking of simple *relief*, not of dining on discourses.'

'I admit, a young man's need for relief at times is pressing. But resort should be had to whores only of the simplest and lowest sort, with one flat fee. Two obols would amply suffice rather than, as our present law indulgently allows, the extravagant sum of two drakhmai! Slave workers, of both sexes, submissive and plainly dressed. In a bare "little house", a cubicle with no cushions or scented ointments. Young men should go in a group, each making his quick deposit and departing. No staying with a whore – male or female – for the night, giving her gifts and cockering her up. No kissing! None of that being babied and coddled and rubbed with oil and such doings. That sort of thing is ruining our city!'

Aristogeiton blew his nose with a kind of trumpet bray, a salpinx heralding the advent of an earnest speech which we could not escape.

'It is true, I tell you all,' he continued, addressing what was by now an audience. 'We are being weakened. Could I rule Athens I should soon put a stop to this nonsense. Nay – worse than nonsense. A *poison*. A poison in the heart of Athens of which we must rid ourselves by fasting and bleeding. All the fine whores, however rich and gaily dressed, boys and girls, I should have flogged. Not prettily paddled – no delicious procession of rosy smacked bottoms – but seriously flogged. Fifty lashes apiece, well laid on, to scar and mar for ever their pretty skins. Then they would be sent to the mines and the ore-washeries, to labour deep in smoke and grime. Any freed persons among them should be accounted slaves as the due of their trade, and subjected to the same treatment. Not a whore among them but would be a slave, proclaimed and marked. The youths who frequented these luxurious folk I would have beaten soundly. Not lashed as slaves, but whipped, as young boys are whipped, and then sent to the borders of Attika to guard the frontiers.'

By now quite a number of citizens had gathered, their attention diverted from the auctioneer to the impassioned politician. A couple of them clapped at the end of this harangue, though not a few looked nervous at such a programme.

'Sparta!' said Aristogeiton. 'Sparta, the land of men! That should be our model. Instead we are drawn to the luxuries and dalliance of the East. We should betake ourselves to plain living and manly courage. Let our men practise war. Let our women spin and weave, and keep themselves veiled. Let married women experience sexual congress as a duty undertaken for the purpose of procreation of good citizens.'

At this point, there was a diversion. The auctioneer appeared to have completed one lot of goods, and was bringing in another. This new household lot included very little in the way of kitchenware or furniture, but it did comprise a selection, if not numerous, of slaves.

'Not bad,' said Aristogeiton's friend, turning his gaze away from the moralist and looking critically at the assemblage of nearly naked bodies. 'I say, that boy's rather fine, isn't he?'

'Human tools,' sniffed Aristogeiton. 'Is he useful? Will his body last and his strength endure? Those are the questions to ask about a slave. Open his mouth, smell his breath, look at his teeth.'

Shoppers don't usually like advice as to how to shop. Most people knew, or thought they knew, how to look over a slave, so a number of shoppers went to the platform where the wares were displayed. In a slave auction it is truly necessary for the customer to get a good close look.

'Good muscles,' said one customer, pinching the shoulder of the young slave he had been looking at. 'You could work around the house, my fellow? Anybody can do that. Would you be useful as a carpenter? *That's* what I need to know. I've trained several in carpentering, and let them out. The rental fees handed over to me have more than repaid the outlay.'

'Here's an old loose-toothed cackler,' said another shopper, disgustedly twitching the veil of matted fabric away from the head of a woman of middle age. It was true, she had few teeth, and her hair was greying.

'What a fright!'

'Ah,' said the auctioneer. 'You don't realize her strengths, gentlemen. She's not for the bedroom or the symposium, I grant you. But she is an *excellent* cook. She has worked as under-cook at a great house, knows the art, and needs little direction. Fish – she scales to perfection. Chickens plucked cleanly – shaved as close as a dancer. Splendid worker. She can also clean clothes very efficiently – saves you the trouble of taking 'em to the fuller.'

Even I was interested on hearing this. But a larger citizen pushed his way forward. 'Just what I've been looking for, I think,' he said, grabbing the woman's arm. 'But I need to know – can you certify that she was born in Attika of a slave mother? Yes? Well that's a point gained. Foreigners caught in war, they can be very sharp and try to give you their lip sometimes. Plain refractory.'

He stood looking at the female, his hand to his chin in thoughtful wise. 'How much? Three hundred? Too much. Question is – is she going to endure? How good is her basic health – really now?' He turned to the auctioneer. 'I'll take her off your hands for two hundred and fifty, but she has to strip. Mind that! I'll not be satisfied until I know she's good enough to last.'

And the woman, blushing deeply just as if she'd been young and pretty, was stripped and turned about for inspection.

'Flabby and lacks tone, but not too aged,' the purchaser decided.

Lacking his assurance and authority, I was too late in coming forward; otherwise I might have made a bid for this woman who could have managed a lot of housework. She looked strong enough to fetch water and carry heavy bundles, despite her age.

'Why, I recognize *these*!' said a voice just at my elbow. It was not a friendly voice, but slightly familiar. I wasn't sure whether it was addressing me. My attention was on the auctioneer, who was leading forth the next item, another youth.

'Here's a good property, sure to develop too in strength and skill. This one can carry burdens for distances, he has served as a slave for a while in Alexander's army.'

'Why has he been released from army service?' one of the onlookers asked suspiciously. 'Too impudent? Or too lazy?'

'He is not serving the army now,' explained the

auctioneer, 'because one of the three men he served, an Athenian, purchased him when he got a military command. This Athenian officer was wounded, and left the service after the big battle near Issos town. The Athenian master came home – to die, as it turned out – with this fellow in his possession. The boy was sold in a job lot to Epikhares after the will was proved. It's all legal – I can show you the writings.'

'I don't know,' said the questioner, looking with dubiety at the boy. 'He must have been but a small sprout at the time of that big battle. Either that or he's a poor grower, won't thrive. That sort tends to eat without anything to show for the feeding.'

'I don't trust no slave as has been in the army!' exclaimed another citizen. 'They know too much about killing, also pillaging and looting. Up to sly tricks, I'll be bound.'

'But – see his muscles!' the auctioneer pleaded. 'Stand up, boy. Turn around. Look, I will strip him; you can see, he's rangy and muscular, a good proportion.'

Like the old woman, the youth flushed at being turned about and inspected while naked. Although passable when stripped, he was not especially good-looking. That can be all to the good. Nothing more tiresome than owning a slave whom one's friends are always trying to flirt with or buy – or jump on. The boy was capable of carrying burdens for distances – always a useful quality. I wondered if this fellow had any ability to answer the door or remember names. It is hard to test the mental capacities of slaves at an auction of this kind, though their physical qualities are clear to all. Some of these physical qualities were particularly clear to the potential buyers, who were by now inspecting him, pinching his arms and testing his joints. One man rubbed the boy's scrotum, and the auctioneer protested.

'There's a limit to how much you can handle the goods before you put your drakhmai down!'

The indefatigable auctioneer was leading forth another man, the last of the lot it seemed. He was tall, thick-necked and very muscular. The hair on his head was greying, but he was very dark about the chin, although slaves are supposed to be kept clean-shaven. Only citizens wear beards. The mark of a brand came through the grime and hair. When this large scowling fellow was spun about, the stripes of the whip on his back were clear for all to read.

'An ugly fellow! A troublemaker!' people exclaimed.

'Oh, he's learned his lessons by now,' the auctioneer said easily. 'And look how strong he is. You want to take the family on a journey? You've got an ugly guard – bandits will think twice before meddling with *this* fellow. And he can carry children, jars of oil, bags of wool. He can handle mules. Why, come to that, he could carry a mule!'

'*Is* a mule, more likely,' said the sour voice near me. 'I recognize him. I protest, these slaves should not be sold this way! I know this lot!'

And I knew who this speaker was, too. Ergokles, the snub-nosed man with the bush of brown hair. The citizen who had been in a brawl with Orthoboulos, and had challenged him in a court of law. Ergokles, whose rival Orthoboulos was now so conveniently dead.

Ergokles was full of a grievance, his quick eyes darting angrily over the scene. 'I *know* this whole kit of ugly servants. I protest! *Unjust!* I declare this to be absolutely unjust! *These* are some of the slaves of Orthoboulos! Orthoboulos' family must be putting some of their slaves up for sale. But they ought to have a whole auction, announced in advance! This hole-and-corner way, they get rid of the rubbish, and hang on to the good stuff. Unfair, I say! Where's the rest of them — their slaves? Answer me that!'

'It's no good working up to a boil, gentlemen,' said the auctioneer. 'That unfortunate family are still entitled to sell what they wish to sell. I have the writings from Krito. Orthoboulos himself had agreed to the sale, before his untimely death.'

'True enough,' another citizen corroborated. 'Orthoboulos had agreed with his new wife to sell his servants and bring some of hers to his house. This plan the family are evidently pursuing.'

'A bad plan!' insisted Ergokles. 'And *not* rightly legal. Not at all — now Orthoboulos is dead. It should have been stopped. That family ought to make a parcel of the whole lot on one day — of all the slaves. The sale should be announced in advance, with the items listed. Here they're trying to do it in little bits. Don't buy any of these — you may be in legal trouble over it.'

He turned to the assembled company. 'If you even think of buying one,' the little man advised, 'think again. Remember, any of these slaves might still be summoned to be questioned about the murder of Orthoboulos — then tortured! The trial impends.

Before you buy these, consider how much torture he or she can stand, and if their health and survival can be guaranteed!'

This appeal made an impression. Some of the potential customers backed hastily away.

'No great loss,' Ergokles continued. 'This lot today – ugly enough to turn milk sour. The lowest of Orthoboulos' slaves – when will we see the good ones?'

'I suppose,' I said, 'you mean Marylla.'

I hadn't meant to say anything – the words just came out of my mouth, as if my tongue were a self-mover without the intervention of thought. Immediately I knew it had been a mistake to speak at all.

'What business is it of yours, young fellow?' Ergokles bristled. 'You, boy, standing there without enough money to buy a piss-pot? What do you know about it?'

'I have no intention of giving offence,' I said meekly.

'But,' said Aristogeiton, coming up to us in his powerful simplicity, 'what this young man says is apt. Stephanos son of Nikiarkhos may come of a fading family – true. Nevertheless he utters only what others are thinking. It must be evident, O Ergokles, that you are wishful to buy Marylla of Sikilia, slave of Orthoboulos. A slave accounted beautiful, over whom the two of you had that unseemly wrangle before. The yearnings of a debased Eros, O Ergokles, have taught you to value what is contemptible. Such low desires do not become a well-born Athenian citizen. It is not for *us* to lose our heads over slaves and such trash. Be proud enough to leave foreign women and low-born persons alone.'

'Oh, write a book about it, why don't you,' Ergokles retorted rudely. 'It's true enough – I want to know where the lovely Marylla is, and when she'll be coming up for sale. That's so. And' – he slipped a piece of silver into the palm of the auctioneer – 'I can reward anyone who tells me straight out.'

'Well, now,' said the auctioneer softly and deferentially, 'if, sirs, any of you are looking for Orthoboulos' pet slave, the lovely girl from Sikilia – why, you might do worse than look in the household of Philinos.'

'He can't have bought her!'

'Not through *me*, sir. I know nothing of it. I know only that it is said – by a few people, anyway. They say that the lovely girl and also the Phrygian butler of the former establishment have both been bought by Philinos in private sale.'

Ergokles looked as if he would burst with rage. His face was transformed into something like an interesting beet, all swollen and red. 'Preposterous!' he cried. 'Unnatural and graceless boy! How could he agree to any such thing? When the whole of Athens knows I have a part share in her! They won't get away with this!'

Ergokles was spluttering like a man caught in a wave. Flecks of spittle gathered at the corner of his mouth and flew away on his words.

'Tush, man! Don't get carried away over a whore,' said Aristogeiton impatiently. 'A Spartan reserve would become your manhood better. This concern for women is weakening the Athenian character.'

Aristogeiton turned to the rest of us. 'Do you see *this*, men of Athens?' The red-cloaked speaker paused, pointing with his finger like a schoolmaster, as if Ergokles had come to the Agora on purpose to furnish an object lesson. 'This man is letting his obsession, his animal desires, take away his manhood!'

Stern Aristogeiton looked at me as he said this, as if inviting me to support this worthy rebuke. Ergokles glared at me at the same moment, with unexpected venom. Ergokles was likely to connect me ever after with the insults offered by the sage Aristogeiton, and love me accordingly.

'Far be it from me,' I murmured, 'to come between two such gentlemen. And, as you say, sirs, I can ill afford such slaves as these and ought not to waste time.'

And in this cowardly manner, I slunk away. Actually of course I had plenty of silver in my pouch, even after my extravagant night. Enough to buy one of these slaves. But I did not want to have anything to do with a servant of any kind from Orthoboulos' unlucky household.

I was not looking forward at all to my further association with this family, and the proceedings leading up to the trial loomed imminent and unavoidable.

I was free to imagine to myself what my appearance at that trial would be like. It seemed to me I could have no other anxiety. (Most untrue. Fate takes us by surprise.) The day after my fruitless expedition to buy slaves, I was feeling much better. I had abstained from wine in the meantime, and my head was clear. The day was cooler but autumn sunshine graced it. I was taking my leisurely way through the agora and had

paused to examine notices posted at the shrine of the
Heroes, when I noticed an unusual stir of excitement.
Some announcement, some description, was buzzing
from lip to lip. There were exclamations, utterances
of astonishment, audible from the crowd a good
distance off. A man came forward eagerly to tell one
of his friends, who was lingering by me at the notice
boards, the latest tidings.

'What is it?' I enquired, bold enough to intervene
with my question before he could reach his friend.

Nothing loath, the man was ready to tell me this
fresh news.

'Astonishing! It is this: Phryne the beautiful is
accused by Mantias and by Euthias of impiety! But it
is really at the motion of Aristogeiton.'

'Impiety!' his friend exclaimed, turning about.
'Phryne? How can that be? What sort of impiety?'

'I don't believe it,' another interjected. 'Perhaps she
has forgotten or misrecited a prayer, or missed the
procession to—'

'No,' said the news-bearer. 'I tell you, it is the most
serious charge possible. She is charged by a written
accusation, a long *graphe*, which goes into the details.'

'Details of what?' I asked, with some contempt as
well as curiosity. It was strange – so it struck me later
– that I did not immediately think of what the details
must be, and how well I myself knew them.

'Well,' said the first news-bearer, happy to develop
the tidings – and now a little group was gathering
around listening to him, so he could enjoy his importance. 'Well, it seems that this lovely hetaira was at a
party one night at the house of Tryphaina. You know,

the madam who keeps the high-class whorehouse. And there, in the middle of the night, amid a crowd of drunken revellers, Phryne mocked the Mysteries of Eleusis!'

'No!' several people exclaimed simultaneously.

'Yes. Truly. The *graphe* alleges that she imperson-ated Demeter and Kore, that she made a speech as Demeter, with corn wreaths upon her head, and then made a parody of drinking the sacred *kykeion*.'

'Oh, no – really?'

'Yes. And more than that, she is accused also of impiety as she has tried to introduce a foreign god into the city. A strange deity called the god of equal shares. And she led a congregation of worshippers in procession, with torches and everything, in honour of this new god, Isodaites.'

'Oh, indeed!' one old fellow said, breathing out in a kind of awe. 'This is a capital charge, then.'

'Yes. Like what they charged Sokrates with. But also mockery of Eleusis – what Alkibiades was accused of in the old days.'

'But Alkibiades fled,' one wise fellow remarked drily. 'He did not stay in Athens to be charged and sentenced.'

'Alkibiades was wise, then,' said the news-bearer. 'For, as Aristogeiton reminded us, and the Chief Arkhon and the Basileus both confirm, death can be the only penalty. Eurymedon says so, and demands that penalty in honour of Demeter. Eurymedon is a devotee of the goddess and among the highest of her representatives in Athens, where he serves at the Temple of Demeter and Persephone. Eurymedon will personally urge the hierophant to incite the court of the Areopagos to move speedily.'

'And what of all those lovely Athenian youths of quality who were there in the brothel-house at the time?' the dry citizen enquired. 'Will they be executed likewise?'

'*Who* was there?' added another. 'In order to press such a charge, there must be witnesses.'

'Oh, they have Euboulos, the son of Xenophon of Melite. A pretty young fellow. He confesses to having been present in Tryphaina's brothel at the time. But he was horrified, and would not rest until he confided in someone his knowledge of the terrible act that had taken place. And doubtless there are many other youths who knew of her offence – offences, one might say. Though the lads may have been powerless to stop it at the time. Some may be found guilty of assisting in the blasphemy. Who knows?'

I could feel my heart sink to my very toes. The trouble that faced me in witnessing to the finding of Hermia's husband's body paled in comparison with the new disaster. For I had no reason to be certain that someone at the party at Tryphaina's had not recognized me. If I were named as present at Phryne's unfortunate festival, I could be had up myself for assisting at the profanation. The thought of Eurymedon was disquieting; I had seen this devoutly single-minded man when he attacked Aristotle, and knew him to be as hard and forbidding as a man made of metal. Eurymedon, truly a devotee of the goddesses of Eleusis, acted as if Demeter's honour depended solely on his own strictness. Eurymedon would be happy to accuse me, since I was known as an associate of Aristotle. A young man like Euboulos would be safe enough because he had a rich and important father (and a living one). And besides, he had volunteered his testimony, acting as a friend to Athens.

'What has happened to Phryne now?'

'They have brought her in and are questioning her.'

'So she will have to go to the prison?'

'She will not be put in the prison, at least not now,' the retailer of news explained. 'There are rich men enough to go bond for her. She is to be put in strict seclusion in a house kept by a woman – but all the portals guarded by armed men – until just before her trial.'

'She is *so* beautiful,' one middle-aged paunchy fellow exclaimed wistfully.

'That's what makes her dangerous,' said another. 'I am a friend of Aristogeiton, and agree with him. Such silly women turn heads. One thinks of the old men of Troy, lining up on the walls of their imperilled city and drooling over their fatal Helen!'

'Well, I tell you one thing,' said the news-bearer, reluctant to give up his importance to the general tide of commentary. '*This* trial is not going to be prolonged, like an assault or a homicide. In a homicide case, there is a family who is offended, but in a case of impiety, it is the gods who are directly offended. Athens, as Eurymedon says, cannot afford the pollution and offence to the gods. The trial of Phryne will come off as quickly as possible. The execution will follow it swiftly, in order to rid the city of the pollution, the danger.'

'We haven't had a trial for impiety and blasphemy for a long while,' one man said thoughtfully. 'It may cause the citizens to become more respectful of their pious duties.'

'Ah, but what a pity!' said another man equally old, thoughtfully. 'It may make a lot of men sad, to see the death of such a lovely thing as she.'

VIII

The Case against the Stepmother, for Poisoning: The First Hearing

I got away from this little group as soon as I could, and hoped that I had displayed no undue consciousness during the recital of this fresh disaster. I had no way of knowing whether Euboulos or any of the others might name me as a witness or accessory to the act of impiety. I hated going about in public. It seemed to me that any moment, someone might tap me on the shoulder and say, 'Weren't you there when Phryne—?'

I could not tell Aristotle about this trouble. He was himself in bad odour with the most ardent supporters of the rites of Demeter and the Mysteries of Eleusis. Eurymedon, so zealous in the cause of Demeter, and so hostile to Aristotle last summer, would not have any friendly disposition towards myself. I remembered how years ago Aristotle had seemed to me a bulwark of defence; of latter days, his friendship had endangered me in some quarters. Now at this point, oddly enough, any association of Aristotle with me might not only do me no good, but might injure Aristotle even more. His enemies, the anti-Makedonians, would be quick to associate the philosopher with any error perceived in me. No help could be had from the Master of the Lykeion. It was my hope to keep out of the matter, though such a hope seemed at long odds. In my favour was the fact that the room had been dark and that the company were numerous and mostly drunken. Also, I was not a regular customer at Tryphaina's and had not given my name. Yet I would have to be guarded, extremely wary. It is, however, ill-advised to appear wary or evasive when one attends a hearing before a magistrate.

As I knew only too well from my own former experience, a trial for murder is preceded by the three prodikasiai in the three months before it. All parties concerned are allowed time to collect, sift, and share evidence, hear each other's witnesses, and examine the facts. All this is to be done with the help and supervision of the city of Athens itself, represented by the Chief Arkhon for religious functions and the Basileus, who presides at the Areopagos. These preliminary hearings take place in a room, not on the *bema* of the Hill of the Areopagos, and are thus less daunting than the trial that will follow.

I had formerly attended a course of such prodikasiai in the position of Defender, though I had been acting for the absent accused. Now I was in the less strenuous position of a mere witness. Phanodemos, Hermia's uncle, acted as Defender. As a woman cannot speak in public, he would speak for his niece. Hermia herself of course had to appear. Although as a well-born lady she was not supposed to speak, she could confer with her deputed Defender, hear what he had to say, and perhaps offer changes or corrections.

Hermia sat slumped in a corner, veiled in the soberest of black garments from head to foot. She was under official guard the whole time – one guard was one of the Skythian archers, the other an official from the prison. Though she had been allowed to remain in the custody of relatives, her movements were strictly watched.

We were too early – or at least the Basileus had not yet arrived. Such an interval was a strain. The two sides kept well apart, under the watchful eye of the prison guard and the Skythian with the barbaric bow. I spoke in a friendly but aloof manner to Krito and to his younger brother Kleiophon. The younger boy hardly responded at all, but then, I had spoken coolly; it was not my part to seem either Krito's partisan or his antagonist. Philinos was present also, which I was pleased to see. As a friend of Orthoboulos he made a suitable supporter and friend for the two orphaned sons. I heard Krito and Philinos conversing behind me.

'How I wish,' Krito said earnestly, with a quaver in his young voice, 'how I wish this were all over! It takes such a long time, these months of hearings. Why does Athens do this to us? Why not punish the guilty party without delay?'

'There is a long delay,' said Philinos. 'No doubt about that, I'm afraid. It serves the cause of Justice –

one does not accuse and punish citizens for such a serious crime without taking sufficient care. But I do fear that means that almost all the questions about the property must be postponed. Certain issues will be left hanging in the air for a while. You were asking me, and that is all I can tell you.'

'It is too bad!' said Krito. 'I am the one who suffers, yet everyone treats me with injustice.'

'Not everyone,' said Philinos soothingly. 'Look, I know that things take a long while to get settled. But if you need to secure some more ready money, you may sell to me some more of your father's slaves. As these did not belong to your stepmother, or to your father's marital household, but were your father's alone – and as he was going to sell them in any case – you as his heir are undoubtedly entitled to make the sale. Other questions remain to be resolved, including who has rights to the property of Epikhares. And there's the dowry. What happens if Hermia is acquitted, and needs a settlement?'

'No – that cannot be!' interjected Krito passionately. 'That wicked woman – she cannot escape the consequences of her crime!'

'We have to consider contingencies, that's all,' said Philinos soothingly. 'As I told you, you had better not try to sell any property of value. Except for your father's own slaves, to which you have clear claim. Now, I have reason to believe you have recently acted without my assistance. Trying to sell some more slaves? Is that true?'

'Well, yes,' said Krito, a trifle sulkily. 'I thought I might get more from public auction. But then that

nasty dirty Ergokles spoke up and made a fuss and
scared people off. They were scared the slaves might
still have to be tortured, and lose value. So I didn't
sell any but one.'

'You should have come to me again, my boy.' I could
hear Philinos trying to soothe Krito by adopting a
paternal manner. 'I admire your wish to be independent, but it really is easier at this juncture to deal with
only one person. Public sales are so very public, they
can incite derisive comment, which those in your
circumstances should avoid. I shall pay a fair price.
You have not found me inclined to haggle. And this
can be done now.'

'I might want to do that, yes,' said Krito slowly.

'Well, then. Consider which ones you could spare.
Not everyone has the cash on hand.'

'Here's the arkhon,' Kleiophon announced suddenly,
as if he felt the kind of grim relief one feels at getting
a bad business under way. The Chief Arkhon for that
year, one Aristophanes (no relation of the dramatist,
but a passable sort of man, if a trifle dull), entered,
accompanying the Basileus, who would preside. The
Basileus has inherited the title of the ancient king of
Athens, but this magistrate was anything but kingly.
Our Basileus for that year was a short, nervous person,
given to meaningless babble and gestures. He fussed
a little, burbling his apologies and wondering about
the heat of the day, about where we were to sit or
stand in the hearing room, and who was to make the
opening remarks. (Of course that had to be Krito.)
Certainly this man was greatly inferior to the Basileus
of the year when I had to appear as a Defender. I

wasn't sure which side this deficiency would help the more, but decided it made for the advantage of the Accuser. Krito had a good strong voice, he had backers with him and when he began to lay his formal complaint he looked the part of the Athenian citizen – his youth adding a becoming touch.

'Men of Athens,' he began formally, 'I am only a young man. Too young to have experience of courts of justice. It is a terrible thing for me to stand here and accuse my own dear father's wife. I cannot even be sure if my father himself, or his shade, wishes me to do so. Yet Justice demands that I seek vengeance against his murderer. It is the right of both my father's children – my poor young brother and myself—'

Here there was an unexpected interruption. Kleiophon, who had been standing attentively just behind his brother, abruptly broke away. He ran across the hearing room to the other side, away from Krito and his party and towards the much smaller party of Hermia and her uncle.

'I – I don't want you to speak for me!' The lad flung his words at Krito. 'I think it's ridiculous – I *know* my new Mama didn't do any such thing. So there!'

'Good lad, do you know what you are saying?' asked the Basileus

'Yes – yes, I do. I want to be a witness for their side. For my Mama's side. And not for *his*. And I have evidence to give.'

'You do not join in this accusation? The accusation against Hermia?'

'No!'

This unexpected interruption had put the plaintiff

off his stride. Such a breaking-out would have shaken an older and more experienced pleader. Krito struggled to express himself, his voice faltering.

'Well – surely to goodness – Kleiophon, I don't know why you're doing this! Really, I don't! And why didn't you say before you were going to take her side?'

'Because,' Kleiophon shrugged. 'Because I was afraid you wouldn't have let me come at all. If you'd known what side I want to be on.'

'Oh, Kleiophon!' Krito stretched out his arms in entreaty, then dropped them. 'You see here, gentlemen, what a difficulty I have. The lad is young and tender, a bit spoiled and grieving for his father. So he has taken this unreasonable stance. I am really amazed! What feelings have led this boy, my full brother by blood, to stand against me? Perhaps he is confusing this woman, this *stranger* – almost a stranger – with his own mother, his real mother, who passed away so many years ago.'

'I am not an idiot!' retorted Kleiophon. 'I know just as well as you that my real Mama is dead. But Hermia is my second mother; my father gave her to us to be our mother. And Hermia gave us a little sister, too. I stand by Hermia. *You* do not care about her at all – you just want her dead so you can get all her property.'

'To get——? Wicked boy! You dare to say such a thing?' Krito seemed really stung. 'These, gentlemen – these are delusions indeed. Or – stay – are they not something worse? Isn't this the concoction of malice against me? Why, oh why?' His forehead puckered, his eyes welled with tears as he gazed at Kleiophon, searching for an answer. Then his brow grew dark.

'I see. A terrible reason. Disgusting. Though I do
not believe that my poor young brother – hardly more
than a child – had anything to do with the plot against
my father. Yet I see and must say what I would be
ashamed to think – still less to tell – in ordinary cases.
What is the reason my brother turns against me? Love!
Love of a disgusting kind! Yes, gentlemen, an inces-
tuous and unnatural love between Hermia and my
brother. He was still young enough to be allowed in
the women's quarters. Unlike myself, this boy could
gaze upon her beauty. How easy for her to soothe him
and soften him with endearments, and entice him to
give her pleasure at stolen moments—'

'You liar!' Kleiophon was turning bright red with
rage. He shook his fist. 'I could *kill* you!'

'That is the only explanation I can think of, gentlemen. This boy must have been seduced by the serpent
who sits there. He is the victim of an unnatural and
poisonous love, foisted on him by the cunning of a
woman accustomed to having her own way. This
woman, Hermia by name, was irritated at my father,
because he would not change his political views and
conform to those of her own family and of Epikhares.
She was also jealous of my father for that he still main-
tained relations with his slave concubine Marylla. As
well as frequenting brothels – that he did so is a fact
so well known by now that I cannot disguise it from
you. So this conceited, domineering and utterly jealous woman had her revenge by seducing Orthoboulos'
younger son – like another Phaidra. Poor boy! It is
for this cause that his mind, still childish, though his

body gropes towards manhood, is deluded and over-cast with a guilty fondness that melts into the fond-ness he would feel for a real mother.'

There had been much murmuring and exclamation in the hearing room. This reaction grew to such a hubbub that the proceedings had to stop for a while. When we continued, the boy Kleiophon had been taken away to collect himself, and the course of events went more normally. It was necessary for me to identify myself publicly as "Stephanos son of Nikiarkhos, dweller in Kydathenaion" and to say that I had been in Manto's notorious house. At least my testimony was now an anticlimax; no danger of my being the centre of the story. I described the commotion at the brothel, the place where the body of Orthoboulos had been found and the condition of the body itself. Manto had also been called, and the freedwoman's statement tallied with my own. Krito had called me as a witness friendly to him. And I saw clearly that my deduction that the unfortunate Orthoboulos had not been killed where he was found played well into Krito's case.

'There! You see!' said Krito. 'Stephanos in shrewd deduction clearly illustrates why we know the murder wasn't done there – though the corpse was brought to that room, in the empty house next to Manto's. As the house was empty, my father's body might not have been discovered for some days. I know, it is hard to imagine that my stepmother, still wearing the mask of respectability despite her tainted seductive ways, could easily leave her home and go unnoticed to such a place as that brothel. But it is not hard to believe that she performed the act of administering the potion

in some other place. Where? Perhaps in some chamber of our own house? Horror to think of it! But no!
There is no need to dread the pollution of our family
home. No sign of such an event appeared in our house.
This woman Hermia had been away for the day; this
was corroborated by my brother and my servants. She
was supposedly visiting relatives. Her witnesses will
swear she did so, but of course they would want to
lie for her, wouldn't they? Most likely it is that Hermia
chose some third place in which to do the deed. The
deed that rendered her the owner of a vast new
property as well as all that she got from her other
husband!'

Krito paused to wipe his eyes and mop his brow.

'Then, after brutally killing Orthoboulos my father
with poison in his drink, and calmly watching him die,
she had him — his corpse, rather — transported to the
room where it was found. There it was deposited,
surrounded by dirty towels and other supposititious
evidence to make it appear that he had died there.'

When asked for further proof of this, Krito was
naturally at a standstill. No real evidence was forthcoming. The chief male slave of Hermia's husband's
household had been officially interrogated under
torture, in the presence of Hermia's uncle (to see fair
play), soon after the body was found; the transcript of
his questioning was produced. Other slaves had been
questioned, without torture, by Krito himself. But they
all, even the tortured butler, stuck to it, to a man, that
they had not been asked to transport any bulky object,
let alone a body, from the house.

Kleiophon was then brought back into the court

and called by Phanodemos as a witness for the Defender's (Hermia's) side. Phanodemos himself, a man not in the first youth by any means, looked tired and drawn, and was unexpectedly awkward when required to be forceful and quick-witted among so many critical auditors. The murdered man's younger son, so Phanodemos insisted, had not much information to give regarding Hermia. Hermia's uncle started the questioning, but Krito soon took the lead.

PHANODEMOS: 'Did you see your mother on the day before Father's death?'

KLEIOPHON: 'Yes. She didn't leave the house much, 'cept to go with Papa – our father – to look after their property. She has – I mean her old husband had – a place in Athens and one in Peiraieus. But Mama was – *is* – good and kind, and she stayed at home and did the weaving and looked after the servants the way a wife is supposed to do. She's too good and kind to do such an awful thing.'

KRITO: 'Answer carefully. Did she – Hermia – leave the house at all on the day that our father died?'

KLEIOPHON: 'She went to visit relatives. They sent someone to call for her, and brought her back.'

KRITO: 'Aha! So you admit – she *was* out.'

KLEIOPHON: 'She was gone in the day, not in the night. And besides, Papa was alive then. Around dusk, I found that he had lain down and gone to sleep in the *andron*. I peeped in, and he was lying down on a couch there. But he wasn't quite asleep, I know, 'cause he muttered, "Go away, boy, and let me doze a bit."' [*Sensation in the hearing room*] 'That was very shortly before Mama came back. So he was quite all right then.'

KRITO: 'So − the poor man could have been dying of the poison at that time? And when was this?'

KLEIOPHON: 'No! Papa wasn't dying − he wasn't sick. He didn't complain of being ill, he wasn't throwing up or anything. I told you it was dusk, the darkness had come on. The room didn't have a lamp lit. But I had a lamp in my hand, and everything looked like usual. The room didn't smell of puke at all. Sometimes when men have drunk an awful lot the *andron* does, but not that evening. And *you* − he turned towards us, looking at myself in particular − '*you* have all been saying that hemlock has a strong smell. There was no unusual smell, no stink, and nothing was disarranged. He was just lying there with a light coverlet over him, the way a man will doze sometimes.'

BASILEUS: [*Interjecting*] 'Especially if he's going out soon and expects to be up much of the night?'

KLEIOPHON: 'I suppose so. But anyway, Mama was out all day, gone for some while when I saw him dozing there. She came back, very soon, and by then he had gone out. But everything was all right. And don't listen to *him*!' [*Pointing an indignant finger at Krito*] He's telling dirty bad stories about me and my Step-Mama − just for spite. He can't really think that! And I haven't done *anything* wrong!'

Kleiophon burst into tears again and was led away to the side of the room. The Basileus tut-tutted about letting one so young give evidence at all. He was undecided as to whether we ought to pay attention to what Kleiophon said or to disregard it altogether.

The first prodikasia broke up in an unsatisfactory state. The Basileus was vocal about his own fatigue, and about the difficulty of the case. Krito looked pale and exhausted, Kleiophon stubborn and teary. As for Hermia, nobody could see her. As she was conducted from the building her foot slipped at the threshold. She must have been greatly fatigued to do such a thing – or perhaps an officious guard got too close to her. But it seemed a bad omen.

IX

Poison in the Prison

I had overheard the suggestion that Philinos buy some of Krito's slaves, or rather, some more; as I already knew, Krito had earlier let two of his most valuable slaves go quietly to Philinos in some sort of private sale. (Perhaps the auctioneer was not supposed to have made that matter public, at least not so soon.) For some reason, so I speculated, Krito stood in need of immediate funds. Just after the first hearing on Hermia's case, we heard as public news that Philinos had bought four of Krito's slaves. I presumed that these were the four I had seen in the slave market the day I encountered Aristogeiton. On my reckoning, then, Philinos had actually purchased a total of six slaves of Orthoboulos' household, even buying the butler or doorkeeper who, however skilled and personable, must have been somewhat damaged, since the man had been tortured.

This transaction put a lot of silver immediately into

Krito's hands. Was it not interesting that the young man seemed to need so much money? Perhaps, however, Orthoboulos had left debts behind him. As the human property just sold were the slaves that, as everyone knew, Orthoboulos had himself intended to sell, they seemed pretty clearly to be Krito's property to sell or keep. His publicly taking the right upon himself seemed a mark of confidence in his case after the first prodikasia. It seemed inevitable, however, that almost everything to do with Orthoboulos' and Hermia's property would eventually be subject to dispute.

'Especially if Hermia were cleared,' I remarked to Aristotle. 'Because I suppose her kindred could take her back *and* ask to have her property – her dowry – returned, since the marriage to Orthoboulos was dissolved so soon. And if that fails – her uncle has threatened – out of the hearing of the Basileus – to sue Krito.'

'Most ill-advised of Phanodemos to say any such thing,' Aristotle said decidedly. 'He is increasing Krito's motivation to win – to gain utter and entire victory. That means destroying the woman. Now Krito will feel that he can have his property free and clear only by sending her to her death. Dear me, I think Krito has sufficient motive already. This case begins to worry me. I wish someone could take that younger brother of his into safe keeping.'

'You can't mean—?'

'I don't suppose I have much meaning.'

Athens was eager for the next hearing, though a second prodikasia is usually not as interesting as the opening one. It would not happen for a month, which seemed a long interval to wait. Events, however, happened with surprising celerity. On the second day after the first hearing, I was in the agora, doing some domestic shopping and exchanging greetings, when my attention, like that of others nearby, was directed to a lively dispute. Krito and Philinos, standing in the cleared ground just outside the Temple of Zeus, were hotly arguing, and had reached the point of raised voices and angry gestures. At least Krito was flushed and angry and waving his arm about. Philinos looked handsome, tall and disdainful.

'I didn't know— You took that girl from my house – my father's house – without telling me about her! I didn't *know* she was a love-mate of yours!'

'Not a love-mate of mine. Maybe now she is. You don't keep a chicken that won't lay eggs.'

'You're insulting my father's memory! You cuckolded him with that girl, you adulterer—'

'Boy, you forget yourself – and your language. Those words are customarily used when *marriage* is in the question. Many men share a whore with no difficulty—'

'*I* should have kept her,' said Krito. 'I should have thought – she might be pregnant, and in that case a child of our house would go to yours.'

Philinos shrugged. 'Maybe. I see no sign of this. I thought you were anxious to get rid of the plaything that reminded you – not always agreeably – of your father. But you can hardly expect a gentleman to go back on a bargain.'

'Who's the gentleman?' Sour-faced Ergokles pushed himself and his snub nose into the business.

'Men may share a whore, indeed – unless one side is unfair and too rich. He urgently shoved people aside with his elbows to get close to the arguing pair. 'Young Krito here may be rubbing a boil close to his own backside. Maybe he thinks this here handsome Philinos is an adulterer – the real sort. A greasy-haired smiler, seducer of wives. A molester of marriage – in the strict sense. Maybe there's reason to think that Philinos had *Hermia*, rather than Marylla. Have you thought of that, boy?'

'Be silent – you are a rascal!' roared Philinos, losing something of his cool demeanor and becoming agitated in turn.

'You – young fellow – Krito. Take a look at those earrings Hermia has, the newest ones,' advised Ergokles. 'If you are wise, you will confiscate her jewel box – tear the rings out of her ears if necessary. Take a good look at them. Ask some questions. Was it Philinos as bought them? And was your dear Pa being diddled all this time – ha?'

'Ergokles, you watch your mouth. I'll have the law on you for slander!' Philinos was seriously angry, his handsome face flushed. He took a step towards the little man. 'You ought to be properly cudgelled, you gutter-picking pig!'

'Watch who you're throwing bad language at,' Ergokles retorted. '*You* mind yourself, or you'll find yourself and your overused cock somewhere you won't care for some day!'

Unfortunately at this point, of all days and seasons, the sad little familiar group of Hermia, blackly veiled, her uncle Phanodemos, and her aunt by marriage –

the whole party accompanied by a guard – were cross-ing the Agora not far from us.

'What's *she* doing out?' asked Ergokles curiously.

One of Philinos' servants replied.

'She's been allowed to collect some clean clothes, and to see her child, who is still living in her – in her husband's house. That's all.'

'Oh, so you allow that,' sneered Ergokles. 'Very sweet, very thoughtful. I should have thought young Master would have prevented such doings. In honour of his deceased progenitor. Not to let the murderess – the adulteress – in at his door.'

Krito flushed. 'I didn't know they were going to do it like that,' he murmured. 'You are right. She must not cross my threshold. Oh – and she should not be anywhere in the Agora! She is prohibited! Ho, there!'

And he strode off to interrupt the sombre little procession. Ergokles followed with eager pace, and so, after a slight hesitation, did Philinos. I followed all three, and so did a number of the other onlookers.

'*You* there,' said Krito, hailing the party in a harsh voice. 'Halt! The whole rag-tag of you is committing an offence. That woman is prohibited from entering the agora! She has defiled the city, and all of you are now defiled for offending with her.'

The little group stopped, and Phanodemos stared blankly at Krito. It was true. Hermia after the accu-sation had no right to appear in the agora or in any other sacred space. But the passage through the agora was so familiar and natural that no one had thought of this, even Phanodemos, who was an expert on religious observances. Nor even the guard, who also stared blankly, racking his brain for an excuse for his own dereliction.

'Please — we haven't come far,' pleaded Phanodemos. 'We have made a mistake. Sacrifices will be offered. Please let us go,' turning to the guard. 'We'll go round the other way, outside.'

'No you won't!' said Krito. 'I've changed my mind. Wicked, polluted and unclean woman, ready to defy the gods — I forbid you. You cannot cross the threshold of my father's house — the house of a man you ruined and killed. That house is now *mine*. None of you may go there. And you, unholy woman, are absolutely forbidden ever to see your little girl.'

'You don't have the authority to give such an order,' protested Hermia's uncle.

'Let the law decide! Meanwhile, this indecent woman should not be allowed into the light of day! My father suffered for her wicked pleasure — with this fellow!' Krito gestured wildly towards Philinos. 'Look! Look here! There is the handsome lover — the wicked adulterer — for whom you have disgraced yourself and committed a heinous murder! You Makedonian murderess!'

The black-shrouded Hermia turned her head — one could make out that much under all the veiling. 'No!' she said, softly yet clearly. 'No. This is entirely a mistake.'

'Oh, yes! You made a mistake, that's quite true!' Krito, full of passion, was waving both hands in the air. His face was red and he was yelling. 'You have brought disgrace upon me and my household. First you tried to pervert my father and turn him from his love of Athens.'

'No, never! You must see—'

'Then you ruined and killed our poor father, you vicious adulteress. *See?* I see enough. You want to see?'

To our horror, the young man leaned forward and grasped his stepmother's veil. 'You want to see? I want to see something too! So take a last good look at your lover!' Krito tore the covering off her head – literally; there was a rending sound as the cloth was torn. We saw – we all saw – the beautiful face of Hermia, pale but with a bright spot in each cheek. Her long curling hair, done up in the back as a citizen's wife's hair should be, was loosened in the attack and came tumbling about her face. Her first impulse must have been again to cover her face, exposed to the eyes of all these gazers, but she stood her ground. Hermia looked neither bold nor coy, but she gazed straight at Krito.

'Krito, you are overwrought. I must ask you to cease from this distressing behaviour – it is not manly in you—'

'Manly? I am the man of the family! And look – she still wears earrings! Adornments given by her lover, doubtless!' Krito again reached over, with both hands tearing the earrings out of her ears. Blood gushed from the tearing wound made on each side.

'No!' her family screamed. The uncle tried to grapple with Krito. But Krito had turned away and was holding the earrings up to the audience.

'Perhaps these are among the cheapest of the baubles that Philinos gave her? But, of course, she was accustomed to such good things, a lover would have to pay many coins of silver and even of gold to keep

Hermia in jewellery. You know, gentlemen, a disgraced woman, dishonoured in adultery, is supposed to wear no ornaments. And if she does so attempt to beautify her wretched self, passers-by can strip them off and slap her face.'

And Krito turned again to Hermia. Turned and struck with his open hand, hard and contemptuously. *Slap-slap!* went his hand against Hermia's cheeks, smearing a face where little rivulets of blood were pouring down from the painful rents in the ears.

'You can all do it to this adulteress – witch – murderess!' screamed Krito. But nobody in the crowd availed himself of the offered treat, not even Ergokles, who was smiling with a certain satisfaction. 'Ah, I see,' said Krito, breathing heavily. 'You none of you want to sully your hands with touching this polluted garbage!'

'It is the part of a *woman* to do such a thing,' said Phanodemos heavily. 'Not of a well-born man. Certainly not a kinsman, and in public.'

'She's no blood nor kin of mine, I am glad to say!' Krito retorted.

The guard, who had stood by during all this action, without defending Hermia or intervening in any way, now seemed to wake up to the fact that he might have something to do. He ordered Krito and the rest to stand aside, commanded the aunt to cover her niece's face again, and told the party to turn about and move. The little party trotted off – in the direction whence they had come. Hermia was now in additional disgrace for polluting the agora. Her motherly attempt to see her little girl had been foiled. Moreover, she was now scarred for life. Perhaps that didn't matter much, as her life would probably be done with in another three months or so.

'Krito is so angry, he seems out of control,' I remarked to Aristotle next day. 'He has turned against Philinos – one can hardly see why. Philinos was a friend of his father, after all. And Krito is against Hermia now, hating her so much that he will believe any evil said against her. I dare say Ergokles has a large part in creating these rumours.'

'Possibly,' said Aristotle. 'This is a bad situation. Tempers are rising, who knows where it will end? It was bad enough when it entailed only the accusation of murder against Hermia. That became complicated by accusations of incest. Now, according to you, we have Krito accusing Hermia of adultery with Philinos, and also accusing her of *political* motives for murder: "Makedonian murderess". I do wonder exactly who has supplied Krito with that notion, and urged him to use it? I fear it is not just Krito but the case which is getting out of control.'

'You know,' I said, 'I wanted Hermia to be guilty, so that when she was found guilty in law everything would be all right. But now I am not so sure that she is guilty. Nor is it clear that anything can prove or disprove her guilt. That bothers me.'

'Also, as this situation ignites, we are going to have at least two more lawsuits arising out of it, setting Athenians by the ears. I don't mind telling you, Stephanos, I don't like this situation at all.'

'It's becoming very nasty,' agreed Theophrastos in his grave manner. 'People whose tempers are not under their own or others' command. And these persons are important enough to cause trouble.'

'Quite so,' agreed Aristotle. 'They threaten the peace of Athens – which is always precarious. This case is giving a loose to pestilential feelings, as well as foul language. Someone is choosing to foist a political cause upon this case. It's like the beginning of a serious boil – one can see the gathering of a strong little group of well-born anti-Makedonians, trying to work political advantage for themselves.'

'Men like Aristogeiton,' I agreed.

'The danger within Athens is a swelling oligarkhy which gains political control. At the worst it could repeat the errors of the Thirty Tyrants. But there are contrasting dangers. On the one hand, Athens – or parts of it – may be working itself up to the rule of an arbitrary and brutal oligarkhy. On the other, the city may be incurring an exterior threat. If Athens gets too lively, it will attract the attention of Antipater, bringing Makedonian power down upon itself. It amazes me that men will deliberately, so it seems, incur a wrath with which they are quite unprepared to deal. These Athenian would-be oligarkhs seem to leave that reality out of their calculations, yet they should *know* from what has happened to so many other cities what the power of Makedon really is. Antipater, without Alexander anywhere near him, crushed even the valiant Agis of Sparta. And Athens could not possibly mount a military effort half as good as the Spartan one.'

Aristotle arose and strode restlessly about the room. 'The trouble is, these Athenians of high rank think

Alexander is less dangerous when he is far away from them. They do not know – as I, alas, have cause to know – that this distance from home is making Alexander more suspicious. More willing to rend people. Nowadays he is more frightened of conspiracies against him than he used to be. And these Athenian patriots in their big talk continually underestimate his regent Antipater, his determination and efficiency. Antipater is bidden by Alexander to keep Attika and the Peloponnesus pacified, and he will do it – even if it means erasing another city. Antipater is quite capable of acting of his own accord to crush what he sees as a dangerous insurrection – even the threat of one.'

'It is too bad that Athens cannot be independent entirely!' I could feel my face becoming hot. 'Free to make her own choices! How dare you make Athens into such a helpless puppet?'

'I am not saying the situation is as I should desire, Stephanos. Not at all. I am merely observing that the men who are stirring things up are not good at dealing with reality. If men are free to choose, they have a responsibility to know what their choice means. I don't think these men are taking account of the likely consequences of their actions. They are not at all prepared to fight with Antipater's men. They cannot have imagined what their city would look like after even a short siege. Oh, it is maddening! Let an Aristogeiton go about dressed in a Spartan cloak, swaggering and proclaiming his adherence to the ancient virtues, if it suits him to play at Spartans. But now that Aristogeiton is moving in the case against

Phryne, he is taking an active political role that might be dangerous.'

'If Aristogeiton or his like rose to real power, then we would all suffer,' said Theophrastos.

'And suffer possibly very terribly.' Aristotle took another short turn about the room. 'An angry Antipater might feel it safest to take very severe measures. I am beginning to agree with Krito – at least in this – that we cannot wait three months for the verdict of the trial of Hermia. We need to do something *now* to help bring truth to light, and quieten the people.'

'Nicely said, but not easy to do.' Theophrastos smiled in his grave manner. 'Now, Aristotle, if only you had some sleepy potion that would sweeten tempers and dampen wrath.'

'The only thing that does that is Reason, which is not at all sleepy,' said Aristotle. 'But Reason is a potion always in short supply. Quite patently we cannot depend on this Basileus, who is – between ourselves – a first-class nincompoop. And certainly young Krito, with his obsessions about Hermia, is not going to bother with truth or justice – nor with details.' He sat down and scratched his beard. 'Orthoboulos, we all agree, was poisoned. First, we really should try to find out where the poison came from.'

It wasn't until next day, when I was in the Agora once again, near the Temple of Zeus, that I thought seriously about how to go about finding the source of the poison, as Aristotle suggested. It struck me then that in the centre of Athens, within a very short distance of where I was then standing, there was a place which presumably housed a quantity of fatal poison – quite legitimately. 'Not far from us,' as my little brother Theodoros had truly said. The prison of Athens is not set apart from the rest of the city; it is at the corner of the agora, beyond the Tholos, near an area of houses and the shops of marble-workers. I suppose it is a good idea to have a prison in such a central position; any prisoner who escaped would have to try to work his way through the throngs, and past numbers of sharp eyes. I walked across the agora to this edifice, which except for its strong external wall didn't really look much unlike any other building (though not of course in the least like a temple). Much of it is one simple storey, with a two-storey part allowing the gaoler's family to live above. The top storey, the living quarters, possesses ordinary windows, but the prison section is distinguished by having very few windows, just slits in the upper wall.

Even when the prison is not inhabited by any criminal, there is always a guard at the door, who is sure to ask one's business.

'What do *you* want to come here for?' growled the guard, who didn't seem favourably impressed by a citizen arriving on a friendly call. 'You coming to look or to buy?'

I ignored his insolence. 'I wish to speak to the person in charge,' I remarked. 'To the governor of this place.'

'He's already busy – he's with somebody.'

'Oh, that will be my friend,' I said airily, and slipped past the guard, heading for the little room on the right which must surely serve as an office. When I got to

the door, and found the chief gaoler in conversation
with another gentleman, I realized that I had inadver-
tently spoken the truth. Or almost. I certainly did
know this gentleman with the square awkward shoulders, brown beard and long patient face, even if I didn't
think of him as a friend, exactly.

'Good day, Theophrastos, and good day to you, sir.'

'Ah, Stephanos.' Theophrastos seemed likewise
determined not to be put out or even to express
surprise. 'I daresay we have come on the same errand.'

'Maybe so,' I responded cautiously.

'I have just arrived,' Theophrastos explained. 'And
I was about to speak to this gentleman here, who as
you know is one of the Eleven. To make some
enquiries'

'Yes,' said the gaoler, with some hesitancy. He
turned to me. 'Did you come to see the prisoner, then?'

'I didn't know there was one,' I said. 'Where do you
keep him?'

'You can look in on him if you like. *You're* a citizen.' Despite this pointedly selective remark,
Theophrastos (who wasn't an Athenian citizen)
followed me and we all three bustled down a short
corridor and across the hall to one of the small rooms.
It was very bare, and not unpleasantly cool. There
was, indeed, nothing one could call furniture – nothing made of wood or any hard object with which a
man might injure himself or others. Just a rough raised
projection, rather like a bench, but made of the same
packed earth as the floor, whitewashed. On this projection there was a thin pallet, rolled up as it was daytime.
The inhabitant of this little room was squatting on

his artificial hill, staring gloomily through the semi-darkness. He looked disappointed; probably he had hoped to see a procession of his womenfolk bringing bread.

'Well,' he said, 'I don't know you, but I'm a citizen. Honest citizen. Men of Athens, I should not be here. I beg you – help me and relieve me.'

'What is he here for?' I asked. Was this poor man destined for execution! Surely not – I couldn't recall any case recently of a capital crime. At least not one in which the criminal had been caught and tried . . .

'He's *here*,' said the gaoler, 'for not paying his fine. That's it. Gives him an excellent opportunity for thinking.'

'All very well for you to say "Pay the fine",' the wretch grumbled. 'What am I to pay it with? I ask you? Can a fine be paid by a man without funds?'

Theophrastos pulled out a couple of obols and made a present of the money to this unfortunate, and we walked back again to the office, which now seemed relatively well-lighted.

'He must needs be glad he is an Athenian,' the gaoler remarked. 'In some states, now, a man so contumacious against the state would receive a little torture to make him disburse the faster.'

'You do inflict torture here, don't you?' I asked. 'On the slaves who are to be witnesses, and on foreigners without sponsors.'

'Yes, indeed,' he replied cheerfully. 'It is administered in order to gather evidence, or secure a confession. The administrators are various officers of the court – including the executioner, our "public man", and the Skythian bowmen who police the city. They do all that needs to be done, usually. The Eleven authorize the activity. My part is chiefly supervisory.'

'What exactly is it that you do to them?' I enquired with a certain curiosity that I knew to be ignoble. I should never have asked this in front of Theodoros.

'Well,' replied the governor of this mansion of pain, 'it varies. With a very valuable slave it is often best to be cautious. A little slapping around and prodding with knives, not to do permanent damage. Though brands or red-hot pincers certainly leave their mark. You see,' he added thoughtfully, 'torture is basically of two kinds: the kind that afflicts the skin and flesh, as with whipping, small cuts, burns and so on. And the more severe and scientific sort, that affects the joints, and disarranges the whole body. To be most effective in interrogation it is best to apply to the joints. The subject can be stretched on a sort of ladder, only horizontal.'

'A mechanical interrogation,' remarked Theophrastos.

'Yes, and so too is the wheel, as you know. The subject is tied to the rim, and the cords pulled tighter and tighter, as he revolves. Limbs are stretched in sudden paroxysms, joints crack. At each revolution, the patient can also be moved slowly over an area of pointed spikes of nails striking upwards into flesh. Exquisitely painful, exciting great apprehension. Much the same effect can be obtained by the basic method requiring only a hook and a rope. The patient is tied up by his thumbs, wrists or elbows, and jerked abruptly upwards. After dangling, he is then plunged down again. The rope passing through a hook in the wall or ceiling, or, even better, over a pulley.'

'Ah. Another exercise owing something to the mechanical arts,' Theophrastos commented. 'And to the theatre. The god in the machine.'

'Such jerks can cause exquisite pain to the bones and joints, even deforming the limbs. The man looks so silly and surprised, flying through the air, his genitals flapping. There's a lot of screaming – of course, these are low types. And they usually come round after, as the men say, "dancing in the air". They'll tell you whatever you wish to know.'

'I suppose,' said Theophrastos thoughtfully, 'in military occupation the interrogators may use some methods even more elaborate and severe. One hears they have also adopted some of the Persian methods. Burial alive – or the threat of it.'

'Happily,' said the prison-keeper, 'I need know nothing of foreign ways. And Athenian citizens should not be tormented, though they can be executed.'

'Indeed,' said Theophrastos, 'that comes to my point. I have been in a manner commissioned to ask you whether you have poison in the prison-house. Or whether you have the ingredients merely, or nothing at all. There is some anxiety in certain important quarters regarding the necessity of preventing the spread of poison in Athens.'

The man blenched.

'Nothing has gone missing, surely!' he remarked. 'We know about the stepmother's poisoning case, of course – and it definitely has *nothing* to do with us. This is a well-run prison. Look, I will show you the store, if you will both witness for me that I do this only to clear myself and answer your enquiry. My assistant is reliable, old and experienced. He should come with us.' He called to a slave, who came quickly. – not the insolent guard, but the unprepossessing 'public man', his short hair grey with age. Once he heard our request, his shoulders drooped. Reluctantly, he led us slowly into an inner room. There was a kind of closet off it, and in that a cupboard.

'Be careful,' said the slave. 'We keep it well stored, but the air of this room is already tainted. And when I bring it out, you will notice the smell. If you get too close, it will give you a stabbing headache. It always does with me. Sure you want to look at it?'

'Yes,' said Theophrastos.

'Get along with it,' said the governor of the prison.

At his master's bidding, the man opened the door, almost with a flourish.

'Death is in here, sure enough,' he remarked. 'But only the makings, as you might say.'

He took out a kind of pottery box and opened it, turning his head away. We approached closer and peered cautiously into the depth of this container.

'Hold them up!' commanded the governor. The slave did so, averting his head. What he displayed was a couple of undistinguished-looking root vegetables, with purple-spotted leaves. The roots were like very gnarled radishes. There was indeed a powerful smell in the air now – a smell something like urine, but more like the stench of a house inhabited by multitudes of mice. It made the air thick. I coughed, and tried to keep down a sense of rising nausea.

'Takes you by the nose and throat, doesn't it?' said the public slave, putting the roots back in their container. 'I dare say I'll feel sick all day. Yet it *looks* harmless, don't it? Like any vegetable. We don't offer our patients the raw *koneion*, of course. We have to make a special preparation, so it can be drunk off. See – here's the pestle and mortar. There are the pots we use. And the cups.'

A shelf in the cupboard indeed held a large stone basin, and a sizeable pestle.

'The celebrated mortar!' I exclaimed.

'Even so – it really exists, and there it is!'

'Famous as the subject of so many vulgar jokes about the death sentence,' commented Theophrastos. 'As in Aristophanes' play where Dionysos is offered passage to the underworld by the "well-pounded path".'

The middle shelf of this poison pantry, like any housewife's cupboard, held a neat collection of pots. There was also a little tray with holes in it, and a small-sized drinking cup of plain pottery set in each of the holes.

'That's all we really need, that and water,' said the slave assistant.'See them little cups with which we serve our guests! I mix it so well, none of my guests has ever needed to ask for a second helping. We keep them cups always here, in that special tray, so no one else ever drinks out of a cup that held poison. Nothing's missing. I work here and I know. Although the hemlock isn't used very often, we get a fresh supply pretty regular, and burn the old stuff – the plant itself. We still have some in liquid form, in a jar. With a mixture of herbs.'

He felt it and shook it, then opened it warily. 'It's half full, just as it was.' He showed us — we stood at a respectful distance. 'Notice how tightly stopped this jar is. We are always careful with this liquid. If we decide it's too old, and want to make fresh, we pour the old mixture into a pit in the earth.'

'We *never* leave it where just anybody could get hold of it,' insisted the gaol overseer. 'Nobody could come at it without passing through the guardroom.'

'So,' I probed, 'you always know how much there is. If there is an execution here, you have plenty on hand.'

'Indeed,' the man in charge assured me. 'We are bound by law and by custom always to have a sufficient supply of fresh *koneion* root. The lethal draught can always be made. We have everything we are supposed to have, and none of the roots is missing. By Herakles! Let us go into the other room — the air in here isn't good for our health.'

We left the fatal cupboard, which the slave assistant had already locked; the fresher air of the gaoler's room was welcome. Though even here a sharp mousy scent seemed to have wafted in.

'So your fellow here,' persisted Theophrastos, 'could make up a new vintage of this poisonous wine at any moment?'

'Oh yes,' said this mechanic of death, answering for himself. 'I have made it before, and used it. I was instructed by an expert when I was young. For an important death, we make up some fresh. That's only considerate-like. No danger of any weakness in the mixture. The faster-acting it is, the better. We're really like doctors, in our way.'

'That's right,' corroborated his superior. 'You are thinking of that lady in the case? The one who killed her husband, so her son says. I would take a special pleasure surely in mixing up a tasty potion for such an iniquitous woman! I'd sooner mix her drink for her, that poisonous wife, than for that lovely girl who's going to be killed for impiety, so they say.'

'It's not sure – there hasn't been a trial in either case—' I protested.

'No it's not sure. Nothing's certain in this world, it's true. But it's likely,' said the governor of the prison, with a certain relish. 'There was nothing in the hearing on Orthoboulos' wife to make us think otherwise. And in the case of Phryne the *hetaira* – well, they do say as Hypereides is taking up the defence. So there will be something worth hearing at her trial, indeed. But she may well find herself coming here to be a patient of ours.'

'Unless,' the slave executioner interjected, 'unless they decide Phryne is too much a foreigner. She is from Thespiai. Now if they treat her as a real foreigner, and a low-life whore to boot, she may be fastened to the tympanon, and be left crying for some kindly hemlock.'

There seemed nothing to add to this.

'No, in all seriousness, gentlemen,' the gaoler said soothingly, 'for an important client, let us say, we make up a fresh batch of our *pharmakon*. And if we had an important person, especially a lady, to give this medicine to, we would put a fair dash of poppy juice into the mix. Makes it easier to bear. Nigh unto painless, and quick as possible.'

'How quick is it, actually?' I enquired.

'Well – I won't deceive you and say it is instant. No, it's reliable, and the quickest method known – for drugs, that is. If you want quickness, don't rely on drugs, but a sharp edge. You can have your head cut off in about the length of time it takes to sneeze! That is, if you have a sharp sword and a good swordsman. The beauty of Athens' method of execution is that it does not disarrange the body. We treat a citizen with dignity.'

'Does it work as Plato says?'

'I suppose so, yes, though I don't recollect what Plato actually said. The *koneion* takes effect gradually, starting with the feet and working up. The patient is unable to walk, and then the legs freeze, as it were. A creeping paralysis. The effect moves steadily up the body, though the mind is awake, usually, until the end or just before. Of course it takes a while, between drinking off the poison and ceasing to breathe. About the time of a good law case in the morning, or the time it takes to have dinner and some conversation with friends. It's an evening, as you might say, but not a long one.'

'So she would have to be in the prison,' I said.

'Not until her last day,' the knowledgeable member of the Eleven explained. 'As the condemned is a woman – and a citizen's wife, in the case of that murderous stepmother. It wouldn't be safe nor proper to leave a citizen's daughter or wife unprotected in the gaol. Her relatives could always cry "Rape!" and "Foul play!" If the trial went against this poisoning female, then she'd still stay with her own relations under guard, as she's doing now. For a day or two after the trial and sentence, to get ready. But the city wants its sentence executed quickly.'

'Ah, yes,' said Theophrastos. 'With all reasonable celerity. Unless there is special cause for delay. In the case of Sokrates, as I recall, there was a period when it was not lawful to execute anyone, until the sacred ship came back from Delos. So Sokrates stayed in the prison an extra length of time, awaiting death for a month.'

'That may be' said the man in charge of the prison, 'but ordinarily the third day after the sentence about does it. Then, you see, the woman would be brought here under guard on the day appointed. With some of her own relations with her, of course, to stay and look after her, and to see fair play and no dirty tricks. Everything would be decent. Matters could be finished very quickly. The hemlock has to be taken by sunset on the day appointed. She could choose to take it at dawn, to get it over with soon, or more likely settle to drink her last at dusk.'

'Up to the patient, as it were,' added his assistant. 'When to take her *pharmakon*, the medicine that ends all troubles.'

There seemed no further reason to stay, so we departed, after grave thanks to the governor of this little house with its poisonous kitchen. The fellow in the cell saluted us as we left. 'Get rid of bad dreams and stomach disorder,' he advised. 'Take some hemlock! Fart your last! Tell your girlfriend to make you some – a good cooling drink on a hot day.' He snivelled and wiped tears away – or pretended to. '*I* wouldn't mind taking some good strong hemlock myself, and doing away with my own troubles entirely,' he whimpered. We refused to throw him another obol. But I realized that of course this prisoner had heard our conversation.

Like ourselves, the unfortunate prisoner would also have been subjected, if to a lesser degree, to the thick mousy odour tainting the air. I crumbled some bay leaves under my nostrils, to try to take the smell out. The chief thing that I seemed to have gained from this enquiry into the prison was a sharp headache that wouldn't go away during the rest of the day.

X

The House of Orthoboulos

Theophrastos and I went together to tell Aristotle of our expedition and to inform him that there seemed little reason to fear that any of the poison had left the prison.

'I believe,' said Theophrastos, 'that the member of the Eleven in charge is intelligent and practical. His assistant has grown old in the service. They corroborated each other. They will make up a fresh batch of poison for the next execution – they have already planned how to make a brew for Hermia, with poppy.'

'Of course,' observed Aristotle, 'it would be as much as their jobs are worth – and more – to let some get stolen. The slave executioner would suffer a very severe penalty, perhaps death. I believe such dereliction might cost the governor all or most of his property in a fine. They certainly would not wish to admit to any such loss.'

'Strange, don't you think,' I enquired, 'that they don't have a supply of that antidote you were telling us about, Theophrastos – Indian pepper, was it? So in case of anything going wrong, or their executing the wrong person, they could cure it before the effects got too severe.'

'I doubt,' said Theophrastos drily, 'if executioners are ever fond of antidotes to executions.'

'Are there other sources of poison?' I asked.

Theophrastos smiled. 'You all seem to think of "poison" as some special thing, set apart. But we are surrounded by poisons! Many plants are somewhat poisonous to human beings. And some plants are good for us in one form and bad in others. If anything natural should be called "bad", which I doubt. Hellebore is medicinal in small doses, relieving sorrowful feelings and oppression round the heart – yet a little too much, and it is fatal. Oleander, so pretty, is a cheering additive to wine, yet it is harmful to many animals, and even kills people. The powers of some drugs become diminished in a person accustomed to take them. Thrasyas even got himself accustomed to eat quantities of hellebore without ill effect. Aconite is lethal to animals, and most animals avoid it. Mixed with a sweet drink with wine or honey, aconite is not noticeable. Yet it can kill a person, sometimes even months after ingestion.'

'That's a problem with poisoning,' I remarked. 'The poisoner could be well away from the victim when the lethal dose at last overtook him.'

'Very true. Not all poisons are quick in effect, like hemlock. And hemlock, as the prison governor said, is not truly instantaneous. A measurable time elapses between administration of the drink, and the death of the drinker. But it is comparatively speedy. Contrast it with common meadow-saffron – a harmless short-lived flower. But this flower of a day can cause a slow and lingering death. Slaves often take meadow-saffron – a cheap way of poisoning themselves. But the dose so wilfully taken may not act for a long time, during which interval perhaps the taker might lose his desire to die.'

'What a horrible idea!' I shuddered. 'You describe a baleful world, full of deathly growths. You bring the realm of Proserpina into the domain of Demeter.'

'Well, they are Mother and Daughter. But my book will emphasize the cures, the help we get from plants – without which we could not survive at all. Thanks be to Demeter! We have benefits innumerable from all this vegetation that springs from the earth in abundance and variety. Perhaps a painless death might be counted amongst such blessings. And plants are very beautiful and interesting things.'

There was no point in annoying Theophrastos, so I assented.

'We are wandering from the point.' Aristotle, who had settled back in his chair to hear Theophrastos, leaned forward again. 'At least from *my* point. It appears we cannot really answer how the poison that killed Orthoboulos was obtained. Evidently if someone possessed as little as one hemlock root, the making of such a poison would be easy – especially to a deft cook. Yet we should pursue this case. I must say, I should like to see this trial brought to an end.'

'It is strange for you to say that,' I remarked, 'as you and your scholars are writing a book on the constitution of Athens, praising the system of our laws and courts.'

'I never said there were no wrongful trials, or mistaken sentences. The case of Sokrates among them.'

'Talking with your scholars, Aristotle, makes me think of things, and then I worry. Perhaps our democracy isn't working properly. It is an excellence of Athens that there can be no monarch or permanent dictator. The city is to be ruled by its citizens, not by one man. Yet – look at Lykourgos. He was voted in for one term of office. But since the laws don't allow him to run again, he put a friend's name down and got that man voted in, but we all know it is really Lykourgos who does the work and administers all the funds in the treasury. He collects the taxes and decides that we will build the new Stadion and so on. So – is that right?'

Aristotle sighed. 'That troubles me too, Stephanos. Lykourgos himself is an admirable man, aristocratic but impartial – relatively. Incorruptible, he is dedicated totally to the benefit of Athens. People say he understands money and how it works. Yet, between ourselves, the city has connived at breaking its own rules and is coaxing itself into being happy with the rule of one man.'

'This evil,' Theophrastos pronounced, 'surely arises in large part from the over-anxiety of the democrats to make positions rotate every year and to determine choices of many office-holders by lot.'

'True. Guarding against oligarkhs, they have ensured

men cannot be elected – or re-elected – to most posts sheerly on account of their particular ability. Hence, all connive at the rise of Lykourgos, because they know they need his particular talents at this time. It *is* dangerous.'

'You need hardly fear,' observed Theophrastos, 'that Lykourgos will do anything rash. He is good for people like ourselves, as he quite likes resident foreigners, yet he is happily above all question regarding lineage. Lykourgos is a man of balance and sober reason.'

'I do not worry about anything Lykourgos himself does or will do,' Aristotle responded, 'but I am concerned that *Athens* has lost confidence in herself. With so many tensions regarding pro- and anti-Makedonian sympathies, at any moment the city is in danger of slipping into conflict, even violence.'

'If the city is an artificial animal, like a marionette,' I remarked, 'then it could get broken.'

'The marionette acting on a wound-up spring won't break – as long as nobody violently pulls or forces its spring. A real animal of flesh has a chance of mending itself after injury, but we see how the artifice of a state can easily break. Sometimes it breaks so hard it can no more repair itself than a vase dropped on a stone. The case against the woman Phryne is dangerous, and brings religious as well as political passions into play. That poor hetaira! I do not necessarily approve of such women, but I must pity her. It is so difficult to *dis*prove a charge of impiety.'

'And she did—' I caught myself in time. Nobody at all – *nobody* – must know from me that I was present at that blasphemous party in Tryphaina's brothel. Not as long as there remained any chance that I would not be found out.

'If Phryne did what she is accused of, she is in a bad way,' Aristotle continued, not noticing my lapse. 'Unfortunately, once people get used to making dramatic accusations of impiety and pollution of the city, they may not want to stop with the sacrifice of one victim. Even the very best of states is always poised by the edge of a chasm, and I fear Athens is nearly teetering on that edge. I think it dangerous for the case of Hermia to take its course.'

'The families concerned are so visibly important,' commented Theophrastos. 'Her case may add more and more fuel to the passions, involving almost everybody in the end − is that what you think?'

'Yes. Hermia's case provides openings for men of various factions − from the most extreme of democratic sympathizers to the ultimate supporters of absolute autocracy.'

'People are much harder on her,' I commented, 'since Hermia offended the city by appearing in the agora. At least some people are, the ones you term sympathizers of the oligarkhs. Her family have had to pay for expensive cleansing sacrifices, and they get themselves hooted at. For polluting the holy place, Hermia in a way is now considered guilty of impiety too.'

'An interesting but not a consoling point.'

'Of course, if she could be proved not to be the murderer, then she wouldn't have polluted anything,' I reasoned. 'You, O Aristotle, seem to wish to abort the proceedings against Hermia. Frankly, I should dearly love to do that myself. Such a stoppage would spare me any further witnessing, and remove the barrier that my future father-in-law has now erected between me and my wedding. Would you believe it! Smikrenes won't let me have his daughter until the trial of Hermia has come to an end – and until he sees how disgraced I have been by it, I suppose.'

'That undoubtedly gives you, Stephanos, a strong motive for wishing that there would be no trial,' agreed Theophrastos, amused. 'Though some married men might suggest you are offered a lucky escape!'

'But, after all,' I argued, addressing Aristotle and ignoring Theophrastos' ill-considered jest, 'Orthoboulos *was* indeed foully killed. Homicide, no question. In order to stop the proceedings against Hermia for murder we must find out who really did it. If she didn't, I mean. *Who* designed and brought about the murder of Orthoboulos – if it was not Hermia?'

'Precisely.' Aristotle arose and started walking up and down. 'We hardly know enough at this point even to speculate. Too many facts missing. We don't really know, for instance, where Orthoboulos had been that day and that evening – or even when he went out, or if he did go out. Is Krito's – or Ergokles' – new idea that Philinos might have a connection of some kind with the case altogether wrong?'

'It seems likely that much of what Krito says is frantic fantasy, based on Ergokles' mean remarks,' I responded. 'There was no need for Philinos to antagonize poor Orthoboulos by poaching either his mistress or his wife. Philinos was widowed young and hasn't remarried. Not yet. But he has many women friends – of the expensive kind. I know – I mean I have heard – that he had an affair with Phryne. We might interview some of his other mistresses, I suppose.'

'I am glad you say "we", Stephanos, as I need your help, though "we" will have to go extremely carefully. As a witness in Hermia's case you will be all too visible. "Tread softly" must be our watchword. But – *where* did Orthoboulos actually die? And where was he when the poison was administered? Those could be two different places.'

'I suppose it might have been the brothel – I mean the next-door house – all along,' I remarked doubtfully. 'He could have been given the poison there, and died where he was.'

'Unlikely, Stephanos, given what you have told us about the condition of the body when you saw it. I have thought about that. Blood was pooled in the head, and the corpse was curved. This suggests that the body of Orthoboulos had been moved – perhaps held head downward – either just before death or just after. Moving him required the body to be bent, and it turned into an arc. If he was moved to the brothel, who moved him – and from where? And *when?* Our enquiries lead us back to the question of the time. He was in his own house apparently until quite late in the evening. His younger son thinks he was well.'

'But,' argued Theophrastos, 'the dwelling of Orthoboulos was inspected after the body was found, and no sign of poisoning was seen. Male slaves testified – one of them under torture – that they had no knowledge of anything unusual in the house.'

'The slaves might have been lying. Or ignorant,' I suggested.

'Yes, quite so.' (It was always pleasing when Aristotle agreed with me.) 'I think,' Aristotle added, 'I will find some excuse to go to poor Orthoboulos' *andron* and look for myself. The murdered man's younger son thinks his father was lying down there, dozing but well. Was he dozing because he was starting to die at that point? Had paralysis set in? Let us see what we can discover.'

The next day, we set off – Aristotle, Theophrastos and myself – to see what we could see in Orthoboulos' house. We didn't set out until the afternoon, however, as Aristotle wished to inspect the interior of that house at around the same time of day that Kleiophon had spoken to his father – at dusk on the day of Orthoboulos' death. At midday, before passing through the city gate to meet Aristotle and Theophrastos and walk back with them, I was in the agora. There I had the dubious pleasure of seeing Aristogeiton again, sporting his red cloak and speaking loudly against the iniquities of Athens, chiefly signalled in the monstrous iniquity of Hermia and the mad impiety of Phryne. Phryne, he was glad to say, was now a prisoner, and would be ending her days nailed to a board, if Justice had her way. Aristogeiton also railed against the luxury and insane cowardice (so he alleged) of Hypereides, who preferred the company of whores and slaves to that of warriors of his own class.

'Aristogeiton is a very angry man, always,' Aristotle

observed, when I described this fresh diatribe as we were walking back to the city gate. 'Proud perhaps, rather than genuinely angry. He signals his difference from other men in his declaration of admiration for Spartan principles. And in his vindictive pursuit of Hypereides. Some Athenians privately think that Hypereides was not altogether wrong about freeing the slaves and arming them and the foreign residents. Of course, at that time he feared a direct Makedonian onslaught against Athens itself.'

'That's why he also wanted to take the women and children to shelter in Peiraieus,' added Theophrastos.

'Exactly. It cannot truly be said that Hypereides lacked concern for Athens. Aristogeiton and his group became extremely excited at the horrific idea of liberating aliens and slaves into citizenship, and proposed a hideous penalty for the man who suggested it. In their eyes, it would not be defending Athens to change Athens so greatly – polluting the blood. Admittedly such an action would certainly have raised enormous problems in relation to property compensation, and even land-owning.'

'But you as a *metoikos* would have benefited—?'

'I can hardly think so, Stephanos, as I would have been identified with the enemy. Yet, despite Hypereides' loathsome treatment of me last summer, I have some slight and abstract sympathy for his current position, especially in contrast to that of such adamantine patriots as Aristogeiton.'

'Who is now determined to cleanse Athens of all impropriety, evidently,' said Theophrastos.

'That concerns me. If Aristogeiton is capable of

such sentiments, he might not be withheld from any cruelty in the name of what he thinks is right. Purity is not without its own dangers. I am reminded of Euripides' *Bakkhai*. In that play, you remember, the righteous ruler Pentheus, prince of Thebes, wants to put down the celebrations of Dionysos and the excesses – as he sees them – of the women who worship the god of wine as Mainads.'

Aristotle threw back his head and began to recite:

"'Those females already seized, hands straitly tied,
My officers now guard in public prison;
The rest I shall hunt down upon the mountains.
These women once cruelly fast in nets of iron,
Quickly I'll end the evil works of Bakkhis.'"

It was strange to hear and see the ageing philosopher piping up with such dramatic spirit upon the public road.

'This prince of Thebes,' Aristotle returned to his normal tone, 'intends to do away by force with irrational frenzy. Instead, Pentheus feeds the frenzy, and is ultimately himself the sacrifice.'

'Many forms of the divine
Many times the gods

'– oh, I cannot remember that last speech. Though I know it does begin with "Many forms".'

I was shamefaced at discovering I could not recall the very last four lines of the *Bakkhai*, when I had really thought I could produce them. And there was

Aristotle, admirably capable of trumpeting forth sets of verses at will. I said as much.

'Quoting was a habit of ours, all of us in Plato's circle,' he said airily. 'And Alexander too – if he liked a piece of poetry when he was a boy, he would get it by heart. He loved best of Euripides' plays the *Andromeda* – he would spout great passages until one had to ask him to stop. I suppose the plight of the Ethiopian princess charmed him. That, and the heroism of her rescuer. He has always fancied himself a Perseus. He sees all of Asia, I think, as the princess in distress, whom he will save from a monster. I'm not sure, however – this is between ourselves – that Alexander was always exactly correct in his quotations, but there are variations, after all.'

'Not now,' said Theophrastos, 'for now we can all consult the absolutely accurate copy that Lykourgos is having made of all the works of the three greatest dramatists: Aiskhylos, Sophokles and Euripides. They say he intends to do the same by the poems of Homer. So we shall always know the utterly correct lines. I suppose that will make it a crime for them ever to be quoted otherwise.'

'An odd idea, in a way,' I mused, 'because many reciters – I mean the professional ones too – put in bits of their own. Especially when they do Homer. Often quite good bits, and some of it might be Homer too – who knows? The reciter has something to do with the story, he is the player and not just a flute.'

'As you say,' said Aristotle, 'that is a pleasure that must disappear when we have such serious texts to turn to. Though the puzzle will be – who decides?

What might happen if somebody were to insist that he heard Euripides himself recite the speech a different way? Would that sufficiently challenge the authority of Lykourgos' copy?'

'He'd have to say his *grandfather* heard Euripides himself,' I pointed out.

It was better for us to be talking out loud in public about the authority of Euripides, a long-dead dramatist, than about the authority, real or potential, of a living and dangerous Aristogeiton, whose own friends might report to him anything we were overheard to say. We were all quieter as we neared Orthoboulos' house.

Orthoboulos' house was, relatively speaking, a mansion. In those days most people didn't build as large and high as they have done later. Older and richer families, however, had originally been able to occupy a good deal of land even within the city, so their houses were more spacious than many later ones. Orthoboulos' house, old enough and in a wealthy deme, took up a noticeable area. It looked like the sort of house with a lot of rooms, and a very spacious women's quarters upstairs.

The house was surrounded by a wall, but the door in the wall was ajar, and we merely pushed it open and walked through. There was a small courtyard in front of the house entry, shaded by a modest tree. Under the tree there was a statue on a plinth, supported by a pedestal of three steps. Not a mere herm, but a real statue of Hermes at full length. On the edge of the lowest of the steps of the pedestal sat a small girl, playing with a doll. This child, who cannot have been much over five years old, was neatly dressed; her clean looks and apparel as well as the toy indicated that she was not a slave-child but a child of the house. It was odd to find her out here, all alone. The little girl looked at us through large round brown eyes, under her fringe of dark hair.

'Good day, child,' Theophrastos said courteously.

'I am Kharis daughter of Epikhares,' she informed us. 'Who are you?'

It did not seem appropriate to engage in conversation with this small person of the house, or to approach her, so without answering we continued to the door. A servant, a butler or confidential doorkeeper, responded to our knock, opening the door suspiciously, only a very little at first. He seemed very upright and correct.

'The Master is not at home,' he informed us. 'I regret.' And he started to close the door again.

I thought for a moment it was absurd of the man to say the Master was not at home when we all knew his Master was dead and buried, but then I caught myself. Of course this was really Krito's house now, though we still called it the house of Orthoboulos.

'I think,' said Aristotle in an easy and genial manner, 'that the little daughter of the house would be safer inside. You notice the street gateway is ajar, and she might run into the street – or someone could come in and snatch her.'

'By Herakles!' The porter blenched. 'You are right!' He turned within. 'Call Nurse to collect the little one as soon as may be – the child's in the outer courtyard.'

'But I want to be *here*,' the little girl protested. 'I have to keep looking out for Mama to come. She said she would come, and I told her I would look for her and run to her as soon as she came to the gate.'

The child came up to us, holding carefully her doll, a creature of terracotta, with movable limbs. The doll had a serene oval face and rippling hair parted in the middle and running from the brow; it looked not unlike Phryne. Kharis herself was dark and solemn. She looked directly at Aristotle.

'Is my Mama coming? Do you know?'

'I am sure she wants to,' said Aristotle. 'And she will come when she can.'

A certain sorrow on the face of the elderly butler told me that, slave though he was, the man was affected by the situation. Of course! This was one of Hermia's own slaves, the new group who had replaced the servants of Orthoboulos. He felt for his absent mistress.

Aristotle must have divined the same thing in the same instant, for he said to the butler, 'You would be doing a kindness to your mistress Hermia if you would let us enter. For the only chance of her refuting this accusation is to have more evidence presented. I assure you, we are sympathetic to the cause of Hermia rather than against her, and would be glad of your assistance. We shall not disturb the servants.'

'Well,' said the butler, reluctantly, 'I don't know as young Master — but he isn't here, and you are known to the mistress, if you say true. So I cannot see what harm it would do to let you in briefly. But what do you want?'

'Just to see the rooms which were mentioned at the first hearing,' said Aristotle. 'The passage and the *andron* where Orthoboulos was lying on a couch.'

'Won't do harm,' repeated the servant, 'as long as I come along and watch you. But it's ticklish watching three. I must ask you, please, not to separate.'

And with a slow and ceremonious step he led us down the hall. I admired the man's deportment – so different from that of my own inefficient slave when pressed into the function of answering the door or letting in visitors. Aristotle slightly in the van, all three of us followed the butler. The little girl Kharis, an uninvited fourth member of the party, came trailing after us, carrying her doll. We went down a hall and into a larger passage, on the right, then paused outside a room door.

'That is the *andron*,' said the servant. 'And' – he bustled in and moved some furniture – 'the couch on which the Master lay would have been just here.'

'There were no lamps in the room?'

'Not that evening, nothing had been lit. But I can light you a lamp so you can have a good view.'

We walked in to inspect. Even with so many of us inside it, the room felt fairly spacious. It was a good room – so much nicer than my own *andron*. The walls were painted red, and the furniture was of a light polished wood, which showed up elegantly against the walls.

'Here was the bed where he'd have lain,' explained the butler.

'I want to find Artimmes,' the little girl said. 'Artimmes is always here, but now I don't know where he is.'

I presumed she was looking for some toy or playmate. We thought it best to ignore her. It is not appropriate for strangers to address the girl-children of a citizen's house, and even in the case of one so young it behoved us to be careful. Kharis played with her doll, whispering to it softly, and holding it up so the doll too could inspect us.

'The old Master, Orthoboulos, as I understand,' the butler continued, 'would quite often lie down for a little while, of an evening, before going out. The couch he lay on was always where you see it placed now.'

'I see,' said Aristotle. 'The couch is not near the window, but on the other side. Yet quite visible from the passage.'

We walked up to this piece of furniture, an ordinary design if of superior wood, suitable for a couch to recline on at a dinner party, or for use as a day bed.

'There would have been a cushion – a mattress, like – on the bed,' said the servant. 'This, I believe, was the identical one.'

It was a good-quality mattress, the cover bearing a woven pattern in black. We inspected it, and Aristotle suddenly sniffed at it. I did the same. It smelt of nothing but mattress, of the straw of which it was made. I then took a deep, if cautious, breath, inhaling and trying to classify the odours of this chamber. It smelled better than most. I also peered about in the dusk to look if I could see anything, but the room had been well cleaned by impeccable servants, and there were no signs of dirt anywhere, nor any smearing of the wall. On an impulse, I dropped to my knees and explored the floor by the bed, and the corner of the wall, sniffing. Some uncaptured dust made me sneeze. I breathed carefully again, remembering that I knew what hemlock smelled like. Surely

I would catch it if any trace of it lingered here in this room.

The little girl burst out laughing. 'You're a dog!' she exclaimed. 'Our old dog did that, sniffing and snuffling.' I thought it wisest to pay her no heed.

'Be careful of that ornament – that statue,' Aristotle warned me. For I had nearly bumped into a niche filled by a sizeable statue, in marble, of a female. No, two females. The stone females appeared to be Nymphs. I could see the base was somewhat discoloured, as by earth and water; presumably this piece had been out of doors at one time. It would have looked better, I reflected, placed at Smikrenes' old shrine to Pan and the Nymphs. The piece seemed out of place here. These bulky if lively young ladies with their voluminous clothing were too large for the place in which they found themselves. One Nymph was so near hitting her head one felt she ought to duck.

'There was another statue too,' Kharis piped up. 'In a different place. This one was Papa's.' By which I surmised she meant the marble Nymphs had belonged to Epikhares, and was not part of the ornamentation of the room as originally furnished by Orthoboulos.

Theophrastos inspected the statue disapprovingly, but then found nearby a stand with two book-scrolls on it. With a grunt of satisfaction, he picked these up and began to examine them, holding them close before his eyes. Then he helped himself to a modest chair, and adopted one of the lamps brought in by the butler to aid him in his reading.

'Now, you lie down on the bed, Stephanos,' Aristotle suggested, 'and I shall go into the passage and be as

Kleiophon.' He did as he himself suggested, lurking in the passage, and peering uncertainly into the room. He whispered, 'Father?'

'I hear you perfectly,' I responded, laughing.

'And I you,' he replied, 'though I cannot truly *see* you. But this is not the best way, Stephanos – what am I thinking of? Your eyes would be sharp and youthful, more like those of Kleiophon. Do you be Kleiophon, and I shall be the unfortunate Orthoboulos.'

So he lay upon the couch, with Theophrastos casting the occasional shrewd glance at us when he was not reading. I also employed one of the lamps brought by the butler, which I held when I went outside into the passage. Little Kharis lurked behind me. Her wide eyes were visible even in this dark passageway; she was obviously taking everything in.

'You need Papa's girl,' she said hopefully. 'Daughter. His one.'

'Keep away, little girl, and don't interrupt us,' I said, as briskly as I could from this odd angle.

'Make it real,' said Aristotle. 'Blow out the lamp – and you too, Theophrastos – so there is no extra illumination.'

I did so. The place was very dusky. I tried whispering, 'Father?' and Aristotle mumbled, 'Go away, boy, and let me doze a little.' As Orthoboulos had done, according to his son Kleiophon.

'I can *hear* you,' I said, 'but I don't really see you distinctly. Just a shape, and a kind of white bit where your face must be.'

Aristotle sat up.

'Well, that tells us something,' he said, rubbing his

leg. 'This is not the most comfortable couch, but then Orthoboulos would not have old bones, like me.'

The remark spread into the silence, reminding us all that the unfortunate Orthoboulos did not have the privilege of living to make old bones.

'The mattress is different,' said the little girl.

'Different?' I asked

'Different from before,' Kharis explained vaguely. 'It has a different cover, and new straw.'

The ears of the butler were sharp. 'What's that you say, child?' He bustled over to us. 'The child knows nothing about it, sirs, she is confusing housekeeping events. This is the same mattress as that on which Orthoboulos lay – that's what you wanted to see, isn't it? Oh, where is that Nurse?'

Nurse was in fact approaching apace; we could hear her coming before we saw her. She was scolding one of the other servants as she came down the passage. 'Letting that precious lamb go into the outside court, whatever was you thinking of! Like as if your heads was stuffed with wool and pudding!' This rebuke was probably intended for the ears of the superior butler himself. She came charging in, a short woman with a wrinkled old face, and great energy.

'And *there* you are, Kharis, my precious! And someone's been letting you talk with strange men, as if we were little better than beggars!' Nurse included us all in her hostile glance.

'She's come to no harm, Kyrene,' the butler said, defensively. 'And I've been with her the whole time.'

'Oh, that's a great comfort, no doubt.' Kyrene's sarcastic tone was as subtle as a saw.

'I'm all right,' said little Kharis. 'I am quite well, Nurse. But I can't find Artimmes. I wanted him to make things for me. I was waiting for Mama, and these men came. They want to look at where Papa was lying. On the night before he died.'

'Filling the child's head with such stuff!' The Nurse was indignant. 'Who are you – whose hirelings? For what? More folks a-going for the mistress and gnawing and gnawing at her,' she complained. Kharis looked as if she were about to cry.

'I assure you,' said Aristotle, 'we are not in the fee of Krito, nor are we antagonists of Orthoboulos' widow—'

'You'd better not be,' she sniffed. 'Or there's gods above us as will strike you down. Little one,' to her charge, 'you'd best come up to the women's quarters, and have a drink of milk-and-water, and lie down a little, perhaps.'

Kharis looked down at the floor, patently not best pleased at this proposal. She manipulated her doll, rotating its movable arm. 'Kharis doesn't want to,' squeaked the doll, rotating her arm madly as if waving away the suggestion.

'Well, you can't stay down here. A prey to all comers and goers! And there's someone else at the door too,' said the Nurse snappishly. Certainly a loud knocking was to be heard. '*Up*stairs is where you're going, little miss, whether you want to or not – you and your doll together,' and Kyrene pulled the child along. Little Kharis made her exit, her doll tucked under her arm, the legs clicking. The child and her attendant were soon out of our view.

XI

Searching for Witnesses

The knocking we had heard did not cease, though the butler, in wholesome fear of the scolding Kyrene, waited until she and her charge had totally disappeared before going to answer. He indicated with a nod that our time in the house was at an end, and we meekly followed him as he carried the lamps along the passage.

'I am not sorry to depart,' said Theophrastos crisply. 'This seems to me a complete waste of time. Except that Orthoboulos had an interesting collection of satyr-plays.'

As we approached the door, we saw that the newcomer, like ourselves, had been able to enter through the unfastened gateway. Impressed with the importance of his own errand, this new visitor certainly had no compunction about knocking loudly. He was now adding calling aloud to his knocks:

'Krito! Krito, I say! Have you no servants to answer this cursed door?'

'Sorry, sir, I am sure,' said the butler with defer-
ence. The person at the door, despite a certain rough-
ness in his speech, was undeniably an Athenian citizen
in good standing, if not luxuriously dressed. He had
a pointed brown beard, and just above the beard a
sizeable round lump grew on his right cheek.

'Who are *these?*' the man enquired, staring at us.
'And who are you?' The newcomer stared at the
servant, measuring him from top to toe. 'I remember
the doorkeeper as a fatter man, a Phrygian or something, quite bald.'

'That's so, sir. I was the servant of Epikhares before
coming to serve the mistress here. Now, these gentlemen are just about to leave,' a gentle hint, as the man
with the wen was blocking the doorway.

'That's as may be,' the man said curtly. 'They might
as well stay, now they're here. Perhaps they too can
answer some questions. Along with Krito.'

Aristotle, Theophrastos and I thought it wise to
remain silent.

'I regret that the Master, Krito son of Orthoboulos,
is not within at present,' the butler said with due courtesy.

'Stand by the gate! Keep a good watch!' So this new
visitor called out suddenly to his own slave, who (as
we now saw) was lurking by the gate in all due humil-
ity waiting to receive his master's commands. This
slave was not humble in bulk or stature, however; he
was built like an ox, and taller than his master, though
the imperious citizen with the pointed beard and round
wen was not short.

'*I* am Theramenes.' This citizen, still standing in

the doorway, stared hard at us. 'Who might you be? You are not members of Krito's household, I know that.'

There was nothing for it. We had to yield up our names.

'Aristotle the philosopher? I have heard of you.' Theramenes did not seem too happy with what he had heard. 'And Theophrastos, I guess he's your assistant. As for you, Stephanos son of Nikiarkhos, frankly I don't recollect you at all. As you are a citizen, however, doubtless you can help me. But we should go in if we are to converse.'

And waving the slave in front of him, this visitor entered the house.

'We were about to depart—' I remarked.

'Yes, they were just leaving,' the butler corroborated.

'This will take only a short while. But we may as well talk within doors. Perhaps Krito will arrive in the meanwhile. I hate to waste time.' Theramenes, taking possession of the passage, chivvied us before him, as a dog may drive sheep along a road.

'I am sorry,' said Aristotle, 'but I really do not understand your business, Theramenes of Athens, or what concern it can be of ours. We are truly in the dark.'

'Dark in here. Lights, if you please, at once!' Theramenes ordered the butler, as soon as he entered the *andron*. He waved at us to indicate we should be seated. This strange man seemed to have forgotten that this was not his house. Yet so unwilling were we to make trouble that we actually sat down, with an

apologetic glance at the old servant. Aristotle and I
sat upon the couch we had been inspecting only a short
time before, while Theophrastos unobtrusively occupied his former modest seat in the background.
Theramenes helped himself to the most substantial
chair in the room, one with arms and a back. The
butler again brought in two lamps.

'It is a matter of such civic importance,' Theramenes
said, 'that I must exceed a little the boundaries of strict
courtesy, both in entering Krito's house and in questioning yourselves. But when time is a factor, and speed
is essential – I am sure you will understand.'

'Ah. I suppose so,' I said awkwardly. 'Perhaps you
would favour us with the exact nature of your business.'

'Certainly. Now, you must understand I am a volunteer. A citizen, acting as a citizen ought – no paid
hireling. I am presently actively engaged in searching
out any young men or slaves, or anyone – even flute-
girls and the like – who were at the party where
Phryne committed her most monstrous act of impiety. I am making a list of names, omitting absolutely
no one, no matter how lowly or unimportant.
Aristogeiton and myself have thought that the best
way of going about things. I have come to Krito not
because of his current problems regarding his father's
death and the charge against his stepmother, but
because Krito himself – a valuable young citizen – may
be disposed to be helpful to us in rooting out iniquity,
by telling us anything he hears.'

'If I take your meaning correctly,' said Aristotle,
'you believe that young Krito son of Orthoboulos

would like to please members of the Areopagos before the trial regarding his father's murder.'

Aristotle spoke with calm detachment. Of course, he had no idea how greatly Theramenes' previous words had alarmed me. A man collecting names – 'making a list' – of those who had been at the party at Tryphaina's brothel – how dire that sounded! I hoped that I had not turned pale. Aristotle had no notion that I had been present at the party in the brothel on the night when Phryne had enacted the role of Demeter. Nor (please the gods!) was he or anyone else ever going to know. I bent all my energies to appearing calm and serious. Fortunately, despite the two little lamps brought in by the butler, the room remained dim, even for observant eyes.

'Exactly.' Theramenes took no offence at the imputation within Aristotle's remark. If he had taken in the implication that arkhons of the court of the Areopagos could be swayed by factors external to the trial in hand, he gave no sign of displeasure. 'Krito son of Orthoboulos is the right age to know a lot of young men, citizens. The sort of persons who were at that party. Krito may well – even in his present state of distress – have picked up some gossip or bibble-babble about that occasion. Even his younger brother, Kleiophon son of Orthoboulos, might know something.'

'But he would be too young to frequent brothels,' Theophrastos observed dispassionately.

'I take your point. One tends to believe a lad of Kleiophon's age is a trifle too young to frequent brothels. Though that's not quite true of *every* lad of fourteen, especially among the lower sort if they're well grown. But the boy still might know something. Kleiophon as well as Krito may have heard some news or gossip, useful to the authorities – or to those acting for them.'

'And you are acting for—?'Aristotle hinted gently

'I am acting for Aristogeiton, and for his friends Euthias and Mantias, who are also concerned in making the formal charge. But several of the arkhons are warmly in favour of our proceeding.'

He leaned towards us. 'The thing is, this charge, once having been made, *must* be made to stick. The trial has got to succeed! Such a charge – the serious charge of impiety – can never be turned into a jest. If the whore were acquitted it would bring Athens into disrepute, and even danger.'

He leaned back in his chair, and opened his mouth for full discourse. Obviously, he felt no trepidation about haranguing the Master of the Lykeion.

'Now, just look facts in the face. This harlot has introduced a foreign god, and endeavoured to make Athenian youth accept this Isodaites, the equal divider, or "god of equal shares", by inducing them to take part in a religious ceremony. She has led shameless revels and involved both men and women in her illicit procession of homage to this god. Thus stirring up trouble in the confused minds of young people, and ignorant slaves. In order to make her foreign deity acceptable, she has ridiculed the religion of Eleusis – long a central pillar of Athenian identity and security. On the goodness of Demeter, goddess of the wheat and barley, depends our ability to feed the people. Our generous religion allows even foreigners to become initiates – even slaves. People near and far love Demeter and the Kore and the worship of Eleusis.'

'Yes, they do,' I remarked, 'and there are statues everywhere, especially of Kore.'

'This love, and the hope supplied by the great Mysteries, must never be profaned. It has always been forbidden to reveal what exactly happens in the holy Mysteries. Thus, of course it is strictly forbidden to mock them. More than the sensibilities of the pious are injured if Eleusis is mocked. The power of Athens is weakened in direct proportion.'

'I see what you mean,' Aristotle said.

'I thought you might see. And you yourself, O Aristotle of Stageira – you have been in danger of offending the city's sensibilities upon this point, in an ill-chosen monument to your wife. Until Reason prevailed.' He nodded, indicating that any reply from Aristotle was not required. 'Do not upset yourself. Many matters come to my attention these days. That uncomfortable occasion to which I allude – all a misunderstanding. Doubtless. In such a delicate situation as yours, you will wish to do all in your power to assist those patriots whose energies are bent upon upholding the cause of our city and our religion.'

'But this,' I said, 'is a court case. The case of Phryne that you are speaking of. The Law will take its course.'

'The Law will take its rightful course if we do not fail the Law. We must not fail. Thus, we need as many witnesses as possible who will tell us the truth about that evening. We must make plain the enormity of the offence.'

'These witnesses,' I wondered, 'those witnesses you have collected already. Will the person acting as Defender – I understand it is Hypereides – have the chance to question them? Of course, he will in open court, at the trial itself. But will he have the opportunity during the advance hearings?'

Theramenes waved a hand contemptuously.

'Totally unnecessary,' he said firmly. '*This* is not like a trial for homicide! The pollution of murder is bad enough, but the pollution of impiety is intolerable. Hearings would repeat the offence by repeating the words. In a case of a homicide, the murdered man's family are the first injured party, and they seek to avenge the death according to the law. But in a case of impiety – why, the gods themselves are directly injured! The participants in this revel-rout should be discovered, and either punished severely, or – if well-born citizens – gently corrected. There must be no more festivals in honour of this Isodaites! Pollution introduced with the new and unauthorized god must instantly be done away with – for the city's own safety. Likewise the perilous pollution invoked in the parody-rite, the insult to Demeter, must immediately be cleared away. The Basileus agrees. Retribution must follow swiftly upon the offence. It is only right that in a case like this the goddess Demeter should be propitiated by the death of the offender.'

'I understand,' said Aristotle, with a dangerous gentleness. (In the past I had heard him say 'I understand' in this tone to a student who was blundering on and clearly knew nothing.) Despite the provocation offered by Theramenes' needless reminiscence of his great personal grief, Aristotle remained calm. Sitting in Orthoboulos' *andron* and being harangued by this ungainly citizen, confronted by that patchy beard and too-visible wen, Aristotle was self-possessed, self-activating and altogether like himself.

'I comprehend now *your* interest in this case, O Theramenes. And it reflects, as I now see, the intelligence of Euthias and the zealous desire of Aristogeiton in conducting the prosecution. Naturally, as Aristogeiton's organ – his instrument, if you prefer – you must wish for success. But I believed you had *already* acquired sufficient witnesses. We are told that the legal action is based on the testimony of those who were at the party in the brothel on the occasion in question.'

'Well, not everyone wants to say that they were there,' Theramenes admitted. 'Natural enough they should like to keep quiet. We do actually have one very splendid witness in young Euboulos. He was there – Euboulos son of Xenophon, of the deme of Melite. That youngster was innocently enjoying himself, as you might say – or at least, if it was foolish and perhaps wrong, still young men will be young men, you know. Euboulos son of Xenophon has certainly behaved in a very manly way in making his statement to us. He was horrified when he realized what was going forward. But of course he alone couldn't see everything. And we need corroboration.'

'The slaves?'

'They have mostly been tortured already – didn't that woman Tryphaina raise a fuss over her brood of pullets!' He chuckled reminiscently. 'Some of the girls prove to be freedwomen, which makes matters difficult, but there are plenty of slaves, from the cook-maids to the flute-girls, and most of those high-class whores. We have had quite a lot of work putting them all to the question! But some of our labourers love their work this time, that's certain.'

He sighed in satisfied reminiscence; I now knew this meant he had seen girls naked and screaming on the rack or wheel, or flying through the air on the end of a rope.

'The pleasure of your work may be compensation enough for you,' said Theophrastos in a calm and civil tone.

'Well, in a manner of speaking, when working for the public good! What the slaves said under the question will be submitted at the trial in evidence. But — at least in some people's eyes — there is always a certain doubt about slave testimony. We need more *citizen* testimony. Men of standing who appear as witnesses, speak straight out and make a good showing. So we are trying to find out more about who was there.'

'Crowds are always a problem,' suggested Theophrastos. 'And then it was late at night, I imagine. The place would be fairly dark and quite noisy, a number of persons milling about. I begin to grasp your problem.'

'You're right enough there — I see you know your brothels.' Theramenes chuckled sourly. 'Hard to keep track of anybody. Trouble is, there was a crowd, as you say — a crowd of drunks, pretty largely. Every one of them can say he ain't sure that somebody else was there, because of the throng and the hubbub. And people moving to different rooms, and the fact that some left the *komos* early. Some people are going to be hard to pin down, we don't know them. Like, there's one Makedonian soldier – a veteran, perhaps. Youngish man who fought in Alexander's wars, apparently, and got a spear wound. We know he existed, but not who he was. And there are so many veterans, many Makedonians.'

'If a Makedonian has offended, then he must pay the penalty. And if a soldier is a witness he should certainly speak out,' Aristotle said with dry impartiality. 'Some people might advise you that it would be better not to attract the anger of Antipater by fixing on members of the military, but I know that is not a consideration with *you*. And I am sure you must rely, too, on Antipater's sense of Justice.'

For a moment the witness-hunter looked a trifle nonplussed.

'We will use what witnesses we can find,' he said. 'That Makedonian was wearing a silly sort of garland, so people didn't see his face clearly. But all those who were present are accountable to Athens to speak up about it. We shall find our true patriots, then – this city needs a careful winnowing. And new leaders! That's what's most important, new leaders, and new spirit.'

'But Athens is known for good leaders,' I objected.

'*Was* known.' Theramenes corrected me with a decided bitterness in his tone. 'I might take a crack at it myself, seeing what a poor crop Athens has had recently. Demosthenes may have won the right to keep his golden crown, but he is much discredited. He talked us into a war at Khaironeia, and then ran away from the battle! Demosthenes took money from the Persians before, and he might take someone else's bribes if it suited him. As for Hypereides – that man went mad after Khaironeia. Trying to persuade us to make citizens of foreigners and slaves! Gone soft. Rendered effeminate by spending so much of his time and substance on the women.'

'You are quite an orator yourself, sir,' I said politely. The man and his sentiments were so unpleasing to me, I should not have been surprised to feel that he gave me a headache. Yet I noticed that I had not had a headache even after sitting so long in this room (not to mention sniffing around it, like a dog, as the little girl had pointed out). If this *andron* had ever held hemlock in any quantity, surely I would have felt that unpleasant dull ache behind the nose and eyes. I tried to focus on Theramenes, waiting expectantly for further remarks from me.

'You are such an effective speaker, sir, I wonder *you* don't conduct the case for the prosecution.'

My propitiatory compliment was effective. Theramenes smirked, looking down his nose. 'I do speak outright,' he admitted. 'It's just that I've a habit of speaking up, and a deal of strong speech at command, for a plain man. Specially when my love of Athens is aroused,' he explained. 'I don't know how it is, but the words come. Yet,' he caught himself, 'Aristogeiton is the chief voice of the prosecution, it goes without saying. And he has Mantias to help write the speeches. And Euthias. Very good with words, Euthias is. And Eurymedon, who knows all about the

Mysteries of Eleusis, is always in their councils, to advise them on the points regarding religion. Nobody wants to cross Eurymedon. An important man, probably the next priest of Demeter.'

As he said the word 'Demeter', a loud hubbub broke out in the hall. A subordinate slave came running down the passage and urgently addressed the butler; that functionary was guarding the door of the *andron*, and listening bemused to Theramenes' authoritative talk.

'Oh – oh, help!' the slave exclaimed. 'He would come in, I tried to stop him—'

The butler opened the door and in came – almost tumbled – the panting household slave and behind him an undoubtedly unwelcome guest. Ergokles.

'What do you here, sir?' demanded the butler.

'Out of my way, fellow!' Ergokles pushed his way into the room. 'I must have it out with Krito,' he declared. 'I'm not putting up with it, I tell you!'

Theramenes, the more displeased as he had been interrupted in his impressive harangue, arose and addressed the intruder.

'What won't you put up with, man? I tell you what *I* won't put up with, it's being interrupted in this brawling way—'

'*You're* not Krito!' Ergokles took one step back, but made no sign of departure. 'Who are *you*, and what are you doing here?'

'We came but Krito was not here,' Aristotle explained, as if the questions had been directed to us. He rose gladly to his feet, and I did likewise. Theramenes sat down and remained stolidly planted, gazing at Ergokles whom Aristotle continued to address in courteous tones. 'Krito was not here, and we were about to leave when Theramenes of Athens arrived. He will explain his mission himself, much better than I could do.'

'I,' explained Theramenes, from his magisterial perch, 'am in search of witnesses to the act of impiety committed at the brothel of Tryphaina. Were you there? Do you know anyone who was present?'

'What a rude fellow, to burst out first thing asking me about brothels!' Ergokles sounded affronted, not intimidated. 'But you're asking the wrong man, let me tell you. I was never near Tryphaina's house. Not me. I've had enough trouble over that tiff at Manto's brothel to last me a while,' he added frankly. 'Tryphaina's brothel is even more expensive than Manto's. No sense in throwing away money at that rate! No, I tell you why I'm here – I'm in search of Krito. He owes me money. Now if you have taken over Orthoboulos' house or are a relation of Krito, I will apply to you.'

'*I?* It was Theramenes' turn to look affronted. 'I have absolutely nothing to do with Krito's affairs, and am certainly no relation—'

'Why, it certainly seemed as if you must be, sitting there in that big chair, and then saying you weren't to be interrupted!' Ergokles exclaimed. 'Made yourself right at home. If you're not a relation then – I say, is Krito got into debt? Are you making a claim to the furniture?'

'No. Certainly not.' Theramenes' tone was icy.

'That's a relief. I don't mind telling you, I'm worried about this family's financial health, and don't understand their doings. Orthoboulos owed me money – real money, I tell you! Now I want to collect.'

'Do you have a document to that effect?' Aristotle enquired. 'What evidence can you produce of the debts you allege?'

'Yes, yes,' interposed the butler eagerly. 'A document – you must bring a document signed by the old master—'

'Don't worry,' said Ergokles. 'I've got *plenty* of evidence. For debts including compensation for the loss of the slave Marylla's services, and a recompense on my investment – not covered by the court settlement. And there's other things, too. Best for me to collect while Orthoboulos' wife still breathes. After *she* is executed the money she brought to Orthoboulos' house will surely be subject to lawsuits. Her family wouldn't miss the chance, and then everything would be in litigation. Vexing – very vexing. But now, while she's still alive, she could persuade her stepson to pay up. And that's why I urgently need to talk with Krito. Though I'd settle for a conversation with Hermia, or her uncle. But it's hard to get at her.'

'Your affairs are profoundly uninteresting to me,' said Theramenes. 'Whatever claims you may have – or think you have – take them up with Krito. And now I shall be going.'

He rose and walked towards the front door, the rest of us following, more or less meekly. At the doorway, the witness-hunter turned back to look at us.

'Mind what I have said,' he pronounced impressively. 'Those who produce witnesses or appear to give testimony will be favoured of gods and men hereafter!'

With this parting shot, which the pious Eurymedon himself could not have bettered, Theramenes turned and strode off towards the gate. The man was doing his best to make an imposing exit. His effect was to be diminished. Before he got to the gateway, another man came bursting through it. This excited individual bounced into Theramenes' hulking slave and almost ricocheted into Theramenes himself. The newcomer was evidently one of the servants of this household. He shouted as he came, addressing the butler, who was again trying to see us all off the premises.

'Oh – terrible news! I must find young Master Krito. A terrible thing has happened! Kleiophon has disappeared!'

'Disappeared?' The butler's face grew pale, but he recovered himself. 'Nonsense. A boy cannot always be found the instant he's wanted – but he cannot truly have disappeared.'

'But – yes, he has. He didn't sleep in his bed last night. He's not with his mother's family, we know he didn't spend the night there either. Krito sent me out to find him, and I've looked *every*where. And asked everyone. He is not to be found.'

'Come now,' said Aristotle, laying his hand on the man's arm. 'I understand your concern, but boys often run off to play or to see the sights. Did you look well through the Agora?'

'Certainly I did.'

'I am sure you have worked hard.' Aristotle was sympathetic. 'But there are many places a boy could go for amusement – even as far as Peiraieus, perhaps, to look at the shipping. You have by no means exhausted all the possibilities.'

'Oh, but sir!' The man looked gravely into Aristotle's face. 'The boy was not happy. He wasn't in the mind to play, or go look at ships for amusement. I know my master Krito would not want me to say such a thing, but I'm dreadfully afraid the poor lad could have made away with himself!'

The butler uttered a loud cry, and put his fingers in his ears. 'Stop! *Stop!* I won't hear such a thing. It's all so dreadful here now, I can barely cope as it is – and the house besieged by strangers I cannot keep out, and members of the family not here!' The elderly man suddenly crumpled, and sank down in the doorway, sobbing.

'I've tried my best,' he said through his tears. 'I don't know what to do any more.'

'It is not your fault,' said Aristotle. He turned back to stand beside the sobbing man, and patted him on the shoulder. 'Stand up, dry your eyes – be diligent,' he suggested. 'Perform your tasks as you know your master would wish. The boy will doubtless return, and your anguish will be for nothing—'

'There's a good deal of anguish to go around in *this* family,' said Ergokles. The snub-nosed man was not rendered in the least unhappy by this latest distress. His quick eyes shot round the scene, taking account of everything. 'What with Papa murdered and Mama about to be executed! Might well be enough to send the unfortunate lad off his head. He may have killed himself, that's true. But more likely it's just disgrace made him flee. You'll find after a year or so that he's just run away to escape the shame of his family. Maybe gone for a sailor, or a pirate, or a bandit, looking for a decent life.'

And Ergokles walked away out of the gate, very jauntily, as pleased as if the bad tidings that had fallen on Orthoboulos' family were some substantial compensation to himself.

XII

The Absent Boy

It was a strange thing, in a way, that the absence of Kleiophon, seemingly so unimportant in himself, became at once a matter of great importance. The news that he was not to be found spread through Athens like a fire. Neighbour told neighbour, slaves and women whispered in kitchens. That a son of the house had mysteriously gone missing seemed to mark another stage towards the culmination of misery doomed to fall on all of Orthoboulos' family — so, at least, some wished to take the matter.

'Orthoboulos' whole kindred is under a curse!' said one excited newsmonger to his companions in the agora. 'Bound for misfortune!'

'"Under a *curse*",' some other light-headed gapers repeated, pleasantly impressed.

'That is all nonsense,' said Aristotle, to myself and Theophrastos. 'We have not looked hard enough, that is all. It is true, as Ergokles so unpleasantly indicated, that Kleiophon might wish to escape his circumstances. If the process is hard on all Athens, it is torment for the young lad, as we saw at the first prodikasia. Young Kleiophon may wish not to escape altogether, so much as to take a kind of holiday from disaster. Yet I do wish somebody could find him!'

If theories about a curse were irritating, there were worse rumours to be heard.

'The boy has been made away with!' said one group. 'Krito and his friends could not bear that the lad should testify against them. Is not this significant? The lad is in their way — and then disappears?'

'I thought of that possibility, too,' I said privately to Aristotle.

'Of course. So have I.'

'Is Krito dangerous?'

'He might be. Whatever he may be normally, Krito's cruelty to Hermia in the marketplace shows that he is in an unnatural state of mind. But, frankly, Stephanos, one of the difficulties of killing someone is disposing of the body. Waysides and rivers often yield up the dead. This gives a rational would-be murderer pause. Krito himself has not been away from Athens. I've ascertained that much.'

The disappearance of Kleiophon seemed at first to prejudice some people against Krito — and also against the handsome Philinos, formerly the close friend of Orthoboulos. This new prejudice against him seemed most unfair, as all Philinos had done was to support the orphaned Krito. Now he was included in the condemnation of Krito by those (chiefly adherents of Hermia's pious uncle Phanodemos) who wished to imagine that the elder son of the murdered man had caused his inconveniently testifying younger brother to be spirited away (or worse). We had, however, underestimated the resourcefulness of Krito's platoon. They rallied by the second day, and spread about a really magnificent story. According to this new version of events, it was *Hermia* who was at the bottom of this suspicious disappearance. But why — when young Kleiophon was obviously Hermia's supporter? Because (so it was alleged by Krito's friends) Hermia's party knew that the lad, once he was examined closely at the second hearing, would be forced to speak the truth, whatever his emotions and beliefs. His later evidence would go to incriminate Hermia, whatever his wishes might be. So Hermia's party had spirited the boy away.

'I cannot say we *know* this,' said Philinos. He spoke as he did everything, handsomely. Tall, well-dressed, his hair freshly cut, Philinos looked just as well in the searching light of a clear autumn morning as he had done by lamplight in the house of Tryphaina, when he had stood by the side of the most beautiful woman in Athens. Philinos, addressing a wondering group of Athenians who had encountered him in the Stoa Poikile, gazed at his hearers, his deep blue eyes expressing more reproach than anger.

I was slightly startled to realize that after that scene in the agora and the tremendous accusations of adultery hurled against Philinos, Krito must have made up the quarrel with his father's old friend. For Philinos said 'we' quite naturally. What, I wondered, could have caused Krito the avenger to change his mind about Philinos? How had pleasant Philinos retrieved the good graces of his deceased friend's son?

'We merely have reason to believe,' Philinos continued, 'knowing our accusations are substantially correct, that Phanodemos and his niece Hermia are aware that they would go down to certain defeat. That is, they would if Kleiophon were interrogated in a systematic manner. Whatever the poor lad himself may feel, his answers will ultimately support our story, because that is the truth. Krito has had nothing to fear and everything to hope from the second prodikasia. So – is it not a coincidence with the second prodikasia coming up that nobody can find him?'

I could only suppose that Philinos' consistency in sustaining Krito's cause against his stepmother, his willingness to attack Hermia (at least rhetorically), had caused Krito to accept that there was no adultery in the case. Philinos certainly showed magnanimity in being so forgiving to the young man. As Philinos was an older citizen of good standing, his statements gave weight and conviction to Krito's cause, and Krito's party was growing, drawing adherents from those who opposed the Makedonian power.

There was another party in Athens – of mainly women and old men – who believed that Hermia had a part in the disappearance of her second stepson, but a benevolent part. According to this version, she could not bear to see the lad so distraught and subjected to such a taxing ordeal as her trial. So she had seen to it that money was given him to help him to travel elsewhere, thus escaping the agony of witnessing her trial and her execution.

This seemed a piece of pure fiction on the part of

the tellers, if largely a sympathetic fiction. Yet there was a general sense that if Kleiophon were still alive, some woman – most likely Hermia – had something to do with his disappearance. This sense I shared, and so, I thought, did Aristotle.

'It's a pity you cannot interview Hermia yourself,' I said.

'I suppose I could,' he said a little dubiously. 'Or at least see her. Ergokles wishes to speak to her – as you know. There should be another witness present, clear-headed enough to remember and repeat what is said. Not a family member, of course, so Hermia's uncle would not do. I might be almost ideal for that part. The pro-Makedonians would find me acceptable, and the anti-Makedonians surely would not care in this instance. It is more helpful to them that the witness be someone distinguished, but not a citizen. Not a voter. They don't want Hermia questioned by any important citizens unless as part of the regular legal case. That must be conducted in the set days of the hearings, under the eye of the Basileus.'

'You have curiosity enough to volunteer,' said Theophrastos. 'I myself have some curiosity to see what you might make of Hermia.'

'Questioning a woman is different – and difficult,' Aristotle replied. 'In most civic encounters, a man in argument or under question makes judgements according to the other man's face. He notes the expression of his eyes, the twist of his lips, and so on. One can tell if the other person is lying, or ill at ease, angry or friendly. One cannot observe these things in a citizen woman, heavily veiled. Really, she is a voice and little else. Yet there is a sense of a presence, after all.'

And so it was that Aristotle came around to thinking that he ought to offer himself as the witness to be present while Ergokles questioned Orthoboulos' widow. I offered to accompany him as far as the house where Hermia endured her imprisonment. As I walked to meet Aristotle, my attention was caught by a group of men talking and disputing at the foot of the Akropolis, near the path to the Asklepion. Dispute among Athenians is scarcely uncommon, but these men seemed truly angry.

'And I say,' said one fellow, his khiton stained with the dust of the stony work which was evidently his normal employment, '*I* say that it's really an attempt by Krito and Philinos to get everything in their hands. Phanodemos was always a friend of the people – and look how they treat him. They persecute his niece Hermia, and thus attack Phanodemos that way. Krito and Philinos are trying their hardest to get the widow of Orthoboulos killed so that they can grasp all the wealth of Epikhares too, and make themselves powerful. Then they'll move against us all. You'll see!'

'It's what their sort do,' agreed another man. 'Tricks of the oligarkhs. As for that poor woman – they don't in the least mind sacrificing her, not they! Probably they poisoned the old man themselves, to get their paws on the money bags.'

'Unjust!' protested another marble mason walking with them. 'Wait for the trial, which will make everything clear.'

'Hah! You think the trial will go by Justice – with

all of them in it, and supported by their friends? While poor Hermia has only her old uncle, the good Phanodemos? You'll see what a fair chance that is!'

When I met Aristotle in the company of Theophrastos, the philosopher and his head scholar were arguing about Perikles, so I did not tell them about what I had overheard. Theophrastos left us, but scarcely had I begun to accompany Aristotle to the house of Hermia's uncle Phanodemos than we two were joined by Ergokles, coming jauntily along, wearing a clean white khiton for the occasion.

'So there you are, old fellow,' was his disrespectful greeting to Aristotle. 'I don't know as you would have been my first choice, but they all said not to waste a citizen on this interview. So I dare say you, my lad, are not going to be party to our conversation.'

I stared at the man as coldly as I could, and said to him formally, 'My name is Stephanos son of Nikiarkhos.'

'Oh, have it your own way – no offence, I'm sure. But Stephanos, I hope you are not thinking of entering the house. It wouldn't be fair for me to have to cope with *two* other questioners, just when I am putting questions to Hermia myself.'

'I suppose not,' I admitted.

'All I want is to get her to say that her dead husband Orthoboulos owed me money and that she knew of it. And to tell her uncle, to my face, with you, Aristotle, as witness, to be sure I am paid out of their estate – and soon. Some women could claim to know nothing about business – but not Hermia. She was ever a manager, *she* knows about money. I have a list––' He waved some waxed tablets he was holding in his hand. 'If the woman could read, she could check it over. But I suppose we'll have to let her poor old uncle do that.'

None too soon, given such an ungracious companion, we arrived at the house of the unfortunate Hermia's unfortunate relatives. Their dwelling was neither very grand nor very poor, a pleasant house in a clean street in a respectable deme. This house had no distinguishing feature – save that the gateway was now guarded by two armed men. The neighbours must have felt bitter about this signal indignity.

'I see no reason,' Aristotle said softly, 'why Stephanos may not wait for us inside the house – though you are right, he should not come near the room where Hermia is to be found. We are expected,' Aristotle added, speaking formally to the soldiers on guard and handing one of them a pair of tablets, containing permission and stamped with someone's recognizable seal-ring. The guard gave a consenting grunt, and we knocked. Almost at once the gate was opened, though not before a heavy chain had been taken away from the entrance. I was not sure whether this reinforcement to the door had been put in by officials or added by the householders to secure themselves against rude attack.

The servant who let us in was a small person, very small, though certainly not a child, and not young. This little man had a hunched back, and a head too large for his body. He had to throw his head back to see us, presenting us with an almost horizontal view of a large flat face, looking up at us like a pale entreating plate.

'We have come with official permission, to conduct an interview with Hermia widow of Orthoboulos,' Aristotle said formally, getting his word in ahead of Ergokles.

'Or rather, *I* have come,' said Ergokles loudly. 'Ergokles of Athens. This man Aristotle, a foreign teacher, is here merely as a witness. This other fellow' – waving a hand at me – 'doesn't count. Let him wait somewhere until we have finished our business. Conduct us to Hermia's uncle at once!'

'Oh dear,' said the hunchbacked slave. 'I cannot move quickly, sir, but I shall act with dispatch.' He clapped his hands and yelled. A female slave, as tense as if she were on trial, came out of some middle region, and was bidden to place a chair so I could sit in the first room, near the house-door. Ergokles nearly stamped with impatience.

'There! Now we are ready!' said the hunchbacked porter. 'I will take you now, sirs, both of you – it is not far, but we must attend to the proprieties. Let me explain—'

His voice faded away as he led the two men to some other region of the house. Not too distant, I judged – they were not going upstairs to the *gynaikon*, so evidently Hermia had been brought down from the women's quarters and would be made to stand in some room contiguous to that in which her interrogators would sit.

I sat alone. There was nothing to look at. This house was not as fine as that of Orthoboulos. Phanodemos had won a golden crown for his contribution to religious festivals, but then, I thought, such expenses as supporting religious festivals could drain a man. The room was austere, unornamented – as if in mourning. As in Orthoboulos' house, I could see a niche (empty in this case) for a statue, and a kind of reverse shadow where one had been. A statue of a youth, perhaps – so I thought, observing the the clean outline on the darkening wall. And there was surely a place where a vase had stood that was no longer here – nor even the table that held it. Yet the ghosts of these objects lingered. Distress for money, rather than the distress of mourning, I now surmised, had removed these things and put them to sale. If Phanodemos were writing a great history of Attika, he might have sold such goods to purchase books, which are always costly. But now he had to support Hermia and her trial and the expenses of the guards – with additional expense in propitiation since their unfortunate trespass into the agora.

I was staring at the empty walls when the dwarfish slave came back.

'Sorry to leave you alone, sir,' he apologized. 'We were used to better days. Call me for anything you might want. They call me "Batrakhion", sir, because when I was a child folks thought I moved like a frog, and that name stuck. Let me bring you something to drink? Water or milk – or wine?'

'No, no thank you, Batrakhion. It is certainly not my purpose in coming to put your house to any more trouble—'

'Oh, sir!' He spread his hands wide. 'Trouble! By the gods we have trouble enough, I am sure. The gods forbid that you or yours should ever see such a terrible time as we are having in this house.'

'This is a very hard time,' I said sympathetically. 'I take it you, Batrakhion, are an old servant of this family, and know Hermia well.'

'Yes, of course. I belong to her uncle. And we've lived here since I dunno when. Of course Hermia's father prospered more than us, leastways for a while, but we always kept a nice home. Dear, I need to get at that wall, don't I – very dusty it looks!' With some difficulty the little fellow dragged a chair beside the wall. Then he briskly jumped up on it, and began to dust the wall and the empty brackets.

'Your master is an admirable and respected man,' I remarked. 'It is sad to see him in such untoward circumstances.'

'That is so, indeed. The Master is good, you see, sir, good and kind. He won't turn his back on anyone who is in real trouble. That's why he bought me. My mother's owners were going to expose me when born, being as how I showed signs from the very first of having a bent back. But Phanodemos saved me from that fate. Bought me for a couple of drakhmai, and I have been a member of his family ever since.'

I realized this dwarfish Batrakhion was not really much older than thirty, though his condition made him seem elderly.

'You can do a lot of work with a bad back, indeed,' the man continued. 'Wasn't the god Hephaistion himself a cripple – and look at all the work he did! You just have to take pains, and plan ahead. That's what I say to all the young servants: "Take pains and plan ahead."'

This advice sounded to me equally valid for good

or bad designs. But I had no quarrel with it. 'And you know Hermia well?'

'In the past, sir. She didn't live here, but I have seen her on and off since she was a baby. Hermia is like her uncle in every good thing – always takes trouble with people, even the least. She thought about making people happy, her parents, and her relatives – the slaves even. She looks after people as was sick, and she always plans work so as to spare the hands. She's too good to die young! Why, she'd no more kill a man than I could hunt a raging elephant! She hasn't got it in her.'

Two eyes in a pale face looked at me beseechingly.

'It is natural,' I said, 'for you to take her part—'

'No!' he burst out. "Tain't "natural"! Not at all.' Jumping down from his chair, little Batrakhion came to stand before me, looking at me almost accusingly.

'You think it's *natural* as a slave would stand up for a master or mistress? When a lot of the time the slaves hate their guts, and would be happy to see that master or mistress put to death – if they could 'scape torturing themselves! Why, some slaves there be so stout of heart and so full of hate they would even stand to be tortured as witnesses, voluntary, if that meant for sure that the law case against the master would go forward to a deathly end! No, it ain't "natural" in your sense that I should speak up for – and weep for – Hermia. It is because she is good in herself. You must see that's the case. Even now – when she's going to die – she speaks so sweetly to the slaves, so considerately to each of us—'

He ground his fists into his eyes. I was startled by his outburst, which contained matter not of the

pleasantest, if one considered it. Yet I was certainly
sorry for this poor little hunchbacked person.

'Yes, yes,' I said soothingly. 'You must not upset
yourself. There are months to go, and much may
happen—'

'Much may happen,' he interjected bitterly. 'But
whatever happens seems like it's only the worst.'

'You are thinking of the boy going missing?'

'That poor boy! Just a lad, not in childhood nor yet
old enough to be an ephebe. Young Kleiophon feels it
all deeply, I am sure of it. Though he was only her
stepson, he has the mistress' nice way with him, he's
just her sort. Not like his older brother at all.'

I noted that this Batrakhion at least used the present tense in speaking of Kleiophon. I was about to say
something more when sounds broke through the bar-
riers of walls and made their way to us. A confused
hubbub, at first – shouting, and a gentle wail of protest.
Then some words came through, clarity arising at
intervals through the muffled verbal noise and
expressed sound:

'By Herakles! . . . A just debt! You cannot repudi-
ate a just debt! . . .'

A higher voice, straining against tears: 'You cannot
mean . . . evidence.'

Anger again: 'Have . . . have the law on you . . .
uncle. Before you die.'

Calm: 'Not . . . any good.'

A yell: 'Why hang on to money now? You are a
dead woman!'

Expostulation. Then the calm voice again: 'For-
bear . . .'

A shout : 'Where's that slave?'

'I'm wanted,' said the pale hunchback, and shot out of the room, like a crab scuttling over a shingle, leaving me to my meditations and the empty walls. I could hear noises still, however, including the slam of a door; soon protesting voices were coming towards me. Retreating from the scene of interview, Ergokles was shouting, as one boiling with anger.

'You will not find your account with the gods in repudiating your just debt,' he proclaimed. 'If you want the favour of the gods – if you, disgraced woman, want to see your boy back – then you should follow justice and pay me what is mine!'

Shocked exclamations from the uncle.

'But I forget!' said Ergokles bitterly. 'That boy ain't yours, is he? So *you* don't care, my fine lady – especially as you're bound for Hades yourself, one of these days – and sooner rather than later!'

Aristotle, his lips compressed, followed, and laid a hand on Ergokles' shoulder. Signalling to me that I should accompany them, Aristotle endeavoured to subdue the fuming citizen.

'That's quite enough,' he said, pushing Ergokles along. Hunchbacked little Batrakhion, teary-eyed, followed us as we two posted along with the outrageous man between us.

'I think Ergokles here is a little overcome,' Aristotle said blandly for the benefit of the guards at the gate. 'You will feel better, man, when you have had some air.'

And with the greatest solicitude he frog-marched Ergokles, still sputtering and foaming, away from the shabby mansion. The hunchbacked slave stared at our retreat and gladly closed the doors behind us, not omitting the chain. It was easy for me to guess what had happened during this interview. Orthoboulos' widow had denied any knowledge of the transactions to which the claimant alluded. She would acknowledge only a debt actually stated under her husband's hand. But all Ergokles had carried was a list of his own statements.

'You may be certain,' Ergokles assured me angrily, 'I did not forget to include the item of the slave Marylla. Orthoboulos cheated me and got the court to cheat me as well. I was never properly reimbursed. That Sikilian woman – I was supposed to have *half* a share. I didn't get my proper half, nor compensation for the months – *months!* – I went without her services. Now she has been sold from under my nose, it appears. But she – Orthoboulos' widow – has the face to deny it – the face I say, with her standing there veiled, but you could see her torn ear! Brazen Hermia had the gall to say that she believed that matter had been fully settled earlier!'

'Be still, be controlled,' Aristotle urged. 'It were more manly to endeavour not to give the whole street an account of your affairs!'

Yet once we had got away from the street of Hermia's uncle, and once Ergokles' foaming and exclamations had diminished to a dull muttering, Aristotle himself seemed interested in picking up the subject again.

'What was it you meant about Hermia's son – rather, her stepson?' he enquired. 'I didn't quite comprehend what you said there: "if you want to see your boy back"?'

'Oh, nothing.' Ergokles shrugged.

'You know something about Hermia's – Orthoboulos' – son?' I urged.

'Nothing. 'Cept everyone's heard he's missing. I was just giving Hermia a tweak, like. To remind her that if she wishes to find favour with the gods for herself and for her family, she'd better *do right*. Do right by *me* – which that family never has done.'

'You feel,' Aristotle suggested, 'that a man whose just debts have not been attended to might well be entitled to aid himself. So, Ergokles, you thought that giving them a little scare might bring them to their senses?'

Ergokles was suddenly wary. 'I only yelled at that woman and told her she will die soon. That's just a fact. If she's not scared of that already, she's duller than I think.'

'And the boy? What do you know about him? Where would you suggest they look for him?'

'How should I know? That family thinks they are so well-born, so respectable. But maybe they should look for the whelp in one of those brothels his father was so fond of.'

Ergokles seemed glad now to go into his own house, and did not invite us to join him.

Aristotle gave him into the care of a servant, with a recommendation that he take a cool drink and lie down.

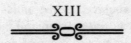

XIII

Pancakes in a Brothel Kitchen

Aristotle and I then went together to my house, not far away, to enjoy a cool drink ourselves. Aristotle, without pressing from me, offered his own description of the interview of Ergokles and Hermia.

'We went into a back room; the widow was in the passageway outside, guarded by her uncle. She was veiled. Ergokles started with a long recital of his alleged debts and grievances. Hermia listened patiently, and then went through the items from memory, saying that three she had good reason to believe fully settled, and that she had no evidence as to the others. Ergokles tried to rattle her by referring to Marylla – I think he has a genuine obsession about that slave concubine. Hermia did not flinch, but said that Ergokles had settled, and after the court case it was at an end. Ergokles demanded some share of the proceeds from the sale of Marylla and even asked for compensation for his other claims to be taken out of the proceeds of the sale of Orthoboulos' old butler, and some other slaves. The widow referred him to Krito.

'It was then that Ergokles – vulgar man that he is – became truly abusive, as you must have heard. He told her she was a dead woman and might as well part with all her money now. This kind and tactful suggestion naturally enough met with no very favourable response. Phanodemos was annoyed – to put it mildly. You heard much of the rest, I daresay. And then I conducted Ergokles from the premises. A useless exercise – or almost.'

'You could form your own opinion of Hermia, even though you had no chance to ask her anything yourself,' I suggested.

'To some extent. This is a very intelligent woman – which makes it all the more strange that she is in such a plight. First of all, I think this woman would be too intelligent to kill her own husband. Murder is so often referred to a spouse. More telling, to my mind, is that I do not sense in her words, tone or manner any hatred for Orthoboulos. Not at all. Even under the provocation of Ergokles talking about the Sikilian Marylla, and that slave's sexual connection with Orthoboulos, she was calm; she referred to her own discussions with her husband in a very normal manner. If she deeply resented – or resents – that connection, she certainly hides it extraordinarily well. The widow never shies away from talking about Orthoboulos, while at the same time she does not bring him up at every turn. I have to admit, I feel favourably impressed.

On the whole, I truly doubt if she murdered him.
Though that's not evidence.'

I told him what the hunchbacked slave Batrakhion
had said about her goodness of heart. 'And,' I finished,
'the little dwarf tells me even now when she is about
to die, she speaks kindly and considerately to all the
slaves. The man began to weep—!'

'Aha!' said Aristotle. 'That makes an impression –
and rightly, I believe. It should be no good in law, but
I am not sure it doesn't count as evidence. Constant
sweetness of temper under severe and protracted hardship is very hard to assume or enact – it is more likely
to be the genuine article. What you say reminds me
of the heroine of Euripides' *Alkestis* – you remember
the play, Stephanos. The queen is about to die in her
husband's stead. On the day of her death, she takes
farewell of her life, her home and the persons she loves,
and she does not neglect the servants. The servant
girl says, if you recall:

> "All the household servants under that roof
>   with pity lamented
> The death of their mistress. She stretched out
>   her hand to each one,
> No one so low that she did not greet, and
>   was greeted in return."

'That has always seemed to me a point that demon-
strates the essential goodness, the real excellence, of
Alkestis. Even when about to die she ignores no one,
and gives her good will to even the lowest.'

'Yes? I must read it again. I do remember that

Alkestis was saved by Herakles, when neither her husband nor his father would die in her stead. But I don't see any miraculous salvation in wait for Hermia.' We both paused in sad thought.

'Ergokles is probably right,' I decided unhappily. 'Correct, if ungracious. Hermia's death is near at hand.'

'It is not only ungracious but in some sense illegal to say such a thing when the trial is only just getting under way. But – I wonder, Stephanos. Is Ergokles being cunning rather than simply outrageous? Might it not be that he punctuates his speeches with such insulting rudeness very deliberately – so that under cover of general rudeness he may say something more pointed? Some of the things he said to Hermia were decidedly odd.'

'Yes. That slightly puzzling remark about how if she wanted to please the gods so she could have her stepson restored, she should pay her debts to him.'

'Exactly, Stephanos. Now – was this the *real* point of the interview? The reason why Ergokles wanted to see her? Not to go over the debts and so on – that was a useless formality, as he well knew. But could it not be that he created an opportunity to speak to her for another purpose? To have the chance to convey in person a threat and a strong hint. Is Ergokles merely an angry man with very little self-control? Or is he actually not in a passion – not in such a *real* passion that he cannot calculate exactly the effect of what he is doing and saying?'

'That is,' I interpreted, 'you are indicating that this might be a plot of Ergokles against that family. Ergokles has spirited Kleiophon away, or helped him to disappear. He needs to let Hermia know this. Hence he arranges the meeting today. But why wouldn't he tell Krito, rather than Hermia?'

'That also crossed my mind. But – suppose Ergokles is really working for Krito? I know this seems far-fetched. But there might be money in it for Ergokles. He might be paid if he could manage to abduct Kleiophon and keep him away from Athens, at least until the trial is over. That would save Krito from having to go against his brother publicly in a court of law, and would deprive Hermia's side of a potentially valuable witness.'

'But,' I argued, 'this doesn't make any real sense of the conduct of Ergokles. If he's playing Krito's game, why would he signal to Hermia that if he gets money from her somehow, the boy could come back? He would hardly want to turn against Krito, having gone out of his way to oblige him.'

'Ergokles is shrewd and mean. But that doesn't mean he is necessarily a good long-term plotter. He looks for immediate advantage. Even if he were collud-ing with Krito, he might want to wring quick extra profit from the situation, and soon.'

'I don't find this a very satisfactory explanation,' I said frankly.

'Nor do I. The second – and to my mind more likely – possibility is that Ergokles is not in the plot regard-ing Kleiophon – if there is a plot. He could be merely trying to cash in on something he senses is going on. If Hermia, for instance, had spirited her stepson away, for the boy's own sake – could Ergokles be indicating to her that *he* knows that is so? Dear me, it is a puzzle trying to read significance into the words of such a man. Yet I feel there is some acting going on.'

'Is Ergokles merely impatient, or does he have a plan?'

'We don't know. We can imagine him exchanging the boy for money, with this one and that one, without any solution— We keep talking about this as if the poor lad were just a piece in a game, while Kleiophon may be in terrible danger.'

'Or dead,' I added gloomily. 'It would be quite possible to spirit somebody away and kill him, and still demand a ransom. But people keep talking about Kleiophon as if he were still alive. The hunchbacked slave in that house referred to him in the present tense.'

'Quite so,' said Aristotle. 'Ergokles didn't talk of Kleiophon as dead. We did get something very like a hint from Ergokles, too – an odd one – at the end of our uncomfortable walk.'

Yes,' I agreed. 'He said "look for the whelp in one of those brothels his father was so fond of". That could indicate that some brothel-owner or brothel-worker knows more about Kleiophon. If there's anything in it, Manto's brothel would be the prime choice.'

'Yes, quite so' said Aristotle smoothly. 'Most alert, Stephanos. And I think you should be the one to investigate. Ask questions, discreetly, at the brothel.'

'I? Look, Aristotle, I am in trouble enough already because of Manto's brothel.' (I didn't add that I was in potentially even more trouble because of the night at Tryphaina's brothel – the episode that Aristotle was *not* to know about.) 'The last thing I want to do is go back there – to Manto's, where they know me by name, and associate me with the finding of the corpse of Orthoboulos—'

'Yes, yes, a nasty matter, to be sure, but certainly not your fault. And brothels are accustomed to seeing their customers again. You know some of the people within those walls, and might be able to divine if they are concealing anything.'

'Easy to say,' I protested. 'You say I am to ask questions "discreetly". Discretion and brothels go very ill together. No, Aristotle, I *cannot* do such a thing. And there is no reason. I am not involved with Orthoboulos' family – save through finding his corpse.'

'And through that woman Marylla coming to your house,' Aristotle reminded me. 'But then, she was seeking me, was she not? It comes back to me, after all.' He rubbed his head, wearily.

At this point, Theophrastos entered the room, though his advent did not prevent Aristotle from completing his statement: 'I do feel involved, because I initially became concerned in Orthoboulos' affairs. Now the case against Hermia has the potential to make a lot of trouble – not for us personally, I mean, but for Athens as a whole.'

'I agree even more than I would have done yesterday,' I said. 'I heard some men arguing today – just stonemasons, coming from the Asklepion.' And I told them of the conversation I had overheard.

'There! That is an example of what I fear,' responded Aristotle. 'The division is not only between those for and against Makedon. The city returns to our old original divisions.'

'You intend by that,' said Theophrastos, 'the splits

and antagonisms that Solon endeavoured to rectify, or at least to moderate – the division between rich and poor. First, there are those who want the rule of a few – the powerful men of good birth and wealth. Then we have those, a majority in number, but not the wealthiest, who want equality. Power to be shared between the rich and the poor, the few and the many.'

'Exactly. There you have the history of Athens – and its constitution. An endeavour to strike a balance between these antagonistic desires. Untoward events may easily tilt the balance. There is always passion on each side, and idealism too. You know, Plato himself as a young man warmed to the prospect of the dictatorship of the Thirty – his own high-born relations were among the group who seized power. He thought they would produce something beautiful, a model of justice and civic harmony. He was soon undeceived. As he told us himself. But there is a threat too from demagogues on the popular side who might like to get their own back on the well-favoured and powerful. Some wouldn't mind leading the people into actions that shake the state. Now, as the conversation you have heard illustrates, some of the lower sort, men of the fourth class, feel that Krito's action against Hermia represents an attempt by the wealthy to take power to themselves by abuse of all ties, including familial relations. I have caught wind of the same attitudes. The charges against the two women are being represented by some fearless souls as attacks on the poor, and on Athenian democracy, by the privileged.'

'That's very odd,' I said. 'It must be a mistake. For we know that Hermia is a rich woman, because of her first husband especially, and she herself is quite well-born.'

'It may be illogical, but it is a political feeling. The two trials are gaining a symbolic value out of proportion to the individuals. I must concede, however, that the prosecution of Phryne was initiated precisely *because* of its symbolic value. Bad – very bad.'

'Don't you think,' said Theophrastos, 'that you may be exaggerating the danger?'

Aristotle smiled and shook his head. 'How I would love to come with you, O Theophrastos, away from the heat of conflicts into the temperate shade! But – no. I don't think I exaggerate, though I hope I do. I think the constitution of the city, its very polity and structure, may be endangered.'

'But what is the worst that can happen? Two women are sentenced, after due process of law.'

'This case – these cases, rather – might cause the whole of Attika to explode like the stomach of a dead camel. A stench that sickens all within range. Do not forget, Athens has been in precarious circumstances before. Arguably, stability is not natural to this city – or perhaps to any other. A period of disruption and popular unrest could be followed by an interval of such tyranny as we would not wish to see.'

'You know too much history,' I said shortly.

He rubbed his head again. 'It may be so,' he agreed.

Next day I decided that I would, after all, go to Manto's brothel. I felt some compunction for my short answers to my good friend, the Master of the Lykeion, though I did not share his sombre views. It seemed to me that law cases constantly came and went, making the whole city fizzle with excitement and then sputtering out, like a fire on a beach. Yet I was impressed with Aristotle's anxiety. I was also curious about Kleiophon, and Ergokles' possible part in his disappearance. Really, it would not be too much trouble to go to the establishment run by Manto and ask a few questions.

I was determined to go during the daytime, and not as a customer. Brothels have a period of busy traffic in the afternoon, and then their biggest rush of customers at night. But early in the morning (unless it is a market-day, bringing eager peasants to the city) they tend to be fairly slack. On this misty morning, not much was astir in the streets save the usual sellers of wares. A small figure huddled completely into its cloak scuttled like a crab along the side-road by Manto's house. A child, late for school – I laughed inwardly, remembering how often I had been a child late for school, delayed by some pursuit or pleasure that seemed important to me at the time. Manto's establishment, as I expected, did not possess its evening appearance. Although the obscured sun was beginning to climb up the sky, sleepy and yawning slaves were still sweeping up. They welcomed me with a prodigious lack of excitement.

'You coming to look for a pertickler?' one asked me, a bandy-legged male slave, resting on his broom just outside the front door.

'Perhaps. Yes, Kynara.'

'You'll find her in the kitchen, most like.' He jerked a shoulder in the correct direction. 'The girls takes breakfast in the kitchen, by the fire, most usually.'

I thanked the man, and walked in, directing myself through twists and turns to the back regions. It was easy to find, because of the hum of voices as well as the light smell of smoke.

The girls were indeed taking their first meal of the day, huddled in rough chairs or benches around a little brazier, warming in the chilly autumn day. A maid-servant was bent over a portable stove, making pancakes. The girls stopped chattering as I came in, and stared.

'Customer? At this time?'

'Well,' I said as easily and suavely as I could, 'any time is a good time, with such beauties. But no – I am not here this moment exactly as a customer. Kynara?' I recognized her with some difficulty. I had not, after all, known her well, and the bevy of young or almost young females looked much alike. They were slave workers, with the short hair appropriate to that condition. Yet, although they were slaves, these girls were allowed to keep themselves clean and even to wear fine raiment. Usually one saw them lined up in the front room, in almost transparent garments, so one could take one's pick. But they had obviously huddled on their most comfortable woollen clothes, well-used and even raggedy, for this morning's domestic ceremony. Kynara came forward.

'I frightened you the other evening, I think,' I said to her, 'when I leaped up and ran downstairs to answer the alarm. And I didn't pay you properly. My apologies. Here's what I owe. And I've brought you a gift – a small thing.' And I held out, as well as the money, a short ribbon, purchased cheaply at the market that morning.

'Oh, a present.' She seemed softened, though the gift was of as little value as I had dared to make it. 'Come here – sit down.' She made room for me on a bench. 'Have something to drink,' she offered. 'It's our own herbed vinegar, with hot water. Clears the pipes these misty mornings.'

I accepted a cup of this hot and thin potation; it was true that it was warming.

'We're celebrating. It's the birthday of Klisia here.' And she nodded at a thin girl with a long neck like a crane.

'It's not everybody who knows when her birthday is,' said one of the girls, cackling with laughter that was not entirely merriment.

'Well, I do know,' said Klisia. 'My mother told me. She was a slave and I was born a slave along of her. But we were together for six years.' She stared idly at the coals in the pancake-maker's oven. 'The master had her sold – lucky old her! I don't know where she went. And the next thing I knew, at night there he was on top of me.'

'A lot starts that way,' said one of the other girls tranquilly. 'You weren't too badly off – you had only one owner, afore you got here. And he fed you, didn't he?'

'Klisia don't look fed, never!' said one of the girls. She went into a gale of laughter. 'By the Two Goddesses, she never does. Demeter knows, she sucks in enough at night to make her fatter in the mornings, but it don't seem to take.'

'Here – have this, dearie.' Kynara consoled the thin and mournful Klisia by popping in front of her a new-made pancake, spread with honey. It smelled very good.

'Want one?' Kynara was quick enough to notice my interest. 'We'll give you one, too.' And she soon spread a very nice pancake, streaming with sweetness, in front of me.

'Sop up that honey, and you'll be in a mood for more,' she advised, making me lick her sticky fingers.

'This had better be the last, we're low on charcoals,' said the cook-maid, smutty and sweating from her toils.

'Oh, the fuel-seller came again this morning, we can all have a second one if we want,' said Klisia of the birthday. 'And I gave Meta a pancake first off, so she won't complain.'

'Is Manto here?' I asked through a sweet mouthful of warm cake.

'Why'd you want *her?*' one of the others asked sourly.

'Oh, no complaints,' I said. 'I just wanted to ask her something.'

'Something about the murder?' Long-necked Klisia leaned forward eagerly, like a crane that spots a fish underwater. 'Do you have more to tell about Orthoboulos?'

'Don't have *nothing* to do with a law case,' one of the others, a well-grown female with a very full bust, reminded her sharply. I realized that of course these women, if summoned as witnesses, would be subjected to torture.

'No, no,' I said, hastily. 'Nothing about the murder. Not at all. Just about selling some honey.'

'That's all right then,' said the large girl, and ate her pancake and honey with evident pleasure. The cook-maid slipped out of the room, bearing a hot pancake on a plate. I supposed it must be for Manto, the mistress, who would eat in state alone.

'And also,' I continued, 'I'm just – just looking for someone.'

'Oh-oh. A special someone? A lost sweetheart. Tell us – don't blush. We'll help you find your darling.' They teased me, and I could feel myself flushing.

'No – I'm not looking for a woman.'

'Who, then?'

'A boy, a young boy.'

'Oh, your taste runs to boys, does it?' Kynara, my interrogator, pretended to cry. 'Too bad for us! But we'll help you to a nice one. Kybele there – that's her with the big bosom you've been staring at – has a little brother—'

'No, not that. I am just searching for this particular young person—'

Some of them giggled. 'How young? There's lots we give their first lesson to,' boasted one. 'We could have given you yours – where was you educated?'

'Hush – here's Manto,' another said sharply. I experienced a slight relief; I was beginning to feel uncomfortable.

The mistress of the establishment bustled in. I was surprised to see her because I had just imagined that Manto would be eating her pancake elsewhere. At first she didn't see me hidden among the bevy, not to mention the apparatus of hot cakes and liquid honey.

'Girls, girls!' she chided. 'You cannot sit about all day. I have been working and haven't had anything to eat yet, and here you are as idle as if you were the city council stuffing your faces in the Tholos! I shall have to send Meta to you. Finish quickly. You've time for some weaving and spinning before the customers come. And clean the public rooms. Oh – you—'

She was nonplussed at seeing me, not expecting customers at this hour, certainly not in the kitchen. 'You, Stephanos son of Nikiarkhos, is it not? What have you come for?'

'It's not about the – the unpleasantness the other evening,' I stammered. 'I am simply looking for some-one.'

'Oh? A nice sort of someone who spends all night and half the morning in a brothel? But there is no man here now. Not at all. Our visitors will come later.'

'Not – not that sort of visitor. The person I am looking for is wanted by his family. A young man, a boy rather, of about fourteen years.'

'No need to beat about the bush,' she said tartly. 'If you mean Kleiophon son of Orthoboulos, everyone's been talking of it. Of course we haven't seen him. Have we, girls?'

They shook their heads. 'No, Manto,' they chorused dutifully.

'Now make haste and do some decent work. Can't have you sitting about like lazy lumps! Off you go now, girls! I am going to have my simple first bite—' She picked up an apple. 'And then I'll be with you all shortly. Meta is cleaning upstairs.'

If Meta had been given a pancake first thing, and was now cleaning, and the mistress hadn't had breakfast yet – who was that other pancake for?

'I wonder,' I said, 'I don't want to get any of your young women into trouble, but you, Manto, are a freedwoman, and in no material danger. So I could talk with you more frankly about the case. I wonder if I could look again at the small house next to yours, the one that belongs to the freedwoman with two daughters who went to Megara.'

'Sorry, but that's *not* possible,' said Manto. 'That woman has come back – of course we all had to answer questions about those premises. Both sides in the law case against Hermia are aware of all the facts. Now this woman and her daughters have retaken possession of the place. Naturally, she's very distressed about what happened there – spent a small fortune trying to clean it and scent it, and purify the room. I doubt she will let me use that house again. So – I am afraid that is that.'

'Forgive me for troubling you,' I said awkwardly, putting down my lumpy pottery cup and rising. I could tell I was expected to depart, and I could take a hint as well as the next man. I tried to look nonchalant as I left, and not like a scandalous young man driven to visiting a brothel in the morning.

'At least,' I said, addressing the broom-wielder, 'I am getting out of this brothel without paying two drakhmai, or even two obols.'

'I congratulate you,' said a charming and amused female voice. 'Was this owing to generosity on their part, young man, or incapacity on yours?'

A young woman was coming to the house, towards the door through which I was just departing. A woman lightly veiled, and wearing a delicately woven khiton under a cloak of softest bleached wool. I knew who it was – Marylla, the beautiful Sikilian. Once the shared property of the angry Ergokles and the dignified Orthoboulos, now belonging to handsome Philinos. Her new master evidently allowed her to go about on her own. Though she was only a slave, I greeted her politely.

'Good day to you, Marylla. I did not come to this house for a – for the – um – the usual reasons. I was searching for a little information, that's all.'

'About what?' She stopped in the entryway, and then threw her veil back so she could look at me. I could see her, with her lovely heart-shaped face and deep grey eyes. It is much easier to talk to a slave woman than to a veiled lady; you know where you are because you can see the reactions and expressions of her face.

'You might think I'd be looking for more details about the murder of Orthoboulos, but actually,' I explained, 'it is about the disappearance of young Kleiophon. You must know Kleiophon – you were formerly a member of his household. And I might ask why *you* are coming here – to a brothel in the morning?'

'I come merely to retrieve a vessel, a silver saucepan, which our house – Philinos' household you know – lent Manto's cook for a party here.'

'I am surprised you did not send a lower slave to pick up such a low object.'

'The mule-boy's already gone,' said the broom-wielder to her.

'That's right, we often use a man with mules for our errands, but the mule-boy has gone. And it is better for me to pick it up – silver pots and pans may not be important to you, young gentleman, but they are to me. Next time, I'll tell Manto, she may turn to her neighbour or to Lykaina or some other woman and ask for her cookware. I will tell you frankly, as a secret: the Master does not know we lent our best pan. You see? I throw myself on your mercy.' I smiled in response to her own entreating smile, indicating that I shared the joke and the secret and would certainly not say anything.

'As for young Kleiophon,' she continued, 'certainly I know Orthoboulos' son. But you must imagine he is endowed with Herculean powers, to begin frequenting brothels at so young an age!'

'Seriously, it occurred to me that someone connected with this establishment might have offered him assistance. Or that assistance of some kind was channelled to him through the offices of somebody here. Perhaps some women were trying to help him.'

'I see.' At this enlightenment her eyes became wider, more thoughtful. 'Are you acting for Krito?'

'Yes, in a way. But not directly. Perhaps for Hermia as much as anybody.'

'Oh, how I would like to help you!' she exclaimed. 'Poor Hermia! And the poor boy, he must have been so frightened, so confused. Just as he had begun to love his step-mama, to see her treated so! I doubt if he had any plan when he ran away. Young people are sometimes driven by impulse.'

'True,' I agreed. 'But if the lad has no outside

resources, he should return when he is hungry enough. And that should be soon – he has been away three days.'

'Indeed, I hope hunger drives him back soon to his anxious family. But you give me other ideas. I had not thought that *women*'s assistance might explain his absence. An interesting notion. My thoughts have run quite otherwise. If I see anything uncommon or out of the way that might lead to— Whatever I see or discover, I promise to tell you. If you promise you will not hand the boy over at once to Krito. Swear you will have only Kleiophon's welfare at heart.'

'I do so swear! Thank you,' I said, a little awkwardly, and stood aside, to allow her to enter to reclaim her silver pan. And so I departed, no better off than when I came, save for a sober potation and a really delicious pancake. There certainly was a market for honey in that brothel, and perhaps we could also supply Tryphaina's workers and customers with the produce of the sturdy bees of our Hymettos farm.

XIV

The Fugitive-Hunter

Despite the damp and foggy day, I walked straight away to the Lykeion, to confess to Aristotle that I had not been successful in discovering anything about Kleiophon. He received me in his old amiable fashion. It was quite like the old days, when I first knew him, seeing a good-humoured Aristotle, no longer in mourning, sitting in his fine room surrounded by books. 'I have failed—' I began.

'Never mind,' he said. 'Sit down, rest yourself.' He turned to the servant, who was already in the room. 'Could you bring us something, Herpyllis?' I was too shy to speak up and say that I had partaken of pancakes in the brothel kitchen, and needed nothing to eat. The slave left and quickly returned with sweet water flavoured with a little mild wine, and some of this season's nuts to chew on.

Aristotle did not adhere to the beliefs of those who hold that all slaves should be kept dirty in order to distinguish them from their masters; he always allowed and even encouraged his servants to clean themselves. This woman's face was washed, and her short hair was brushed into its natural curls. I knew this round-faced woman with the sweet face and patient smile, as I had seen Herpyllis before. She had come from the family of Aristotle's mother and tended his wife Pythias in her last illness. Pythias' favourite slave was then kept on to look after Aristotle's little girl, the young Pythias. I could see that this woman Herpyllis had now become general housekeeper too. How I wished I had a slave so reliable – one who moved so silently and touched things with such deftness and delicacy.

'I'm thinking that the slave I must buy should be an older female,' I remarked. 'Cheap, but they're very hard-working, and my wife – once I married – would not be jealous.'

'That might be a good plan,' he said absently. 'Herpyllis, do you think young Pythias would like to come in? Stephanos could see her and she could eat a few of these nuts with us.'

Herpyllis, beaming, obediently fetched the little girl, who ran straight to her father, with a cry of 'Papa!' The child was young enough to be allowed into an *andron*. As she was now six years of age, she would not sit in her father's lap before strangers, but stood at his elbow, eating walnuts. She had no shyness about introducing her own topic.

'Papa, what is a camel? Herpyllis says there are camels.'

'I will explain – no, I shall do better than that,' said

Aristotle, taking up a waxed tablet. 'I will draw a camel for you, as I have seen them. The beast lives in desert places in the East, and people ride upon it. It has long legs, and a hump – like that! Dear me, Eudemos or even young Demetrios could have done better. Still—'

'I would like to ride on it. Can I have a camel?'

'No, child. Expensive to keep around the house, we don't have them in Athens.'

'But Alexander's army has many, many camels,' I added. 'Five hundred together, sometimes.'

'Alexander is now in the Caucasus, so we hear, and has probably dispensed with the beasts. Not good at ascending steep mountains, I imagine,' said Aristotle drily.

Pythias was glad to keep the picture, but then, having had enough new information, asked Aristotle to play a game. In talking and playing with her briefly we forgot our troubles, or at least Aristotle did. Herpyllis watched us, sitting on a stool near the door and working at her distaff. She kept her eye on the Master of the Lykeion, and at a motion of his hand she took Pythias the younger away.

'I have been giving you an object lesson in praise of family life,' said Aristotle blandly. 'In the hopes of counteracting the effects of all this brothel-attendance. Now, what happened?'

'I did visit Manto's brothel,' I explained. 'I tried, but I couldn't seem to say the right thing, or elicit any information at all.'

'Awkward, I should imagine, making enquiries in a brothel,' said Theophrastos, who had entered at this

juncture. This scholar himself was so stiff and proper
I couldn't imagine him in a brothel at any time for
any purpose.

'Never mind,' said Aristotle. 'I expect you did the
best you could.' There seemed no point in going on
about the morning's oddly pleasant breakfast, and I
didn't like talking about such things before the dignified – and not uncritical – Theophrastos.

'I have a fresh concern,' Aristotle announced
abruptly. 'I was going to tell you Theophrastos, in
strictest confidence, but I don't see why Stephanos
should not be included in that confidence. I have
received a puzzling note from Antipater. Here it is,'
and he read aloud:

> '"*Aristotle son of Nikomakhos. Greeting from
> Antipater, General of Hellas.*
>
> *I trust you are well. I am sending to you a person
> with unusual abilities. Employ him I beg and his
> payment will be my affair. You will know him if you
> mention the Lenaia.*"'

'A very crisp note,' said Theophrastos. 'The writer
certainly wastes no time in chat.'

'Oh, that is like Antipater – he is always so busy,
and in any case a certain brusqueness is his style,' said
Aristotle. 'The tone of the letter has little significance.
The General doesn't believe in conveying too much
in any one epistle, lest it fall into the wrong hands.
You see, he has not even stated in his letter the name
of this person whom he wants me to employ.'

'He tells you to mention the Lenaia,' I added. 'But

doesn't indicate why you should mention the name of the winter drama festival. It's not so important as the Great Dionysia, in the spring. And it's not as if *you* could have been at the Lenaia.'

In the case of the Lenaia, the smaller and more old-fashioned of the two Dionysos festivals, foreigners and foreign residents like Aristotle are not allowed to attend rituals or performances. As this festival is held in the cold month of Gamelion, ambassadors and other foreigners do not greatly object to being deprived of a chance to sit through performances conducted in the frost and cold rains. But the plays of the Lenaia can be as good as those of the Great Dionysia — at least sometimes.

'We shall doubtless understand the reference at once, as soon as we are faced with the man,' said Aristotle. 'But this letter tells me — if I read between the lines — that Antipater already has some wind too of recent affairs here in Athens, and is concerned. He wants an agent on the ground whom he trusts. That could be very awkward in itself. Nothing would fan the flames of anger more than for some of the patriots to know there was a Makedonian spy around.'

'There are probably quite a number already,' said Theophrastos. I recognized with a shock that this observation was most likely true, though hardly consoling.

'No Athenian could want Makedonian spies around!' I exclaimed. 'Antipater doesn't say this person is a Makedonian.'

'No — but obviously Antipater wants somebody on his own side here. But why this person? Obviously, it must be someone who can do something which I cannot. "Unusual abilities." He has skills which nobody else possesses. I do hope this is not a troublemaker.'

'We shall know soon, I think,' said Theophrastos. 'I hear your servant Phokon coming to the room now, with another person behind him. A person with a very decided tread.'

We sat staring at the door. It opened soon enough.

'There's a person for you, sir,' said Phokon. 'He would not give his name.'

'Let him in,' said Aristotle, with resignation. The door was flung open, and a man entered.

How can I describe someone who came to seem both a saviour and an incubus? A man who was going to play a very distinct part in the history of Athens, though many historians do not care to mention him.

At that moment I saw a man just above the middle height, yet seeming tall. He held himself very erect, and his body was well defined, with square shoulders, and every sign of a muscular torso beneath his simple khiton. Yet he appeared long-legged and lithe, as if he might easily begin dancing at any time. His dark brown hair curled in little wings around his well-shaped head, a large and very round head. His face too was quite round, furnished with a well-shaped nose and large brown eyes. 'What a good-looking young man,' you might well say to yourself as soon as you saw him. Yet he gave me a certain unease, this person whose suppleness was oddly combined with a bull-like neck, a head round and hard as a great boulder, and very long sinewy arms. He mixed the forceful and the graceful very oddly, a combination of Herakles and Apollo that was not quite beautiful, nor even quite comfortable to behold. He walked into the room with the slow elegance of a well-bred man, but his bearing suggested the confidence of one who could fight his way out of trouble.

'Good day, Aristotle of Stageira,' said this newcomer. 'Antipater will have written to you about me.' He glanced over at the table on which lay the waxed tablets. The tablets were folded closed, but it seemed as if his sharp glance permitted him to read through the wooden covers. His eyes flicked around the room. 'Who are these persons?' he demanded.

Aristotle rose. 'I am Aristotle son of Nikomakhos, Master of the Lykeion,' he said formally. 'This is Theophrastos, my second in command, as it were. And Stephanos son of Nikiarkhos, citizen of Athens and a good friend.'

'You perhaps already know me,' said the newcomer easily. 'At least you, Stephanos of Athens, may know me, for you are not a foreigner and thus can attend the Lenaia. "Where the rainy winds drive us fast through the spray."'

'That's true,' I agreed. And now I could indeed at least partially identify the person who spoke to me. Now that I heard his voice, and caught the quotation from a recent drama.

'*You* were an actor in the last Lenaia,' I exclaimed. 'On the day when it rained so hard. Of course I cannot recall your own face, as I saw you in a mask. But now I recognize your voice, and something about your movement is familiar also.'

'And that is all you remember of my performance in the Lenaia?'

'Oh – you were very good. And, yes, you won a prize.'

'Quite right. I won the prize for best actor,' this young man said complacently. 'I am Arkhias the actor. Antipater himself has been taken by my ability. I wonder if I might take a chair?'

'Oh, my apologies. Yes, do sit down.' Aristotle returned to his own chair by the desk, while Arkhias helped himself to the best armchair. He filled it imposingly.

'Well, Arkhias the actor, what can we do for you?'Aristotle smiled a little. 'I fear I have no play to produce, am not even writing anything I could offer you. But the roles for the next Dionysia are being cast now, and I could put in a word –'

'That would doubtless be useful,' said Arkhias, waving a hand gracefully to dispose of this offer. 'But matters are already in train. My professional success, if I may refer to it in those terms, is fairly well established by now. The life of an actor, however, is precarious. It is a profession which has won great glory for some, and wealth for a few. Yet it is not a lifetime work. Not, in that respect, at all like an art or a craft.'

'No, indeed,' said Theophrastos, amused. Arkhias raised an eyebrow.

'Yet it *is* an art and a craft. The skills required are unusual, and the techniques difficult to perfect. Acting necessitates good memory, enormous stamina, a strong voice – all this goes without saying. But it also requires constant, even tireless, observation of human beings, Beyond that, it calls for the rarer ability to melt into another person, another character. Even someone of a different sex or race – or someone not human at all, like a bird.'

'Yes,' I agreed, somewhat hesitantly. 'Of course the masks and costumes help. And a dramatist tells us a lot about who the character is supposed to be. I don't know how it would work without a mask-maker, and lines to say.'

'It is regrettable,' Arkhias said, 'that the wonderful gift which disguises even itself is overshadowed by the ostentatious and glittering poetic knack of the drama- tist, and even by the drudging competence of the mask-maker. In reality, it is the fire in the actor that makes dramatic performance. Without the art that brings the character to life, there is no theatre.'

'Except,' Aristotle interjected academically, 'the khoros, which is probably at the bottom of all theatre, in the early time – ritual and chant of an entire group—'

Arkhias was not interested in this scholarly disquisition.

'We are talking about *now*, not olden times,' he corrected. 'It is part of the genius of Antipater, Alexander's general and regent in the Greek main- land, to be perceptive and far-reaching. He had heard of me through an associate. Of course, though the men of Makedon may not openly attend the Lenaia, they still need to know what is going on here. Antipater summoned me to him when he was at Korinthos. With the help of some underlings, I performed several roles that I had undertaken for the Lenaia, privately, for the regent himself and one or two of his friends. Antipater admired me, complimented me, showered gifts upon me. Yet the most surprising thing is his suggestion: that I employ these unusual abilities, at least part of the time, to the service of the good of the state.'

'You mean, be a spy,' I said bluntly.

'It's more than that,' Arkhias said, sitting upright in his chair and never taking his eyes off Aristotle. 'As we all realize, the master of a household should be able at any moment to lay his hand on any of those who belong to him – wife and concubines, children, slaves. He should know where they are, what they are doing, and be able to call them to account in a moment. He says, "Fetch the black horse," or, "Command my younger son to present himself," and is obeyed at once. So, too, a king, or ruler of any state, needs at any time to be able to lay his hand on any of his people. If he doesn't, in certain cases, know where to find them, he should know those who know *how* to find them. With my ability, I can pursue a person and capture him – or her – before my quarry can know that I am near. For I do not, if you take my meaning, pursue in my own character.'

'A bounty-hunter!' I exclaimed in disgust. 'There are a number of people who do that, go after runaway slaves – but it's considered a low occupation, and—'

'The work of pursuing runaway slaves is not fully congenial to myself,' Arkhias agreed, patiently. '*That* is not what Antipater meant. I see he has already sent you an introduction to me. The regent has singled me out. I gave up the chance of the next Dionysia to work with him. I have taken instruction in the arts of war, to add to my other abilities – he even sent me to Pella and to Dion. I have been spending the spring and summer there, learning the use of weapons and other things from masters of his army.'

'But what precisely does he want of you?' Theophrastos asked gently.

'Antipater needs – *we* need, I perhaps should say – we need to be able to locate and take hold of any persons whose absence or whose activities in absence might be detrimental in any respect to the well-being of the state. Exiles, victims of kidnapping, hostile spies, fugitives.'

'A far-reaching task,' murmured Theophrastos, coughing lightly in a manner indicating some disapproval. The newcomer paid no heed to him, but continued with his absorbing self-description.

'Take your own work, for example.' Arkhias looked at Aristotle. 'An heiress is missing. You go after her – and fairly soon you find her. Antipater knows all about that case and was impressed with your results, O Aristotle son of Nikomakhos. But you, the Master of the Lykeion and a well-known figure, can hardly run away on a leave of absence at any moment. And you are also ageing, if I may be so frank. I am young. You can see for yourselves, I am in perfect physical condition. I can swim, wrestle and run. And ride a horse very well, and even manage a chariot. Now I have been trained in warlike exercise, I can wield a sword or javelin or sarissa as well as a soldier.'

'A tower of strength,' said Theophrastos.

'Yes – as you imply, these are merely skills of strength. Though they might come in very useful, these are the skills frequently found in athletic young men without a thought in their heads. I, however, am not like them.'

'They usually know no plays,' I agreed, laughing. Arkhias spoke seriously and did not laugh at all. He stood up in order to make more impressive the recital of his capacities.

'I have studied with good rhetoricians, I can use logic and employ eloquence. But I am no mere rhetorician. In fact, I am unique in my combination of abilities. My art rests on a keen and constant observation of human behaviour, emotions, mannerisms and so on. I can dissimulate. With the most ordinary pieces of costume – and of course with *no* help from a mask – I can make myself into somebody else.'

'I don't know about that,' I said dubiously. 'As soon as you began to speak, I recognized you.'

'Yes, Stephanos son of Nikiarkhos, you did – because I wanted you to. Had I wished you *not* to recognize me, you would not have done so. I adopted the voice with which I had played the part, even quoted a line of the drama you saw. But I can become a different personage at will, even in voice and movement. Listen! I have the most perfect Athenian accent. Yet I come from Thurii, the colony far to the West, in Greater Greece. If I had let nature rule, I naturally would speak like a Thurian.'

'I don't know if I have heard of that place,' I remarked.

'It is very well known,' Arkhias insisted. 'Built around the ancient town of Sybaris. The great Herodotos was one of our founders. Good soil, lovely wines. Poseidonia is full of barbarians now, but *we* are all Greek, with Greek arts, Greek pottery and sculpture, and schooling in true Greek literature. We call ourselves the Italiotes. Our cities are banding together now in a League of Italiotes. Once we kick the men of Karthago out of Sikilia, and make it entirely Greek, we shall unite with Sikilia. And then we can take Karthago itself. While Greek power spreads to Asia, do not neglect the West.'

'But you have not remained in the West,' Theophrastos pointed out. 'Fortunately for ourselves, I am sure, you are giving us the benefit of your skills and presence here.'

'True. I have left the western colonies and come to Greece itself, seeking my fortune. I have succeeded here, in the very home of the arts. Antipater honours me in sending me to your city. Here I am. Make use of me, then, for the peace and tranquillity of Athens.'

'Am I to understand,' Aristotle enquired, 'that you would undertake tasks at my request or suggestion?'

'Yes.'

'But you might also undertake tasks for Antipater separately – of which I knew nothing.'

'Yes. You were a spy once, yourself, in Asia in the old days, I think – so you understand.'

'A dangerous man, you are, Arkhias. I fear,' Aristotle sighed heavily, 'I fear Athens will not be the same again, after we introduce in peacetime such a spy. A spy not upon a foreign enemy but upon ourselves. Athens is the greatest exponent of freedom; its concerns are conducted openly. The strength of this city lies in openness – in laws publicly debated before they are passed, in trials openly conducted by laws on which the people agree—'

'Very nice, I'm sure,' said Arkhias. 'And nothing will happen to disturb all that. But if anyone plots against Athens, it should be known to the authorities. And if anyone needs to be found, I can find him. You should consider me above all as a skilled hunter, who tracks the most excellent quarry. The highest prey – which is man. I go into the forests, as it were, to do my work. You will not always see me. I work on the periphery, finding what is out of place.'

'There is that case right now,' I said 'The case of the missing boy, Aristotle. Why don't you tell Arkhias about that? And then we would see.'

'Aha!' said Arkhias, his nostrils flaring. 'You wish to set me a test? Very well, I have no objection. But do not forget' – he held up a finger – '*Never* mention anything of this. To you as to everybody else, I am only an actor, well versed in poetry.'

XV

The Golden Girl

'A dangerous man,' said Aristotle, shaking his head,
after Arkhias had departed. His departure was
certainly not abrupt. The Master of the Lykeion had
offered Arkhias food and drink while the actor heard
about the case of the missing Kleiophon.

'A dangerous man,' Aristotle repeated.

'But he's on your side,' I pointed out.

'My side? I wonder what side I have. Must I choose?
O Stephanos, I value so much the nature of Athens
itself. This is my home, the home after my own heart.
I have rejoiced that the Makedonians spared this city,
and I desire it to continue in peace and prosperity. But
if what we call "peace" is built on constant spying and
informing, that is a high price to pay. It certainly does
not put an end to the divisions of which we were
speaking. I rather wish, Stephanos, that you had not
mentioned to him the case of Kleiophon.'

'I had already begun to think that was a trifle rash,

myself,' I confessed. 'Though you must admit, we are
at a stand as to the whereabouts of this boy – and also
as to who took him or abetted him. Hermia's trial
cannot properly proceed without his being found. And
the lad may need rescuing from some brutal captor!'

'The deed is done,' said Theophrastos calmly.
'Arkhias knows about the missing boy, and he will be
a dog on the scent of Kleiophon from now on. That
doggedness carries at least this advantage, that while
this Thurian is investigating that case he will not poke
his handsome nose into other affairs.'

I thought, but did not say, that it was as well the
Thurian actor was not poking his handsome nose into
Phryne's case or the persons attending the party at
Tryphaina's brothel. I had not been so rash as to draw
the concerns of Theramenes to Arkhias' attention.

'Meanwhile,' Aristotle continued, with an uncanny
aptness, 'we are fast driving on to the trial of Phryne.
It's almost as if they were trying to combine the
charges against Sokrates and Alkibiades. Sokrates was
charged with disrespect to the city's gods, chiefly in
introducing a new god – his personal *daimon* – and
corrupting youth. And Alkibiades was accused of
mimicking the Mysteries. Phryne is accused not only
of mocking the Mysteries but also of introducing a
new foreign god and corrupting young people. The
charge of blasphemy and impiety is so easy to bring,
and arouses so much anxiety, rage and fear. It appears
to be harder to conduct such a trial rationally and
civilly than it is so to conduct a trial for murder.'

'Alkibiades,' remarked Theophrastos, 'became an exile,
in order to avoid a trial, abandoning his leadership

of the Sikilian Expedition. If he hadn't, that attempt to take Sikilia might have succeeded. Some did not wish him to be too powerful. And Sokrates – unlike his self-indulgent pupil, he refused to be a fugitive; as a reward for standing his ground, he was convicted and killed. Impure motives, political passions, drive such charges forward.'

'But a woman is so seldom connected with politics,' I sighed, thinking of the beauty of Phryne, and her joyousness.

'Perikles' hetaira Aspasia of Miletos was prosecuted for impiety,' Theophrastos suggested. 'Whether this were brought about by enemies of Perikles or because she was an adherent of Sokrates is not certain. Later, the Athenians relented and turned about face – as they so often do – even legitimating Perikles' son by Aspasia. But Phryne isn't accused of mere association with some other offender, and her alleged new god of "Equal Shares" won't go down well with the two top classes of citizens. Hypereides speaking as her Defender will have his work cut out for him. It is said that Aristogeiton and Eurymedon hope not only to defeat but to humiliate him.'

'Bad, and getting worse,' commented Aristotle. 'Of course, this trial is a mode of attacking Hypereides – and frightening any others who might be too self-confident and free-speaking. That seems essentially the object, not merely to kill a wealthy hetaira. Hypereides and I can never be on good terms after – after the insult to Pythias' monument. His cruel behaviour in that dreadful encounter in the Kerameikos—'

Aristotle passed his hand over his eyes, and remained silent for some moments.

'I never thought to converse of my own volition with that man again. Yet even I must admit, Hypereides now seems a bulwark against disaster. For if Eurymedon and Aristogeiton and the rest convict Phryne, their blood will be up. That extremely pure group of patriots will see their clear pathway to oligarkhy – simply by bringing more accusations of the sort.'

He stood up. 'No, it won't do. I will send to Hypereides myself and arrange a meeting.'

'What good can that do?' I enquired.

'Not much, very possibly. But I cannot simply do nothing. I may have some advice to give him.'

I couldn't imagine that Aristotle's advice would be much regarded by Hypereides, considering how this statesman had treated the philosopher. Hypereides himself had a very good reputation as an orator. The subject of Phryne's trial was unpleasant to me – even fearful. The brutal truth, so it seemed to me in my worst reflections, was that I myself would not be safe until she was tried and executed. After that, people would stop chattering about and digging into that evening at Tryphaina's house. Until that point, I would always be in danger of being dragged in myself. Not only could they make me a witness, but at this point the very fact of my not having spoken up before would make me appear suspect. It would not be very hard to charge me with deliberate complicity, even impiety. Consciousness of guilt on my part, I realized, would be not only inferred but alleged to explain why I had not spoken. Masquerading as a Makedonian soldier would not be helpful to my cause, but the reverse – it would be disgusting to Makedonians as well as to Athenian patriots. At any moment of any day, some-one could recollect my face and fit it to the face of one of the revellers at that now famous – or rather, infa-mous – party. Other brothel customers, the whores, not just the fine hetairai, but the poorest slave *pornai* and the slave attendants who worked there – any one of these might recognize me. I had not given my name that evening, but I had not taken off my face. If only it were possible to go to a brothel in a mask!

I went to a barber, several times, for very vigorous trimming of beard and a shortening of my hair. Then I began to worry whether I didn't look too much like a soldier, with hair too short. I thought, belatedly, I should have grown my hair long and simpered in an unsoldierly and un-Makedonian way with perfumed locks. But in that guise I would look like the kind of man who hangs around in brothels. I didn't need more of that reputation, either.

'Heard you have taken to having your breakfast with the whores,' gibed my old schoolfriend Nikeratos. 'Eating honeyed pancakes, so I hear? What a sweet tooth! Did you get plenty of honey?'

'Ridiculous the way news gets around and gets completely distorted,' I said contemptuously. 'I presume you yourself have been to Manto's brothel, where you have picked up this fine tale.'

'Oho, so it was *Manto*'s brothel, was it?'

'Boys,' said his father, laughing, 'it is not seemly to

talk of such things in front of a parent. Respect my grey hairs!'

'Come, Father,' said Nikeratos, 'it is not as if you know nothing of what we get up to.'

'No,' he agreed. 'And you graceless youths think you can teach your fathers and grandfathers about life, never realizing that we have done the same – and more! But the girls of Athens are not as pretty as they used to be, not as alluring and delicate. The new style is bolder. And to my mind, not as good.'

'Oh, Father,' said Nikeratos, 'you cannot say that Phryne is not most beautiful! She is extraordinary. The goldsmith Khryses is making a statue of her, all in gold.'

'Ah, Phryne,' said the older man. 'Yes. She is an exception. She came up suddenly, like a summer plant. I remember her well when she was a little barefoot slip of a lass, her legs scratched from the briars, going about the lanes and fields looking for wild capers to sell. Her family was hard up, you see. Yet even at that time, she was as pretty a little thing as you could see, with a voice like a bird. But then, while she was doing such tasks, her full beauty broke out, like a plant bursting into flower.'

'You are turning quite poetic, Father,' Nikeratos said affectionately.

'No, I'm no poet. But – little Phryne! She always spoke nicely to everybody, and she sang when she was walking through the ferns and briars and leaping over ditches. It seems a dreadful shame, you know – a terrible shame. Little Phryne!'

The old man was not the only one of the Athenians

who echoed this sentiment. All sorts of people produced recollections of Phryne in different phases: the child, the young girl, the woman. The goldsmith who was making the gold statue of her had set about his work well before the accusation, and at first had worried that his project would be rendered worthless. He need not have been concerned. If the image of Phryne had been interesting before, it now gained in wonder. Phryne herself, the woman about to undergo trial, was daily a more disturbing marvel.

'I believe——' Aristotle said to me. 'Tell me if you think this wrong. But in order to help Hypereides, I should like to see Phryne myself.'

'You are as bad as all the rest,' I said, laughing at him, but with a sick feeling. Suppose Phryne was to let slip to Aristotle that *I* had been there? No, surely she did not know my name.

Aristotle misinterpreted my dubious silence. 'Not to gape at her, Stephanos,' he assured me. 'I need to know her – what and who she is – before I advise Hypereides. He is so desperate he is willing to see me, privately and briefly, but I need to know whether the advice I might like to give be right or not.'

'You won't be able to see Phryne alone,' I cautioned. 'She has some old woman with her all the time, as well as friends and protectors.'

'Well, then, think of me as like Sokrates when he interviewed the famous hetaira Theodote. Told that her beauty was beyond the power of words, Sokrates went to see her, saying, "Therefore I must go and see this woman for it is evidently not possible to judge her beauty by listening to you." And when he met her, he talked and jested with her in a civilized fashion.'

I could not tell whether Aristotle himself were jesting or serious. He added, 'I do not require nor expect the woman to be alone.'

'You know Phryne is now in the prison?' I asked. 'She has been allowed to stay in a house, like Hermia, until recently. But the prosecution insisted that three days before the trial she be moved to the gaol, and strictly guarded. Their argument is that although freeborn she was not born in Athens, and is neither a citizen's wife or mother. Therefore she has behind her no real property, no land or high kindred, to give surety against escape. So the girl lies now at the prison.'

'I know that. Do you want to come with me?'

'I – no! I shall leave you to your own perceptions and reflections of the beautiful Phryne. I had rather,' I asserted boldly, 'go and view the famous golden statue.'

So we went in different directions that day: he to see the flesh-and-blood Phryne in the prison, I to the goldsmith's shop to look at her golden image. The crowd this day was bigger than before – now, a couple of short days before the trial itself, interest was hectic. People who knew Phryne and people who did not flocked to the goldsmith's shop to behold the display. Women were among the spectators, not only women of a certain occupation, but virtuous wives, fully veiled, who had persuaded their husbands to bring them to this marvel. I had to wait to get in; a throng of people was moving into the small workshop and only slowly did the viewers move out again. Once arrived at our goal, we were allowed to stop and gaze our fill. Khryses the goldsmith, with pride in his own art, was exhibiting his creation. It wasn't, strictly speaking, his creation; it was based on a sculpture in bronze executed by another and greater artist, now transformed by a first-rate goldsmith who had not spared his materials.

The image of gilded bronze was tall. It was nothing like life-size, but sufficiently large to allow the artist to do justice to the height of the body, the long moulded limbs, the graceful turn of the torso. The figure was decently clothed in flowing draperies – appropriately, for Phryne herself always went about very decently clad, so it was difficult for any man not paying for the privilege to see her. But the slender statue's flowing garments did not conceal the beauty of the form. The sculptor had outdone himself with the turn of the head on its graceful neck. The face with its golden features really did have a look of Phryne – a Phryne slightly amused, expectant, ready to be joyous.

'Ahh!' said most, gazing on her.

'Like a nymph at dawn!' said one poetical gentleman.

'Lovely! Poor thing!' said a woman near me.

'It is an image of Beauty itself,' said one man, a philosopher, instructing his younger friend and companion, who was ready to be impressed. This speaker was evidently intending to say much more, but other people had their own remarks to make.

'It has quite a look of her, to be sure,' said one middle-aged citizen, with a critical and remembering eye.

'A shame that such a beauty should be a whore and

a good-for-nothing,' said a woman among the spectators. 'Stealing husbands from honest women, and
encouraging impudent behaviour.'

'True,' exclaimed the deep voice of a gentleman
behind her. Looking over my shoulder, I saw the figure
of Aristogeiton, in his unmistakable uncompromising
red cloak.

'Disgusting spectacle!' he exclaimed. 'An imperish-
able memorial to the incontinence and folly of the
Athenians!'

'Quite right,' said the woman, emboldened by this
seconder. 'How can anyone want to look at such a
thing when the woman is a wicked woman?'

'But when it – she – is so beautiful – as she is,' a
man pleaded.

'Not so,' Aristogeiton pronounced. 'That is a perver-
sion of the word "beautiful".' He pronounced the word
itself with a certain distaste. 'Nothing is beautiful that
is not moral and proper, and in harmony with the
health of the state.'

'Such a piece of folly!' The decided woman waved
an unbeautiful hand at the golden form. '*I* wouldn't
give such a piece house-room.'

But instead of applauding her, Aristogeiton now
frowned.

'No women at all should be attending this degrad-
ing spectacle,' he pronounced. 'Certainly not citizens'
wives, respectable females.'

'I only brought her,' explained her husband hastily,
'I mean, I made her come only so as she could see
what a bad example this is, and a warning. To show
her what our daughters are *not* to be.'

Looking at this red-faced fellow and at what I could see of his thin wife with the chapped hands, I could not imagine that their daughters were in any danger of untoward beauty. To give the husband credit, he probably produced this justification on the spur of the moment purely for the benefit of Aristogeiton – who refused to be appeased.

'Get you home, in the name of decency,' he advised. 'All females with a claim to respectability should depart forthwith. Any women remaining will be judged as women without reputation – as whores, in fact. And they should be treated accordingly. It would be better if respectable men departed likewise.'

He was now standing directly in front of the golden statue, and glared at it.

'This is a menace.' He was muttering rather than speaking loudly as before. 'A menace to our community, our customs and sacred laws. An offence to good manners and behaviour. A poisonous thing!'

Khryses blenched. I imagine he was in terror for his statue, fearing the scowling spectator in the red cloak was about to deface it. Aristogeiton, however, did nothing to harm the object, only turning to favour it with another scowl before going out of the door. He had thinned the room of some of the spectators, so the rest of us could see better.

'At least,' said the middle-aged philosopher, now able to carry on his address to his companion, 'this image will remain when the girl herself is gone. Whether she is poisoned by hemlock, or tortured on the *tympanon* – such disagreeable details are best left unconsidered. That beautiful form of flesh and bone

– alas! – will cease to be. But the object will remain. It will tell succeeding generations about beauty. This image, itself a symbol, points the way to higher things. You see, Myrtilos, that Beauty itself does not belong to the mortal world.'

'So, Hermodoros,' asked youthful Myrtilos in response, 'it doesn't matter if there are beautiful people or not?'

'Of course,' said the bearded Hermodoros, stroking his companion's downy cheek affectionately, 'of *course* it matters, in the sense that it is delightful. You, Myrtilos, so often called "Myrtilos the Beautiful", should know as much. But human beauty, like the beauty appearing in natural objects, is only a reminder of the higher and more perfect. Beauty itself is not a thing of base matter – not like flesh, nor even like the hard bronze material, gold-coated, of which this statue is constructed. Beauty is a form, a truth, perceived but not possessed by a thing, or located in it.'

'You know so much,' said Myrtilos, impressed. 'So this is the true philosophy?'

Aristotle came in as this pair left. He cast a glance at the statue. 'Remarkably like,' he murmured, and did not linger. I came away too, though I was glad to have seen the bright image. Yet that semblance did not strike me as a consolation for the vanishing of Phryne herself.

'It is a magnificent image,' I said to Aristotle as we were leaving. 'Yet – I don't know how – it is not the same—' I caught myself. Why should I confess that I had seen Phryne herself, close to? 'I am the more certain that Hephaistos the artificer found his golden girls a poor substitute for Aphrodite.'

'Perhaps. But many men have to make do with substitutes of one sort or another.'

'Did you see Phryne?' I asked once we were out of the press of the crowd, and had a chance to speak privately. 'How was she? What did she say?' I was still slightly anxious that Phryne might have mentioned me to Aristotle, but Aristotle's calm if grave responses soon allayed these fears. Foolish fears. How could Phryne have known anything of me? I had not even spoken directly to her on that memorable night.

'As to *how* she is – that is difficult to say. I have never been with someone who is under sentence of death and yet not dead. I wasn't with my dear friend Hermias when he met his agonizing end in Atarneos. As a medical man and a friend, I have looked upon people dying – even, as you know, seen my wife, my dearest Pythias, die. However terrible the parting, death from illness or age remains natural. A death sentence is different. Someone under sentence of death who is in full health and going to die—! Extraordinary!'

'But Phryne isn't under a sentence. She has yet to be tried.'

'Strictly speaking, you are right. Not according to the letter of the law. She is waiting to be tried. But I hear on many sides that the accusers and many of her judges – that is to say, the arkhons of the court of the Areopagos – feel that the propitiation of the gods depends on a speedy determination of her guilt, and a swift execution of the sentence of the court. So she may have but a day's grace – or less – after the trial before the final end.'

'So – by this calculation, her death is now only four days away from her. Or really, three. Today is already going, the sun is beginning to decline. Strange to watch a day draw to an end when one has so few!'

'If I were a moralist first and foremost, I should remind you that we all have but a few. The real difference between the condemned man and ourselves is that he knows what we do not – the exact date of his death. Somebody in Athens who is drawing breath at this moment will die before Phryne – of an infant's croup, of an old man's apoplexy, of a falling tile. We shall all go, but do not know the manner and date of our going.'

'You are philosophical, too,' I said, thinking of the lecturing Hermodoros. 'But it is not very helpful.'

'I agree – all this is beside the point. None of it changes the fact that Phryne, a healthy young woman, is facing imminent death.'

'Was she alone?'

'No. There were a number of people with her, as well as guards sent by her friends to see she is not molested while in prison. The room was almost crowded, in fact. She has some women friends to look after her. She is certainly not alone, and I daresay having an audience heartened her – a little.'

'How was she? What did she say?'

'Phryne, I am told, is known for wit and playfulness. Such a circumstance as hers certainly tends to depress the spirits. Yet, I could still glimpse flashes of what I imagine was her old gaiety. She reminded me that Sophokles in old age was enamoured of Arkhippe, who came to live with him. And when a former lover asked another man what Arkhippe was doing these days, the answer was, "Like an owl, she sits on a tomb."'

'I've heard that story before. Not very polite to *you*!'

'She was teasing me. And she gave it a good and witty turn, for she said, "But in my case, the opposite is true. For you all come to me, curious about my death. You come as owls come to tombs – but they usually don't all flock on the *same* tomb."'

'And you said—?'

'Oh, I said something about our being owls of Athena, you know, and that we are most visible in twilight. Whereas she is beautiful by noonday. She *is* still lovely, though vicissitudes have cost her complexion some of its glow. She needs to wash very carefully in olive oil, and her special maid must be sent to do her hair. Phryne herself referred to this matter.'

I remembered, a little sadly, the hands pushing the locks back, the jesting voice saying 'It will cost you a mina to do my hair – unless you're my maid.' The face, the hair, I should never see again.

'Doing her hair well cannot help her,' I observed. 'Nobody will see her. For she will be entirely veiled when she appears before the Areopagos.'

'Just so. You are right, of course. Now I must have the talk I dread – with Hypereides. I shall not go to his house, but to the house of a friend of both of us. A very short interview. At an hour when I can hope to be unobserved. His credit would not be improved by being seen with me. Nor would mine fare the better for consorting with him at this juncture. I hate to speak to that man at all. But there – the times are too desperate to permit one to give pride of place to a grievance, however justified, however deep.'

It was puzzling to me that Aristotle would overcome, at least to this extent, his grievance against Hypereides – a justly based grievance, entitled to persist throughout a lifetime. It must mean his concern for Athens was not only sincere but great. Or else his concern for Phryne.

XVI

The Trial of
Phryne for Impiety

The autumn morning was cloudy, with a lowering and
sullen dawn, and splashes of rain. By the time we set
out, the rain had almost gone, but the skies remained
unfriendly. Not an easy day on which to appear in a
trial for one's life, I thought. A jury that has to sit
outdoors in inclement weather may be inclined to feel
discontented with their circumstances. Discontent and
chilliness can render men spiritually cool, apt to seize
on faults and be severe.

Not that this jury is easily to be rendered enraged
or gratified, since trials for impiety, just like trials for
murder, are argued in the court of the Areopagos.
Members of the Areopagos are praised as possessing
the advantages of age and judgement; these former
arkhons tend to be somewhat old and thus less subject
to spurts of passion than the young supposedly are.
Well settled in life, their fortunes made, they have less

need than others to seek for gain. Not but what it is a kind of impiety in itself to speak as if any member of any jury in Athens – let alone an arkhon – might be biased, or susceptible to the allure of potential partnerships and patronage, advancement or advantage.

We straggled and pressed towards the Hill of Ares, under whose warlike patronage Phryne's case would be heard. The jury of arkhons had come early, in duty bound, and by the time I arrived most were already in their place, looking elderly and severe. The rest of us citizens struggled to gain places (some sitting, more standing); there was soon a huge throng of people crushing one another. The ceremonies on the top of the hill began, and the Basileus as his own herald made the formal proclamation: 'Foreigners away! Let only citizens draw near to hear!' As cases of impiety, above all, concern the city's relation with its own gods, it is only right that such important trials be conducted solely for and by the citizens of Athens. Sacrifices having been performed in due fashion in the Temple of Ares, Accuser and Defender took their oaths, and the charge was made. The Accuser, Aristogeiton, took his place standing on the historic Stone of Accusation, and now we saw a woman's shape, all muffled, standing on the Stone of the Accused.

Then the whole party moved down to the flat space and the *bema*. Around it were grouped officials, including the Basileus (sitting) and the attendants whose duty it was to mind the water-clocks. Space for the general audience was extremely limited, and men were still pushing and shoving; it was the biggest crowd I had seen at such an event. Aristotle, with other resident aliens, was standing in a remote place beyond the barrier, whereas I enjoyed a fairly good view, and could hear without strain. There was a slight disturbance as some women tried to come into the place where the foreigners were standing, but they were hustled away.

'Bunch of whores!' said one of the men near me. And of course he must have been right. No decent woman would appear near the court of the Areopagos.

'I suppose they are some of Phryne's friends and companions,' I responded.

'*Those* chickens!' The man laughed. 'They're all at their prayers today. Some have gone to the Temple of Athena to offer sacrifice, but many more have gone to the Temple of Aphrodite. Or special shrines. And much good may it do them!'

The herald announced the case again, for the benefit of all who could not hear the ceremony upon the Rock of Ares.

'This is the trial of Mnesarete daughter of Epikles of Thespiai, a woman commonly known as Phryne, on the accusation of impiety. She has mocked the sacred rites of the Mysteries of Eleusis, thus offending Demeter and the Maiden. And this woman Mnesarete has introduced a foreign god, not one of the gods of the city, by the name Isodaites, the Equal Divider. In unlawful celebration and in his name she has called men and women together in ritual dance and procession. In doing both Mnesarete has displayed wanton and unmistakable impiety,

corrupting the young of Athens who consorted
with her and who followed in her train.'

So Phryne had a real name! I had come to think of
her so naturally as 'Phryne', her nickname everywhere,
that I was surprised to hear she had a normal name
like 'Mnesarete'. Being tried under her real name
might not be helpful to her, I thought. 'Phryne' was
a woman of whom many knew and some were very
fond; 'Mnesarete' was an unknown person who might
be knocked down and stamped on without qualm.

The muffled form was brought in. Phryne herself,
not visible as herself, but draped in black from head to
foot, and heavily veiled. She looked much as Hermia
had done at her trial, save that Hermia was slightly
shorter. The tall woman was attended by another, much
shorter, also muffled and veiled. At least, I reflected,
the accused young woman had been allowed to keep
another female by her at such a time. But just as I was
thinking this, Euthias and Eurymedon stepped forward.
They both spoke – I caught the clear cool tones of
Eurymedon. The Basileus nodded reluctantly, and
summoned the guards to remove the female attendant.
Women really are not supposed to come near the court
of the Areopagos – only defendants. (Slaves are customarily tortured and questioned elsewhere, and their testimony read aloud in court without their appearance.)

So Phryne stood there alone, muffled, like a pillar
of cloth. It was as well for her that the day was cool.
There she had to stand, speechless and unmoving, at
a corner of the platform during the whole of the
proceedings, with no one to hold her arm or whisper

encouragement, not even her own slave to catch her if she fainted.

Hypereides came separately as Phryne's Defender, or the voice of her defence; of course he could not stand with Phryne before his turn to speak came. While his opponent was speaking, he stood on the ground, arms crossed, a manly firmness in his countenance. He did not look at Phryne then, and when at last he did ascend the *bema* he was many arm-lengths from her. Both Aristogeiton and his ally Euthias appeared as the Accuser. This dual appearance was unusual, though not unknown.

'Euthias wrote the speeches,' said a man near me, hissing the news to an older companion, who seemed to rely on his information. The news-monger seemed fully informed. 'Euthias wrote, with the help of Mantias and Eurymedon. Euthias is the better manager and understands argument *much* better than Aristogeiton. But of course *he* isn't so strong in public. So he has coached Aristogeiton behind the scenes. Two nights ago they were up all night, going over and over it.'

This was believable. Certainly Euthias, though noted as a logician since his schooldays, lacked height and presence. Yet if puny, Euthias excelled at arranging information, and was listened to in the Ekklesia whenever he reported on facts and figures. His monotonous voice and unimpressive appearance, however, militated against real success in the oratorical line. Euthias had a new thick cloak and his wispy beard was freshly cut and anointed. Behind him stood Eurymedon, champion of the Mysteries of Eleusis, a man tall and glacial, unmoving as an antique tragic mask. Eurymedon, often spoken of these days as a future chief priest of Demeter, already looked the part of the hierophant: he possessed a perfect profile with a long straight nose, and a face dignified and indestructible as an ancient bronze helmet.

Throughout the trial Eurymedon gazed with implacable disdain at Phryne and even at the witnesses who described the night at Tryphaina's brothel. Beside him, also prominently on view, was the less beautiful Theramenes, his wen glowing with excitement. The witness-hunter looked pleased with himself and often whispered to Eurymedon, or even to Euthias, who seemed annoyed every time the too-familiar Theramenes did this, as if a tool should insist on drawing attention to itself. Impatience on Euthias' part was forgivable, for he would have enough to do, not only to listen to Aristogeiton perform (and to estimate how well his speech was received) but then also to listen keenly to Hypereides so as to offer instant advice about changes in the second speech of accusation.

Aristogeiton, who was to act as the speaking Accuser, made a truly eligible prosecutor, possessing good height, and a magnificent carrying voice, as well as a strong projection of presence. On this occasion he looked important, even tremendous. He had acquired a new haircut, so his locks, though they flowed in the aristocratic fashion, did not straggle. His beard was well trimmed. Somebody had also had the thoughtfulness to suggest paring his nails, which were customarily broken and rather dirty. I had expected to see Aristogeiton wearing his Spartan red cloak, but today (presumably under good advice) he had dispensed with that interesting garment; instead, he wore an unbleached cloak of homespun wool, slightly irregular in the weave and almost ostentatiously plain.

As the Accuser, Aristogeiton of course had the right to the first speech. This is a critical piece of oratory: the first speaker can set the tone of all that follows. If he is both thorough and impressive, then the Defender has his work cut out for him. And the next speech, the first spoken by the Defender, can be no longer than that of the Accuser. Thus, the more elegantly terse the prosecutor manages to be, the more neatly he hamstrings his opponent. The clerk of the court set the *klepsydra*, and Aristogeiton opened his mouth.

ARISTOGEITON: FIRST SPEECH FOR
THE PROSECUTION OF PHRYNE

'Men of Athens, I come before you as one of you, appealing to your honour and justice, your religion and sense of piety. Who among us cannot value the decrees of the gods, the services we owe them, the gratitude we feel to them? All who value Athens and its religion have a stake in the proceedings of this day.'

So far Aristogeiton said, to the best of my memory, exactly what is set down in the texts that soon circulated (or were circulated by him and his party) after the trial. But in many instances 'speeches' as delivered to the public in writing differ markedly from what was actually heard in court: Aristogeiton's first speech against Phryne is no exception. I obtained the purported records and annotated them at the time; these documents I preserved, but have taken leave to vary from them – in the case of all speakers – where

I believe my own memory serves me better. My account, so I believe, is truer than those circulated by either Accuser or Defender after the famous trial.

Aristogeiton's (or Euthias') opening sentences went well. Nobody could take issue with this pious first statement, so his auditors sat as serious and attentive as he wished.

'We meet today,' he continued, gathering strength and power, 'to determine whether to keep pollution and poison in our midst or to cast it out. We are judging the case of Mnesarete, commonly known – and she is very *commonly* known as well as often *known* – as Phryne. This woman, a notorious courtesan and harlot, has had the audacity to defame and set at naught the most holy religion of Eleusis – our religion, the prop and stay of Athens, and of all Athenians, who in gratitude support the rites of the most adored goddess Demeter and her devoted Daughter, the Maiden. This harlot is strangely named Mnesarete – strangely, for the name means "memory of virtue". How wrongly named, for there is assuredly nothing of excellence or virtue about her. Better to term her "Phryne", this woman doubly impious. She has led most shameless revels, in introducing a new god: Isodaites the Equal Divider, or as she calls him also, "The God of Fair Shares". This unhallowed, unknown and dangerous deity is not one of the gods of Athens, yet Phryne as priestess has led a revel-rout, a religious procession, tossing torches and playing music, both men and women celebrating this alien entity which she has perversely introduced within our walls to infect us.

'The seriousness of the charge is measurable by the

very fact that the trial is held *here* – in the Areopagos. Now, some say that this harlot called Phryne – or Mnesarete daughter of Epikles of Thespiai – being a foreigner should not be tried here. As an alien, if resident, a *metoike*, she should be tried in a lesser court. But the gravity of her crime – the crime of impiety, which necessarily entails the most final of punishments – necessitates her presence *here*. The national nature of this crime which afflicts us all bids Athens try this Boiotian female – rare privilege! – as if she were an Athenian. The woman has been allowed a Defender to speak for her. This is a measure of our extreme effort to be just, our own generosity of spirit.'

He paused to run his hand across his forehead, while my talkative neighbour whispered, 'They *chose* the charge of impiety because it would mean the Areopagos, and certain death.'

'Certainly,' continued Aristogeiton, 'this woman has all the benefits to which she may or may not be entitled.' The speaker betrayed a very slight self-consciousness here. He must have been aware that he was walking on a thin crust over a chasm, for not a long time ago it had been argued in court (in a truly notorious case) that as a persistent debtor to the state Aristogeiton himself was not open to all the privileges of citizenship. The Accuser pressed on, rather hastily.

'Now, some may say that I, no meek or mealy-mouthed person, am a curious choice to lead the prosecution for impiety. Yet it is my own sense of piety that drives me to this measure. I am well known to you all, a plain speaker, and an advocate of a plain and serious way of life. Is it any wonder that I am offended by the meretricious defilement of our sacred city by a gaggle of impudent and luxurious courtesans? Is it any wonder that I am almost confounded by the deliberate impiety indulged in by this light-minded foreign woman? An impiety in which she has coaxed others to join her, calling a malediction upon Athens and all within the city.

'Some of us must make the effort to purge this poison, expel it from our midst. I come to you as one who is determined to rescue the city most dear to the goddess Athena. Is not our protectress the Virgin Goddess the most undeniably chaste of virgins?' Here he looked piously up at the Parthenon. 'I come to rescue Athens, a pure maiden, from the monstrous toils of vice and impiety. Our city is a hapless Andromeda, chained to the rock and at the mercy of the monster of destructive vice and baleful ungodliness. I am come to set her free. Even as my ancestor Aristogeiton the tyrant-killer struck a fatal blow to set Athens free. Surely the serpent of vice and the monster of impiety are better worth striking down, more worthy of eradication from the earth, than even a tyrant ruler himself? I am a plain man, simple and sincere, a man of few words, preferring deeds to words. It is my happy lot to come to you, sword in hand. Behold me striking at the serpent head of a tyrant which has our city in its thrall. See in me not the man you know, nor a man activated by any personal malice, but the liberator of our maiden city!'

'And then I woke up,' said a voice in the crowd.

This is an old piece of waggery, but it was extremely effective at this point. Ripples of laughter ran through the audience, including the jury of elders. Aristogeiton flushed, and began to realize he had better get away from the dear topic of himself.

'But – ahem – the nature of the case is – the centre of the – the issue is the well-being of Athens. This must be our primary concern. That well-being is deeply bound up with the proper observance of our religious rituals and festivals, and respect for our gods who have protected us so well. We do not recognize foreign gods, unless their worship has been officially approved by the government of Athens. The illicit or secret introduction of a new deity – or rather what is claimed to be so – is a distinct and terrifying offence rightly punishable by death. Phryne has introduced a new god at her own whim, a foreign thing which she has induced others to worship in celebratory procession. For this she deserves death.

'But she likewise deserves death for her mockery of the rites of Eleusis, a mockery which prepared for the installation of the unclean thing. Our great religion, the worship of Demeter and her Daughter at Eleusis, in the Mysteries of Eleusis, is at the core of Athens' prosperity. If offended, the Two Goddesses will withdraw their favour from Attika. The crops will fail, people will go hungry – hundreds, perhaps thousands will die. To save the future children of Athens, you must have no mercy on this vile woman.

'There is no doubt what ought to be the sentence of the court on any person who introduces new gods or profanes the Mysteries. The only question, the only matter to be determined, is this: Did this woman commit these acts? Let us go swiftly into this determination.

First, I call as witness the brothel-keeper Tryphaina. Her testimony has already been registered, and will be read.'

FIRST WITNESS FOR THE PROSECUTION: TRYPHAINA
Mantias read aloud from a short script :

'I Tryphaina, a freedwoman whose mother was once a slave to Pherekrates of Athens, attest that I am the keeper of a house of resort for purposes of entertainment and prostitution. I affirm that I have knowledge of the woman called "Phryne" who was at that house on the night in question, and did lead a revelry there. What went on I don't exactly know, I wasn't in that part of the house at the time. There was no unusual disturbance. I know that she called for wine (to be mixed with pure water) and barley bread, which she said she would pay for. She said to give equal shares to all. I believe she meant, give everybody some food. The woman called Phryne is very generous, well-bred and polite, and not likely to give trouble. Yes, Phryne is a woman who gives sex for hire, though she is very good-mannered. I don't know that she charges more than two drakhmai. Men give her presents, very expensive ones. She has sometimes hired a room herself in my brothel to entertain a man of her choice.

Tryphaina's testimony was thus produced as women, even freeborn, are, like children and slaves, lacking in honour and cannot serve as witnesses in open court. I thought the interrogators might have screwed some more damning statements from Tryphaina, but then, this brothel manager was probably under the protection of powerful people who did not wish her put out of business.

SECOND WITNESS FOR THE PROSECUTION:
GROUP OF SLAVES IN TRYPHAINA'S BROTHEL

A sheaf of testimony derived from questioning the slaves was quickly put in evidence. All of this testimony had been digested by Theramenes. While many of Tryphaina's girls, even under torture, had disclaimed any means of knowing what had been going on (one woman insisted she had been in the kitchen; another, that she was in the jakes, or in another room) there was enough to make it clear that Phryne had put ears of corn upon her head, had sipped a porridge made of wheat taken from the hand of a flute-girl called Thisbe, and spoken of herself in a kind of rhyme or song as the sorrowing Mother. One or two remembered the 'god of equal shares'. They acknowledged Phryne had also led a procession through the house, with music and torches.

'If we turn to the character of the accused,' said Aristogeiton with a grim smile, 'it is hardly necessary to bring more testimony to what nobody in their senses denies : the woman Mnesarete, known in streets and alleys as "Phryne", offers sexual favours of all kinds in return for money or gifts. The woman is a prostitute, simply. She should be given no more credit for her way of life than the commonest girl who makes her living lying on her back in some stinking alley-way, or urine-soaked corner of the city walls. For the deeds of this Phryne stink in the nostrils, regardless of how much Egyptian perfume she may apply.'

We all sniffed a little, as if trying to catch a waft of the scent that Phryne might be wearing.

'Not only is she of the basest profession but this woman is a foreigner, from Thespiai, a treacherous city which supported Makedon in the destruction of Thebes. Well might such a dirty creature want to put in a claim to all kind of good things by assuming the protection of a "God of Equal Shares". Such a foreign innovation might have led the common people to revolt or make untoward demands. Dangerous to think such thoughts, unhallowed, unsuited to Athens. For the deeds and words of that fatal evening, we have witnesses. I call upon the chief of these. Euboulos son of Xenophon, of the deme of Melite.'

The person thus summoned was the joking and slightly swaggering young man who had played such a significant part in the night of revelry at the brothel. He seemed more nervous now, and much more modest than merry. He was clean and neat, dressed in a pure white khiton, and looked altogether like a fine specimen of young Athenian manhood.

THIRD WITNESS FOR THE PROSECUTION:
EUBOULOS SON OF XENOPHON OF MELITE

'I saw Phryne at the brothel. I had come from a party at Arkhimedes' house, and we were laughing and joking. Yes, we had come as a *komos* – we danced through the streets to Tryphaina's house. We had all had a good deal to drink. I don't know if the woman Mnesarete had been drinking, or where she had come from that evening. Then Phryne – Mnesarete, that is – suddenly said that she was Demeter. Nobody could stop her when she started chanting one of the hymns to Demeter. And somebody in the kitchen gave her stalks of wheat to put around her head. No, I don't want to recite everything she said, in case it is impious of me. But she began a hymn – or it *sounded* like it – like this:

"I sorrowing Mother, I desolate Demeter seek—"
And towards the end she said,
  "Now I eat the *kykeion*,"
And she was eating a dish of gruel at the time – some slave's dinner which she made part of her play. And then she said, "I believe in the god of Equal Shares." And she led us in a procession— Yes, I was one, I didn't realize how wrong it was until next day. And there were torches and musicians playing all kinds of instruments.'

There was a grand indrawing of breath. This was bigger than many had supposed. The offence fully explained and confirmed by a citizen youth! Aristogeiton was triumphant.

'There – do you hear this? You all hear! You *see*, men of Athens! This is no minor scrape, no little infringement, no scamping of a prayer or so. This is deliberate and awe-inspiring mockery of the most sacred moments of our holy ritual of Eleusis! An enactment – a travesty. To wean them from our great religion to her own foreign god! Impieties uttered in the ears of our young people, corrupting them in an unauthorized and illicit worship in which they then participated. What shame to our great city! What more is there to say? But lest you think the word of this young man of good blood and fine demeanour does not suffice, I call for other accounts.'

Theramenes had not been idle. He had found

another citizen youth to act as a witness. This was a young gentleman named Kalippos, who nervously added some details of his own.

FOURTH WITNESS FOR THE PROSECUTION:
KALIPPOS OF PAIANIA

'Yes, I was there, and I heard Phryne — I only just found out that her real name is Mnesarete — singing or chanting this hymn-song to Demeter. It was public; there were many people present at the time: slaves, like the flute-girls and some of the whores, and a lot of harlot freedwomen. And of course customers and people drinking like Euboulos and myself. Yes, I drank rather a lot. I think Phryne had come from a symposium. I am from a country deme and I know few people in Athens. The young men looked like citizens or citizens' sons. There was a rather silly-looking soldier of Makedon with a green wreath over his eye. I don't know who he was. Somebody said he had been wounded by a spear in the wars, I remember that. I remember Euboulos asking should he dance the *kordax*, and Phryne making some silly joke or other. Phryne did as Euboulos has said. Yes, this performance she did as a show for a roomful of people. And she said "I eat the *kykeion*" and took a sup of the porridge in a bowl. And then she said something about "Equal Shares for all" and we had drinks and danced and she led us in a procession round the house by torchlight.'

'There!' said Aristogeiton, triumphant. 'No more needs to be demonstrated. The matter is plain. For what happens in the Mysteries? The hymn to Demeter is sung. And at an important part of the ceremony the *mystai* drink the *kykeion*, the mixture of grains and herbs sacred to the goddess. These observances were founded by the great Demeter herself, and are never to be defiled. This woman of Thespiai is certainly guilty. Mnesarete has mocked the Mysteries, made a travesty of them, just prior to introducing her foreign god and having him followed by men and women in religious procession. She must and shall pay the full penalty.'

Having brought his case off with great effect, Aristogeiton sat down, savouring the plaudits of a crowd certainly deeply impressed.

Not everybody was well-disposed, however. 'Hah!' said my chatty neighbour. 'He had to sit down, the water-clock is almost out. He'll save the big bag of wind for the second speech. That's what they all do.'

Whether Aristogeiton were a sympathetic personality or no, whether he had more rhetoric to spend or not, there was no denying that he had created an impressive case, not only flourishing in oratory but also substantial in evidence. His audience, taken by surprise by the vivid tableau of impiety presented by the witnesses, was disposed to be convinced, even if some might accept conviction with reluctance.

Hypereides' task in his first speech was undoubtedly a hard one. He could hardly bring in evidence in the shape of witnesses to demonstrate that Phryne had *not* done what she had done. He had to change their perception of what had happened, and of Phryne herself. Hypereides' face showed the pull of anxiety, skin stretched taut over his cheekbones. Though the orator tried to summon up his usual good-humoured smile and easy style of address, we all could see that these attributes were not natural, but cost him an effort. His voice too seemed strained, his bearing stiff. But he started off with firmness and energy.

HYPEREIDES: FIRST SPEECH FOR THE DEFENCE OF PHRYNE

'Men of Athens, I am astonished to hear my opponent claim that he is an expert in all matters pertaining to citizenship and good citizenship. For his own dutifulness has often been called into question. Not only so, but his citizenship has been in doubt – debated in public court, as many here well remember. Born indebted, Aristogeiton has done his best to shift his burden of debt to the state so that he can go about his business like a normal citizen, even when he is mortgaged up to his chin. Moreover, he has made others assume the name of debtor in his place so he could keep on appearing in law courts, as he loves to do. No man was ever more insistent on going to law – and no man more often in the wrong! I know you are too wise to be confused by him when he claims this woman is not an Athenian and shouldn't be in this court, yet insists a big trial before the Areopagos is legal. Does Aristogeiton himself not heartily enjoy playing a leading part in a trial before the Areopagos? And does Aristogeiton not care whom he catches in his toils – as long as he can have the enjoyment of bellowing out big speeches?

'You have heard Aristogeiton proclaim how averse

he is to bad women. One would think he had run into a great many bad women, at the rate he goes on. Perhaps that is so. Is it not true, O Aristogeiton, that once, and not so long ago, you were closely associated with that truly memorable female, Theoris of Lemnos? Her maidservant was put to death for sorcery and poisoning, and Theoris herself was tried for impiety, Demosthenes prosecuting. At one time, however, Aristogeiton and his brother were well affected not only to Theoris – reputedly a woman very generous with her favours – but also to her guilty servant, the reciter of spells. These men were purchasing charms and drugs from both the Lemnian women. Some say this was in order to do away with accusers or rivals. Aristogeiton's detestation of women of bad character seems of recent date. Perhaps he was bitten by experience of much greater evil in womankind than can be found in the brothel of Tryphaina.

'Nobody denies that the woman named Mnesarete daughter of Epikles – better known to many simply as "Phryne" – is a person who lives by the money men give her. And those men who give her gifts often receive sexual favours from her. Nobody denies that Phryne was in Tryphaina's brothel and that an evening's entertainment there turned slightly rowdy as a revel got under way. But revels are a normal part of Athenian life, like drunkenness and flute-girls. Let the art of our vases painted in generations past bear witness that what pleased our forefathers still pleases ourselves.

'The matter at hand is – what did she do at Tryphaina's brothel on a particular night, not long ago? And how, if at all, does it come to be associated with "impiety"? First, let it be clear that we are not at all clear about what did or did not happen. We may agree that there *was* a party at Tryphaina's house. The fact that there was a party does not mean we can be at all confident of knowing what took place there, or even who was present. The brothel inmates from whom you have heard are either whores – many of whom were in the upstairs regions – or hard-worked kitchen slaves who had only a partial view, or were not in the room at all. The many revellers of whom you have heard have shrunk into only two. These two young men who so gallantly testified for Aristogeiton, Euboulos and Kalippos, admit they were very drunk at the time. This is a poor basis for any allegations.

'And *what* is alleged? All that is told amounts to this: Phryne sang a song, she took a sip of porridge. Anybody can sing a song – anybody may sip or spoon up gruel or porridge whenever they like. No injury is done to anybody. Then Phryne made offer of wine and bread – only barley bread – for everybody who wanted it. She said jokingly that everybody should have an equal share. You hear this from the evidence of Tryphaina, called by the Accuser as witness. As Phryne offered her friends the bread, and the wine mixed with water, all to be paid for at her own expense, she told the manager of the brothel to give everyone an equal share. Then she employed the term often used of the great and beloved god Dionysos, the "Equal Divider". Dionysos is certainly not an unknown or new god in Athens! Some of our friends seem to take fright at the phrase – perhaps thinking that a political meaning is intended. In their fantasy they see thousands come to grab their fat lands, instead of one woman in a brothel one evening, with men grabbing at her.

'Phryne is merely a woman. On that occasion, she was trying to do a kindly act. A woman being hospitable, enjoying giving food to people. A womanly and natural thing to do. After that, the brothel party danced as such drunken groups do dance. And if you're moving around at night, lamps or torches are necessary, but torches give better light and keep one from stumbling. A silly and harmless party. A drinking revel, such as most of the members of this court have been to after a symposium. That Mnesarete, better known as Phryne, offered to introduce a new god that evening is laughable – patently false.

'What else is said against her? That she profaned the worship of Demeter. Our problem here is partly one of definition. How can the worship of Demeter be profaned? Why, comes the answer, "in mockery of the Mysteries of Eleusis". What are these Mysteries? Nobody who has not been a *mystes* can know. A person who has been initiated cannot speak of what he or she has experienced and seen. I shall ask the accused to indicate by a sign an answer to this question – with permission—'

The Arkhon nodded, and Hypereides turned towards the muffled black shape that was Phryne.

'I ask you, Mnesarete daughter of Epikles, have you been initiated into the mysteries at Eleusis?'

Modestly murmuring a negative, the black shape also made a vigorous sign for 'No'.

'The accused is clear on the fact that she has never been an initiate. Now, this must indeed be true, for had she been enrolled as a *mystes* the priests and Guardians of the Mysteries would have a record of it. And that has never been alleged.' He looked directly and even defiantly at Eurymedon. 'So – we are on safe ground when we say that this woman, daughter of Epikles, has *not* been an initiate. You remember that our great dramatist Aiskhylos, when rebuked for giving away some of the secret rites and mysteries in one of his plays, replied, "Oh! I didn't know they were secret."' [*Laughter*] 'Had the tragic poet been an initiate, his reply might seem feeble. But it became clear he had *not* been an initiate, so he was acquitted. Aiskhylos would have known only what everyone knows – what it is *permitted* to know – about the procession, and the celebrations. We all see many images that pertain – or could be made to pertain – to the Mysteries. A bowl, a torch – these are not secrets. An ear of corn is often produced in monuments and paintings, sometimes merely as ornament. Now, admittedly, there are indeed clear allusions to the religion of Eleusis in the plays of Aiskhylos, citizen of Athens and author of greatly honoured tragedies. Yet we did not persecute our great Athenian who wrote such beautiful plays to honour Dionysos. Neither did we prosecute Aristophanes the dramatist, though he has drawn further upon material of Eleusis. And not even for tragic but for comic purposes – in *The Frogs*, to take just one very noticeable example.

'Not being an initiate in the rites of Eleusis, then, *how* can Phryne profane or even truly mimic them? Men of Athens, *it is impossible to profane what one does not know.* Neither has she been guilty of divulging material that must remain secret. Even the accuser's allegation cannot really say that she told any secrets. All this woman could know of what goes on at Eleusis is what everybody knows – in short, it is the common knowledge and bruit, the public side of the Mysteries. So, even if she said what is alleged, her position is in this respect like that of Aiskhylos and Aristophanes – she has referred merely to the elements of the Mysteries that are common knowledge, and has not profaned them, nor revealed any of the secrets of Eleusis.

'There is no necessary relation between her alleged action and impiety. She offered her acquaintance gathered there a light meal at her own expense, in which all present, slave and free, could have an equal portion. It is on record that this woman, the daughter of Epikles, has attended temples, made sacrifices, paid heed to public days and honoured the gods of Athens. A trifle of harmless and foolish sport in one evening does not amount to any assault upon the divine, or upon the Mysteries. It is part of the greatness of Athens that it does not turn the power of the state against individuals to gratify private malice. Nor does it turn our great religion, so universally acknowledged in its ability to nourish and console, into a weapon of offence. This case should never have been brought. I ask the arkhons in their good judgement to dismiss it and free the poor woman.'

Having come to a good stopping-point, Hypereides stopped, mopped his brow, and sat down.

What Hypereides said was indeed rational. Yet I could feel that he was not making the good impression he usually contrived to make. His assault upon the character of Aristogeiton had not gone over well on this particular occasion, although usually Athenians savour such attacks. And his rational argument seemed even to disappoint an audience expecting a more exciting dispute. I caught even myself thinking that Hypereides might actually have been better off had he argued something truly preposterous – for instance, that it wasn't the real Phryne who was there that night, for she had been spirited away, but someone else acting in her stead. Hypereides needed to supply the jurymen with some justifying excuse for contradicting and displeasing not only Aristogeiton but Euthias and the powerful and pious Eurymedon. Had Hypereides really given his jury what he – and they – so badly needed? I was certain he had not. Hypereides himself looked strained. While he was speaking, I had noticed for the first time signs of age, not only in his face but in the greying of his hair.

The weakness of Hypereides was sensed by Aristogeiton, who was pawing the ground in impatience to get to the *bema* and begin his second speech. He was sure that he could nail his opponent to the earth; we all sensed this as he strode up and delivered his rebuttal.

ARISTOGEITON: SECOND SPEECH FOR
THE PROSECUTION OF PHRYNE

'The noble Hypereides, men of Athens, has stooped to personal attack upon me. I cannot stop to speak against that nonsense, point by point, yet I cannot stand here patiently being slandered by him and not defend myself. I am a citizen of Athens, and a lover of my city. This patriotism has been offensive to some who were not so staunch. A group of despicable persons, enemies, once conspired against me to rob me of my most valued, even sacred, possession – my citizenship and rights as a full citizen. You all *know* they have not been successful. Now, it is my patriotism that stands between Athens and disaster. You must rely on my patriotism to defend Athens, and to speak out against the iniquity.

'When we sift from Hypereides' speech the vulgar elements of personal abuse, all that my opponent has said amounts merely to this: that a person who offers free drinks cannot do so in an impious manner, and that a person who has not been an initiate cannot ridicule the Mysteries. That argument is weak and irrational on the face of it. It is true that many people have heard something of the Mysteries – and, I agree, partly through the indiscretions of poets. But think of this. Suppose you were to argue that a spy could not tell – would not be able to tell – a foreign ruler where an Athenian naval warship was unless he had been on that warship as a member of its crew? Absurd, is it not? It is equally absurd to argue that only an initiate could profane the Mysteries. The essence of the charge is not that this woman, this harlot Phryne, has revealed the secrets of the Mysteries, but that she *profaned* and *mocked* them. That she certainly did. She had grain stalks in her hair, ears of wheat, and she said she was Demeter. By the gods! It horrifies me even to speak these words! And she mocked the holy *kykeion* by taking a bowl of a slave's pottage and pretending that it was the food of the goddess and her initiates. What worse did we have to say against Alkibiades?

'Yet this accused, this woman, is not a valuable person. She gives nothing of worth to our city, as did the dramatists Aiskhylos and Aristophanes, or even Alkibiades, who with all his faults was a brilliant general. This creature is one of the lowest of the low – woman who gives sex for money. A cloacal pit of semen, as dignified as a latrine. Though not a woman of Athens, this Boiotian Mnesarete, or "Phryne", is a sewer of Athens. Or rather, let me say, a toad in a sewer, an obscene toad in a damp secret tunnel, sitting on excrement, whatever jewels she may bear on her forehead. This female who stands cowering before you is not a decent woman. She may be a clever one. So clever she thought herself as to be above the law! In public she introduced a foreign unknown god, after mocking the religion of Athens. In public – with foreigners present, like the Makedonian soldier of whom you have heard, his drunken stupid head wreathed in triumph! The dirtiest bird fouls its own nest. Let us give a clear warning to all Athenians and all who come to us to partake in the Mysteries that we tolerate no loose play with our religion. Let us state this clearly in the face of the world, before gods and men. We do not permit prostitutes to put us in danger of the wrath of the gods by foully polluting our city.' There was a little more in that vein, and some more high-coloured abuse of Phryne in partic-ular, and her cohorts and their way of life. But

Aristogeiton worked briskly and strongly towards his conclusion, which was most effective.

'When you think of it, men of Athens, this crime of Phryne is like a murder. No! This is *worse* than murder! For a murderer, a vile person, kills one human being, and must suffer for it. A truly impious person, with no reverence for the sacred but rather with a design to defy it, endangers a whole city – puts thousands into the risk of their lives! She has denied the gods and foisted in some foul and dirty bird of her own raising in the place of the gods of Athens, leading young and foolish persons to join her. Mnesarete prepared her foolish young folk to forsake the gods to whom worship is due by a travesty of the rites of Eleusis. Were Demeter to take heed of this offensive action on Phryne's part, the priests and leaders of her religion tell us, the goddess could desert the city. Demeter offended could quickly bring famine upon Attika. Surely to invoke this destruction is a worse crime even than killing one citizen! I have clearly demonstrated that Phryne is impious, having led most shameless revels to introduce a new god and holding illicit religious celebration within the same house wherein she also profaned the Mysteries. I ask you, men of Athens who love Athens and her prosperity, go home and look your wives and children in the eye and tell them you have spared the city from such evil by judging this harlot guilty and dealing with her as she deserves.'

I knew then it was all over with Phryne. The only question could be – would she die by hemlock or by being nailed to the tympanon? I read boards and hammers in the eye of Aristogeiton and his fellows.

In this hopeless condition of things, the tired and defeated Hypereides rose to speak his last speech.

HYPEREIDES: SECOND SPEECH FOR THE DEFENCE OF PHRYNE

'Men of Athens, I – I cannot know what to say after such a cruel ending. It is hard to speak.' He stopped and swallowed. 'There are those who think they know how to read the mind of the gods, and that the gods will be pleased by the killing of an innocent woman.' Hypereides looked up at the sky for a moment, as if searching the heavens for inspiration. It had stopped drizzling and blowing, and the clouds, separated, were blowing swiftly across the sky. He shook himself, as if he were about to plunge into the sea. Then, having made a decision, he turned to us.

'What pleases the gods, gentlemen? Is it cruelty and destructiveness? Is it killing people on a trumped-up charge that is delightful to them? I do not believe that Aristogeiton realizes to the full what he is proposing. I ask that the accused woman be allowed to approach where all can see her.'

And he nodded to the soldiery, who formally brought black-draped Phryne close up to him where he stood on the *bema*.

'Look!' he ordered. And he approached the woman. 'Look! – but the trouble is you cannot *see*!' And with his own hands, he abruptly threw off her veil. Phryne's lovely face appeared, and her hair, parted in the middle and pulled back from her brow, her glowing locks

braided and coiffed in the back. The hair and head of
a free woman, certainly not a slave.

'*This* is the woman!' cried Hypereides. 'Behold her!
The woman you wish to condemn on the strength of
a peevish conspiracy against her. Even if she used the
phrase "the Equal Divider", it is untrue that Isodaites
is a foreign god, as this term is used of Dionysos,
whom we all love and honour. Ridiculous charges have
been made, on the slight basis of a brothel party, with
terrified slaves' evidence – really slight – and the
evidence of citizen witnesses scraped up by the zealous prosecutors – witnesses who were quite drunk at
the time. A conspiracy of those who are using her as
an easy but famous target in order to cause trouble
in Athens – and to begin a reign of tyranny, a time
when they may choose whatever victim they please
and cite him or her for vague offences. Look again, I
say, at the real woman!'

Some or most of the jury did indeed turn their
heads and bend their gaze upon Phryne. The clouds
clearing, a watery light had succeeded, which made
the act of vision easier than it might have been. A few
sober men looked away, ostentatiously. I thought the
Basileus would speak – and so did Hypereides.
Evidently afraid that he would be forbidden to do what
he had determined to do, he laid hold on Phryne's
garments once more.

'And look – *here!*' He tore open the fastenings of
the front of her cloak, tearing it off and with the same
lightning movement rending her fine linen dress.
Under the thick cloak Phryne was wearing nothing
more than this light dress, not even a breast-band.

Her beautiful bosom was at once laid bare. The rest of her clothing, torn and rent apart, fell slowly to the ground, revealing more and more of her perfect body as he spoke, so it was like seeing a divine wonder come into being. She looked indeed like an Aphrodite, arising from the waves formed by the folds of the garments, black cloak and foam-white dress, that fell from her thighs to her knees, and then from her knees to her feet. Like a peeled willow wand, the bark curling back from its whiteness, or like a spring bud escaping from its green covering, Phryne, entirely naked and divinely shaped, was in the midst of us. Not gold, not bronze, but flesh and blood in the most beautiful of moulding.

'Look there!' cried Hypereides. 'Look upon the beauty which has been vouchsafed to us!' His voice cracked. A thin ray of sunshine came down to the empty space and touched Phryne, so all could see her clearly – a striking moment and a thrilling sight.

'I tell you what is impiety!' cried Hypereides. 'It is impiety to destroy this beauty, this wonder, for peevishness and civic spite!' His voice cracked again and tears rolled down his cheeks.

'I ask you all – as earnestly as I could ask anything of man or gods, including my own life! – I ask you all to spare this lovely woman. See how sweet she is, how beautiful, how graceful and gracious. She stands here before you not as a person shamed but as a goddess vindicated. Lo! Here is a sign and here is a wonder. The goddess Aphrodite has given Athens this great gift. Aphrodite has caused her own qualities to be realized and incarnate in this beautiful being who dwells among us. And you are about to say to Aphrodite, "No, no, take back your gift! We despise it, we trample on it! We will not only do without it but we are determined to destroy it."

'Why, oh why, men of Athens, do you wish to offer the goddess Aphrodite such an outstanding insult? Aphrodite has never injured us. No, she has been helpful always, blessing not only our vegetable gardens but also, most centrally, the genial bed where man and woman lie. It is Aphrodite who has bestowed upon us the blessing of steady procreation. Generation upon generation, the race of Athenians has not faded from the earth. Strong and beautiful people are born to us by her divine help. We have soldiers for the field, and reapers for the grain. Aphrodite's own husband dwells with us and teaches us the making of instruments of skill and ornament. We go to the goddess' temple and make sacrifices of doves and incense, offering her thanks for betrothals, for weddings, for the birth of fine children. We pray individually to her for lovers, for husbands or wives, for children. And for love, for *Love*—' Hypereides was talking almost wildly now, his arms flailing, and tears coursing down his face. 'For Love which we are going to kill and put away in the dark grave for ever and ever – to deny the pleasures of the bed, the tenderness that ought to exist between man and woman!' He wiped away his tears, and continued.

'For love that moves the universe. Eros who was before other things. With bright Erato we sing songs in praise of love and fulfilment, of beauty and desire. Aphrodite provides all this for us – and Athenians

wish to spit in her face? Not for any true love to
Demeter, who in harmony with Aphrodite gives us
food and sustenance. But out of spite, malice and pique,
for fear — fear of I know not what. Should we not
rather fear that Aphrodite will turn her head away,
and deny the pleasures of the bed and the gift of prog-
eny to citizens of Athens who have so insulted her?
Aphrodite might perhaps cause the genial powers to
fail. How horrible it would be if each man were to find
his member incapable of doing as he wishes. Only those
impotent men already settled to their unexciting fate
can think of insulting Aphrodite with perfect peace of
mind. How can you face going to your grave without
children? Do you wish to spite the goddess by lying
always alone? Or do you fear that as a punishment
upon you?

'Men of Athens, as you see I can hardly speak, I am
so greatly moved. And moved afresh at the sight of
this glorious beauty which we are about to insult and
throw away. How — how can we do such a thing? It
is not like a true Athenian! What would you say if you
saw a man go towards a beautiful marble image — an
image of the goddess indeed — with an iron pick, about
to hack deep holes in it? Or, if you saw him going up
to a bronze statue with a sharp awl and watched him
scrawling lines and gouges in it, so that the loveliness
was quite destroyed! You would think of such a man
as a madman. If you saw him approaching the lovely
image with his pick or awl, you would endeavour to
wrest the weapon from his sacrilegious hand. Is this
not so? How much more, then, ought we to prevent
this act of wanton destruction, and spare beauty.

'If we do as Aristogeiton wills, we shame ourselves and insult the goddess Demeter and the goddess Aphrodite together. A strange and horrible thought, to offend the divine Giver of love and laughter. I ask you for the sake of pity, for Justice, for the love of Beauty, and for the honour of Aphrodite, that we declare – as in reason we ought – that this woman shall go free! Let the glowing work of the goddess in its perfection remain undamaged by us, and let us give thanks for it to the gods!'

By this time, the jury as well as the rest of the audience were in an uproar. Some were yelling at the speaker that what he was doing was outrageous, but more were craning their necks to look at the naked woman, even while listening with all their ears. Some among the audience, even many among the jury of sober ex-arkhons, were changing seats and climbing over others to get a better look. Phryne stood there, naked in the cool autumn sunlight that fell around her, as quiet as a statue (though those who were nearest said later that she trembled slightly). Even among the viewers most eager to look there was a sense of awe, as if they were looking at a divine manifestation.

Hypereides ceased speaking, but did not sit down. Aristogeiton and Euthias were sputtering and expostulating. A few – notably Eurymedon and Theramenes – were shouting curses at Hypereides and at the woman, while others told them to stop. The Basileus could scarcely quieten the jury long enough to put the formal question. The votes came instantly, of course – and the votes for acquittal were a great majority. Only a few hardy spirits (not necessarily the oldest, either) had withstood the charm of beauty, the awe of the goddess, or their own rising sense of pity.

As soon as it was clear that Phryne was acquitted and was not sentenced to death, the turmoil grew louder and more complicated. For now, some of the jury, not content with giving their verdict alone, ran over to congratulate her personally. With charming graciousness, Phryne, still naked, spoke a low word to each one. The men were surprisingly decent, not laying a hand on her even when they were close to her bare and shining body, but a few she touched on the hand or gave some other sign of respect and affection, if they seemed to wish it. Her female companion rushed out into the field, with no one to say her nay, and started to rearrange the lovely woman's attire, throwing a cloak over her. But Phryne would not leave until she had spoken to each man who wished to speak to her. Then, at the end, she looked at Hypereides, who by now sat exhausted on the edge of the platform, sponging off his face. They did not touch or embrace. But a long look, an extraordinary look quite as substantial and compelling as an embrace, passed between these two – and then Phryne departed. The goddess was gone, and Athens was saved from insult to Aphrodite.

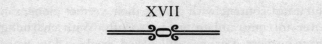

XVII

Statues and Dolls

Naturally, there was a great outburst at the end of this trial. While the arkhons were congratulating Phryne, other citizens were shouting and calling, standing on tiptoe or jumping to get a good glimpse of her, especially those denied perfect vision at the striking moment of revelation. Commentaries and exclamations were not lacking. Most expressed a sense of relief, even pleasure.

'It's like a good tragedy, where you fear the hero will die, and you're on the edge of your seat, and then at the very end there is a rescue. It's like the tragedy of Alkestis, brought back from Hades,' I heard one man say.

'Well,' said another, with some satisfaction, 'I don't know if they've finished the official count yet, but I would bet my best mule that Aristogeiton and Euthias did not get one-fifth of the votes for their side!'

'They'll have to pay a fine, then,' another rejoined. 'Aristogeiton never has any money, he's in debt already.

What fun they will have, trying to squeeze money out of him!'

An old man being led along the sloping path by his son raised his aged voice in querulous complaint.

'I told you, boy – I *told* you – we should have come earlier. We were too far back! And – oh, these eyes of mine, my poor old eyes! If only I could have my young eyes back again.'

Yet nobody who was there that day, even the aged fellow with the poor eyesight, could say it was not worth it.

Phryne's salvation did not please everybody, however. Predictably, Aristogeiton, Eurymedon and Euthias were enraged, Aristogeiton bellowing his rage so he might have been heard all over the city. 'That *dog* Hypereides! A dog's trick, dropping his shit in a sacred space! Bringing the brothel to the law court – insulting the Areopagos. Degradation of Athens – I'll be even with him, I can promise that!'

Those arkhons who had been staunch enough to vote for condemnation, withstanding the pleas of Hypereides and the vision of beauty, were greatly incensed, and so were some common citizens. Ergokles, who had taken a place of vantage at the front of the crowd, registered his loud displeasure within the hearing of both Phryne and Hypereides.

'Nothing but a sham!' he declared. 'An outrage!' Ergokles turned to Theramenes for support and vindication.

'Disgusting, it should not have been allowed,' Theramenes heartily agreed.

'I have lost money on a wager on this trial,' Ergokles

announced peevishly. 'And so has Krito. Pity, for that is really *my* money you're wasting, Krito. The funds you and Hermia owe me. It's true, isn't it?' turning to Philinos for corroboration. 'I hope *you* haven't lost money too, Philinos, in wagering on the outcome.'

Philinos said nothing but looked amused; Theramenes, taken aback, protested, 'Surely no true man of Athens would cast frivolous wagers on something so important! As serious as a trial at the Areopagos!'

'Though how *serious* it was today is an open question,' another added with disgust. 'All those prostitutes should be considered slaves. Hetaira or alley-crawler, treat 'em alike.'

'Exactly,' said Theramenes. 'Though they're slippery to deal with. You'll find even the lowest slave-girl, if she's good-looking, may know a thing or two.'

Ergokles laughed. 'A true word,' he remarked, in his always too-loud tone. 'Isn't that so, Philinos? Many a lovely slave knows a thing or two. And now because of wagering against this terrible Phryne, I am low on cash. And yet I *need* money. I need money to buy me a slave – even if she's not lovely.'

Philinos drew away from this crass fellow, but Ergokles moved a little closer to Philinos and Krito, repeating, 'Just to buy me a slave – just *one*.'

'Don't waste your money on female slaves. Go to the brothels for your needs,' one sour citizen advised. 'Brothels have less folly and low cunning than our performance today.'

'You must,' said Ergokles, 'no, *we* must make sure there is nothing of the same mummery in the case of Hermia. No hoaxing and coaxing! Let that next trial be a *real* trial of a murderess, and prove that the citizens of Athens are men.'

Ergokles was not the only man to express such an opinion.

'Disgraceful! Such a display should never be allowed,' said one tall man with a commanding presence of his own. 'That Hypereides – he has outdone himself. The vulgarity!'

'Shameful! Crying in public and talking about love!' agreed another man, scowling ferociously. 'Such nonsense will give Athens a bad name.'

'Must talk with Lykourgos about this,' the tall citizen insisted. 'We shall get a proposal up for the next Ekklesia and make sure that such a ridiculous exhibition is never again allowed. We must make a new law: *No pleader is to display personal emotion.* Weeping and crying – not to say bellowing and blubbering – ought to disqualify any pleader from speaking further. And permit no man to be related by sexual tie to someone for whom he pleads.'

'Can we rule that a husband must not plead for his wife?' his friend asked dubiously. 'That might be difficult – a man being his wife's natural defender.'

'Well, we can rule out keepers of concubines and patrons of whores, perhaps.'

'We must also ensure,' insisted another man joining them, 'that the dignity of Athens is insulted no more in that outrageous way! As if the court of the Areopagos were a public bath! Assuredly, we shall make a law: *Absolutely no person who is party to a trial is permitted to undress!*'

While these opinions were being exchanged, we

were slowly descending from the Areopagos towards the agora by the Eleusinian Way, the first sloping part of the road that leads worshippers (going in the reverse direction) to the holy site of Eleusis. As we passed by Athens' own temple of Demeter and her Daughter, I glanced in at the great and graceful image. The goddess herself looked so kind and bountiful that I found myself wondering how a mother so gentle, so good and so generous to mankind, could be so eager to punish and demand blood. Demeter herself had suffered so much in the loss of her child. Why should she wish others to suffer a like grief? But doubtless Eurymedon and his fellows had good answers to this.

When we arrived at the foot of the hill and entered the agora, we found everyone abuzz with the news of the case, down to the very lowest sellers of greens and bread. Hungry after the morning's events, a number of us stopped by these stalls, and by the bread-selling women hunched over their ovens, who were doing a fine trade today. Little gaggles of prostitutes clustered together, rejoicing in the fact that Phryne was saved. Their tone was of course very different from that of the discontented men thinking up new laws.

'Thanks be to Aphrodite!' was a general exclamation. 'I have promised the dear goddess a special piece of jewellery if she would save Phryne,' one girl said. 'And now I shall give her the very best! For the goddess has splendidly displayed her own beauty and power to all.'

'I was at prayers this morning, too,' said another, whom I recognized as one of the women at Tryphaina's party. 'Phryne herself has been *so* splen-

did in not talking about other people. Always generous and kind. Now the gods have delivered her! Thanks
be to Demeter and Kore! Thanks be to Aphrodite and
Eros!'

'Eros – yes,' said an elderly man with an almost juve-
nile enthusiasm. His handsome and yet unlined face
shone, as if he, like the worshipping women, had recently
had contact with the goddess of beauty and joy.

'I have had a vision and revelation,' this man
announced to his friend, as they stopped by a stall
near us for a nuncheon of bread and olives. 'The other
female figures I have done have all been clothed. That
image that the fool goldsmith has choked with gold –
even that is nothing, *nothing*, to what I shall now do.
If my life is spared long enough to fulfil the vision in
my mind, I shall create a wonder. Now I shall make
a new sculpture, *entirely* new, in honour of Phryne. I
shall create a statue in the most perfect marble, based
on Phryne herself. The goddess Aphrodite – naked.'

'Oh, Praxitiles,' his friend protested through a
mouthful of flat bread, 'Athenians would *never* buy a
statue that did such dishonour to the goddess.'

'Not dishonour, but the greatest honour. The greatest beauty displayed to the full. And I think I could
find purchasers. The liberated Greek cities on the coast
of Asia are all getting richer, and desire works of
Athenian art. Kos has a temple that needs a statue.'

'*Naked!*' a quite different man was snorting to his
companion, as they both stood by a leather shop.
'Displaying the female naked – like an animal or a
female barbarian! A naked woman in the midst of an
Athenian assembly – the shame!'

'Yes,' his companion agreed, fingering the sole of a leather sandal. 'An indecency. She ought perhaps to be punished for it. Well slippered.'

'I thought I should have died of shock,' asserted the first snorting protester, 'absolutely *died* of shock when Phryne bared her bosom – *both* breasts fully presented – for all to stare at in the light of day!'

'And her buttocks too,' his friend added. 'I hope you got a good look at her posterior. Most charming! Utter elegance!'

'This case,' said a heavy-set authoritative citizen, now joining them, 'this case of Phryne makes Athens a laughing-stock. And for what, I ask you?' The heavy-set man threw his open hands wide in a gesture of bitter astonishment. 'For what? A set of holes for sale! Hypereides snivelling – dripping tears on his grey beard – over a whore! Repulsive! This disgusting miscarriage of justice makes it all the more necessary that Hermia the poisoning widow of Orthoboulos be properly sentenced. By Zeus, we cannot lose our reason and go soft on all women! We must make sure she does not get off.'

'But,' objected Theophrastos, who was coming to join us, 'that seems hardly reasonable, unless the two cases were connected.'

'Who asked *you?*' said the heavy-set citizen, glowering at the interloper. 'I don't know as you deserve an answer, but I will give you one – because Hermia is another bad woman.'

'Besides,' added a man with a large black beard, 'you must know that Hermia, like her first husband, is a supporter of the Makedonian enemy.'

'But Phryne herself is not particularly in favour of the Makedonians,' said Theophrastos, smiling.

'She is a wretched Thespian. All Thespians alike are snakes. They live among their flat vegetable gardens, and envy bigger cities. The people of Thespiai joined with Alexander to attack Thebes. And, I repeat, who asked *you*?'

The heavy-set man elbowed his friend, saying, 'Beware. Lots of Makedonians about,' glancing at Aristotle. Theophrastos shrugged and came to join us.

'So much passion,' he remarked. Then he looked at Aristotle, rather severely.

'Did you, O Aristotle of Stageira, advise Hypereides to commit that act – to exhibit the naked girl?'

'I shall not trouble to deny it. The occasion seemed to call for strong measures.'

'Like a mere rhetorician, you encouraged the man to weep and spout in that fashion? O Aristotle – I can hardly believe it. You have betrayed Reason. You who have taught us to despise being "swayed by claptrap and emotion" – as you have said yourself. Who could expect to see you a pander to emotional display, the love of sensation, the ejection of all logic? Total shame-lessness – against all the principles of Athens' consti-tution! I could not be more amazed.'

Aristotle, though he looked serious, made no pres-ent reply. We hazarded no more comments about the case, being surrounded (as Theophrastos belatedly realized) by overhearers. I volunteered to walk part way to the Lykeion with Aristotle and Theophrastos; it would be good to have a little walk after standing still for so long. Besides, it seemed better to keep a

third party between the two friends while
Theophrastos was in this censorious humour.

Just before we went through the city walls at the
Diokhares Gate, we encountered a man – or rather he
encountered us. He seemed to have been hurrying to
speak with us; being elderly, he was out of breath. This
was not a friend of mine, nor, I thought, of Aristotle's.
Yet there was something familiar about him. The aged
lines, the tired look, the pallor, the rigid expression
the miserable wear when they are putting a brave face
on things . . . Yes, now I certainly recognized him.
Hermia's uncle, Phanodemos.

'Ah, sir!' he said. 'Ah, sir!'

'Yes?' said Aristotle kindly. 'Do take time to catch
your breath. But when you have done so, will you walk
a little way with us?'

'No time,' said the man, still panting a little. He
nudged Aristotle and indicated that he wanted to move
to a quiet corner, an angle of the wall near the gate.
Such corners are, as had been pointed out by
Aristogeiton today, usually dirty and foul-smelling, but
some privacy could be afforded by this coign. And if
Theophrastos and I stood on the outside of Phanodemos
and Aristotle, these two could have a conversation without being overheard by chance passers-by.

'You are wise, O Aristotle,' said Phanodemos. 'I hear
– never mind how – that your words brought Phryne
back to life.'

'Your kind courtesy makes you exaggerate,' said
Aristotle. 'It was Hypereides who did it. Not to
mention Phryne herself.'

'Help *us*, please,' Phanodemos begged. 'Help us in

any way you can. I don't know what to do. I was once respected,' he added bitterly. 'The People honoured me. Gave me a gold crown because of my knowledge of religious law and customs. I have worked always for Athens and Attika. In giving religious donations, especially for the Sanctuary of Amphiaros. In writing my big *History*.'

'You have long been a benefactor to Athens,' said Aristotle. 'Everyone knows it.'

'People looked up to me formerly, Lykourgos delighted to honour me. Now old friends drop off. Nay, we are hooted at in the streets! All the expense of keeping Hermia and paying for the guards and so on is borne by me — as well as sacrifices to atone for our mistake in entering the agora. Meanwhile, people won't even pay me what they owe. Perhaps they think I myself will be under sentence and they will never have to pay! I ask your help not only for Hermia herself, but also for myself, for my own wife and our family. I fear we shall all be in danger if Hermia goes under. Kleiophon's disappearance makes everything much worse.'

'I see that,' said Aristotle sympathetically.

'People wildly imagine what might have happened to the lad, and throw the blame on his stepmother — oh, for all sorts of things. You'd think she'd boiled him in oil and eaten the bones, the way some of them go on! But, dear heart, she is innocent. Help us to bring her off.'

'I don't see my way clearly,' said Aristotle. 'I am really not certain that I can help.'

'With a madam and a brothel? Surely it is easy to blame a brothel! We shall insist that Orthoboulos did die in the brothel where he was found. He *was* killed there — he must have been! His home had nothing to do with it. *Nothing*. Tie to that, and you will be in the right way. And if you have any clue about where the boy is, please let us know.'

'I should do that in any case,' said Aristotle. He patted the man's arm, reassuringly. 'I regret that I cannot do more,' he added. 'What I can do, I will. But your best hope lies in yourselves. Prepare the best case you can. Ask a rhetorician for assistance. Krito is a difficult opponent — his youth speaks so loudly for him, people will forgive any mistakes he makes, or rough- ness of temper.'

'You have no need to tell me so,' said Phanodemos. 'The ingratitude! For Hermia was truly a second mother to both of the boys. It seemed like such a good marriage. Would to the gods she had remained the widow of Epikhares!'

He shuffled off, back towards the city, while we passed through the gate and advanced into the greener and leafier regions. At this time of the year many of the leaves were beginning to depart. A fresh breeze blew from the abrupt tall hill Lykabettos, and the sound of the gently chattering stream flowing down its slopes was pleasant.

'Poor fellow!' said Aristotle abruptly.

'That you offered assistance to Hypereides seems to be known,' said Theophrastos. 'Not necessarily a good thing. I had no idea the extent you would go to in assisting the orator in this case. What on earth persuaded you to give assistance to Hypereides — of all people!'

'Well, it is not the same thing as giving assistance to Eurymedon. No.' Aristotle stopped walking, briefly, and stared at the hill and into the distance. 'I thought myself after last summer – the insult, the episode, you know – that I should never speak with Hypereides again. But circumstances are powerful things. The prosecution of Phryne is – was – part of a plan to intimidate the people of Athens, including even some leading citizens. As one would beat a dog in front of a lion. Phryne herself has many connections among important men, and yet she offered a very easy target.'

'I can scarcely see it in quite that light,' said Theophrastos. 'I heard no proof that she was innocent of the deed of which she was accused. In fact, it seems evident to me that she did exactly what those youths say she did. She was impious, in short.'

'Yes. I may have colluded in saving someone who is guilty of some kind of impiety – whatever that is,' Aristotle admitted. 'The charge of "impiety", so easily abused, is as you know a charge I don't at all care for. It was used against Sokrates. Often this charge of impiety is brought out for the most nakedly – if you'll pardon the expression – *nakedly* political purposes. I do not say my own action was the best. It was a response to circumstance and contingency. General principles, applied to a real and thus particular situation at a particular time. That's what political activity is. And you must realize, both of you' – here he started to walk on again – 'the case would not have ended with the execution of Phryne herself.'

'Why not?' I asked

'Because Phryne herself is an image, a symptom

and a symbol. Her death would have been a public spectacle long remembered. As soon as she was destroyed,
our party of freshly eager patriots, such as Aristogeiton,
combining with their staunch supporters among the
religious, like Eurymedon, would have been swelling
with pride and power. Such a development – what shall
I compare it to? It is – oh, it is like watching a puny
infant grow overnight into a swordsman and a bully.
Things can happen so quickly. This party of newly
powerful men could then go unhindered, freely terror-
izing citizens and non-citizens with charges of impiety, or the threat that such a charge *could* be made.
Anyone – anyone thought to be too sympathetic to
Makedon, for instance – might be brought to heel in
this manner. The rule of the Thirty Tyrants teaches
us how once a group of oligarkhs starts getting into
killing mode, it is easy for them to continue.'

'So,' said Theophrastos, his voice still disapproving,
'*you* excuse the nauseating spectacle of this day – which
you have helped to create? A citizen of over sixty years
weeping for his doxy? Confess your exact part in this
iniquity.'

'I did see Hypereides, as we had arranged. Our
meeting was short and very cautious, brittle on both
sides. He cannot love me, particularly as he knows he
injured me deeply. On the other hand, he was greatly
upset, obsessed by the fate of Phryne, a woman whom
he almost adores, one with whom he has shared the
pleasures of the bed and some of the confidence of
friendship—'

'She is obviously more to him than just a *porne* for
the night,' I agreed.

'Hypereides was not lying when he said that he was pleading as heartily as he would do for his own life. He would do almost anything to get her off. I suggested to him the image of the man attacking a beautiful statue with a pick. I suppose he got the irony – or it will come to him later – in relation to his former insult to me. But he was not too proud to use it.'

'But talking about a statue is different from stripping someone naked!'

'You remember, Stephanos, early last summer – before the terrible episode – I tried to suggest to Hypereides that one way of defending the little man defrauded by a cheating perfume-seller would be to display the charms of the woman Antigone, showing how she had beguiled him into signing the false contract. On this occasion I suggested a similar strategy, put to the reverse effect. I put the suggestion to Hypereides – but *only if all else seemed to be certainly failing*. Remember that. I suggested in that case that he display Phryne herself and praise Aphrodite. And when the case was obviously going against him – in fact, as good as lost – that was exactly what he did.'

'So much for the upholder of law and reason! O Aristotle, Hypereides was but the obedient actor, and you are the khoregos whom we have to thank for producing this spectacle!'

'But a wonderful spectacle!' I interposed. 'How glad I am that I got a good place! Many have gone away satisfied.'

'Aristotle, it will be said you requested Hypereides to unveil – nay, to strip – his mistress merely so you could have a good look at her.'

'The benefit was not mine,' protested Aristotle. 'I had to stand afar off, and my own eyesight is not what it was in my younger days. But I daresay Stephanos is right, and many have left the trial feeling pleased.'

'And many have *not*,' said Theophrastos. 'It is impossible to reconcile this performance with strict law. Let alone how some of the jurors are going to reconcile themselves and their verdict with their wives.'

'But it is not strict law to execute Phryne,' said Aristotle. 'What she did was thoughtless, but the rational defence – the same as was used for Aiskhylos – is the right one.'

'And as you must see for yourself, there is a drawback, Aristotle,' I felt obliged to point out (perhaps picking up some of the censoriousness of Theophrastos). 'The unexpected victory of Phryne has just made all these men the more determined against Hermia.'

'Yes, indeed,' said Theophrastos. 'You heard the citizen who said this made it all the more necessary that Hermia should not get off. They will press harder for a death sentence. You have not made it easier for her!'

'Perhaps not,' Aristotle responded without heat. 'Yet, had Aristogeiton won against Phryne, Krito and his new backers would be absolutely *certain* that they could get the death sentence against Hermia too. And her side then would be so cowed and upset that it would be all the easier for the party backing Krito to win.'

Aristotle stopped in his walking and turned to confront us both.

'The plain fact is – there was *no* way in which the

trial of Phryne could end well for Hermia. But they have not succeeded in the case of Phryne – no matter how many rebukes are tossed around.' Here he smiled at Theophrastos. 'That is important. They did *not* win. Despite their blustering, they can lose a cause. And people know it. Had they won against Phryne, I doubt whether any witness or any friend would have stood by the hapless Hermia and her poor old uncle.'

'And are you proposing to try to help – as Phanodemos has asked you to do?' enquired Theophrastos.

'Since Aristotle has been so much involved in the Phryne case, and behind the scenes, too,' I suggested, 'it might now be more prudent for him to abstain from dealing with Hermia's case.'

'There is good sense in what you say, Stephanos. But perhaps my curiosity – or my anxiety – will not let me be guided by it. And remember, now we have the fate of that poor youth Kleiophon to consider as well. Where is he? He should be found. Phanodemos' allegation that the murder of Orthoboulos must have taken place in the brothel – or the extension to it, the house next door – does not really satisfy me. If that were so, we should be able to *prove* it. I think I should go back to the house of Orthoboulos.'

'I shall not accompany you,' Theophrastos said decidedly. 'A waste of time – I would rather be teaching, or reading, or working with my plants. I must say, that kind of thing seems most ill-bred. Crawling around a man's floors and his furniture! Sniffing mattresses!'

'I would be willing to go with you,' I said to Aristotle, ignoring Theophrastos, 'but not today. I need to go to the agora now and buy something for our dinner. I'll go with you tomorrow.'

'Incorrigible, you two are,' said Theophrastos.

Next day, at the time when most people are doing their marketing in the agora, I met Aristotle near the mansion of Orthoboulos. Together we entered the gate, and passed the Hermes statue. I suppose we both expected to behold again the form of the little girl Kharis sitting on the plinth, but she was not to be seen. Again we confronted the correct old butler, who seemed more dishevelled and sorrowful than before, bowed down under the weight of the family troubles.

'You recognize me, I think,' said Aristotle, giving our names nevertheless. 'And we would be happy to speak to Krito.'

'The Master is out,' said the servant in a voice without inflection or expression, as if speaking the words made him tired.

'I shall be glad to leave him a note. If you allow me to sit for a very short while in the *andron*, I can set a message down in my tablets.'

This ruse to get us back into Orthoboulos' *andron* succeeded to a marvel. Without further question, the servant led us to the apartment of state, and lit a lamp to assist letter-writing, though at this time of day we could still see each other well enough. Aristotle took out his tablets and began to write. I stared about the room, wondering what I should be looking for. I noticed a new statue, a small copy in bronze of a celebrated Hermes, that now occupied the niche in the wall into which the two marble Nymphs had once been crammed. Kharis, I remembered, had told us that there had been another statue.

'I see you have a different statue here,' I remarked to the butler. 'What have you been doing with the Nymphs?'

'The Nymphs, sir?'

'The young ladies in marble that were here before. Interesting, how a statue leaves its mark on the wall behind it,' I went on, staring at the wall. 'A sort of ghost, but the reverse, if you see what I mean – brighter and cleaner where the wall was hidden and protected by an ornament. This piece isn't nearly the size of what was there before.'

Both Aristotle and I looked at the place where the large marble Nymphs were not dancing.

'Everyone likes a change, sir. Those marble Nymphs belonged to my old Master – Epikhares, I mean. The piece used to be outdoors by a spring in the old country place, but it was brought here. We tried it out in this room, but then Master Krito had the big Nymphs taken away. It didn't fit, as you say, sir. And in a time of mourning and trouble it hardly seems right to fill the room with pretty things. It's not as if there will be any dinner parties here.' The old man sighed, a sigh that might have come from the soles of his feet.

'Have you had any word from Kleiophon?' enquired Aristotle, casually, but pausing in his writing.

'No. Oh, no.' The aged butler wrung his hands. 'Wicked lad! To put this trouble on his poor mother by running away at such a time!'

'Of course,' Aristotle pointed out, 'you came to know him only recently, is not that right? As you have just come to this house and this family with Hermia, the boys Krito and Kleiophon would have been practically unknown to you. It might be easier to understand the lad if you had known him from a baby.'

'That's true, sir, I am sure.' The old servant was not disposed to quarrel. 'But all I can think of is the mistress, and how this runaway makes everything look so much worse.'

'Perhaps,' I suggested, 'the boy is aware of that now, and that makes him afraid to come back.'

Aristotle picked up my suggestion. 'It could be. And if some sort of message could be got to him – a message of reassurance—'

'As you say. But how is any message to be got to him?' The butler's tone indicated a lack of confidence. 'And you know – there is worse.' He lowered his voice. 'Krito sometimes thinks his brother will come back, but sometimes he says the boy had been kidnapped, carried off. And I believe the mistress herself thinks that Ergokles has him.'

I was startled. 'She told you that?'

'Not exactly. There were other people in the room. I went to take some clothes and things to the mistress, but the guards were there, as well as Phanodemos. She just said that if Ergokles came to give him anything he wanted. "*Any*thing." That was what she said.'

'Interesting,' said Aristotle.

'But nothing comes of it. Hearts will ache and Kleiophon will go on missing. Things never come right in this world, it seems to me. We don't even know if he is alive. And if he's dead — and *I* think he is — it would be a disgrace to the family not to bury him.'

'Yes, yes,' I agreed, 'but it's not a disgrace if you can't do it straight away. Burials don't always get performed immediately, in wartime and disturbed times.'

'When they bury people they put them in the ground. And then they don't get up again,' said a small strange voice. I looked but could see no one. Then I looked down, and saw that the child Kharis had entered the room.

'O Kharis daughter of Epikhares!' exclaimed the butler. 'You know you should not be here! This is the room for men. And besides, you should not be wandering around downstairs without Nurse—'

She paid no heed at all.

'Will they have to bury Kleiophon?' she asked.

'No, no,' I said soothingly.

'If he's dead, they *have* to bury him,' she insisted.

'Let us hope that there is no need of a funeral at present,' said Aristotle.

'I want to see Mama.' The little girl levelled her brown eyes at him and spoke reproachfully.

'I know. Be patient. One day your mother will certainly come and see you, or be able to send for you and have you come to see her. But right now we all want to know where Kleiophon might be. Did you know him at all? What did — what does Kleiophon like to do?'

She shrugged. 'He likes running and playing war.

He liked the farm – he's going to have a farm when he grows big. And he likes horses – but not so much as Krito. Krito is going to buy a lot of horses and he is going to have chariots at Olympia. Kleiophon likes mules – very much. When they came with the lanky boy, we used to look at the mules. I patted one.'

'Very good, O Kharis daughter of Epikhares. The young man becomes clearer to my eyes. Anything else? What other things does he like?'

'He plays knucklebones – he let me play with them sometimes. And he likes new bread, and pancakes with honey – and me too.'

'So do I,' I agreed.

Ignoring the agitation of the old butler, who endeavoured to induce her to leave, the sole offspring of Epikhares sat on a footstool in front of the chair of the man of the house.

'You will have to have some clothes, dear, to go to the funeral in,' she said, startling me until I realized that she had her doll with her. It swung its pottery arms in a carefree manner, though it was certainly suffering from lack of sufficient raiment, wearing only a narrow strip of woven cloth about the neck. Kharis untied this lumpy ribbon, as if preparing her for new vestments.

'Don't *want* to go to a funeral. Not again!' squeaked the doll. She raised both her arms in protest.

'But if everybody goes, *you* must go,' said Kharis, in her grown-up tones. 'We will find Daughter-Lady and dress her up. Then we will all go. That is what people do when a deaded is put in the ground!'

'No!' insisted the doll. 'Leave me. Go away! I will

have a nap. And you can tell me about the funeral. And I won't get dressed up! I have to look after my baby!'

And at this point another 'doll', not professionally made but contrived of a lump of baked pastry about half as big as my thumb, set up a wail and cried, 'Don't go, Mama, don't go!'

'Is that Artimmes?' I asked, looking curiously at the rather grubby 'doll' of pastry. I remembered now her statement the last time we were here: 'I can't find Artimmes, I want to find Artimmes.'

'No!' she said, turning on me a look of scorn. 'Artimmes is all grown up. He's *bald*.' She turned back to her poppets, rocking and soothing the baby of crust. The lady doll kicked rather jealously.

'Tsk tsk!' said Kharis. 'What are we to do with you?' And she shook her finger at the disobedient doll, who ventured a sly kick once more.

'Kyrene is coming!' said the butler reproachfully. 'And she will give you what-for!'

He was a true prophet; Kyrene bounced into the room.

'Kharis! Well – of all the disobedient girls! Come along, my young piglet.'

'I want to stay,' the child said. 'My dolly wants to stay and look for the Daughter.'

'Your doll doesn't have to look for you! You are right here! Pick dolly up and let's walk. Come, come! It's not proper, not like a girl well-bred, talking to strange gentlemen – and in the *andron*, too. Come away, missy, and behave like a proper girl of a good family.'

'I *am* a proper girl' said Kharis, jerked to her feet by the mastery of the nurse. 'Oh no! My girl – she will be hurt! Oh, don't step there! My baby—' And with anguish she picked up the broken crumbs of the pastry 'baby' now irrecoverably damaged by the nurse's foot.

Kharis' lip trembled and she started to cry.

'Now, child, don't make a silly fuss about a dirty bit of crust!'

'My little baby! My baby's dead. And my little girl is *hurt*—' Kharis picked up the jointed doll, which had been tumbled out of her lap to the floor when the nurse abruptly compelled the child to rise.

'There, there!' she soothed the doll, who appeared quite unharmed, and gazed at her with perfect serenity and absolute composure from under her strangely grown-up hair, parted in the middle like Phryne's.

'Don't carry on like a little baby yourself,' rebuked Kyrene. 'Your doll is well enough, you see. But, gentlemen—' The nurse Kyrene turned her reproachful eyes and dared not only to address but also to rebuke us. 'You are surely men of good family, good Athenian citizens, and you know you should not demean the family – just because we're in trouble – by encouraging our child to come and entertain gentlemen. Believe me, she isn't that kind of girl at all – not what she's bred to! So say no more words to her, and if you come again – which I hope to Herakles you don't— Sorry to disoblige, but to be honest – I'm a tribeswoman of the Atlas mountain people, and we are minded to say what's in our hearts. If you come again, I say, make pertickler sure you *don't* see the daughter of Epikhares.

Don't you never ask for her, and if she comes send her away at once and don't try talking with her, which is a dangerous game for a female at any age.'

And holding Kharis firmly by the arm she swept herself and charge and the underdressed doll out of the room.

'You must pardon her, sir, she's old. Kyrene was Hermia's nurse before,' said the butler sadly. 'Not but what there's truth in what she says, and I told the daughter of Epikhares not to come here, I'm sure I have.'

'I can bear witness that you did,' I said placatingly.

'Sorry for any trouble we may have given you. Make your peace with Kyrene,' said Aristotle, slipping the man a couple of obols along with the tablets addressed to Krito.

'What did you write to Krito?' I asked as we got out of the gateway and into the street again. Fortunately this time we had not been detained by Theramenes the witness-hunter, or any other intruder.

'Oh, a formal and bland message. Just to say that I should be happy to help in the search for Kleiophon and would be glad to talk with him, especially if he could give me any more information about where the boy might have gone, and when exactly he disappeared. But I don't truly expect Krito to respond to me.'

'I have an idea,' I said. 'A slender clue, I know. But the little girl says her stepbrother loved pancakes with honey. When I was asking questions at Manto's brothel – as *you* told me to do – they said they knew nothing of Kleiophon. That morning the girls were eating pancakes with honey. Meta, I was told, had already had breakfast. Yet one pancake was taken away on a warm plate, and not accounted for. A little mystery there: *who* was enjoying the pancake I saw the maidservant taking out on a plate? I thought it was for Manto, but she came in just after, and hadn't yet eaten anything that morning. She shut us up and set us all packing, as I explained before. I couldn't ask more questions. And when I came to see you, Theophrastos came in and then Arkhias, so I didn't go into trifling details. Yet I have thought of that pancake since. Might not Kleiophon have been in hiding at the brothel, in the care of one of the girls?'

Aristotle stopped in his tracks.

'Very good, Stephanos. Not a very substantial clue – thin and sticky to be sure. But it points to a possibility. Yet, if the boy was in that brothel on that day, we can be sure he is not there now. He would have perhaps received some help there, maybe even pieces of money – but sent by whom? And then he would be conveyed on his way. To where? Of his own free will or under compulsion?'

'Since we heard Ergokles' threat,' I stated, 'the idea that Kleiophon has been abducted – kidnapped – and that Hermia is being blackmailed seems the likeliest explanation of all.'

'There are probabilities weighing on that side. But abductors would have to take him first to somewhere in Athens, and then out of it, in order either to hustle him off or to kill him. It would be easier to kill and bury him deep in the countryside. The little Kharis is right – if he is dead, he would have to be buried.'

'By the way, Aristotle, do you think it right to delude

that little girl by saying she will see her mother?'

'I am not deluding her, Stephanos. One of these days, little Kharis will assuredly see her mother. Either Hermia will be freed — in which case, no question. Or Hermia will be condemned. In which case, the gentry of Athens are not so cold-hearted as to deny the opportunity for this citizen's daughter to say "farewell" to all her family. Including of course, her child. So Kharis will see her mother again, at least once.'

'That's hard!'

'So it is. I am sorry for the child. And Kharis is a person whom I must respect, for she has given us much valuable information. On our first visit, the child told us — a helpful tip, which we were slow to pick up — that another statue had been taken away. The marble thing was too big for its site. Odd, how statues once used out of doors for religious reasons are now moving indoors! But there was another statue there before, one we have not seen. Somebody, I think, used that first statue and didn't want it noticed. It was taken away and the Nymphs substituted.'

'You realize what you say points to Krito? And there are some other odd things about Krito. He burst into a tantrum and accused Philinos of adultery with his stepmother in the most dramatic way! But now he and Philinos are on good terms again, and working together on the trial. How did Philinos win him round? I ask myself. And then I answer, Philinos could give Krito more money — he seems to be the source of supply, with all these "sales". And Krito might need more money now because he has to pay the kidnapper of his brother.'

'There is an interesting mystery about the rapid reconciliation with Philinos. Certainly, Krito seems to want money, and his father's estate is somewhat tied.'

'The statues – they point to Krito. He is master of the house and can order statues moved in or out as he pleases. But – no, I can scarcely believe— Worse than Oedipus! The Nymphs looked wrong; probably it was merely good taste that caused Krito to remove that piece.'

'And now there is a third statue. A modest Hermes, too small. The wall behind it, your bright ghost – very finely observed – indicated the height and bulk of the statue that was formerly present. *Before* the arrival of the marble ladies and their draperies.'

'A disappearing statue – a murder weapon? But no. A statue of bronze or marble might kill someone by striking him, but that was *not* how Orthoboulos died – I saw his corpse.'

'No. He died of hemlock poison. I trust your observations. But he died somewhere else, not the spot where he was found. And I now believe he was not in the house when Kleiophon spoke to him.'

'What do you mean? He answered the boy—'

'The boy saw a shape on the bed, and heard a voice saying, "Go away, boy, and let me doze a little." The voice would be muttering and sleepy. Kleiophon was fully satisfied that he had addressed his father and his father had bidden him to depart. Little Kharis' actions just now, her drama with her doll, opened my sluggish eyes. *She* did the speaking for her doll, and she could even move its arms. It is not necessary for the doll to be a living thing for Kharis to give her that kind of life. So I realized – and I should have thought of this sooner – it was not difficult for someone to lay a statue in that bed, under the coverlet, and then – hidden in the darkened room – to supply a voice for it.'

'A kind of show, a game – with an image?'

'Just so. And you see, this demands that we have *conspirators* – more than one person. Someone must have been looking after Orthoboulos – by which I mean killing him – outside the house, at another place. But another person meanwhile moved the statue, presumably with a third person acting as assistant, and performed this brief impersonation.'

'The murder was well planned, then.'

'Ah, but we knew that anyway – hemlock is scarcely the choice of the impetuous killer acting on the spur of the moment.'

'We are still no nearer to knowing who it was.'

'Nor do we know where Kleiophon is. Does his disappearance have anything to do with the plot to kill Orthoboulos – does he know too much? Or is this disappearance the effect of another crime? Or has Kleiophon simply run away? We probably ought to suppose that there is a plot involved. I imagine that Arkhias, who by profession is in love with plots, is working on that assumption.'

'But – Hermia? If Orthoboulos was not killed at home – that is what Phanodemos thinks – that might help her. But a conspiracy in the home does *not* look good for Hermia.'

'Exactly.'

XVIII

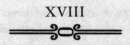

Papa's Daughter

Well might Aristotle agree that things did not look well for Hermia and her family. Yet at that point we did not know exactly how very bad things were for them. We were soon to learn. After departing from Orthoboulos' house Aristotle and I were crossing the agora, in the general direction of the road to the Diokhares Gate, when we heard an animated noise nearby, beside the bronze statues of the Heroes. This is the site where public notices are posted, and legal announcements made, including of lawsuits and engagements to marry. So this spot is of constant interest to anyone who wishes to keep up with what is new in Athens.

Aristotle and I steered our course towards the centre of the hubbub. 'What is it?' I asked. 'Hush! A new charge – of homicide, they say!' replied one of the onlookers. When we got to the railing behind which are the plinths and the statues of the Heroes, we saw two men whom we both knew – though we did not care for either: Theramenes the imperious witness-finder, and Ergokles, the little man who was such a tireless enemy to Orthoboulos. I was surprised to see these two men in partnership. Yet, I supposed, Ergokles, so shrewd in his own way, had spotted in Theramenes a good source of help and support. The verdict in favour of Phryne left Theramenes temporarily without a job in which to employ his zeal, so it might have been easy to tempt him into another cause.

'Ours is a search for *Justice*,' I heard Theramenes say. 'Justice – which is so scarce in Athens, and has recently been denied in favour of whores and dancing-girls. We will reward any witnesses – not slaves – who come forward to tell what they know of the wicked abduction of the boy Kleiophon by Hermia and her family.'

'I share your concern,' said Ergokles. 'I too ask for justice against this family. I have been insulted by Hermia and her uncle. From Hermia and her stony-hearted and devious family, nothing good comes.'

'Besides,' said Theramenes, 'we must make every effort to rescue the boy Kleiophon – assuming the poor youth is still alive! Or to bury his remains and honour him with revenge, if he is dead!'

'That's right,' said Ergokles. 'All Athenians will wish to save the boy – or avenge his death! We are united in our desire for Justice – united now with Krito against his truly wicked stepmother.'

At this cue, Krito strolled forth and joined the two men standing against the railing just below the stat-ues of the Heroes. Ergokles and Krito joining in the same cause? Hard to believe! Yet that these two men were together was undeniable. Krito's usual supporter Philinos (a supporter once more since their puzzling reconciliation) was standing near at hand. I saw him at the front of the crowd, where he was attended by Marylla, the beautiful slave who went veiled. I pointed them out to Aristotle, who only nodded. I could see another slave also, the beefy attendant of Theramenes. He also stood quietly, arms folded, yet patently alert, as if it would be a pleasure to him to bang the heads of all around him, slave or free, as soon as his master Theramenes gave the word.

'You will be surprised, men of Athens – or at least some of you,' began Krito, 'to see myself and my father's former opponent Ergokles together on this occasion. But we thought it best to appear together, as a sign that the enmity between my father's blood and himself is to be considered at an end. For in this emergency it is my duty to unite with all men of good will to save my brother and defeat the machinations of a wicked woman. How truly wicked she is the gods alone know! And all her family, stony-hearted, devious, are as bad. That woman and her ingenious and malevolent uncle Phanodemos have conveyed my brother Kleiophon secretly away. Despite our best endeavours, they keep him hidden. Why? You may well ask—'

'Stop speechifying! You're not in court now, at any rate,' said a voice from the crowd.

Krito blushed to the roots of his hair, but stood his ground. 'You would not call it "speechifying" if you could feel how my heart aches. How anxious I am for the fate of my young brother! O men of Athens, help us to save him! The motive of our enemies is not far to seek – they endeavour to injure our case against Hermia. So Hermia and her gang have stolen Kleiophon. Likely they conveyed him out of Athens and then – how horrible! – it is too easy to believe that they made away with him.'

'So much has been left for Krito, this fatherless youth, to do,' Theramenes supplemented. 'Now a number of right-minded men of good will are supporting him in the new lawsuit, which is the only resource open to him at present. Krito formally accuses – tell them yourself,' with a nudge to Krito.

'I accuse my stepmother, Hermia, widow of Epikhares and of Orthoboulos, and also her uncle Phanodemos, of conspiring to abduct my brother Kleiophon, son of Orthoboulos.'

'And I formally charge—' Theramenes prompted. Krito scowled.

'I was coming to that.' And he took up the ritual statement: 'And I formally charge Hermia widow of Epikhares with the crime of murder through counselling homicide, and I charge Phanodemos of the deme Thymaitadai of the crime of homicide. And I charge both of you to keep from all legal and holy things, from holy water, from wine and libations, from the agora, from the courts, and from all sacred places!'

So henceforth, I realized, Phanodemos as well as his niece must avoid the agora. It would make it harder for him to conduct any business, including his niece's defence, or (now) his own.

Krito and Theramenes posted the written statement of the charge on the wooden fence, Ergokles fussily assisting. People crowded to read the notice, and Krito was the object of many questions and commiserations.

'Well, I daresay there's no need for me to linger,' said Ergokles, speaking loud against the babble. Indeed, there seemed no reason why he could not depart. 'You know where to find me,' he said jauntily to Krito, and walked off beyond the public herms towards the Stoa Poikile. His little form was soon lost to view amid the traffic of the big road at the point where it properly begins to be the Panathenian Way.

'It's unfair, the way those men are hounding poor Phanodemos,' I said to Aristotle. 'Trying to do his duty by his niece, he is accused of this hideous crime!'

'I cannot quite see how any legal case will go anywhere unless they produce very strong evidence as to what happened to the lad.'

'Chiefly, a body – the poor boy's corpse. Impossible to have a homicide trial without it!'

'Not impossible. A court can try someone on a charge of homicide without a corpse – at least in theory. But a jury does not care for it. Not unless you had something very strong to support the accusation – for example, if a trustworthy witness had seen the unhappy victim thrown into the sea.'

'One of the worst ways to die! No burial – one cannot get across the Styx! That does not make me feel any better about Kleiophon. And how strange that Krito should have joined with Ergokles.'

'Most interesting that Ergokles should have joined with Krito.'

'I should have thought Krito would keep clear of Ergokles — who is *not* a nice man. Ergokles holds grudges. But perhaps, so it strikes me, Krito has felt it better to pay Ergokles what he asks, even if the debt is unjust, in order to get rid of a nuisance. That would explain why Krito has turned to Philinos again, as a source of the money he needs.'

'But how does Ergokles comport himself with Philinos? — given that the quarrelsome little man still thinks himself entitled to the Sikilian slave, or compensation for her.'

'He must be resigned by now, as Philinos was there with that slave woman this morning, and Ergokles said nothing,' I remarked. 'The woman Marylla was veiled, almost like a citizen woman. Though a slave, she acts more like a free person in some ways. The morning when I went back to Manto's brothel to see if I could get any more information, I noticed she was fully veiled. Though she unveiled her face when she spoke to me.'

'Marylla was at Manto's brothel? You surprise me — the beautiful Sikilian a worker there? Surely not!'

'No, no. She was just coming to the door, she said they had to return a silver pan they had borrowed of her — from Philinos' household. It was lent to Manto's cook.'

'Then Marylla must certainly know Manto, if they are on pan-borrowing terms.'

'I suppose so. But my point is that she now follows Philinos about, veiled like a proper lady. It's as if

Orthoboulos never existed. I conclude she is now Philinos' permanent companion. As she's not freeborn, but purchased, she's not a hetaira, but, rather, his slave-concubine.' I considered this. 'How strange it is that Philinos should exhibit his infatuation with a mere household slave! He is so handsome and well-born — and well-to-do — he could marry well.'

Aristotle demurred, but with a hesitancy unusual in him. 'Well, but — Stephanos, the woman is very beautiful, the relation seems to be continuing. Marriage is difficult, and does not bring quite the same satisfactions.'

'That's true.' I had to agree, thinking of the brothel, and of the beautiful display of Phryne's breasts.

I felt I had sufficient excuse to conduct more investigations at Manto's brothel, spurred by the recollection that little Kharis had said that her stepbrother Kleiophon was fond of pancakes with honey. Of course, many children were, but it seemed wise not to leave unsolved the riddle of the extra pancake. I returned to Manto's large house the next day, not so early as last time. There was some midday traffic, but the press of customers was not great as yet.

'Well, here is Mr Breakfast,' said the girl with the long thin neck.

'Less of the smart sayings,' I retorted. 'It isn't your birthday any more, Klisia. Lucky for you. Birthdays will come fast enough. Too soon wise, you know, too soon old.'

She gave me a penetrating stare. 'Does your mother know that you come here so often? Doesn't she scold?'

'Hush, Klisia,' said Kynara gently, laying her hand

on my arm. 'He's mine you know, for now, and only I
am allowed to bite him.'

'But you are right,' I said placatingly to the former
birthday girl. 'I still remember those pancakes. Indeed,
I have an interest in a farm which makes very good
honey – in Hymettos – and I hope to sell some of our
produce here.'

'Ah. A man of business. Nothing without a profit.
It's Manto you will have to deal with – *we* can't help
you.' She turned her head away.

'You have to forgive our Klisia,' said Kynara, 'for
she is expecting a customer who was supposed to come
at midday and still hasn't turned up. Name of Ergoklès.
Little fellow. Do you know him?'

'I do, as it happens. Haven't seen him since yesterday. In the agora.'

'It will be fine with me,' said the long-necked girl
with a sniff, 'if I never see that little runt again. Don't
mind me.'

'Come, come,' I coaxed, sitting on a stool with
Kynara on my lap, and offering the other girl a hemi-
obol. 'No harm between us I hope, have some wine at
my expense. I would just like to know the answer to
something that has been puzzling me.'

'Yes?'

'When I came and you were having breakfast the
other day, a pancake, well plastered with honey, was
taken out of the room. You were all here, so I thought
it was for Manto. But then she came in and had taken
nothing to eat as yet. So – who was that extra pancake
for?'

There was a pause. Klisia of the long neck laughed

nervously. 'Asking questions! You came here last time
I remember, asking questions. And *what* a good housekeeper you are! Counting pancakes! Enquiring into
waste – even in a house of pleasure. The sweet was
for anyone who wanted it, I suppose.'

I couldn't see how to proceed. There was an
awkward pause, and I jumped up. 'Well, I will talk
with Manto some other time. I must be going.'

Kynara restrained me. 'Not so fast – what need to
hurry away? Where could you go worse than here?
Have some wine and water. We can go upstairs.'

'No need – I wasn't coming for—'

'Well, that is too bad!' she pouted. 'And I *know* you
went to that other place – Tryphaina's – and spent a
lot of *silver*. One of Tryphaina's poor girls told me.'

This was a disagreeable surprise. So at least one
person at that luxurious brothel knew who I really
was, though I had not given my name at Tryphaina's.
Athenians are very good at worming out such facts.
And if I had not been known by name at Tryphaina's,
my face had been identified by at least one individual,
probably Kleoboule. Hard for me to believe that my
face and figure could be memorable, but some people
recollect everything.

'Poor girls,' Kynara continued, with a light emphasis. 'You don't want to go *there* for a while. I say "poor
girls" of course, because most of them have been
tortured. They can hardly move, some of them, and
won't be good at their game for some time. Still,
Phryne got off!'

'That is a cause for celebration,' I said heavily,
accepting her nudges and prods in the direction of

upstairs. Certainly, I should spend my money on this girl and put her in good humour.

'Come along,' she said. 'Woof, woof!' and shaking her head like a dog coming out of the water, she lightly bit my upper arm.

'There,' she said, turning back as she led me away, with a triumphant look to her long-necked friend. 'I told you. *I* am the one allowed to bite him.' I did not feel I was winning the battle.

Although I may not have been winning the skirmish, by the time we came for a bout on the bed I quite enjoyed it. I was careful to ply Kynara with money, and promises of more, while indicating that I valued privacy, and did not wish to be talked about. She indicated that she quite understood, and would rather have me come again than be scared away by too much talk.

'Girls who talk too much get left,' she said sadly. 'The women in Tryphaina's house did not talk much, even when put to the question.'

'Such a sad thing,' I said. 'Phryne's ordeal is over, however, and so is theirs. Aristogeiton will have to pay a fine, and he is in debt already, so that may keep him subdued. But you might help me in other ways, perhaps.'

'Whatever you like, little Papa.' She indicated, through gestures not fit to be specified in words, that she was willing to oblige me in everything.

'I think,' I said, when we had arrived at a breathing space, 'I think the extra pancake with honey was intended for a visitor who wasn't a customer – a sort of boarder. I think it was a young man, a man or boy just too young to enter into the lists for the games of Aphrodite.'

'You think a great deal,' said Kynara. '*Now* you think you can get further by not questioning so directly as last time.'

It occurred to me that I had underestimated her shrewdness.

'*I* think a lot too, when I have the time,' she said. 'I think about how I would like a nice man to take care of me. To buy me away from here and set me up in a house on my own, kept just for him. And maybe make me a freedwoman later.'

'That is quite a large proposition,' I retorted.

'Well you are a gentleman – with land, you say, in Hymettos. And I wouldn't want too much – no jewellery, or fine clothes. I don't eat much! I wouldn't expect to be a household concubine and confidante. Just not to be in the brothel, and to have only one man to please, and some time to myself.'

'Oh, I thought you girls rather enjoyed being together.'

'We may be friends with each other, but there's no one hardly who doesn't wish she was out. Oh, we all dream of being free! To weave and spin for my own benefit, and sleep alone when the one man was not with me. To be free from the whip! Not to be tortured if there is any law case! Oh, what a release to the soul.'

'You are asking too much, girl. You have no idea how straitened my circumstances really are at present – indeed, I cannot promise this.'

'Well – think about it. You are well-born, and landed, you have prospects. You have a lucky face, and you are

still young. I'll say this for you, you don't lie and lead
a girl on, and promise what you can't perform.'

'Not in any department,' I replied firmly, pinching
her, and she dutifully giggled.

'I will trust you, and hope you will make me a return,'
she offered. 'I shall tell you what you want to know –
but you must never say *I* told you. You are right about
the pancake – what a silly thing to remember! There
was a young boy here at that time, someone I never
saw, but I heard about him. I thought he might be a
relative of Manto's but one of the girls said he spoke
in a very fine manner, which doesn't sound like Manto's
family. He was here for only two days.'

'And where did he go?'

'I do not know.'

'Perhaps,' I said with careful casualness, 'you are
right and he really was a relative of Manto. Where
did Manto come from originally?'

'She was born in slavery. I think it might have been
in Paionia – way out there where there are so many
fields and farms and sheep.' Kynara waved a vague hand
in quite the wrong direction. 'But Manto is really a
Spartan woman, her mother was from Kythera. Where
Aphrodite was born. She says her mother told her she
had an awful voyage from Kythera. When Manto was
a little girl, the owner of Manto's mother set her free,
and Manto too – she has been free since she was young.
Her mother ran this business, and Manto inherited it,
though of course the heir of Manto's first owner owns
the actual land and house. Manto has an older half-
brother who is still a slave, but I believe she has a
younger sister who was born free. A sister somewhere.

That's all I know. It isn't good manners to enquire into Madam's life.'

'I quite see that,' I agreed. I realized I had got further without mentioning Kleiophon's name.

As all desire was quite satisfied – including (temporarily) Kynara's desire for more money from me – it was time for me to move on. Now I had some solid information, though I must be chary about sharing it; I intended to keep my promise not to mention my informant's name. I must also be chary, I reminded myself, about any more such visits to this brothel; they were expensive, and might prove even more costly. Were Kynara's comments mere chat or strong hints? Was she even planning to extort money from me because she knew my secret – that I had been at the party where Phryne performed? Surely, I reasoned, she could not have known this the last time I had seen her, before Phryne's trial. For that would have been the best time for her to extort money from me for her silence. To keep my name out of the trial for impiety. Probably it was only after the trial that she had learned of my presence at the fatal party from one of the suffering inmates of Tryphaina's tortured establishment.

Only a few days ago, the announcement that someone had this piece of knowledge would have been most alarming. I was quite willing to face any opponent in a fair fight, but the law, in which people like Eurymedon can enmesh one as a fly in a spider's web, did put fear into me. Even though Phryne's trial was happily over, I had to admit to myself that it would do my character no good for the history of my presence at Tryphaina's to emerge into the light. A witness-catcher like Theramenes working on other cases, perhaps with people like Eurymedon or Aristogeiton, would have no qualms about making life difficult for me on another occasion.

I had plenty to think about as I made for the doorway of this not very lucky building, musing so that I almost bumped into another visitor departing from the brothel. This was a country man, judging by his gait, and the manure on his boots. Some dogged peasant come to Athens for the market and indulging himself in one brief spurt of pleasure. But then . . . I paused. Something about the way this person moved, something about the round shape of the head under the hood – this was familiar, and did not belong to the country. Also, there was just a hint of fine perfume – of course, he might have caught the scent from the girl he was with, but Manto's brothel had not yet quite arrived at top-notch Egyptian perfumes. Herbs mixed with olive oil for a wash, yes, but not . . . I had put these details together by the time we left the house.

'Well, Arkhias,' I said, 'I did not know you were such a good customer.'

'Hush!' He looked daggers at me. 'Do not talk until we get away.'

We walked in silence until we reached a deserted spot where he felt it safe to speak.

'Really, Stephanos of Athens, you should *never* address me when I am working!'

'Oh – that's what it is? I thought you were playing.'

'Certainly not. I am – you may notice – in disguise.'

'Well, if you think *that's* a disguise,' I retorted, 'it is as well you met me. For I can tell you it isn't.'

'Really? What's wrong with it?'

'Your head has a remarkably round shape, and that is perfectly evident. Sometimes you move like a countryman and sometimes not. You hold yourself more upright than a peasant farmer or country labourer would do. Your hands are too clean — especially the fingernails. Worst of all, you smell. Of some lovely scent — it makes its way even through the manure. It's too good for the inhabitants of this brothel.'

'Ah!' He smiled, and looked at me with reluctant admiration. 'Stephanos of Athens, you should enter my profession too. Not as an actor — you could never do that — but as a spy. Your criticisms I shall take to heart. Wonderful! You have a good nose. I used perfume yesterday, but it evidently has not worn off. Alas, I shall have to cease its use — lovely, the scent of water-lilies of Egypt. A friend from Naukratis gave it me.'

'Give it to a girlfriend,' I said heartlessly.

'You are very good,' said Arkhias, 'very kind, to give me all these tips. For I must ceaselessly practise my vocation and get everything right, down to the minutest detail. I am most grateful for your help. How few could explain all the points at which I have erred as clearly as you have done! For this assistance you will have the thanks of Antipater as well as myself.'

'Don't mention it,' I said, with irritation. It was not my idea to get entangled with this spying person, or tied to the pro-Makedonian party. Both he and Antipater could keep their thanks.

'I hope you had a good time in there,' I said caustically. 'Found what you are looking for?'

'Passable – I don't think the girl suspected anything. And I may have some information. I will tell you one thing – in confidence – as a reward for your advice.' He lowered his voice. 'I am on the track of several individuals. But one of them is the other butler – the Phrygian slave.'

'Whose Phrygian slave?'

'Orthoboulos' servant. He – his house, I mean – has a new chief house-slave now, an old man formerly belonging to Epikhares. Hermia brought him. So he's gone, the old Phrygian—'

'Don't tell me his name was Artimmes?'

'Quite right.' Arkhias looked briefly disappointed. 'I am trying to find out where he has gone. It occurred to me that an old family slave such as that might be used by young master Kleiophon in running away.'

'An interesting idea!'

'I have many others. And I may have some good information. Though I shall let that wait until time proves whether it is really helpful or not.'

Of course it was with Aristotle, certainly not with the redoubtable and irritating Arkhias, that I wished to speak of what I had found out. It was surely important. There had been a boy hidden in Manto's brothel, three days or so after Kleiophon's disappearance. I was pleased to find when I got to my own house that Aristotle had sent Olympos, his second male slave, with a message. The Master of the Lykeion wished me to come to him as he had something important to discuss. A private conversation seemed assured. I was about to set out on the familiar walk to the Lykeion when Phanodemos came unexpectedly to my door. The unfortunate uncle of the even more unfortunate Hermia looked older every time I saw him.

'Please, O Stephanos,' he said, almost without greeting. 'Have you seen Ergokles?'

'There's no reason why I should ever see Ergokles. I saw him in the agora, by the monument of the Heroes, when Krito laid the new charge against you.'

'Yes, terrible. Terrible! If everybody takes against us, we are undone! For who can prove that something did *not* happen! How can we prove——? We cannot *prove* that we did not have the boy abducted, or made away with altogether!' He shuddered. 'I *must* find Ergokles. Nobody has seen him since that – since Krito's scene at the agora. I can no longer go to the agora. Hermia is certain that Ergokles is covertly threatening her, hinting that she has disposed of the boy and must pay him money to keep quiet. Ergokles is quite dreadful when he appears – but he is most unnerving when he does not appear. We need to find out what he is really doing. Does he truly suspect us, or is he just trying to make us pay him?'

'You'd be making a great mistake if you tried to pay off someone like Ergokles.'

'But if he thought we might bargain, he might be less willing to support Krito, even though now he seems to have thrown himself in on that side. Maybe it was only to frighten us. Or perhaps Ergokles himself knows where Kleiophon is!'

'I cannot help you,' I said gently, laying my hand on the elderly man's arm. 'At least, I am busy at the moment and cannot go looking for Ergokles. If I see

him anywhere, I shall certainly tell you. I have hopes
of doing something to assist you, you may be certain
of that.'

And I pushed him gently away from my door. How
I wished I could tell him that I had found Kleiophon
– alive.

I walked quickly to the Lykeion, and told Aristotle
of my discovery. Shortly after Kleiophon's disappearance, Manto's brothel had been briefly the lodging of
a strange but well-spoken boy. I was not going to
inflict on Aristotle the recital of irrelevant brothel
events, but I thought it only right to mention
Phanodemos' anxiety. As I finished relating all this, I
was suddenly overtaken by another thought.

'Aristotle, who is Lykaina?'

'What brought her to mind?'

'I just remembered – when I was investigating
whether Kleiophon could be at Manto's house – not
this time, but the time before – I met Marylla, as I
told you. And she said that next time Manto's people
could borrow a pan from Lykaina. And I suddenly
thought, there is this woman called "Lykaina"
connected somehow with these families, and we
haven't found out exactly who she is. Marylla once
said she was a mistress of Philinos. We have heard of
her but not laid eyes on her.'

'Perhaps we should set our hunting dog Arkhias on
the case.'

'I think he is busy enough looking for Kleiophon
still.' I passed on to Aristotle not only my sighting of
Arkhias in disguise, but also the news that the
'Artimmes' searched for by little Kharis was the old

Phrygian butler of Orthoboulos; I mentioned Arkhias' idea that Artimmes might be concerned in Kleiophon's disappearance.

'It is best for Arkhias to pursue that course,' said Aristotle. 'I have pursued my own course, and have something important to show you!' He stood up with his usual restlessness, and looked at me with dancing eyes. Then he dramatically pointed to something draped in cloth standing in a corner of his *andron*.

'I sent one of the scholars to look for this,' he explained, still looking towards the mysterious object. 'Theophrastos refuses to be interested in this kind of thing. So I gave instructions to Hipparkhos of Argos.'

'Oh yes, Hipparkhos. That serious young man who looks like a horse.' Hipparkhos, with the low monotonous voice, and unintimidating manner, might be a good person to send on delicate errands. Little danger of his attracting personal interest. 'But what did you want him to look for?'

'The missing statue, of course! The statue that was once in Orthoboulos' *andron*! This image – we can call it "Statue the First" – was, I believe, moved on the evening of the death of Orthoboulos. Taken away from its niche and put into the bed, to be covered up with a blanket. Then the hidden watcher would whisper, hoarsely imitating Orthoboulos' sleepy voice. But – what happened to Statue the First? It is my supposition that it got damaged – perhaps when someone tried too hurriedly to move it back from the couch to its place again. If that happened, I surmised, the conspirators might simply have thrown the image away. They could move some other objects around the room to disguise the loss for a while.'

I thought about this. 'The conspirators, as you call them. The murderers. They alone would know that very soon the house would be plunged into mourning, so people might not be concerned with household objects. Later they introduced the marble statue of the Nymphs which didn't quite fit the space, and Krito – or someone – seems to have removed it again.'

'Yes. It does not necessarily follow, however, that whoever inserted the marble Nymphs into that niche was among the conspirators.'

'They might blame the fact that an object was missing on the funeral. When a lot of people come for the laying-out and funeral, it is not unknown for valuables to disappear. And there's been a lot of theft in Athens lately.'

'True. But a statue cannot be made off with easily, like a little cup. It is not only costly, but heavy. "Statue the First" would be in an inventory somewhere – but we forget that these two households only recently combined. Thus, some objects wouldn't be missed by the boys, who were not used to seeing them anyway. The statue that disappeared from the scene most likely belonged to Epikhares, not to Orthoboulos. Epikhares, who was not only richer but a man with more taste – or more ostentation – than Orthoboulos. And if you think about it, you will realize that the statue that was moved to the bed is unlikely to have been of marble.'

'It could not have been marble, but it could have been bronze,' I thought aloud. 'Bronze statues are usually not solid, they can be made with a hollow core.

Marble is solid – and weighty. A marble statue of any considerable size is too heavy for one or often even two persons to move. And this had to be, if not life-size, of *some* size in order to be long enough to impersonate a man—'

'Good. And what else must be true of the statue?'

'It has to be a male statue – what god? One wouldn't expect a large Poseidon in a private house, and a Zeus would be too much. A statue of Pan is usually small—'

'The statue did not have to be of a male in order for it to *represent* – or, as you say, "impersonate" – a male, Stephanos. It was not to be naked – it was to be covered with the blanket.

'Again, little Kharis offers us valuable information. "You need Papa's Daughter." She said that to us, or something like it, the first time we visited Orthoboulos' house – when you and I were clumsily trying out the impersonation game. And again, in our recent second visit, she said something like "I want" – or rather her doll wanted – "to stay and look for the Daughter."'

He twitched the wrappings off the still form that stood in the corner.

'Behold!' he said. 'The Daughter-Lady! Epikhares' Kore, Papa's Daughter!'

And there was a statue of Demeter's glorious daughter, Persephone. The Kore, *the* Girl, *the* Daughter. The second half of the Two, the Mother-and-Daughter, Demeter and Persephone. This aged bronze image was shapely, well executed, with a smooth green skin. But the image had suffered damage – the right hand had been broken off recently, revealing bright bronze in contrast with the colour of age. The toes on the right foot were bent or broken, and there was an unattractive dent in the side of the face.

'There! The damage indicates why the conspirators could not put it back in its niche as if nothing had happened. The statue was their marionette, an inanimate agent. An awkward marionette, because of its size. Perhaps one person tried hurriedly to move it on his or her own, and dropped it. A nuisance. For then, somebody had to dispose of the damaged statue.'

'How?'

'The simplest way. It was thrown into the dung-heap at the end of the road, and well covered.'

'What a stinking thought!' I regarded the image with disfavour.

'It got rid of the problem for the immediate interval, which was the important time. Of course the dung-collector for this deme found it eventually. The experience would not have done the image much good, but he quietly cleaned it off, and then he sold it, at a very low price, to a man in Peiraieus, the sort of person who mends and sells dilapidated objects. It might have been sold to another owner – but if it didn't sell quickly, it was going to be melted down for new bronze. Hipparkhos was just in time.'

'"Papa's Daughter"! A Kore belonging to Epikhares that had passed into the possession of Orthoboulos, and into his *andron*. So that's what it was.'

'So I believe. And this pleasant bronze person was used as an accomplice in the homicide of Orthoboulos.'

'But why? Why would somebody go to so much trouble over the statue impersonation?'

'Because the *time* at which Orthoboulos died was going to be important. To somebody. So somebody went to extra trouble. I should think that is obvious. Whoever could persuade others to act in accordance with this impersonation was the leading spirit in the murder.'

'And this poor object was mutilated in the process.' I walked around it. 'What hubris! To use Demeter's Daughter as their marionette. I cannot bring myself to touch this image, thinking of the dung,' I confessed. 'I would never want to see it in a room of my own.'

'Unfair to the poor Persephone, Stephanos. Bronze is a clean and enduring material, but its elements are of the earth. We ourselves, less clean and enduring, are of dungy earth; we make stinks every day and someday shall stink entirely of mortality. And is not Persephone true to her calling? She disappears, is eclipsed in a nether world, and then returns.'

XIX

Run to Earth

'I think,' Arkhias said to me reproachfully, 'that you might have told me you were going to see Aristotle.'

'I didn't exactly know that when I met you,' I said. 'Anyway, I often see Aristotle. I imagine you see him sometimes when I don't. So what does it matter?'

He shook his head. 'It is important that we all share our knowledge. Not go off in different directions. Now, I have some tidings – or rather, I divine the possibility of tidings – and I wish to ask your help.'

'What do you want me for?'

'I believe we may find more news of Kleiophon if we go in the direction of Megara. But we need some transportation. If you have a donkey, I will hire it of you – Antipater has given me funds for expenses – and I shall ask you to accompany me.'

The possibility of hiring out the little ass was tempting. Taking a trip with Arkhias was not.

'Why do you need *me*?'

'Much better to have an Athenian citizen. And you may have an errand or two?'

'I could take a couple of honeycombs to sell.'

'Excellent. Of course, I shall be in disguise.'

'Of course, are you not always so?' I replied with heavy irony. We arranged to meet at the Dipylon Gate, and I went home for the donkey, which had not been doing much for the last couple of days. Quickly I arranged some honeycombs in panniers, covered with some leaves to keep the flies off.

When the honey-laden donkey and I got to the Dipylon Gate, it took me a moment to spot Arkhias. The actor wore a slovenly threadbare old cloak covered with fish scales, and bore upon his back a creel containing two lampreys wrapped in wet leaves; in his right hand he carried a stick from which depended several fish, gazing at us with glazed reproachful eyes. Arkhias gazed at me with only slightly more expression, silently indicating that we were not to exchange greetings or recognition. He fell in behind me and we walked in procession, the donkey first, then me driving the donkey, and then (a good way behind me) the supposed fish merchant. Other people got in between, but I did not bother turning my head. A certainty he'd turn up, right enough. After we were well past the Akademeia, Arkhias drew level with me.

'Yesterday I was a peasant selling vegetables,' he explained. 'Today I am a fish-seller.'

'I can see that – as well as smell it.'

'I need to vary the roles, to have a number at command.'

'Very good. Not all roles smell so strongly. Please don't stand upwind of the honey.'

At the next village I did sell some of the Hymettos honey, which pleased me, and Arkhias, seeing me in better humour, took it upon himself to be conversational.

'It's not really Megara, you understand.'

'What isn't?'

'Where we are going. Just a little way beyond and behind Eleusis. A distance, but we should do it easily.'

'Do what?'

'Get there.' This all seemed pointless; I privately considered that we were getting nowhere at all. I let us jog on in silence. Occasionally Arkhias burst into a minute lecture on the art of disguise, but my lack of response would induce him to be silent again – until the next time.

'We're coming to a village now, we should turn to the right here,' he remarked at length.

'We're always coming to villages. Is this the one where you had news of Klei—'

'Hush!'

I was able to sell the last of the honey in this village, and Arkhias got rid of another one of his fish, which was just as well. Now I should gladly have turned back and gone home, but Arkhias gazed at me reproachfully.

'Only a little way further. I am sure you will be glad to go just a few more paces.'

We went on into the countryside again. Eventually we passed a little low-lying house, set well back from the road. I could hear geese cackling.

'Shouldn't we call in there and get something to drink?'

'No, no,' said Arkhias. 'Let us not waste time in doing that. The householders would not be pleased to have to be hospitable. Too poor. Not good customers for honey or fish.'

We continued on our way – or Arkhias' way – past little cultivated strips and a few untilled fields with sheep in them. The sun had come out and it was quite warm again for the time of year. Some late birds sang. Some late wasps made their presence known about my sticky panniers and Arkhias' smelly fish.

'There!' Arkhias suddenly tensed. 'What's that?'

'What?'

'In the ditch over there – a bit of cloth, moving in the wind—'

'Some peasant – some *real* peasant – taking a sleep in the middle of the day,' I suggested. 'Or a man overcome with too much wine. Pay no heed.'

'How can you say so? Why don't you investigate?'

'Investigate it yourself.'

'Someone may be hurt. Was that a groan?'

I rushed to the ditch and peered in. Homespun cloth had appeared above the ferns and furze, blending with these in their autumnal dry colour. But under the vegetation and the cloth was a body. Not warm. A human body, quite cold, though not stiff. With a sinking feeling I imagined having to tell Hermia that her son was dead. Reluctantly I cleared the furze away from the head, and turned the face upward.

'Ergokles!'

The swift-darting eyes were still enough now, and glazed. The snub nose had shrunk, and something had pecked it. As I moved the head, something very disagreeable happened. The head wobbled, flopping this way and that. I suddenly recollected how when I was a very young child I accidentally cracked my mother's distaff (though not quite through), and remembered the dismaying feel of the broken pole and the fuzzy head of wool flopping in every direction.

'Is he dead?' Arkhias asked.

'Yes. It is Ergokles, no doubt about that. And someone has broken his neck for him. The way he was lying – no, I think somebody else has already been here and disturbed this body.'

I dropped Ergokles' head with indecent haste, and turned to face Arkhias.

'You? It's *you*! You knew Ergokles' body was here all the time. He certainly couldn't groan – you made that up. Either you killed him yourself some while ago, or he was already dead when you found him.'

'Of *course* he was already dead. I did not kill him. But it is important that I shouldn't be the declared finder of this corpse.'

'You found him in this ditch? In this place? When?'

'Yesterday. I was on the same route, taking this side road around Eleusis. I spied the cloth, and came up and touched it just as you did. Moved the body and the head waggled, and then flopped back again in a different position, so it wasn't lying quite the same way. Very observant of you to spot that, though.'

I bit back a remark to the effect that I had experience in finding corpses. This was not something of which I wished to remind either fellow-citizens or foreign interlopers.

'Strange that Ergokles should die here,' I mused.

'I'd have thought he would have died somewhere cosier. A brothel, maybe. The bugs and birds have been at him.'

'They would be. Your panniers will provide an excuse for the interest of the flies. Ergokles smells worse today than yesterday. You see how good it is that I am so smelly today. I think we should take him back to Athens, on your donkey.'

'So *that* was why you wanted my poor beast! You planned for me to be the finder of the body. What about Kleiophon?'

'There's nothing to do with Kleiophon here. I just told you that, because then I knew you would come.'

'Are you sure,' I said carefully, 'that you are not of Cretan descent? I know you told us you are from those western regions near Sybaris. But is it not possible that there were Cretans among your ancestors?'

'Why?'

'All Cretans are liars,' I muttered through clenched teeth, as I set to the job of hoisting the very dead and lolling-headed Ergokles upon my unhappy donkey. Arkhias gave some help in getting the dead man into position. We covered the body with its own clothing and the fishy cloak of Arkhias. A cloud of flies surrounded us.

'Stop!' I said. 'We should investigate the place where he was killed.'

'Don't bother about that. The — this you-know-what — should be taken directly to Ergokles' house. His family can inform the authorities,' Arkhias advised. He gave my donkey a smart slap to start it on the road back to Athens, and I had to proceed with them.

'Ergokles' family can then pursue the matter at their leisure. I don't know if this area is under Athenian control, but I imagine so.'

'Yes. But — right now we are *here*, the place where he was killed. We should investigate what happened here first, before going back to the city.'

'How do you know where he died?'

'I don't. But he most probably was killed nearby. He didn't just fall down in a fit. Somebody broke his neck and then packed him carefully in a ditch.' I glanced about. The region was not very populous. But I heard the sound of geese somewhere.

'Look!' I required my hands to flap flies away from my head too much to spare them for pointing out what I meant. 'There is that little dwelling we saw before. Set back from the road, but in this lonely spot it's the kind of place that might be a sort of tavern. A house whose inhabitants offer drink and a bite to passers-by for money. Not like the real farmers, who are truly hospitable.'

'Perhaps.' Arkhias didn't seem especially concerned. 'But it's likely not inhabited, or if it is, it could be the den of some really poor creature with no information to offer. Considering our burden, we should proceed forthwith.'

'Suit yourself,' I said haughtily. 'Walk on ahead, or stay and mind the poor ass.'

Arkhias muttered, under his breath. I didn't heed him, but proceeded up the path to the little dwelling. Happily the geese were in the back of the house, pent within a makeshift fencing of sticks and furze. Beside them lay a little garden, baking in the heat, with seedy lettuces long bolted and gone. The house was very simple, roofed with furze instead of tiles. It was not much higher than I am myself, yet it had a kind of rambling spaciousness, enough for somebody to sleep, eat, and store tools – even animals. Just behind the house, under an apple tree near the goose-pen, I saw an old man.

'Good day. Fine geese you have here. Do you sell drink to travellers?'

The old fellow blinked and then arose and shuffled towards me.

'Oh yes, sir. We have a very good well, wine and good water, mixes lovely. I'll get you some, and bring it out.'

'Oh, I may as well go in,' I said, and walked within, ducking my head at the very low doorjamb. It took a while for my eyes to become easy in the interior darkness. But I saw the room was set up for visitors, if transient visitors. There were chairs and a table. I heard a sound between a groan and a snore, and looked about for somebody. Not finding a snorer in the central room, I glanced into the lean-to which was spread with a little very ancient hay and hinted at the ghost of a long-absent donkey. In this apartment I spied one lone animal, a young sheep, uncomfortably sleeping. Behind me, the old man unexpectedly set up a loud cry and an old woman came slowly in from the next room, a small chamber opposite the lean-to. This ancient female seemed unperturbed by his yelling – I fancy she was very deaf. She was also bent over, her chin almost touching her chest.

'Something to drink?' she said to me. She did not

look directly at me, not out of modesty but from physical necessity: her back curved forward like a bow and her bent head was far down. Rheumy old eyes appeared to search the floor, which was far from spotless. The geese evidently wandered in from time to time. The young sheep snuffled heavily, snored and farted.

'Don't be startled. Just a sick lamb,' the old woman said. 'It's taken to its bed and has gone into a stupor, like.' With fair dexterity, she poured out a thin wine, mixed with water from a cracked hydra, and shuffled over with this offering. She smiled – grinning in a terrifyingly toothless manner.

'Don't be frightened,' she said encouragingly, seeing me hesitate. 'The water's fresh out of our well. Very good water. Or if you pay for it you can have a hot drink. Soup, even. Once that sheep has died, we'll have stew.'

'No, he can't!' cried the old man. 'No fire this time of day. Waste of fuel.'

His aged spouse glanced towards the corner, where a little charcoal was neatly piled.

'If he paid for it, he could,' she said. 'Fuel-seller came.'

'No need,' said the aged householder crossly while I earnestly disclaimed any interest in hot drinks.

She took the water-jug back to a short table used for kitchen work, and I saw that in a pan of water lay some fresh beets. Aside from bolting lettuces and a few herbs, I had seen no sign of such things in their little garden.

'Did anybody come here earlier – a day or two ago? An Athenian with a rather snub nose, and straight brown hair?'

She did not answer, taking refuge in her deafness. I repeated the question to the old man.

'Lots of people come by,' he replied.

'Did you buy those beets from a vegetable-seller yesterday?'

'May have done,' he said uneasily. 'Can't say I remember. Little thing like that.'

'Want to buy a goose?' piped up the old woman unexpectedly.

'No thank you, not at present. But I do want to know where my friend is, the man with the snub nose and the plentiful hair.'

'Lots of people,' she said, in her cracked voice. 'They come and they go. *I* don't want any more quarrelling or messes. If it didn't help bring in a few obols, I wouldn't do it.'

'That's right,' her husband remarked. 'If it didn't bring in a pitiful little bit of money to help us in our old age, we wouldn't let all and sundry into our house.'

The man gave me such a meaningful look that I felt constrained to bring out an obol and gratify him. Since I had been paid for the honeycombs, I could not say I had no coins with me. The aged wife took it from her husband and put it for safe keeping into a cracked jar on a high shelf. But the cracked jar slipped from her trembling grasp, and crashed to the ground, where it shattered.

This piece of aged pottery had held only a few coins, and these were tossed about the floor. I picked up my own obol to give it again. The embarrassed old couple had better treasure than that, however, and pursued it about the earthen floor among the goose turds,

uttering little cries. I was surprised at the nature of
the coins thus revealed. As well as the bronze pieces
– a few obols and half-obols – there were several
silver drakhmai. Most amazing, the old wife had in
her pot a grand silver coin, the tetradrakhma. No –
not one, but two . . . no, five . . . of these four
drakhma pieces, each with a fine portrait of Herakles
(or Alexander looking like Herakles), his head
adorned with a lion's skin. Some of the coins had
fallen with the other side uppermost, showing Zeus
sitting on a knobby chair, apparently talking to an
eagle sitting on his right fist. The silver shone finely,
even on this dark floor among goose droppings and
feathers.

'I am glad to see you do not badly out of your little
business,' I remarked. The old woman, flushed with
effort and shame, shovelled together the coins picked
up from the guilty floor. 'It's the *geese*,' she insisted.
'We sell the geese! And their down. We can get some
things in exchange for goose-feathers.'

'That's right,' said the old man. 'That's all we have
to live on.'

'Don't you have somebody to take care of you?'

'My nephew, curses on him, took the farm, and the
good house, and left us to get on as best we can. May
lightning blast him!' The old man certainly didn't hold
back.

'Don't curse, deary, what's the good? Only brings
bad luck,' said his aged spouse. Her rebuke was miti-
gated by the fact that she was so bent she seemed to
be addressing her own feet every time she spoke.

'I see,' I remarked. 'That vegetable-seller with the

beets,' I turned to her, 'did he bother you? Was he asking questions, too?'

'They *all* ask questions these days!' The poor old trembling woman seemed on the verge of tears. 'They bother and bother. Like the wasps. When you shoo them off one thing they're on to another. I don't know – I just don't know—'

'What don't you know?'

'Nothing!' roared the master of the house, animated for all his bleary eyes. 'We know *nothing*. You understand that, young fellow?'

'Quite,' I said, rising. Gratefully I emerged from this hut into clearer air. The geese honked and hissed, but nobody else said anything. I walked off back down the path to where the fish-seller and the nervous donkey with his burden were waiting sheltered by a scrubby tree. We started to trudge along, us and the donkey and the body and the flies. A few late wasps settled on what they could reach of the late Ergokles.

'They need nourishment, that old couple. I'm glad you sold them some beets,' I remarked. Arkhias didn't rise to this observation; his cheeks flushed a little, but he said nothing. 'You don't want to share your information, I can see that. But somehow you found that Ergokles had been in that hedge-tavern. Is that right?'

'Why should I share information with you?'

'Because Aristotle may be displeased if you do not. And he has had the ear of Antipater longer than you have done.'

Arkhias walked along in silence, considering this. But I was not going to drop the matter.

'You asked questions of that old couple. And you

found out – what? That Ergokles had been there? Is that right?'

Arkhias nodded.

'And he was there alive – and had a drink in that place, probably.'

Reluctantly, Arkhias opened his mouth.

'Yes. And the old woman indicated he didn't seem to be feeling well when he left. But in truth that's *all* I know. They wouldn't tell me more. I suspect some other people were there, but they left no trace that I could see. And that old couple aren't very forthcoming.'

'Hmm.' I thought of the silver coins. Somebody – possibly, suppose – had paid the old couple for the use of their dwelling – just a room. Or had Somebody conversed with Ergokles outside at the back, beside the geese, invisible from the road? Ergokles and Somebody would have shared a drink. Had Ergokles been killed in that wretched cottage? Or had he been alive and walking when he got to the place a short distance away? About a parasang's distance from the little dwelling. Had he been quickly dispatched and then left in the ditch?

'Don't mistake me, Stephanos of Athens,' Arkhias continued. 'I have a high respect for you. I conceal only when my case is not complete. And this case is sadly incomplete. I cannot set the deficiency down to my own incompetence, but I have not found the boy. I will confess to you that I was not looking for Ergokles – so I will not triumph in finding him. No, I never intended or expected to find *Ergokles* dead. You are correct in your deduction: I did speak to that old couple. And I am sure that Ergokles was there at that place, not long before some person murdered him. But everything is too opaque and dim to be blurting out disconnected facts. Instead of a proper clew, I have pieces of yarn that are too short and don't match.'

'It is our duty to report the finding of the corpse, and get Ergokles' family and the authorities to look into it.'

'Yes. Maybe. But that old couple——! Hard to inter-rogate. They can be deaf – or feign deafness. It's a nuisance, but they are technically free, if the lowest of the low. That pair cannot legally be tortured in Attika. You have no idea how difficult it is, anyway, torturing creatures as old and frail as that. They may fall off their tree before the arrow hits, as it were. No, it would be better to have more time in which to look for hints and signs.'

'One corpse is a big enough sign!' I retorted. We plodded on our dreary way. It would have been, I reflected, almost unthinkable in the height of summer to undertake such a journey, if the flies were so thick at this time when the summer had departed. And yet I had only too recently had a journey full of flies and bad smells, walking in Asia . . .

'I hope you will be all right,' Arkhias remarked with concern as we drew near the city walls.

'I hope so, too – but in what exactly?'

'You must take the – this – to Ergokles' own house. If I were you, I should just say you were selling your honey in the countryside, and stopped when you saw the clothing in a ditch, and wondered if someone were ill. I don't think you should be suspected. Ergokles has obviously been dead longer than this morning, and presumably several people knew you were going out with the donkey and the honeycombs today.'

'I? Certainly there is no reason why *I* should be suspected!'

'That's all to the good. Let Ergokles' family deal with the case. They are bound to suspect Krito eventually, I should suppose. Don't you reflect or make any suggestions aloud. Just be polite and don't add anything.'

'Well, you will be there to back me up about the finding of the cor—'

'Hush! We're getting within earshot of folks now. No. No, of course it wouldn't do for me to appear, as myself, in a case in which I have been working in disguise. Extremely awkward. Ruins Antipater's whole plan for me! *My* name must not come into it – you must understand. It would be the same thing as dragging Antipater into it, and you wouldn't want to do that.'

I was taken aback, and truly angry. To think that this foreign actor was using me as an agent! Not to say as a tool. I vowed inwardly that I should be even with Arkhias for that at some point; I was glad that I had not told him about the silver coins in the old woman's jar. But these thoughts did nothing to mitigate the task of delivering a corpse to the door of an Athenian house, and asking heavily for the person in charge. The master of the house had come home, but not in a way he would have liked.

XX

The Fuel-Seller

It is never a pleasant task to deliver a corpse to the
right address. Naturally the inmates of Ergokles' unre-
markable dwelling were dismayed. Ergokles was a
widower, not rich in relatives, and I was requested to
wait until his brother-in-law came. I insisted they
convey the corpse within doors, where the female
slaves could start working on it, but I remained outside
with my poor little ass, which was perturbed at what
it had been forced to carry, and was now hungry as
well. There was no browsing on Ergokles' stony
street. Eventually the relative came, with an arkhon
to whom I made a report. That Ergokles had most
patently been dead for longer than a morning was of
great assistance to me; happily (as Arkhias had
predicted), no suspicion attached. I related nothing
more than the bare facts, how I had been selling honey
in that area, had seen the fabric in the ditch, and on
investigation found the dead man. No, I said, I could

not tell at all who had killed him. I said nothing of the hedge-tavern. It was clearly incredible that either the old man or the old woman had wrung the neck of a healthy active man in early middle age. (Although must not one or both of them be in the habit of wringing the neck of a goose?)

All this took the rest of the day, so it wasn't until next morning that I went to give Aristotle the latest news, fearing that Arkhias would have got ahead of me. Happily there was no sign of the actor-spy, and Aristotle had not heard of Ergokles' death. He insisted on a full account of the discovery – which I gave, including the presence of Arkhias in disguise, and his earlier discovery of the body.

'Arkhias must have gone in that direction the day before you did because of some suspected connection with Kleiophon,' Aristotle remarked. 'If we believe Arkhias to this extent – that he did not expect to find *Ergokles* – then he expected to find some clue regarding Kleiophon. Now, was Ergokles aiding the lad – helping him to run away? What would be the profit in that? Or was Ergokles himself searching for the boy? More probable. As we mentioned before, if Ergokles still hoped to profit from Krito, he might believe that finding Kleiophon would please the boy's brother. But on the other hand, he might think to help Krito's cause, and merit solid thanks in some sort of payment, by doing away with Kleiophon, or huddling him out of the country. Hermia once executed, Krito, now sole heir to a lot of wealth, would be grateful. He could cover his continually paying Ergokles off by saying he made periodic settlement of the alleged "debt". So at least the disagreeable little man might have thought.'

I hesitated. 'It's complicated; I'm not sure Ergokles himself was the same as he had been – I mean, not quite on the same side.'

'Explain?'

'First, because when we came down the hill after the trial of Phryne, Ergokles exclaimed that he had lost money in a wager on the outcome of the trial. He said he now needed money, to buy a slave. I think, looking back on it, he was talking more to Philinos than to Krito. He was saying something about "a lovely slave" – still going on about Marylla, I suppose. We've already discussed how odd it is that Ergokles suddenly turned around and was backing Krito, when the new homicide charge – making away with Kleiophon – was laid against Hermia and Phanodemos. I think Krito must have already paid him, substantially anyway, with perhaps promise of more to come.'

'Right, Stephanos. Motives shift. What you suggest is that Krito had come to a composition with Ergokles – just to get the troublesome man out of his way. Then Ergokles' pointed remarks and attempts at extortion might be directed against a new target – Philinos.'

'Exactly. Philinos took the "lovely slave" that the little man once shared with Orthoboulos, and Philinos has offered him as yet no compensation. Ergokles has an obsession about being cheated over that slave.'

'Ergokles loves – loved – grievances,' said Aristotle. 'His chief activity was collecting grievances and then claiming compensation for them. If the world went awry with him, he felt someone must pay. He had very

poor judgement How many has he harassed?
Orthoboulos – now dead. Krito – Hermia –
Phanodemos – and now Philinos. Poor Ergokles, so
unlovable. Quite a number of people might want to
get rid of him. And any one could be his murderer.'

'Not Krito, I think,' I said slowly. 'If Krito had
already settled with him. This event points again at
Hermia. Alas! Think, O Aristotle – we both heard
Ergokles at that interview when he was surely trying
to extort something from Hermia. If she suspected he
knew where the boy was, she might have had the nasty
little man followed, and then killed.'

'Surely far-fetched.'

'No – you don't realize, she is already suspected.
Right now, Ergokles' family – that is his brother-in-
law and his second cousin – have decided to go to law
to lay a charge against Hermia's family for the murder
of Ergokles. They will lay the charge directly after
the funeral.'

'Oh, by Herakles!' Aristotle slapped his forehead.
'The gods grant us patience! So Ergokles' relatives
wish to be in the fashion? Absurd!'

He stood up and walked restlessly about the room.
'Will there be no end of homicide charges? This is
ridiculous. We must find that boy, Stephanos! That's
the only way to begin to untie this knot. And yet –
where to begin? What connects all these people and
events? What points to the direction the boy has
taken? Let us go over everything we know together.'

And so we did, for a long time, recalling conversations and trying to connect details. Once more I
dredged up my recollections of the brothel colloquies,

especially on the memorable day of the pancakes. For I was reasonably sure it must be Orthoboulos' son who had been in Manto's brothel on that day.

'He was there, I think at that time,' I assured Aristotle. 'I didn't see him – I saw a small schoolboy scuttling along, but nobody the size of Kleiophon. And shortly after that, I think, the lad was spirited away from the brothel. But by whom or how?'

'You say Marylla came shortly after, just as you were leaving. And her story was that she came to reclaim a pan. A lame excuse that seems. For such a well-treated concubine as she has become could send a slave to fetch a utensil. And who can believe Philinos would be seriously annoyed about pots and pans?'

'You don't know what some men are like about housekeeping goods,' I said doubtfully. 'You are not only relatively rich, Aristotle, but careless about things you think beneath your attention. Women and slaves do those things all the time with each other – lending and borrowing – but are afraid of the master of the house knowing.'

'Well, perhaps you are right. I daresay I should ask Herpyllis to make me a complete kitchen inventory. Yet Marylla's presence strikes me as odd, and therefore interesting. Anything else?'

I racked my brains. I tried to envisage again the narrow kitchen of Manto's house, the untidy girls in their raggedy morning wear grouped around the pancake maker, the little portable oven and smoky cook-maid—

'"The fuel-seller came this morning." That's what they said,' I recalled. 'It's a normal thing, but still –

there *is* the fuel-seller. He has come up twice. But then a fuel-seller does show up, particularly as the weather begins to turn cooler.'

'Ah! Where else does the – or a – fuel-seller show up?'

'He had come to the old people's hedge-tavern, that dirty rundown place near where the corpse of Ergokles was found. Odd – that very poor couple could afford so much charcoal. But then they could easily pay for it in goose feathers. And someone had paid them real money.' I described the old couple, their dwelling, and the contents of the cracked jar.

'Someone – perhaps more than one person – paid them handsomely, in new silver coin, very recently. Over twenty drakhmai worth of new Alexanders! That money might possibly connect them with Ergokles' death, but surely not with Kleiophon. How would the boy come by coins like that? And would he pay it for lodging in that hovel if he had? Hard to believe a gently-reared youth would want to stay there long, with the goose-turds on the floor and the poor young dying sheep in the lean-to.'

Aristotle, who had been pacing now sat down again, and stared at me.

'This is new. Tell me about it – not the goose-droppings, but the little sheep.'

'Not much to tell, really. It snorted in its sleep and wouldn't wake up, though it could certainly still shit. The old woman said it had gone into a stupor. They would make stew of it when it was dead.'

'But it might not die of its ailment, Stephanos, if it were only in a stupor. Suppose . . . if something to bring on sleepiness had been introduced so that Ergokles drank it . . . and the sheep in some fashion got access to the remainder, and innocently drank? This is drawing a bow at a venture, to be sure. This hovel you describe – I am sorely tempted to relate it to Ergokles. But again, no thread, even fragile and fine-spun, connects it with Kleiophon.'

'Unless it was Kleiophon who killed Ergokles,' I said gloomily. 'It's hard to see how a boy could just disappear like that. If he is dead, somebody has done a good job of disposing of the corpse. And if he is alive – why, he could be anywhere.'

'Yes. He could have fled to another city. But first he would have been in Athens – at the beginning, within the city walls. He would need to be able to move around – or be moved undiscovered. That is, if he were his own agent. If somebody else were moving him, that person – whether enemy or helper – would have to find a way to make him movable.'

'The mule-boy!' I said. '"The mule-boy's already gone" That's what Manto's slave, the one sweeping outside the door, said to Marylla. Kleiophon could have gone about as a mule-boy. There's a charcoal-seller on the slope of Lykabettos who sells to well-to-do homes, where people don't want to shop for things like charcoal in the marketplace, but have it brought to them. And that charcoal-seller of Lykabettos has a mule-boy. Because that man goes about on a mule, sometimes with two or three. And he takes a boy with him to tend the animals.'

'I know the man you mean – his name is Ephippos and he lives not far from here!' Aristotle jumped up.

'Theophrastos last spring looked into all the fuel-sellers and their prices. Ephippos sells fuel to Orthoboulos' house — I believe he may also serve Manto's establishment. Let us find him!'

Aristotle was right. The fuel-seller's dwelling on the lower eastern slopes of the absurdly abrupt hill of Lykabettos was not far from the pleasant groves of the Lykeion. Well outside the city walls, Ephippos rented a spread of land, affording plenty of room for burning charcoal, and for storage of charcoal, large jars of oil, and mules. Using wood collected on Lykabettos, this charcoal-burner also went on occasional expeditions to better-wooded parts, like Akharnai, where he dealt with local burners. He also sold olive oil for lamps, as well as sticks and furze, and dry olive stones for little stoves.

We could smell the smoke and the hardy scent of mules as we neared his establishment; perhaps Ephippos made extra money out of selling the mule dung, of which he enjoyed a goodly supply. Two mules stamped irritably as we passed by, each tethered in his own space, with a space between them. Working mules are not to become accustomed to roaming at will.

'Well, men of Athens, what can I get you? You come for charcoal, perhaps? Or would you like a good measure of dried olive stones?' The fuel-seller himself came out to greet us.

'We hear of the good quality of your charcoal, O Ephippos,' said Aristotle, 'and we have thought of changing our supplier at the Lykeion.'

'But you changed your supplier last spring, did you

not?' This man was no fool. I suppose the local fuel-sellers maintain an observation of each other's customers.

'That shows we are capable of changing,' said Aristotle with a beguiling smile.

He cast a glance around the goods of Ephippos. As well as stables, there were low sheds tidily arranged for keeping fuel from moisture and wind.

'We hope to find that your oil is clean, your charcoal good, and you yourself above reproach. Pray, can you tell us the names of some of your customers to whom we might apply for information?'

'There's too many,' said Ephippos, with a sharp glance.

'Well, let us say, one or two might do,' said Aristotle soothingly. 'Were you not the supplier to Orthoboulos' mansion? The one that now belongs to Krito?'

Ephippos looked at us steadily for a space, then nodded to himself. 'I did serve that house,' he said. 'Matter of fact, still do.'

'And you also serve the house of Manto?'

Ephippos cracked a broad grin. 'You'd better be careful about talking of *service* in that establishment,' he said. 'You know it's a girls' factory, and no mistake! But brothels are good business, they're always awake at night.'

'Quite so. And you are, I can imagine, a kind and generous man, as well as perspicacious. You not only sell warmth, you are warm-hearted. When the boy appealed to you for help, you did not reject him—'

'Here, stop! You go much too fast for me, Aristotle of the Lykeion. What a jump from charcoal to boys!'

'Yes, but you took the jump,' insisted Aristotle. 'Not because you are venal, however, for I think you did not get much out of it except the service of a lad to tend your mules. Did your other servant leave – the one the little girl called a "lanky boy"? For your muleteer, who was certainly taller and older, changed into someone who was but a boy indeed.'

Ephippos spat. 'The other one, the tall fellow, ran off. Said he could better himself doing something else, even going for a soldier. He weren't no slave, but my second cousin's son, so I never set catchers on him. But I was doing rounds on my own, when up this boy pops and says he'd like to work with the mules. So I let him. I had a big delivery to take round-about Athens, and I knew later I'd be going past Eleusis, Megara direction. So I was main glad of his services.'

'But you knew who he was?'

'No, not I. A lot of children talk to the mules – I don't pay 'em much heed. This lad came to me, in distress like. His clothes were tore, he was hungry and he needed something to live on. Told me his name was "Simmias". Said his father was a potter, dead, and his older brother beat him. So I took him on.'

'But you did not keep him.'

'He needed a better life, and I could see he was not real happy about staying in Athens. So I sent him to Lykaina. Thought she could get out of young Simmias what his trouble was. That's a woman friend of a friend. Very jolly and nice, helpful sort and kind to children. So he went off to Lykaina's house.'

'Have you heard from him? Have you seen him

again?' Aristotle interrogated sharply. 'Come, man, why equivocate?'

'I think he is doing all right. But I don't know no details. You'd better ask the woman Lykaina.'

'Even though he is riding your mule? Your third mule, Ephippos. Of course you have a third mule. We can see the space it occupies. You've lent or rented it to him.'

He nodded. 'I rent mules to folk and that mule is rented out. But you mistake — *I* don't have the boy. Ask Lykaina.'

'I should willingly do so,' said Aristotle. 'I gather she is not a citizen's wife or daughter — but the kind of woman to whom any man can talk?'

Ephippos nodded. 'You may do that right enough. Not but what Lykaina may be some gentleman's peculiar fancy at present. Time not altogether at her own disposal.'

'Let us go to her at once,' said Aristotle. 'That is — where is she? I have no idea where she lives.'

'Well,' said Ephippos, 'she's main far away, not on this side of Athens at all. Lykaina lives well outside the walls on the other side. Towards Mount Parnes, on the outskirts of Akharnai. It's a weary way if you ask me.'

'Not so bad if one rides,' Aristotle observed. 'Rent us the two mules.'

After some ritual haggling, this was agreed to. The fuel-seller gave us some directions as to the location of Lykaina's dwelling. 'Her house is small and sits on the edge of a piece of waste ground,' he particularized. Then we were mounted and set off towards the city gates in order to pass through Athens and out the other side.

Though certainly swifter than walking, going on muleback is not altogether comfortable. These brutes had very decided backbones, and very decided objections to doing anything difficult, like rounding a corner. In every neighbourhood through which we passed, they made the inhabitants a copious gift of manure. I hoped folks would regard it as a gift for gardens. Unkind remarks pursued us as we tried to press through traffic, while members of the populace both walking and riding seemed determined to slow to a snail's pace before me, or even to stand still under my mule's nose. I was treated to pointedly personal analysis from people we bumped into, comments reflecting unfavourably on my looks, cleanliness and ancestry. We tried to keep away from the middle of the road, but then my mule seemed to have a desire to slide my foot briskly along a wall, perhaps to see if it could break a bone or two. At other times the animal trotted along well enough, but then it would get into conversation or something with Aristotle's mule, which always endeavoured to stay in front. Sometimes mine tried to catch up, which made Aristotle's mule trot the faster, looking back with a wicked gleam in his eye, and bumping the Master of the Lykeion about most sadly. Both beasts seemed amused by this. It is difficult, riding on mules who are personal acquaintances and enjoy relations and rivalries of long standing. The mules seemed to understand each other much better than we did them.

It was a considerable distance to the area in which

Lykaina lived, on the outskirts of the village or town of Akharnai, the largest deme in Attika, one of the many outside the city walls. Akharnai crouches along the feet of the peaked Parnes hills to the west. Akharnaians, rather like those low mountains, are prickly, cool and independent; Aristophanes the playwright imagines one of them defying the central government in Athens and making his own peace treaty. We turned our mules' noses to the north, parallel to the Parnes, and began to look for the landmarks mentioned by the fuel-seller. There was the monumental marble-cutter, with the unfinished tombstone. There was the shop of the potter who made uneven bowls, and the large house with its many hens. Our mules trotted along as if the way were familiar — as they naturally would if Lykaina was supplied by their master with fuel. We turned right and left again, down a long lane, a lonely place. As the lane trickled to an end we found ourselves looking at the waste ground to which the fuel-seller had referred. And on the edge of that waste, on a slight rise, was a solitary small dwelling.

The dwelling of Lykaina was not of the most contemptible class of building. The roof was tiled, and there was a stout wooden door. Yet, if nicer than the hedge-tavern of the old couple, it was not much nicer. The house was small and appeared unkempt; I could see a gap in the roof where one or two tiles had cracked and slipped. Behind the house was a wild yard, its boundaries delineated by a few piles of brushwood. A shed with only two walls, containing some ancient hay, was mouldering quietly in a corner; as there were no beasts pertaining to the establishment, the shed was perhaps a slave's quarters. Beyond or behind the shed were a few rows of vegetables, by now completely finished. Among the ruins of yellowing leaves and withered stalks one solitary hen scratched, more as a diversion than as a practical means of making a living.

It was a painful pleasure to climb down off my mount, the mule uncharitably looking me as if to say, 'This is a welcome relief, but sadly belated.' Now we were arrived, what kind of woman were we about to meet? What might she reveal? The day, which had been almost too warm for the time of year, suddenly became cloudy, and I sensed a coming rain. We walked up the path beaten in the grass and dirt, slowly approaching this unknown place.

'What do *you* want?'

I started, and I could swear Aristotle did likewise. A man had come round the corner of the house and was now confronting us. A slave, a tall and burly slave. He was dressed in a meagre grey homespun slung over a splendidly muscular torso. His short grey greasy hair was powdered with dust, and dark whiskers poked through the grime on his chin. The man's ox-like neck was encircled by the iron ring that announced his enslaved station. Not every slave has to wear one, so this was an indication that he was dangerous or likely to run away. It was clear too that he had been branded – so he was a runaway who had been recaptured. A desperate fellow, an insensate brute most likely, but not a creature whom it was advisable to irritate.

'What you staring at?' he enquired gruffly, addressing himself to me in particular.

'Have I met you before?' I wondered.

He spat. 'Nah!' he said with finality.

'We are seeking Lykaina, the mistress of this house,' said Aristotle pleasantly. 'We have business with her.'

'Don't know if Lykaina mistress of this house has any business with *you*,' said the slave. 'I ain't seen neither of you before. What kind of business might yours be?'

'Hens?' I suggested, perhaps too brightly. He gave me a ferocious scowl.

'You let that hen alone, d'ye hear?' Maybe the poor mangy chicken was a kind of pet of the brute's.

'Let us go in and see her – Lykaina, I mean,' suggested Aristotle, trying to slip past the guardian. But the burly fellow thrust out a huge arm and held Aristotle back.

'*Nobody* goes in now. She don't want nor need visitors poking around. Now, can you write a note?'

'Yes,' said Aristotle, rather blankly. 'But I haven't anything to write on, unless – oh yes, I did bring a pair of tablets with me.' He fished out a pair of battered wooden tablets. 'I'll write a short note, if that is what you think she would like,' he suggested amiably, trying to erase what was already imprinted on the soft wax. Swiftly he wrote a few lines and folded up his tablets. His mule farted loudly and began to move towards the remains of the vegetable garden.

'Back to the road!' ordered the surly one. 'And get them animals out of there. *I'll* take that, if you please. Now, stay where you are, and don't move.' Snatching the tablets in his huge paws, he walked away. Although the house was small it must have had a door at the back, for he went around the corner and disappeared from view.

'Well guarded, this female, whoever she is,' said Aristotle. 'I wonder if she's somebody's treasure. And I wonder too that her lover, the person who must insist on all this privacy, hasn't made her the present of a dog.'

We were waiting in a nowhere for nothing perhaps – I could not imagine for what. A shifting wind blew across my skin with sudden clammy coldness, and I could feel gooseflesh rising. A little while ago, I should have thought it very agreeable to be slightly chilly, but it did not seem so now. My shoulder throbbed and ached from the strain of pulling at the mule and jogging up and down; the cold air gave the spear-wound fresh twinges and twirls. I felt sorry for myself: waiting for nothing, wounded and full of aches, a good distance from my own house – with a storm about to break. Yet even I really knew the wait was not very long. The huge slave returned but not with any woman, nor any invitation to enter. The man simply thrust at Aristotle a pair of tablets – not the ones he had handed in, but a new pair, of good wood.

'You take that there letter and be off,' said the slave. Aristotle hastily opened the splendidly waxed tablets, and I peered over his shoulder to read the unexpected epistle :

> To the honoured Aristotle of the Lykeion, Greetings
>   from Lykaina his servant
>   This is not the end of your search. I am but a
> humble instrument. I too think it is time that what
> is missing ought to return.

*For the information you seek, you could apply to
the mother in the question. Yet, as her distress is too
grievous to be disturbed, I urge you to take this
letter and apply to the oracular lady who lives in
the house of weaving women, and she can explain.*

'Amazing,' I said. 'A woman to write a letter. As
long as that.'

'An accomplishment indeed,' Aristotle remarked.
'Not only clearly inscribed in a good hand, but the
sentences are not bad. One would think some man
might have dictated this. But who—'

'Be off, both of you, right now,' said the big slave
impatiently, 'and don't stand puzzling over that-there
writing, as if you could read no better than your mule!'

And indeed, one of the mules seemed to be trying
to read over our shoulders.

Thinking it best to take the man's advice, and not
to tarry longer at the house of the strange Lykaina,
we got on our animals once more (not without difficulty) and moved off. The light was going rapidly
from the sky, and the wind continued to blow,
whistling off the peaks of the Parnes. Dark clouds
menaced us above. But when I looked back at the
house of Lykaina, on its little slope of waste land, it
seemed to be in a pool of sunshine while all around
it was getting darker.

We made our way back to Athens slowly on our
tired steeds. 'What does that strange note mean?' I
asked as we jogged along. 'I can see that "the mother"
must mean Hermia. I know no mistress of a house of
weaving women. Who is this she-oracle?'

'You do know her. The mistress of an establish-
ments of girls who weave – when they have nothing
else to do. Manto – whose name indicates an oracle
or divination – is surely the person indicated. Mantic
Manto.'

At this moment the heavy rain burst forth from
those dark clouds, and the wind was driving sheets
of water across Mount Parnes – and across our road.
We had not brought cloaks with us, so we were
severely dampened. The actual rainstorm did not last
long; by the time we got within the city walls it had
softened to a drizzle, but riding was exquisitely
uncomfortable.

We were in such a damp and unpleasant condition,
smelling no doubt horribly of wet mule, that I thought
we might each go straight home. But Aristotle had
other ideas. 'We ought to go at once to Manto's. If
she has information, there may be no time to lose.'

So we proceeded on muleback to Manto's house,
causing astonishment to the slaves keeping the gate
and to the evening visitors who were beginning to
arrive, as well as to the gaggle of lightly-clad beauties who came to look at us as we came in. They could
not restrain their laughter, nor stop wrinkling their
noses at the smell.

'Tsk, girls!' said Meta, marshalling them. 'No need
to be so unwelcoming. Mules smell of money, remember that!'

'I am sorry, I do not wish to trouble any of you,'
said Aristotle, with but a courteous glance at these
women in almost transparent gowns, 'but I am – we
are – in urgent need of speech with Manto.'

'It's the honey man! On honey business again?' said one of the girls, lifting an eyebrow at me.

Fortunately, Meta told us at once that Manto would receive us in private. We followed her, and found Manto in a respectable little chamber, without a bed. A full loom was set up, and the loom weights indicated that she did her own work. Two small folding chairs were set in place, while she remained on her weaving stool, facing us. She had asked for lamps to be brought in. The room was a trifle close and smelled of wool, but not of perfumes.

'This,' said Aristotle, 'ought to perform my introduction.' And he handed her the tablets given us by the large and surly slave.

Manto examined the letter carefully. I was not sure if she could really read, or was merely looking at the style of writing and the signature to identify the scribe.

'We hope,' said Aristotle boldly, 'that you will fulfil the wishes of Lykaina who writes you this letter, and tell us about young Kleiophon, without forcing us to disturb his mother. But you know that his absence is now making things worse, not better, for Hermia.'

'Very well,' Manto sighed. 'I have been good at keeping the secret, but I too am concerned about the boy himself, and what might happen to him. I think he might actually be safer in Athens. I do not know everything. All I know is this. I received the boy, disguised as a lad attending mules; he was carrying a message from a woman called Lykaina, written like this one. She said that Hermia would be in contact with me soon, and please to attend to her wishes. The mother, Hermia, sent me money privately—'

'How?' I interrupted. 'How did she know where to send it?'

'Lykaina told her,' Manto replied with a touch of impatience. 'The fuel-seller had taken him to Lykaina, who was able to set everything in train when she sent him back to Athens again, and to me. The boy's name was *never* mentioned in this house, though some of the girls knew a lad came attending the mules. He was here for about two days only—'

'Eating pancakes,' I interjected. She looked surprised. 'Or one pancake anyway,' I amended. 'With honey.'

'Very likely. As I was saying, Hermia sent me money—'

'How?' I asked. 'Just how could she send money?'

'She had someone bring it of course, someone trust-worthy.'

'Of course!' I exclaimed. 'The slave Batrakhion, the hunchbacked servant in Hermia's house. He's devoted to her – and she could trust him. On the day of the pancakes, I saw a funny little figure by the side of your house, all wrapped in a big cloak. I thought it a boy late for school. But the way it scuttled along – I should have realized it was Batrakhion.'

'Yes, quite true. He is the slave who does Phanodemos' shopping and errands.'

'So the guards at Hermia's – Phanodemos' – house would suspect nothing unusual in the little fellow's going out,' I commented, happy to reach a patch of unusual clarity.

'Just so. As I was saying,' Manto reiterated with some asperity, 'Hermia sent me money, wrapped in a cover from Lykaina, so it couldn't be detected as a message from herself. She sent word that the boy needed to get away. Then we – I – passed the money on to him as well as a message from his mother saying she loved him – you know the style of thing. And the boy left, on a hired donkey. I think he was going to go to Korinthos – or rather to one of the two ports serving that city, and then away by sea. Peiraieus is too much part of Athens, people might recognize him.'

'So – how do we get in touch with Kleiophon?'

'That I cannot tell you. But I do not believe he is in any other person's control, and I do not believe you have any cause to fear that he has been injured in any way. At least, he departed in good health, with his mother's help and blessing.'

'We shall need to have more words with the fuel-seller,' I said shortly. We should have to take the mules back to Lykabettos – the very thought made my back-side wretched.

'That is all I can tell you,' said Manto, turning her head back towards her loom, suggesting a desire to return to privacy. Though how much privacy could you get in a brothel, I thought, hearing a flute beginning to warm up, the loud buzz of voices, and a certain significant thumping from the room above our heads.

We took our leave, and returned to our damp disconsolate mules. The road back to Lykabettos was very splashy, and the going slow. The fuel-seller was not there, and we had to haggle with the servant as to how much wear we had inflicted on the animals. Muleless, we made our way on foot through puddles to the Lykeion. The city gates being closed, I accepted

Aristotle's offer of a good meal and a place to sleep.
I could also have done with a medicinal bath and some
ointments. Herpyllis was kind enough to see to it that
I had warm water, and sent the slave Autilos with
olive oil (good quality) with which to rub my tired
body. She was also kind enough to suggest to Aristotle
that he should lend me some clean garments.

'Let us at least rejoice in a good dinner,' said
Aristotle, making libation before pouring the first
wine. Herpyllis had brought in to us fresh bread
accompanied by a savoury stew. But we were stopped
before we started by a knocking on the door. Phokon
hurried to answer, and I heard his voice in the hall
objecting that the Master was at dinner and could not
be disturbed. But this insistent visitor paid no heed.

Quick young feet came towards us, and without a
knock a quick young person entered the room. A
travel-worn young person, much sunburnt, with long
hair and a wisp of whisker.

'Good evening, O Aristotle,' said a voice, a boy's
voice, slipping as boys' voices do.

'I am Kleiophon son of Orthoboulos.'

XXI

━━━◦§◦━━━

The Mule-Boy's Story

'Kleiophon!' we both exclaimed. Even Aristotle was astonished at this advent. 'Yes, I recognize you – but you have been missing for so long, and we have been worried about you.'

'*Who* has been worried?' the youth demanded practically.

'Many people,' said Aristotle. 'Sit down, young man. I shall tell Phokon my servant to see that you are brought something to eat immediately. Do not alarm yourself,' seeing that the boy was getting up again. 'Phokon is reliable, and discreet. Are you unsure whether you have returned to Athens for good, or no?'

'I suppose I ought to return and stay,' said Kleiophon. 'I have been thinking – perhaps it was rather cowardly of me to run away.'

'That shows manliness,' I approved. 'So you are ready to take your part in the hearings – and in your stepmother's trial?'

He sighed. Despite a certain improved confidence and even more mature bearing, he still seemed vulnerable, and very young. His face was very dirty, more like that of a slave than a citizen, and his clothes stank of mule. Aristotle, with true Greek hospitality, kindly made no objection to a person in such a pickle occupying his *andron.*

'Yes, I suppose so. Krito frightened me so I didn't think I could bear it! He told me that Papa's ghost would come and haunt me as long as I stayed in the house. He said I was a traitor. And as good as a *murderer* for siding with Hermia. That's what Krito said.'

The lad shivered, and looked whiter under the sunburn and the dust.

'Phokon, please inform Herpyllis that I have visitors and she is not to come in. But please bring us yourself some more wine, and another spoon,' Aristotle ordered. Turning to the boy, he spoke authoritatively. 'I do not wonder that you were alarmed by these brutal hints,' he said, 'but that kind of thing, as you probably realize, is used to frighten slaves and children. By now I imagine you have seen through the foolishness of some of your terror.'

The boy straightened his shoulders. 'Yes,' he said proudly. His eyes grew brighter as the food approached, and Aristotle poured him out a generous goblet of wine well qualified with water. 'Yes. I am not a child now,' Kleiophon announced, just before his teeth sank into the food. We waited respectfully until the edge of his hunger was dulled.

'I was so unhappy then,' Kleiophon explained,

taking another gulp of the wine and water. 'It was very dismal, Papa's dying. It would have been very sad anyway – but then to find that he was murdered, and in such a way! Everybody in the house was very miserable. Of course it wasn't so hard on Kharis, my little sister. Because it wasn't her real papa who had died. She's only my stepsister,' he explained.

'Quite. But I imagine Krito himself was quite overcome.'

'Yes. I understand it better now. He was upset partly because he thought he had to *do* something about it. So he accused Mama. Krito never liked the idea of having a stepmother anyway. *He* wanted to be the one that Papa always looked to for help and advice, now he had got older. Krito was very important to Papa during that stupid trial over that dreadful man Ergokles! We all hated Ergokles, of course, but that didn't keep us together. In fact, it made trouble. Maybe we'd have got along better if Ergokles' accusation hadn't poisoned things.'

'What were the chief sources of trouble?'

'Well, Papa was ashamed, and very worried, sometimes he didn't attend to things. Krito became very fault-finding – even with Papa. And bossy and important. Krito thought he was in charge of the family sometimes. Then when Papa got married, his new wife – Hermia – was used to handling money and managing a household of servants. She didn't pay much attention to what Krito said.'

'So – we can begin to understand. Once your father was dead, your brother's growing dislike of Hermia fitted well with his need to find someone to accuse.'

'Yes. *Somebody* had to be – has to be – guilty of the murder. So Krito thought it must be Hermia. I am sure he truly means it. Krito was always like that – always. Once he gets an idea in his head, he really believes it and you can't get him to think anything else.'

'You resented his headlong decision to accuse Hermia?'

'I hated him at the time – because Mama had been so good to us, especially me. I don't want to lose a mother again! And then Krito had other men around him to bolster him up, and Mama had hardly anybody.'

'It was brave and manly to attempt to stand by her.'

'But then, if Krito had known in advance I was going to stand up for her, he would have kept me out of the first hearing. I thought it was quite clever *not* to say anything much until the prodikasia, when we were actually in front of the Basileus. And then I could show my loyalty to Hermia, and argue for her side.'

'That was intelligent,' Aristotle said. 'I take it that what you said at that first hearing – about speaking to your father the evening before he died – was true?'

Kleiophon, his mouth full of bread, nodded.

'Then you did quite right to mention it. It added new and important facts to the evidence; such details need to be carefully sifted.'

Kleiophon nodded again, in emphatic agreement. 'Mama was out that afternoon, when Papa was resting. And I heard him go out a while later – I heard the door close. The old butler we used to have was not always there all the time in the evenings—'

'Ah!' I said knowingly. 'Artimmes, the bald Phrygian.'

'Yes, that's right. The butler we have now belongs to Hermia, I mean he came from her house. He wasn't put in permanently, though, until they took Artimmes away to question him, after Papa died.'

'But the change of servants had already begun? Or was at least talked of?' Aristotle enquired.

'That's right. But that night Artimmes was looking after the door – when he wasn't pottering off to the cook to get a bite, or finding bits of wood to make things for little Kharis. The woman Marylla was still part of the household – she was upstairs weaving with other servants. The housekeeper spoke to her. Marylla wasn't very hungry, didn't want to come down for dinner, so the maids stayed with her and the housekeeper took her up a piece of bread. Hermia had gone out to see her uncle Phanodemos and his wife. Just after Papa left, then she came home. And I *know* that Hermia came home after calling on her uncle and aunt. I really believe she had nothing to do with Papa's death, nothing at all—'

'We understand this,' I broke in. 'But what did Krito do to make you determine to leave – and in the middle of the proceedings leading to the trial? You left your stepmother alone.'

He cast his eyes down. 'I know that was not a noble thing, to run away,' he said. 'But when he got me at home after the first prodikasia, Krito scolded and mocked me. He told me I was a murderer, or as good as, and said all that about a ghost. Then when I cried he said I was crazy. Unless I were declared to be crazy and locked up, he said he would see that I was put on trial for my life next. After the trial went against

Mama. People said she would be killed. Krito told me
– he described – how they would do it.' He trembled
a little. 'I could not bear it!' he cried, his voice crack-
ing. 'I could not bear to stay here in Athens and go
through all that! I just wanted it all to *stop*!' He put
his head in his hands.

'Of course. Very natural,' said Aristotle soothingly.
'Yet although you felt almost driven out of your wits,
you were in sufficient command to devise a plan of
escape. It must have been a good one, as nobody caught
you.'

The lad took his hands away from his face – on
which dust and tears now combined in a kind of paste.
'Yes,' he said reminiscently. 'It was good, wasn't it? I
had thought about it before, actually. Because the fuel-
seller came around our house regularly, with a mule,
sometimes two, even three. He had a tall sun-burnt
boy to tend the animals, and I thought what fun that
would be. And then the fuel-seller came and I heard
him complain to the servants that his mule-boy had
run off – the lanky one. So I slipped out of the house
and caught up with the fuel-seller. Not by our house,
I didn't want him to know who I was. And I had put
raggedy old clothes on, and some dirt on my face, so
he wouldn't think I had a good home and make me
go back.'

'Resourceful Simmias,' complimented Aristotle.

'Yes – how did you know? Did Manto tell you that
was the name I took? I worked a couple of days as
just his mule-boy. I got to know the animals, and I
fed and cleaned them. Sometimes I got to ride! And
I saw different areas of Athens. At last I was able to

go outside the walls!' His eyes lit up with pleasure. 'But I knew this couldn't last, and I could see the fuel-seller – his name is Ephippos, by the way – might guess I was well-born and not really a mule-boy sort. Though I scraped my hair back, and kept dirty and ragged.'

'Disguise,' said Aristotle. 'Appropriate under the circumstances. Though had you called at your own house, your dog would have recognized you at once.'

'I don't have a dog. My really good idea was to get away to a port – not near Athens, too many people who might know me. But to get to one of the ports of Korinthos, and then go off. But I had no money to do that. And I also didn't want Mama to worry about me.'

'And so?' I prompted

'So – I asked Ephippos, when I was looking after his mules – still being careful what I said, you know. And he suggested I share my troubles with Lykaina, a female he knew, who lived out near Akharnai but was often in the city. So I went to see this Lykaina.'

I leaned forward. 'You did?' I asked. 'What was she like?'

'Well – like nothing. You know what women are, they veil themselves. She was veiled. Though I saw some of her hair, shiny and black. I suppose she is a freedwoman. She was nicely dressed, like a lady almost, but her house was really tumbledown. Lykaina has a pretty way of talking, but it was sometimes difficult to hear her, she spoke so low and quiet. And not much. But she was kind, and swore to keep my secret. And she told me to go to a certain house in Athens, where there were women who'd look after me. And she promised she would at once get word to my mother, who could send me money and a message there, at the strange house in the city.'

'At Manto's establishment!' I said triumphantly. 'And I trust you enjoyed the honey pancakes?'

'I only had one.' He looked surprised. 'How did you know? I was hungry. The first day when I left Lykaina's and came to Manto's I had a headache and wasn't hungry at all. Very strange house, that is. Lots of women around but hardly anybody came to see me. I saw one great girl, though, when I peeped out!' He chuckled reminiscently. 'She had a thin dress on, and really big tits, to make you want to play with them. Manto shooed her away. Manto is very proper and she does a lot of weaving. Otherwise, I would have thought I was in one of those houses the boys talk about at school. It was rather lonely and there weren't any books, at least not in the little room I was made to stay in.' He stopped grinning and looked thoughtful.

'It was probably as well that nobody in the house met me, except for Manto. I needed to keep secret. Then Mama sent me a message and some money.'

'By Batrakhion,' I said. 'Did you know Batrakhion before?'

'Oh, that little humpbacked fellow. No I'd never seen him before. But Manto let him come to see me, and he told me he was a servant of Phanodemos and knew Mother well. "I must be her eyes," he said in his funny way. He gazed at me, kind of goggling like a frog, so I'm sure he had a good look and could tell her I am well.'

'So your stepmother had sent money?' prompted Aristotle.

'Quite a lot of money. So I knew I could escape to Korinthos. And she would know that I loved her and nothing bad had happened to me.'

'Did you write to her?' I asked, thinking that such a letter from her son might help Hermia.

'No, I forgot, I was in such a hurry. And I'm not good at writing letters. The woman of the house helped me set off with a hired donkey. I went in the Megara direction, where I had gone a few days before with Ephippos and his mules, delivering charcoal. I had money and I could get to Korinthos on my own. I got to the last place where he delivered the charcoal, at the end of his route, and thought I'd stop there for a rest and something to eat. I remembered there was a funny sort of tumbledown cottage place with a lot of geese and a couple of old people in it, and a little sheep frisking round the yard.'

I was all ears. 'Go on!' I urged.

'It wasn't very nice but it wasn't the sort of house where people were likely to find me. I bought food off the old couple – they weren't hospitable, they *sold* things. I got some bread and cheese for the journey – I had already got a leather wallet to put stuff into. And I was at this funny place when somebody I knew came in!'

'Let me guess,' I said. 'Somebody you knew – a person whom you didn't wish to see you. Could it have been Ergokles, by any chance?'

He looked at me with astonishment. 'Yes,' he said. 'That's *exactly* who it was. I certainly didn't want him to see me. He was blustering and carrying on in his nasty way. That old couple can hardly hear even when you speak loud, so they didn't pay much attention. He was waiting for somebody, and ordered some wine, and then he got impatient. I was outside, sort of feeding the geese and looking as much like a house-slave as I could, so he wouldn't notice me. Though that old pair have no slaves, can you believe it!'

'Yes, I can, easily,' I said.

'But you'll never guess what happened. The people Ergokles was waiting for turned up, at least one of them did. He talked as if he was expecting a couple of people, and one of them at least a man, but the person who came was a woman. And I knew who it was, as soon as I heard her speak – Lykaina!'

'Really?' Both of Kleiophon's hearers were surprised and interested.

'I wasn't sure whether to speak to her or not. But as she was with Ergokles and somebody else might be coming, it seemed best not to. I stayed hidden. Luckily, the deaf old woman asked me to kill one of the geese for her, to sell to these travellers. So I killed the goose, by wringing its neck. I wanted to look at home, like the slave who does all sorts of odd jobs. And I put goose feathers all over me, so I would look like somebody who spent his time with the geese, and was goose-bespattered – you know what I mean. Nobody would wish to know me. But Lykaina! I was surprised that she didn't know me straight away. She ought to have recognized me. Maybe her veil was too heavy.'

'She was veiled?'

'Yes. Though she half threw off her veil when she talked with Ergokles. I could see her shiny black hair tumbling around. She actually sat down beside Ergokles and talked with him while he was eating! He was sitting at a little table outdoors, where it was cooler. Women are supposed to stay in the kitchen and out of the way when men eat, but it didn't seem to bother him – or her. Any more than that silly little sheep playing around. They had something to talk about, I guess. But the geese were a nuisance, and set up quite a racket. She drew him indoors, and then she got up and went outside to the well. She got some water in an old cracked hydra. And she poured it into a jug on the little table, and told me to take it in and give the man a drink. So I poured Ergokles a drink of water – still acting as if I was a house slave, you understand. And I gave the rest of the water to that stupid sheep that came nosing up to me.'

'And then?'

'Then I found Lykaina really *did* know me. She must have recognized me when I spoke to the sheep. She came up to me – we were outdoors, away from the old couple. She had made them stay in the lean-to where an old ass used to be kept – when they had one.'

'Aha!' I said. 'So the old people could always say they knew nothing of what happened. And perhaps that was true, in a way.'

'I suppose so. They weren't curious at all. Out in their village, maybe nobody had heard much about a missing boy, and these broken-down old people, partly deaf – they aren't the sort to get the news anyway.'

'A shrewd deduction,' said Aristotle. 'Yet somebody

else could have deduced the same thing. That they were old, deaf, poor, and out of the way. An admirable couple, in some respects. And the hovel an admirable house for secret dealings.'

'What else did Lykaina say to you?' I asked.

'She told me to keep my money carefully in a pouch round my neck, with a talisman. And she told me to take off right now, get going on the road to Korinthos. "Escape!" she said. She said that was what my mother wanted, that it was truly important that I should get clean away from Athens. And there would never be a better time than now.'

'Then – why are you not at sea? Why did you not do as she advised?'

'I did what she said. I rode off on the donkey, but the donkey was hard to manage, so I walked a lot of the way. And I really thought I would go. But then, as I got nearer to Korinthos, I began to wonder. I wouldn't know anybody, or where to go. And if I was a boy on shipboard I would be treated as a servant, perhaps like a slave, and big men might want to use me in all sorts of ways. If only I were eighteen! Seventeen, even. And then I thought about seeing Mama, my stepmother again, and little Kharis. And I thought maybe the trial would go well, and in any case I should not be running away from Mama's trouble. So I came back.'

'So you came back,' Aristotle repeated.

'And I went back to the place where they hired the donkey for me, near Manto's, and sent a message to her, and she sent a message back saying you, the Master of the Lykeion, had been looking for me. Maybe that meant I should run away again. But I thought, instead, that I would come at once and talk with you.'

'An admirable and straightforward course,' said Aristotle, 'if not perhaps totally well-advised.' He pondered, looking at the boy.

'There are additional complications,' he said eventually, choosing his words with care. 'Matters have changed since you were in this city – at least since you were here as Kleiophon. Ergokles is dead, for one thing.'

'Ergokles is dead? But that's a good thing, isn't it? Excellent news!'

'It might be – and might not. I must tell you, Kleiophon, though I applaud your decision to come and aid your mother – stepmother – I think your wish should not be granted straight away. You are in greater trouble than you know. You could injure your stepmother more right now than ever before.'

Aristotle stood up.

'You must and shall leave straight away,' he announced. 'I shall give you sufficient funds to travel with. The only thing that you should do first is write a letter. In a moment I shall give you some tablets and you must compose a quick letter to your mother, explaining that you are well, and will write again soon, but that you plan to go abroad. I shall send this epistle to Hermia once I know you are safely away.'

'Oh, no! I can't take money from you—'

'Yes you can. Don't trouble me with thanks, you can pay me back later. Then I am going to put you into the care of Phokon. You are both of you to walk down to Peiraieus, as two slaves together. Understand?'

'Yes, but—'

'No buts! This must be done, and at once. Phokon will put you on a ship bound for one of the ports of Korinthos, and he will ask some other passenger to keep an eye out for you until the end of the journey. In case you need assistance or supplies within the city itself, I shall give you the direction of a friend dwelling in Korinthos, to whom you may turn for help. But while in the Korinthos region, communicate with nobody else. If you wish to take a ship leaving one of the two ports of Korinthos and go into the world on your own, that will be best. But please, if you can, leave some sort of written word with my friend. On your travels, you had best adopt a name other than your own. Not "Simmias".'

Kleiophon looked aghast.

'Then I cannot help Mama—!'

'You will be *truly* helping her by writing your letter, and then keeping out of the way. You could do her and yourself great damage if you remain. It will be said that you and she plotted together to murder Ergokles. You yourself will be greatly endangered, and your danger will aggravate the troubles of Hermia. The growth of a case against her will certainly ensure her early death. Your best service to her, to yourself and your whole family is to get out of the way for a prolonged space of time.'

'But I could stay with Ephippos as a mule-boy—'

'No. Not safe any more. There is somebody else looking for you. A young man, physically strong and able, who is shrewd as well as indefatigable. Within three days or less you would certainly be tracked down.

I repeat, the discovery would injure you and Hermia very greatly. Go, I tell you!'

Kleiophon seemed cowed and impressed. 'Well, if—'

'I am sorry.' said Aristotle, gazing on him with a kind of kindly sadness. 'Indeed, I am *very* sorry to appear to baulk your best impulses, which I esteem. You will grow up and become a good man. But to preserve your future, you must go. One last thing – I shall tell my servant Phokon that if the waiting time for a ship to Korinthos is long, or if he suspects you are being followed, or might be recognized, he is to put you on the first ship about to depart from Peiraieus – no matter what the destination. Now, I shall tell Phokon.' And he vanished, not before he gave me a warning look, unspoken advice not to say too much to the boy.

Kleiophon looked at me, still aghast.

'Am I not to see Mama?' he said.

'Better not, not now,' I replied. 'Safer for her. Anything that makes *you* safer and happier will be good for her.'

He subsided, and paid me no further heed, writing his dutiful letter and then staring thoughtfully at the wall as if trying to read a vision of his future.

'Phokon knows all about it,' said Aristotle, coming in again. 'Here is a cloak for you. No, don't thank me! It is a slave's cloak. Wear it on your way to Peiraieus, and on the ship. Nothing closer than Korinthos will do. Give me your letter to Hermia, and take this letter of introduction.' He handed the lad some plain tablets bound with twine. 'This epistle introduces you – under another name – to a man in Korinthos, a goldsmith from Asia. You may find his accent a trifle bizarre, but he has a very good heart, does not want courage, and owes me a favour. Now, go!'

The pair set off, and Aristotle sat down, then got up again, pacing restlessly about.

'What a pretty problem we have here! I shall not be easy until Phokon returns. It will take them some while to get to Peiraieus. I didn't dare to lend a horse or mule, nothing that might be identified. It is better they should melt into the crowds of trudging foot-passengers.'

'Kind of you,' I said 'to take all that trouble, and go to all that expense.'

'It is,' he agreed gloomily. 'And I am not sure myself what good will come of it. I realize that I have put myself in some danger. Talk about finding the kidnap-per – it is I! But I couldn't just let this unfortunate child wander into his fate.'

'You mean,' I said, 'that he could be tried for the murder of Ergokles?'

'Oh, yes. Undoubtedly. Kleiophon really is involved, however innocently. He has in fact been an agent in the killing of Ergokles. This boy was used to give that unfortunate Athenian the drink in which a narcotic or soporific poison had been mixed, so that he would fall into a stupor. You note that the little sheep you saw was well enough when the lad first arrived. The sheep was fed the rest of that drink and succumbed to the torpor in which you saw it. I'd like to know, by the way, if the beast awakens, and cheats the old pair of their stew of diseased mutton! I don't know how we could easily find out, however, without one of us going back to those old peasants' place. That sleepy poison itself I think most likely not lethal. But a stupefied Ergokles was easy to dispose of; someone could then break his neck with impunity.'

'Our poor boy had nothing to do with breaking the man's neck.'

'Quite true. But it would not be hard to convict the boy out of his own mouth. He hates Ergokles – or hated him, "that dreadful man". Kleiophon blames him for trouble in Orthoboulos' family. Once Kleiophon admitted to giving a drink to Ergokles, people could readily assert that the lad had added the poison himself, and that he had excellent motives for doing so – and then for personally breaking Ergokles' neck.'

'I suppose,' I said, 'it could not escape the notice of accusers or of the jury that the lad had just wrung a goose's neck before giving the drink to Ergokles!'

'Exactly. How I hope our poor gosling never gets into the clutches of the law! An honest antagonist could make out a good case against him in the murder of Ergokles. There's no love lost between Ergokles' folks and Orthoboulos' family. A weak Basileus would assuredly let Ergokles' family's accusation run its legal course without urging them to look further for those truly guilty of conspiring against Ergokles.'

'Well,' I said, 'we found the missing boy, and are no better off than before, but rather the worse. For Kleiophon can be of no help, but is rather a liability. You have the letter from the boy to Hermia, and that will clear her – if the Basileus and the prosecutors are reasonable – of the ridiculous charge of killing Kleiophon. But you cannot send that letter till you know Kleiophon is safely out of Athens. The evidence Kleiophon gave at the first prodikasia may go for little or nothing, as he cannot repeat it. Having been a party to the murder of Ergokles, the boy cannot defend his mother in the case of the murder of Orthoboulos – about which we know no more than before. Also, the group who lost the case against Phryne still burn to deliver a knockdown assault against Hermia.'

'A succinct summary. But – are we no better off? I think we do know more. Certainly, we have been given new light. If I think, fresh illumination will perhaps come to me.'

'And our new light is called "Lykaina".'

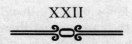
Phryne

'Yes, the recurrent Lykaina. Marylla mentioned her as Philinos' mistress, when she came to plead with me to help Orthoboulos. It is Lykaina to whom the fuel-seller Ephippos sent his new "mule-boy" for assistance. And Lykaina – in her written message – told us that we should approach Manto for further information. Lykaina must have known as much as Manto – yet she sent us to Manto to tell us that the boy had received the money from Hermia, which appears to be absolutely true. Strangest of all, this Lykaina is seen at that low cottage or hedge-tavern on the Megara road, the one kept by the deaf old couple. Kleiophon sees her there, talking to Ergokles. And it is Lykaina who prepares the drink poisonous or stupefying to Ergokles – so we believe, if the boy speaks the truth. But why? *Who is Lykaina?* Ephippos, somewhat evasive, leads us to believe she may be somebody's kept woman at the moment. What other access do we have to the woman Lykaina? I wish we could find some person not mixed up in all this to help us. To give us clearer information, and even arrange an intro-duction.'

I had already decided, though with a knot in my stomach, that I should at last mention a certain fact.

'O Aristotle, I *do* know someone who was – who does – know Lykaina. The hetaira just tried for impi-ety. Phryne.'

'And how do you know this?'

'She said so. At a – when – on a night when I was with a group of people, people of her own sort, and she was at ease.'

'"Of her own sort." Aha! So you, Stephanos, actu-ally *are* a reveller in brothels, an all-night drinker and carouser among the whores! A side to your character quite new to me.'

'Not exactly. I have to have some pleasure now and then,' I muttered defensively. 'But I probably shouldn't call on Phryne today. Not proper.'

'No, no. Come and support me. If I, an old man, may brave ridicule to see the glorious creature, I don't see why you should not. After all, Stephanos, Sokrates himself went to see the lovely Theodote, and chatted with that celebrated hetaira. By all means, let us make our way at once to Phryne's door. Perhaps she will provide a golden key to unlock the invisible door that stands between us and the unknown Lykaina.'

It was not hard to find Phryne, for she had her own dwelling near the centre of Athens, as I knew, though I had never visited it before. She lived in a decent neighbourhood in a well-made house. The owner who rented it to her gave the ground floor over largely to a freedwoman and her man; these persons took care of Phryne's wants, and kept an eye not only on the slaves who served her but on all the comers and goers to Phryne's own apartments.

One of the household slaves was a tall muscular fellow, not such a burly brute as the one who had served Lykaina, but presumably expressly chosen; he could certainly make sure that nobody the lady of this mansion did not wish to see was allowed to enter. Aristotle told him our names and sent him upstairs; it was not long before we were called to the upper region. Phryne came to greet us – or rather to greet Aristotle – with warmth.

'I shall never forget,' she said, pressing his hand, 'any of those who supported me during the time of hardship. Hypereides most of all, of course, but all the others who helped me through danger. You came to see me in the prison, I remember that quite clearly. It's like sitting up with someone on a sickbed, a kind thing to do. Do sit down – and your friend too, of course.'

We sat down. It was a very pretty room, kept beautifully clean; there were elegant wooden tables and stands, supporting small statues and a couple of antique red pots with black figures on them; one was a picture of Paris with the three contending goddesses, giving the prize to Aphrodite. This room was as good as many a wealthy man's *andron*, but of course it couldn't be called an *andron*, I thought. Neither was it a *gynaikon* or women's apartment, as it was so large and handsomely furnished, and men came here. We did not have the lovely hetaira to ourselves; we found her entertaining visitors. A couple of rich men, who looked as if they might be rival lovers, sat about in what must have been their best clothes. They were elaborately courteous to each other, which is always suspicious.

'I don't know,' one of these wealthy-looking men was saying, observing with a jealous eye the place close to herself that Phryne had reserved for Aristotle, 'why ageing Hypereides should be the only favourite. I would have done as much for you as old Jug-Face if I'd been there. I was known for orations at school. It was just my misfortune that I was in Delos at the time. On business. Buying more slaves for our marble-working concern.'

'But,' said Phryne gently, 'of course I have reason to be grateful to the people who were in Athens. And not in Delos.'

If Phryne looked as lovely as ever, I thought, she also looked slightly different, a trifle thinner and paler than she had at the unmentionable party. If this change were the result of her sad experience, yet it also became her. Her great eyes still expressed their gentle humour, even bright flashes of fun, and yet there was a sadness in them. Not just sadness, something else, the look of someone who has recently contemplated death. This look gave a more glorious and arresting beauty to that beautiful face with its calm symmetries.

'It's odd,' said the marble merchant's wealthy rival, playing with a carnelian and gold bracelet which he kept passing through his fingers. 'Strange, that you should look more irresistible now, Phryne, even when you look more serious. If we didn't know what you really are, a man would swear that you were noble.'

'Ah!' said a voice from the corner. 'But she is more than merely noble – Phryne is divine!'

'A divine freckled toad,' murmured the first man.

'Phryne *is* divine!' repeated the owner of the voice, emerging from his corner. I saw now that he had an assistant with him, a youth who carried a basket. 'Divine! A vision of beauty that quite elevates one into another realm, as Plato said—'

'Tush!' said one of the other visitors loudly. 'Plato did not mention a word about looking at pretty prostitutes. The true lover looks at the fresh beauty of a young man – a beauty already with its intellectual and noble aspects. And then the lover advances to a knowledge of beauty in its own right, and gains an idea of the divine, without the help of any mortal flesh whatever. It is a great deprecation of the divine Plato to make him the celebrator of any prostitute's charm – however worthy and naturally attractive.'

Hermodoros, the philosopher of beauty, having offered us this brief lecture, bowed to Phryne, whose eyes danced as she returned the compliment. She would not have been so amused, I thought, had she known of the same man's complacent resignation to the prospect of her death. I remembered Hermodoros' disquisition in the shop of Khryses in front of her gilded image.

'Oh, that's all stuff and nonsense. Plato's fakery,' said the man with the bracelet. 'All that stuff in the *Symposium* that you think so fine is said, to Sokrates supposedly, by a woman he calls Diotima of Mantineia.

Someone told me – I forget who, but it's someone whose grandpa knew Plato pretty well – that this character was a secret jest.'

'How – a jest? Does the divine Plato make jokes?'

'The real "Diotima" was a whore – a hetaira, you know. Originally her family came from Sparta. Very lively and opinionated. This Spartan girl is called "of Mantinea", as she is a diviner, a "seeress" in the same way as our Manto the brothel-keeper – who can tell you who your next girlfriend or boyfriend will be. By the time Plato wrote his famous dialogue, this woman had grown old in the service and had retired. But she hadn't given up talking to men, and speaking in public as Spartan women did – and do. *That's* how this "Diotima" character knows how to talk so well about gazing at male beauty. *She* knew the game. Old Plato himself admired her – when he was not so old.'

'I thought he went in for men – youths chiefly,' said the young man carrying the basket.

'Yes, of course. But he was not above taking an apple from another tree, if the apple was pretty and firm-fleshed.'

'Whoever Diotima was – and surely she is but a voice for Plato,' insisted Hermodoros, 'what she is alleged to say is obviously right. And I too pursue the Beautiful – that is why I am so willing to go about in the wake of Praxitiles here.' He bowed to the elderly bearded man. 'Let me introduce you to him – Praxitiles son of Kephisodotos. He thinks about beauty, albeit in a mechanic way, and he sees things more than other people.'

'And if you want marble, my good fellow,' added the wealthy merchant, turning to the sculptor with condescending graciousness, 'I am sure our works could supply you. For you mechanic workers always are in need of heavy materials – metal or stone.'

'You folks don't use your eyes, it seems to me,' grumbled the elderly artist, good-humouredly. I remembered how I had seen him in the agora, eating bread and olives after Phryne's trial. 'My life has been a great pleasure to me, as I have been allowed to exercise the power of looking at things. Now I am nearing the end of my life, and even my eyesight is not what it was. But – this is both sad and exciting – as I come nearer death, I am freshly inspired by life and have new visions of great wonder.'

'Would we could all see them!' exclaimed the man who loved beauty. Praxitiles paid him no attention.

'I am grateful to Phryne, for she has given me a new vision. I shall produce a work entirely new, if the gods let me live so long. Not gilded nonsense, but marble, smooth and glowing like living flesh. I have already begun to sketch what will be my greatest sculpture.'

'You have produced many great sculptures,' interrupted Hermodoros. Perhaps he was the more anxious to utter compliments since he had been snubbed. 'Your Satyr. And the statue of the youthful Apollo killing a lizard. Everyone praises the delicious "Lizard-Killer"!'

'All that is past doesn't interest me,' declared the sculptor, passing his hands rapidly through his hair so it stood upright, and gazing earnestly at Phryne.

'Except that I can make *you* a gift, O lovely one, of a recently completed work. Which would you take – as a free gift?'

She smiled. 'Beware, dear Praxitiles, of offering gifts, because I always take them. Or almost always.'

'I know. I want you to accept. Take my Eros, with his bow. It is much the best piece still remaining in my workshop. He's done in my new way, better than the old ones. And who but you would be fit to hold or keep Eros?'

She rose and made a graceful acknowledgment. 'With great gratitude I shall accept – in front of witnesses – if you truly mean it.' She stepped forward and took his hand. 'Dear old friend, do you truly want to give me such a valuable piece? It is incomparable – and irreplaceable!'

'As are *you*. Please take it. For I shall take much from you, before our story is done. I shall take your beautiful body and make you the ideal of Aphrodite and all the women who come afterwards!'

'Well then, as I am contributing so much to your welfare and the welfare of all men – I do accept.'

'This is *too* much!' exclaimed the man with the gold and carnelian bracelet. 'I don't see why people are to be allowed to make gigantic presents of such a nature. It's not fair!'

Phryne ignored him, and continued to address Praxitiles.

'I shall give your glowing Eros a suitable home,' she continued. 'Not this little house, but a temple at Thespiai. For poor Thespiai lacks any great works, and this Eros of yours may cause pilgrims to turn out of their way to see it. And then the people of Thespiai will have visitors, and fame.'

'So be it. Though I would pray you to keep it in Athens until after my death.'

'Which must *not* be soon.'

'Which must not be soon, for I have my great work yet to do. A naked goddess. Completely new!'

'Preposterous!' exclaimed Hermodoros. 'How are you going to justify presenting the goddess in nakedness — like an Amazon or barbarian captive?'

'It will be the goddess at the bath, alone, you see, just stepping out—'

'Oh *no!*' The beauty-lover was quite shocked. 'Oh no, Praxitiles, I pray you do not commit this horrible deed. What a bizarre thing to do to a goddess! Poor Aphrodite! Shown at a bath — you will have to include water jars, and a large towel — oh, no! It's too commonplace, it affronts all one's ideas of the beautiful and great.'

'Nonetheless, it's what I have decided to do,' said Praxitiles cheerfully. 'I have been making sketches, large and small — in wax, on wood, drawn with charcoal on papyrus. The basket is full, as you see, carried by my assistant — my son Timarkhos, gentlemen. I have used Phryne as my model. Now my son and I must depart so I can go back to work on the first model. I leave the substance to commune with the shadow. Goodbye, Phryne — but I will be back someday soon,' he announced loudly and cheerfully from the passageway, as he and his son proceeded on their way.

'Unbelievable!' The man who loved beauty put a

hand across his brow. 'One can hardly bear to think of Aphrodite in proximity with – a towel. I must go away, I fear, mistress, to get over the shock.' So there was another visitor gone.

The two rival lovers – or would-be lovers – realizing that Aristotle meant to outstay them, made preparations to depart, greatly to my relief. I was uneasy the whole time I was in Phryne's room, for fear something of my presence at the dangerous party should leak out here in this company. The man with the bracelet was the last to go; he seemed wishful and abashed. He had not offered his piece of jewellery to Phryne. Inadequately armed with such a conventional bauble, he doubtless found it impossible to contend with something as magnificent and singular as a new statue of Eros. Presumably this visitor even feared his bracelet would be sneered at and rejected. He was soon disabused of any such notion.

'Oh, my dear friend,' said Phryne, following him to the door, 'must you go so soon? I am sorry we have not had a chance of a long talk. But' – she turned her eyes towards the bracelet, now almost concealed in the palm of his embarrassed hand – 'might I enquire if you brought something, some little gift meant for me?'

'Well, yes,' the citizen mumbled. He turned slightly red, and scraped with his feet like a schoolboy. 'But I did not know – I did not think it would be acceptable—'

'Foolish boy!' Phryne tugged at his ear, and pretended to pout. 'You think I am overcome with the offer of enormous statues? Is that it? But such statues may be difficult to house — even images of bronze, let alone marble. You see that I shall have to offer the image of Eros to somewhere more stately, like a temple. But a delicate, wearable lovely thing, from the hand of a friend — what could be more welcome?'

'Here. It is yours, Phryne. Please take it. I meant it for you. The quality of the gold is excellent, and the stones first-class, I assure you.'

'Oh, dear man! Let me put it on straight away!' she cooed. 'There, does it not look nice? Now, you won't stay away and leave me to worry that I have offended you, will you? You see I must talk now with this old philosopher, but come in two days. I shall shut my door against all other comers, just for you.'

And with further sweet farewells, she saw him, now beaming, to the door.

'Heigh-ho!' she sighed, wandering back to her former seat. She took off the bracelet and inspected it critically. 'Since there is not to be a God of Equal Shares, it's as well to keep it. I have a use for all such valuable things,' she declared, tossing it on a table. It is true, I thought, all such women are harpies.

'Are you going to sell it? What do you need it for?' I asked, rudely.

'Oh — you know I have now to rebuild Thebes, since I promised to do so.' Phryne looked mockingly at me, then turned to Aristotle, who had said nothing but sat serenely, watching.

'You, O Aristotle of Stageira, obviously have something particular you want to say to Phryne of Thespiai — otherwise you wouldn't have stayed through all this chat. And I think you disapprove of women having money, and of my sort, and of me,' Phryne surmised, looking at 'this old philosopher'. 'Obviously, therefore, what you have to say is a matter of importance. Something you don't wish to say before others.'

'Quite right. And as you, Phryne, are a target for all the arrows of Eros and have many visitors, we must make the most of our time. Therefore, I shall be blunt, and ask you for a clear answer. My friend here says you have mentioned Lykaina. What do you know of her?'

'Of Lykaina? I don't think I have talked with you of Lykaina, have I?' She paused and looked thoughtfully at me. I felt myself beginning to turn red. 'Ah. Yes. I thought so. The ill-fated – I was right, *you* were at that party; you know about Thebes and you heard me mention Lykaina. Let us see—' She snatched an olive wreath from the table, a wreath from a party of yesterday, most probably, and jammed it on my brow. 'Not the same kind, but it will do. I begin vaguely to recognize you.'

'Oh?' Aristotle was watching me acutely. 'What is this? "The ill-fated—" Oh! *The* party in fact – you were one of the *komos* at Tryphaina's!' He slapped his thigh. 'I have it now. The "Makedonian soldier"! With a wound. That was *you!*'

I said nothing. I was heartily glad that all the others had left the room, but I wondered whether somebody might not overhear us next door, or down below. The blood rushed ever more hotly to my face.

'We must not tease you,' said Phryne sweetly. She reached over and squeezed my hand. 'Never mind me, I have a wretched memory for faces and names –

especially of people who give me no presents. I cannot say who exactly was at any party I have been at for a long while. But Lykaina – I may have mentioned her at several different times and places. For she is an old friend of mine.'

'What sort of old friend? Who is she?'

'Well, it will not surprise you, gentlemen, to hear that she was in the same line of business as myself. Though we are not from the same city – not at all. For I come from Thespiai, that humble town among the vegetables. And Lykaina was ancestrally from Kythera, the delightful island where they make purple dye. Many say it is the birthplace of Aphrodite.'

'Hesiod says so,' interjected Aristotle. 'Though others say Paphos in the island of Kupros.'

'Well, Lykaina believed she came ancestrally from the birthplace of Aphrodite. So you see, we are different, Lykaina and I. She is Spartan, I Boiotian. She is endowed with rich curling black hair, and I with yellow hair. But we both found ourselves in Athens, and in the same line of work. We grew into acquaintance in an odd way, because we found we were both sharing the same man!' She laughed, a little trill of delight. 'We got together and shared a good laugh as well, and talked over the fellow and his preferences. And then we talked of ourselves, and became friends on our own account.'

'When was this, exactly?'

'I don't know, exactly. A couple of years. Some time ago. After Alexander took Tyre, I remember people talking about Tyre around the same time.' She looked at me.

'Yes, I think it was at *that* party that I told the story I like to call "The Tale of the Generous Women". A true story. You remember – the two women who were generous to each other in the way they shared the man? Well, the women Plangon and Bakkhis in that story were like Lykaina and me.'

'How strange!' was all I could think of to say.

'That was in the past. And then – last spring – didn't the same thing happen to us again, here in Athens! But not very seriously, though the fellow was very good-looking. I told Lykaina that she could have him, no matter how good-looking he was. I didn't want to be taking anything from her. She said it was just because I was proud, and there is something in that. But she was laughing – she had that wild free way that Spartan women have. It certainly didn't injure our friendship.'

'Ah,' I objected, 'it is not a young man from Kolophon that you were dividing between you. Nor did either of you have to give up an inimitable necklace studded with gems.'

She laughed. 'Not exactly. But women are always giving up something. We wished to be free of trouble. We thought this time the man was not worth it, even though he was excessively handsome. I was not sure he was fully interested in women, or whether he did not have yet some third woman on a string. But just as I gave him to Lykaina, she decided she would change her life. She wanted to find someone rich and generous enough to give her a permanent establishment. She thought she might find better luck nearer Asia. So Lykaina went to Byzantion. And that's the last I heard of her.'

'To Byzantion? When did this happen?'

'Oh, last spring – or early summer. I can't quite – oh, around the time when the case of Orthoboulos and Ergokles was decided. When the roses were blooming, and it was safe to travel by sea. Lykaina was not entirely without acquaintance in Byzantion.'

'And you have heard from her since?'

'No. I am a little surprised, for she can write, as can I. Lykaina may not write as well, but she could certainly scrape out a letter. I looked to hear from her before now. But if she has fallen into difficulties in the new city, she might be too proud to let me know. On the other hand, she may be having such a good and lively time that she has no opportunity to send letters. I hope that's the case.' Phryne got up and moved restlessly about her pretty room, touching various objects as she passed them.

'What does Lykaina look like?' Aristotle asked.

'She is handsome, not too tall but well set up. She is physically active, like most Spartan girls; she can run, and leaps when she dances. Lykaina has lovely curly black hair, and eyes of an odd golden brown, very fine, with dark eyelashes. She sings beautifully, and can play several musical instruments – though she is not "a flute-girl".' Phryne pronounced this last phrase with distaste. 'Lykaina is good at weaving, and makes beautiful clothes in her free time.'

'Don't you think,' I suggested, 'that if she had stayed in Athens instead of going to Byzantion, you would have caught a glimpse of her by now?'

'Yes – yes, surely. She could hardly disguise herself from me – but what would she want to do that for?'

'It is possible,' said Aristotle, in a judicious tone, 'not certain, but *possible*, that somebody is going about calling herself "Lykaina".'

'Oh, well, you know — "Lykaina" is a name not uncommon to our sort of people. I should call it a nickname, rather than a name. As you both know now, "Phryne" is not my name, but something I go by. "Lykaina", "Kynara," "Naiara", and so on — these are names for business.'

I realized suddenly that my poor Kynara, whom I would take good care never to see again, must have a real name, and that I should never know it.

'Neither I nor my friend would be upset if we found there was another "Phryne" or "Lykaina",' said Phryne. 'Bound to be. I just hope there isn't another "Phryne" too close by, or it might be awkward. I should perhaps have to adopt some other term as a nickname.' She smiled impishly, showing all her pearly teeth.

'Perhaps,' she suggested, 'in view of my trial, I should take a hint from a predecessor, and call myself "Klepsydra". She got named after the water-clock because she set up a water-clock in her own bedroom and timed her customers by it!'

Aristotle arose. 'We will trouble you no more at present,' he said. 'It has been kind of you to receive us.'

'Not "*kind* of me". It is what I do. Receive gentlemen.' She stood up. 'But your visit to me in the prison was truly kind, and deeply appreciated. I desperately needed to be able to sit up and talk rationally on that day, before the trial. I was so afraid of going to pieces! For when I was by myself, I had terrible mental pictures of the fate in store. I thought they would rend me on the tympanon, with nails and staples and merciless exhibition.' She whirled about where she stood, and shuddered. 'I do not know how the spirit can bear that – why it does not take flight at once! But sometimes I thought they would be merciful and accede to my friends' pleadings, and give me the hemlock poison.'

'More likely,' I said soothingly, not at all sure I was right.

'But that was not cheerful either. Someone once read aloud to me the story of Sokrates' death. It took a long time. To lose the use of my limbs, my legs and arms, before I am actually dead! It would be easier to be murdered, quickly – if someone thrust a dagger into you!'

'Be careful what you ask for,' said Aristotle drily. 'The enemy – or friend – who thrusts the dagger in needs to know what he is doing. There are slow tormenting deaths on the battlefield. Pain, terrible thirst. Death, though he comes, will not come at once when called for.'

'Oh well,' said Phryne, tossing her head. 'I should not have started us talking of such horrors. I prefer the kind of parting that ends with a bracelet. Or at least a kiss!'

And before Aristotle could do anything to prevent her, she raised herself on tiptoe (though she was his height) and kissed him a butterfly kiss on the cheek and on the mouth.

'There,' she said. 'Let this take away bad thoughts. No, not for you, young man – *you're* still too young and haven't earned it.' She turned, and signalled to her attendant, who decorously saw us out.

We were not seen by anyone we knew when leaving Phryne's house, which I counted among pieces of good fortune. But when we were passing through the agora, we were suddenly halted by a commanding voice.

'Aristotle! Stephanos! Excellent! Glad I have found you.'

It was Arkhias, this time not looking like a pedlar but like a well-to-do merchant.

His beard was combed, even lightly scented with sandalwood, and he wore a fine-woven cloak. Antipater, I thought, must have given him not only funds but chests of clothing to enable him to assume so many roles. Arkhias boomed out greetings as if he were the merchant he resembled, but dramatically lowered his voice to say, 'I must speak privately.'

'Shall we walk to the walls and see if we can find a secluded spot?' I suggested

'Full of whores, garbage and beggars. Let us go to your house, Stephanos.' Arkhias appeared not so much to suggest as to command. With an ill grace I invited Aristotle and this fine-talking disguiser to my house, where we sat stiffly in my *andron*. I saw Arkhias looking around my room and pursing his lips, as if he didn't think much of it. All its shabbiness was more evident to me than ever, the crack in the wall, the dust on a side table.

'Now,' said Aristotle, perhaps almost as impatient as myself. 'In what manner can we be of assistance, Arkhias?'

'I thought you would wish to keep up with any news,' Arkhias said reproachfully. 'The boy – you know' – with a glance over his shoulder at my innocent doorway – 'the boy Kleiophon. I think I spotted him. But unfortunately just too late!'

'Too late?' I repeated, while Aristotle more practically asked, 'Where was he?'

'Well, let me tell you.' Arkhias settled into his instructive mode. 'I should say that I picked up an important clue very recently. There was an old Phrygian butler who belonged to Orthoboulos. He was tortured, actually, in an unprofessional and lax fashion, when they were investigating the house just after the murder, but was determined to have little of interest to say. This man was bought by Philinos. But I have discovered that this slave—'

'Artimmes,' I suggested.

'Yes, this Artimmes has been sent away by Philinos. I was told that he had been sent to the new city that Alexander is having built in Egypt. That seems highly significant! It occurred to me that Artimmes might have been sent off to accompany Kleiophon to some remote destination. If only that information had come to me the day before! For I was proceeding to carry out my planned investigation pursuing Kleiophon's whereabouts.'

'What did you do?'

'First I went back to that hovel of a tavern that you, Stephanos, know of. There I questioned the doltish old couple, like one in authority – though not laying a finger on them, I assure you. People often tell the truth of their own accord, even from simple surprise or nervousness. And I found from them that a boy had been there, looking after their geese for a little time. He *killed a goose* for them. Wrung its neck. Significant, is it not? But *why* did they need a goose killed? Because this old couple were expecting to serve it for dinner to a good visitor or visitors. I didn't find out who that was, the old people were tight-mouthed over who exactly came. Claimed they had spent their time in the lean-to and didn't know who came or went, but that a "nice gentleman" came and "a nice lady servant" fetched water and gave it to the boy to give visitors. Then another man came, they thought. But the old people insisted they were resting in their retreat and couldn't exactly see these new visitors. They must have been well paid!'

'Most interesting,' said Aristotle.

'What about the lamb?' I enquired. 'How was that doing?'

Arkhias frowned at me. 'I wasn't there to attend to animals, Stephanos, but to get information. There was a rather stupid-looking sheep staggering around, and geese cackling so you could hardly hear! But we are wandering away from the point.'

'Which is—?'

'Why, that the boy who was there – probably only briefly – could well have been the murderer of Ergokles. I believe that boy was also my quarry – the boy we are all looking for. He most likely came to that hovel by prearrangement. The boy's overwhelming desire to kill Ergokles explains why he has hung about in the Athens area instead of going away. He may have some murky associates. There are persons connected with this plot that we don't yet have a handle for. The "nice lady servant" for instance. And then there's that strange Makedonian soldier, a man with a wound, at Tryphaina's party. Turned up only the one time, and nobody seems to know who he is. Might *he* not have something to do with these other strange occurrences? I keep asking myself.'

'There are so many Makedonian soldiers,' said Aristotle. 'And surely none of those would want to call attention to himself by engaging in any nefarious business in the city. Antipater would hardly be pleased at your blaming Makedonian fighting men — without any facts, too!'

'However that may be, I was determined to pursue this boy. I got on his trail again, because somebody had seen the mule-boy with a charcoal-seller. And somebody else saw the boy later on, going from the Eleusis area towards Athens, still in the guise of a muleteer, but with some goose-feathers on his clothes. Once I got back to the city, however, the lad wasn't with the fuel-man. That boy had broken loose.'

'So what did you do then?'

'I try to think like my quarry — I can do that better because of the acting. I thought to myself: "What is the boy likely to do?" And the answer I came up with was this : "Make his way to Peiraieus." The nearest port, if he had given up going to Korinthos. So I went to Peiraieus, but that is always so crowded. Difficult to spot someone. It would have been much easier had I been following him on his way there. Yet, even so, I caught a glimpse of a boy on a ship that was setting sail. Just a short glimpse – but I am sure it was our lad. Kleiophon son of Orthoboulos.'

'Really? Remarkable. Don't you find it hard to believe it really is the same boy?' Aristotle sounded dubious. 'After all, a number of days have passed since the lad first disappeared.'

'And you wouldn't recognize him, really, as you don't know him,' I pointed out

'He has been described to me. And I have seen his brother,' Arkhias declared. 'That should suffice, if I am good at my job. I think he was disguised as a slave when he went to Peiraieus and got aboard the ship, but – I would *swear* by the gods! – it was Orthoboulos' second son. How I regret that I was too late! Very slightly, but I must confess I was too late. At least we know where the ship is going, but that may not be of much use, unless we could get an official demand that it be sent back.'

'I doubt that a naval trireme will be sent in pursuit of a boy,' said Aristotle placidly. 'Where is that particular ship bound for?'

'Egypt,' groaned Arkhias. 'Hard to pursue! It's not as if he were going to Asia with stops at all those islands.'

'Ah, Egypt,' said Aristotle. 'He will find it hot. Perhaps he will bring us back some perfume. Or even a monkey.'

XXIII

Lykaina

It took Aristotle's considerable skill to soothe and remove the disgruntled Arkhias. After much praise of his indefatigable work, however, Aristotle was able to send him away, happy at the prospect of looking into the business interests of Ergokles, which Aristotle suggested as an immediate project. Then he and I sat in my dusty *andron*, looking at each other.

'Phokon must have suspected they were being pursued and watched,' said Aristotle. 'He took decisive action, as instructed, and got the boy aboard the first departing vessel. Egypt, fortunately, is a long way off. Too far even for Arkhias. The lad won't have any friends in Egypt however,' he added ruefully. 'So much for my plan of using our old acquaintance Theron of Halikarnassos, now a goldsmith in Korinthos.'

'Lykaina,' I said. 'Before we went to see Phryne, you indicated Lykaina offered new light. But now we know both less and more. For the Lykaina we know cannot be the one that Phryne knows! That woman has already gone to Byzantion.'

'So Phryne says,' Aristotle agreed. 'And Phryne's friend writes badly. The letter we received under the name Lykaina was well written.'

'But perhaps she got someone else to write it for her.'

'Perhaps. In that case, who? You notice something else connects Phryne's friend with our case. Phryne and Lykaina recently "shared" the same man, if briefly. And that man is superbly handsome.' He got up, strolled to one of the little tables, and absently fingered a pot. 'Cast your mind back to the first appearance of Marylla − in this very room. It was then the end of spring, beginning of summer. She said something like this : "Lykaina, mistress of Philinos, has told me she knows he is worried about how this case will turn out." Both Phryne and Lykaina, then, we may hypothesize, shared the handsome Philinos.'

'That makes sense,' I said. 'I saw Philinos there − at that party we mustn't talk about. He left before the troublesome events. But Phryne said something to him about already having made their voyage − in a way that meant that the love affair between them had ended. A pity in a way, they looked so beautiful together.'

'So they would. That strengthens my contention that Philinos was shared by these two women. But in the spring, around the time that I took on an interest in Orthoboulos' troubles, Lykaina − according to Phryne, who has reason to know this woman quite well − went away.'

'So why is Lykaina still here? But Phryne has suggested a perfectly obvious explanation – that there are two different women with the same nickname.'

'Not impossible. But consider: Philinos was Orthoboulos' best friend. Now why does the mysterious Lykaina – the *second* Lykaina if you will – also take a strong interest in Orthoboulos' family? A sufficient interest to be instrumental in the care of Kleiophon – if not actually in abetting his escape from home? We should find an answer to this.'

'And you suggest?'

He had turned about, in his restless fashion, and was walking to and fro.

'The only remedy is to find Lykaina ourselves, and work out who she is, and what is her real part in the events of the past few weeks.'

'Luckily, we know where she lives.'

He shrugged. 'We know where the fuel-seller *said* she lives. The fuel-seller has also played an instrumental part – is he a villain, a sympathetic bystander or an agent? Yet I agree, we must go back to that house near Akharnai. I say "we", hoping you are willing to come. I would prefer not to tackle Lykaina – or her brute of a slave – on my own. It is some distance, so I think I shall hire mules for the two of us – but *not* from our cheerful Ephippos.'

I said I was willing, though I was more nervous of the mules than of the burly slave. We could not make an early start on the morrow, however, because of Aristotle's engagement to give a lecture and to meet with his own scholars, so it was after noon when we set forth. The sun in autumn was no longer scorching, and the day was pleasant enough. No day spent on the back of a horse or mule is altogether pleasant to me, however; on that day my wound still hurt when I pulled at the creature's bridle and tried to direct him. As we made our way to the north-west, I recollected that Akharnaians are especially brave, and have a big temple to Ares. If this Lykaina had Akharnaian fighting men as friends or in her employ, an encounter might not be too pretty. Yet, as she was a woman who sold herself for money, it was more reasonable to anticipate hospitality, and I hoped for a fairly agreeable encounter and perhaps some refreshments.

We arrived at our destination, the low-lying house in its patch of waste ground. It was quiet. The hen must have gone to sleep somewhere. We dismounted. Boldly, Aristotle started across the yard towards the door. He was intercepted by the big branded slave who had made such an impression on me before.

'What do you want? Shedding dung over other folk's yards!' the man enquired. Indeed the mules were making the most of their opportunity. We might have retorted that the yard (not to mention the withered vegetable patch) would be the better for our animals' donation, but Aristotle remained civil, and asked him to take a message to Lykaina. He accepted the tablets in his bear-like paws, and we both expected that he would go within the house, but he did not.

'She ain't here. I'll deliver it for ye. But go away. There's a mastiff now within the walls,' he warned. 'And the neighbours ain't specially loving to strangers. It'll take her a while to send an answer. Not today. Go quietly home, you two. And take your beasts with you.'

The man walked off with sturdy step and long stride, but not until having waited to see us meekly mount and turn to go. Aristotle and I proceeded in a direction different from that the slave had taken.

'No use in following him,' said Aristotle. 'We cannot be inconspicuous on muleback, and he would merely get angry, and refuse to deliver the message. Wait until he is further away.'

We waited. A few late cicadas sang mournfully, and a remnant of crickets were chirping in the autumn fields.

At last it seemed safe to go back to the small house of Lykaina. Aristotle asked me to tie up the mules somewhere out of sight, and we returned to lurk in Lykaina's yard, hoping she might, after all, return. It was very quiet. Time passed. There was no sign of anybody.

'Funny, the dog – the "mastiff" he mentioned – doesn't bark or whine at all,' Aristotle observed.

I picked up a stone and hurled it against the shabby unanswering door. It bounced off. There was no reaction whatever from within.

'I don't believe there is a dog. If there were one, he would certainly have barked. Shall we enter, Aristotle?'

'I have thought of that, but it is breaking the law in a most flagrant manner to break into a house. I could not bring myself to do it. Moreover, my position as a *metoikos* makes me especially vulnerable to any legal action. Exile is a high price to pay.'

'That's true,' I agreed. 'And with everyone so nervous about all the burglaries and robberies in Athens these days, it is best to be careful.'

We were left to the dubious pleasure of gazing at this structure, noting again the cracks in its walls, one by one, and the places where broken tiles had slipped. Time passed, and the sun began to decline.

'I might break in,' I said. 'I could say I heard someone crying "Help!" as we passed by. And I broke in all by myself, and then I cried out, and you had to come to help me.'

'Ingenious,' was Aristotle's only comment. We waited again. The sun did not stand still but continued his rapid autumnal descent.

'Well,' I said impatiently, 'shall we stay or go?'

'I am more tempted by your plan, Stephanos, but — hsst! Someone is coming.'

We ducked out of sight among the sparse bushes. Someone was indeed coming. It was a woman, a veiled and decent shape, carrying a small bag. She walked quickly, but not hastily, with a light step. Aristotle stood up and pulled me round so that we also would appear to be approaching the house like proper visitors, not lurkers. We walked across the yard and accosted the woman about to enter this poor dwelling. She threw back her veil just as she reached for the latch, and opened the door.

'Greetings, mistress.'

'Yes, sirs — oh!' She turned. A face gazed out at us from the framing of the thrown-back veil, a lovely face, with short ringlets and large thoughtful grey eyes.

'Marylla!' I was astonished, yet pleased at being able to identify exactly who it was. 'What do you do here? And what has happened to Lykaina?'

While I was speaking, Aristotle rather rudely had

gone ahead of us through the now-opened door.

'Lykaina? Oh, Lykaina – yes, it is her house, as you know,' Marylla responded cheerfully. 'She has gone away again. I have offered to look in, and pick up any notes left for her.'

Marylla followed Aristotle into the house, and I followed her.

'Dear, it does need airing out!' she exclaimed, throwing the door wide open and unlatching the shutters on two windows. 'One can hardly breathe!'

That was true. The air inside this hovel was thick and choking, stale, and full of rot. The roof timbers were presumably letting go where the rain had slid through the tiles. There was a pervasive scent of privy, and the even more horrid smell of a dwelling that has housed not only mice but rats for too long. The feet of a hundred rats must have trodden on everything. Certainly there was no sign of a dog.

'She cannot really have been living here!' Aristotle too wrinkled his nose.

'No, not to say living,' Marylla responded. 'Lykaina *has* let this place go, hasn't she? Ugh! There's a dead rat there, I see. Could one of you throw it out?'

I obliged, though with an ill grace. But I could hardly make her pick the thing up – Marylla was somebody else's slave, not my own. I certainly did not want to stay longer in the same room with this large and very dead rodent. The smell made me gag.

'I have nothing to do with looking after the house, of course, Lykaina has a slave to do that. Do sit down – those two chairs are all right.' She quickly dusted them off.

'We know the slave you mean,' I told her. 'The branded fellow. He's looking for Lykaina with a letter from us.' She bustled about, trying to make things more livable. At least the two chairs were clean. Between Aristotle and myself she introduced a quickly dusted small table.

'I come,' Marylla repeated, 'just to pick up letters for Lykaina. Her slave cannot read. Some of those are notes from lovers, and of course Lykaina doesn't want to lose track of those. A matter of business.'

'Where has she gone?' I enquired bluntly

Marylla laughed, a pleasant and sweet sound. 'Lykaina? This time? Oh, I suppose to Korinthos or around there. But she will be back now and then. From time to time she is here, so she doesn't want to lose touch with old admirers who could be useful to her.'

This sweet talk while the air was so foul was disturbing to me. I left my clean chair and walked to the corner, whence some of the worst of the smell emanated. 'Great Herakles!' I exclaimed. 'There is a mattress here that smells of sick! Why don't you burn it? Throw it out?'

Aristotle quickly joined me. 'There's some residue on the wall,' he said quietly. 'Someone has been sick here. Unusually so.'

'Oh!' said Marylla in great disgust. 'That would be that slave. Great ox of a fellow, drinking and eating too much – he must have been sick. Usually he sleeps outside. I told him long ago to throw that old mattress out and burn it. I suppose he simply emptied out the straw and refilled the ticking, and used this pallet to sleep on himself – lazy fellow! He's supposed to sleep in the shed, but he probably brought this thing in here when the rains began.'

She approached and looked with disgust at the object. 'We ought to burn that, as you say. I'll see it done tonight.'

Aristotle's hands closed over hers. 'No. Mistress Marylla, you have much more to explain. Let Stephanos throw this pallet outside.' I did so, retching, while he gently forced Marylla to sit down. I returned, and at a nod from Aristotle closed the door. With regret, as the fresher air was wanted, and much missed.

'It is all discovered,' Aristotle said gravely. 'This is all the evidence we need. For it is not the residue of a normal sickness that is on that pallet. It smells of deadly hemlock. *This* is the place where Orthoboulos was really murdered!'

'How could I know?' protested Marylla. 'That is really far-fetched! But even if someone died here, *I* had nothing to do with it. This house belongs to Lykaina.'

'Yes. To Lykaina. But which Lykaina? The black-haired prostitute with the brown eyes, the woman who has gone to Byzantion? Or to a new Lykaina? One who has soft ringlets and grey eyes? Very beautiful grey eyes.' Aristotle looked at her with compassion, almost with tenderness. 'What is in this bag?' He opened the bag she had carried in with her, a small pouch with drawstrings. Within were a few simple garments. But at the top there was a mass of dark hair that tumbled about. Aristotle drew it out and held it up. 'A wig. Egyptian, perhaps? What a strange thing for a woman who has beautiful curly brown hair touched with gold. And she wears clothes of Sikilian and Phoenician weave, the garments of the lovely daughters of Sidon.'

To my surprise, at hearing these gentle tones, tears began to course down this woman's face.

'What a creature!' I said in astonishment and disgust. 'She kills her master, she kills Ergokles, and now she thinks tears will move us.'

Marylla arose, with dignity, shaking off Aristotle's hands.

'This is horrible. And – it is too shameful!' she turned crimson. 'Please, let me go! I need to urinate right now, most dreadfully!'

'No, you cannot escape into the yard,' said Aristotle. 'Is there not somewhere you can do your business here?'

Blushing, almost sobbing, Marylla led the way to a very small curtained-off closet, into which she took a large plain receptacle. We stood on guard. The poor woman, harassed by her circumstances, could hold out no longer. She made a very plenteous evacuation. When she left the closet, she was holding the noisome pot and making for the door.

'No, you don't go out,' said Aristotle. 'Throw it into the yard, Stephanos.'

'Throw it yourself, you're the medical man!' I retorted. And to my surprise, Aristotle meekly did so, while I kept an eye on Marylla. She went to the other side of the room, a kitchen area where there was a large hydra. She poured some water out and washed her face, neck and hands, very thoroughly, then retreated to her chair, with a little sigh of relief.

'That's better,' she murmured. Aristotle returned, and strode over to the woman.

'Now, you must tell us the absolute truth,' he said warningly, taking hold of her.

Marylla arose with dignity, shaking off Aristotle's restraining clasp.

'There is no need to hold me. I know you are too strong for me, and that *he'* — she looked at me with some venom — 'he guards the door.'

'I think I can begin to work it out,' said Aristotle, 'now that I start with the firm premise that you did kill Orthoboulos. He must have come here fairly early in the day. Not at night at all. You had killed him — or else the process of his murder was advanced to its final stages, without your needing to be present — *before* the unfortunate man was supposed to be speaking to his younger son. Then you at least were fully accounted for during the latter part of the day and the night during which Orthoboulos was supposed to have been killed.'

'Whispering,' I rebuked, 'playing a child's game, speaking for a statue laid in a bed with covers over it! I am ashamed of you — using Hermes in such a way!'

'It was Kore—' She caught herself but it was too late.

'There,' said Aristotle. 'Proof positive.'

'And not even with torture!' I exclaimed. 'Arkhias is right.' She shivered.

'Control your fears, Marylla,' said Aristotle. 'If you make a complete confession, then we may be able to spare you the worst of torture. Light interrogation will suffice for the court.'

'But I am a freedwoman!' She lifted her head.

'Since when?'

'Since two days. My master gave me my freedom.'

'Philinos did? Yes, he has reason to treat you well. All the better if this is true and legal – though Philinos would have to witness to the fact. Is it registered? And you haven't been listed as a foreigner living in Athens; you would have to be registered at once as a *metoike*, and not as an Athenian freed person. But if you have been set free by your master, you will be unlikely to be tortured at all – *if* you cooperate.'

'And if you talk with us,' I suggested, 'we will know who all the people involved are, and already understand many of the events, so it will be easier.'

'Stephanos has a very good point,' Aristotle emphasized. 'It will be easier, quicker, and less painful to tell us all than to be taken first into the city to be questioned. You would have to deal with bunglers new to the case and to you.'

Marylla gazed at us steadfastly and sorrowfully, her lovely face and sweet curving chin, her eyes sweetly grey as an autumn sky or sea, clouded with the shower of tears. Her honey-coloured hair curled damply around her temples – she had been sweating in her distress. She stood alone in the centre of that ugly room, and raised her hands in a gesture of prayer and entreaty.

'To you, O Goddess! To you I make my last appeal! You who loved, vindicate your servant!'

Her great eyes searched upward as if she could see beyond this fragile and falling vile roof.

Then she turned to us, with an amazing effort at self-possession.

'I shall tell you all, gentlemen. *All*. But I am thirsty. Let me have some wine and water, and sit down while I speak.'

'Yes, yes,' we said together. She moved again to the kitchen end of the dull apartment, where there was the great hydra, and some water pots standing on a table. There were also some goblets and pitchers on a shelf. 'The water is not bad here,' she said, 'as it runs from the high Parnes. And the wine is better than you would think. Can I serve you with some?'

'No,' we said in unison. I could not have borne to eat or drink in that stinking place anyway, even had I not feared my hostess. She poured herself a drink, and quickly drank it off. Then she poured out another and returned to the place where the chairs were, setting her goblet down on the table, before she sat down in the most comfortable chair, the one with arms.

'As you will not drink with me, I must drink alone,' she said. 'I pour a libation—' and with a few words of prayer she poured some drops of the wine and water to the dirt floor. 'And now I drink. Thanks be to all the gods!' She drank deeply.

'I needed that, my throat's dry,' she said, setting the goblet down. 'Now, what can I tell you? Where to begin?'

'Why did you have to kill Ergokles?' I demanded. 'I know that's not the beginning but near the end. But what had Ergokles got to do with it?'

'What makes you say *I* killed Ergokles?'

'The boy,' Aristotle answered. 'Kleiophon told us. I suppose when you were his father's servant and concubine he was not allowed much access to you, so he

didn't know the woman he had met in this house was
Marylla. But he encountered you here as "Lykaina",
and he was sure it was dark-haired Lykaina who came
to that old people's hovel. You – as "Lykaina" – made
Kleiophon carry the poisoned water to Ergokles, so
that he fell in a stupor. And then you – or your male
accomplice – broke the man's neck.'

'Oh dear.' She shook her head. 'That silly boy! So
Kleiophon foolishly returned to Athens! Yes, I made
him an accomplice – thinking that a sure way to make
him keep away from the city. Had the lad gone on to
Korinthos, as he was supposed to do, he would have
received a message telling him to fly because of the
murder of Ergokles. You see, Kleiophon had become
troublesome, with everyone looking for him. And he
had made an impression anyway at the first hearing,
which everyone would remember. If he were questioned too much, he might break down, under pressure from Krito, and deny what he had said. Or people
might begin to suspect the trick whereby we made his
father appear to talk with him. When the lad took that
foolish start of running away, it seemed best to keep
him gone.'

'But why Ergokles?'

'Ergokles had nothing to do with it all at first. Had
he kept his stupid head out of Orthoboulos' affairs, it
would have been well with him. I loathed Ergokles of
course, because of his treatment of me when he had
me to use as half his own. But soon I was free of his
nasty bed. What happened later – it's Ergokles' own
fault! He's the sort who will never give up – never go
away! Look at all the business of the trial of

Orthoboulos. Even after he lost that, Ergokles kept sticking his head in, trying to find some way of blackmailing somebody into giving him money. He wanted to charge people just for his leaving them alone. He tried extorting money from Hermia, saying she had spirited the boy away.'

'We know he did that.'

'Yes. Well, he was also trying to extort money from Krito. Poor Krito got tired of Ergokles always insisting that Orthoboulos owed him money. Krito had hoped to get rich enough to buy horses and a chariot, you see, but he found that Orthoboulos' wealth mostly wasn't his to touch yet, and then he had the strain of Ergokles pestering him.'

'So he wanted any money that Philinos might be able to give him,' I said. 'He sold his father's slaves to him. But then Krito turned against Philinos for a while.'

'Krito became quite possessed on the subject of Hermia,' Marylla agreed. 'He got into one of his rages, and started accusing poor innocent Hermia of adultery with Philinos. But it was Ergokles who first put that silly idea in his head. Krito had to back down soon and come to his senses. Philinos had been a good friend, and could help him a lot.'

'Ergokles really failed, then, at persuading Krito that Hermia was an adulteress as well as a murderess,' I remarked. 'But it did Hermia great harm.' I thought regretfully of her torn ears.

'Ergokles made himself disagreeable to everybody. He pestered the unfortunate Hermia for compensation, and Krito too. Krito at last settled this false claim and paid him off, on Philinos' advice — which was really *my* advice. But you couldn't get rid of little Ergokles. He was just never satisfied. I should have known. He was always mean — cruel and persistent.'

'True,' said Aristotle. 'He was not satisfied, and turned his extortionate eyes upon Philinos, I suppose. As Philinos has some wealth to pick on.'

'Yes,' Marylla said slowly. 'That was so. The sun is going down.' Although it was still day, the sun was sliding away from our windows. 'May I light a lamp?'

She lit the lamp. Her hand trembled slightly as she did so. She looked at her hand meditatively. 'I never used to be easily frightened,' she remarked. 'But it's funny to look at your hand and think it will be dead and buried soon.' She shivered. 'I believe,' she remarked, 'that I am going to feel cold in a little while, when the sun goes down.' She turned to me.

'There's a little portable stove there, and some charcoal. Would you mind lighting a fire? I am not good at it. There's a firepot in the kitchen with a coal to start it with. I should be glad of the warmth — I am the sort who always feels the cold before other people do. Perhaps because Sikilia is so warm. A fire will dry this place out. It's damp because the roof is going.'

Rather surprised at her request — I was a man, and a citizen, and not her servant, after all — I did as she requested. It were best not to interrupt the flow of her story.

'You were working with Philinos,' Aristotle said, in a voice that prompted rather than accused.

She sighed. 'Yes, I admit that. But it was all my idea — he merely fell in with it because he loved me.

I promised him that if Orthoboulos were dead we could be truly together; he would never have to share me with another.'

I interrupted. 'Did not Philinos have many women friends? I have heard that he was in love with the beautiful Phryne. And wasn't he keeping – or at least sleeping with – the real black-haired Lykaina at the same time?'

She laughed. 'Oh yes, that's true. I think, you know, Philinos wanted the reputation of being a tremendous man for the women. They *all* want to sleep with Phryne, it's so good for a man's reputation. Because, you know, she won't take just anybody, even with lots of money. And Lykaina was very handsome. But that comedy was just for a season – less. Phryne dropped him and Lykaina said she was leaving. Going as far as Byzantion, in fact. So that left it clear for Philinos to begin a new affair, and to decide he would take me.'

'So – you were Philinos' tool, then. The law may go easier with you because you, a slave, were merely his agent—'

'I was no man's agent,' she retorted proudly. 'Nor a tool. Philinos wanted me. But the price for me proved to be very high,' she added bitterly. 'For it was to kill Orthoboulos. And now – alas! – I am betraying my poor Philinos. The killing, however, was my idea entirely. And the only death we intended was that of Orthoboulos.'

This was a shocking sentence to hear from her pretty mouth. She stopped for a rest, after having said it, her eyes now fixed dreamily on the dirty wall.

XXIV

Eros

There was a long silence as all three of us held our peace. It was true. Marylla had said it. She was the murderer of Orthoboulos.

'As you have admitted this crime,' said Aristotle in an altered tone, 'I believe one of us had better make notes of what you say. As I am not a citizen, Stephanos, it had better be you. Are there writing implements?'

She nodded. 'In the basket atop the little cupboard. Lykaina wrote notes. So do I.'

I found a collection of usable tablets, and brought them back to the table. 'Write as Marylla speaks, but skip the digressions,' Aristotle instructed. 'Set down "It was my idea. And the only death intended was that of Orthoboulos."'

'That is correct,' said Marylla, 'Ergokles, of course, was never an object. Until he made himself unbearably disagreeable.'

'I know how Ergokles was killed – I found his corpse

in a ditch,' I told her. 'I take it,' I paused in my writing, 'that at the old people's hut you first gave the disagreeable Ergokles a potion that would stupefy but not in itself kill him. That's why the sheep that drank it was in a stupor but is now staggering about again. It was your Philinos who broke the man's neck.'

'I admit nothing for Philinos,' said Marylla. 'I saw nothing finally done. I might have thought of a better place to hide the body than in a ditch, where a corpse is sure to call attention to itself!'

'But you planned the death of Orthoboulos? You enticed him here, to this place, for one thing?'

'Yes. It was tidier and nicer then, of course. Lykaina had already left. She had a caretaker, a young freedman, but that young man whom she told to look after her house took ill and went home to his mother. A poor dim-witted being! And really, the neighbours don't know Lykaina. They just saw a woman who went in and out. So I became "Lykaina" and had another life from time to time. I wore the black hair when I was being her. At other times I would come as myself, doing errands "for Lykaina", especially collecting written messages.'

'So you persuaded Orthoboulos to come here?'

She laughed, low in her throat. 'That was easy. I, as myself, Marylla, told him about this gorgeous hetaira who was mistress to Philinos but was pining for him. But this unhappy black-haired beauty didn't know how to meet him. I told him I loved him so excessively I was willing to help him to this great treat, without jealousy, and also to put this woman out of her pain. I begged him, for her sake, to come.

Just once. He came. And he found just me. And I
pouted and said the only way I could get him to come
somewhere outside of his own house for some exciting and noisy love-making was to say it was for
another woman. So we made love – although it was
plain daytime – and had a little meal.'

'A poisoned repast?'

She nodded. 'It was a very nice nuncheon, though
it was poisoned. I put some sleep-inducing drug in it,
to make it all easy. But the *koneion* coming on the top
of food and the poppied stuff was too much. I daresay that was why he puked after dinner. One is
supposed to take my medicine only on a moderately
empty stomach, and to evacuate bladder and bowels
first. He did the latter, fortunately, before we enjoyed
his last meal.'

'So he died here?'

'Yes. I didn't even have to stay with him all the
time. I told him that he had been sick because of too
much food and excitement, and perhaps the wine, and
he should lie down and sleep it off.'

She laughed drily. 'A surprise for him, waking up
on the banks of Styx instead of in this old house. He
went off to sleep, snoring, while his limbs stiffened.
Then his breathing got bad, and then it got really bad
– and then at last I believe it just stopped.'

'How did you get the body to where it was found?'

'Phi— my associate waited until he was dead. At
least, he was pretty sure the man was dead. And put
it on a mule, covered over with other things, so it
would just look like a load.'

'A load of oil and charcoal?'

'No. A load of sheepskins and things.'

'So that is certainly why the body had the strange shape it did,' I said. 'As if it had tried to turn a somersault. Thrown over a mule's back, head one side, feet the other.'

'That explains the pooling of blood in the head,' added Aristotle. 'But let us get this straight, Marylla. You poisoned Orthoboulos here in the middle of the day, then in the late afternoon had Philinos take his corpse by mule to the house next to Manto's. By the time it — they — arrived it would have been getting dark. Meanwhile, you went home in daylight to stay demurely in Orthoboulos' mansion. But to clear yourself, you played with the time, by creating an imaginary live Orthoboulos who spoke to his younger son at dusk.'

She looked guilty and said nothing.

'This enacting of Orthoboulos was quite elaborate,' said Aristotle. 'We know you and your accomplice took a statue and put it under the blanket, then you or your accomplice whispered. I believe this was your second male accomplice.'

'That,' I decided, 'must be Artimmes, the Phrygian. One of you whispered in the voice of a drowsy Orthoboulos. What I don't understand,' I added, 'is why one of you didn't just get under the blanket and impersonate Orthoboulos, without the trouble of the statue.'

Marylla sighed. 'You don't think as a slave has to think,' she explained. 'Any slave found lounging on the master's couch could get into *terrible* trouble — for insolence, for acting outrageously! Whereas if the

statue were found in the bed, the punishment would
not be so severe. One could have any number of expla-
nations: "It's a game to amuse the children"; "I put it
down while I looked for spiders" – that sort of thing.
But it was difficult, that statue. Artimmes was good
at mimicking Orthoboulos' voice, but he had to leave
when called, and I dropped the statue. It was too
damaged, so we had to throw it out.'

'It's been found,' I told her curtly.

'I feared its absence would be taken more note of,'
said Marylla, 'although I knew we could count on a
lot of household disturbance very shortly. And then
with the funeral and everything, nobody missed it.
Krito didn't care till later, when he ordered a marble
thing, some outdoor Nymphs, to be put up. The ugly
piece filled in the space.'

'Can you tell me this?' Aristotle enquired. 'How did
you persuade Artimmes, the Phrygian butler, to assist
you, and be your voice – did he know it was for a
murder? Was he your tool merely, or was he angry
that he was being sold to make way for the servant
from Hermia's household?'

'I have nothing to say about him or anyone,' said
Marylla doggedly. 'I must admit that Philinos did us
all a good turn – *not* accidentally – when he persuaded
Krito that his household could have nothing to do with
his father's death. He pointed out that only a weak
man allows his own servants to be tortured. So Krito
didn't allow any of us – at least Orthoboulos' old
servants – to be put to the question. Except for
Artimmes, when people were investigating the murder
the first day. He was tortured, but it was just with

pincers and slapping about, and beating with cords, and he was able to withstand it. Anyway, Krito was obsessed with Hermia alone.'

'You sent the corpse of Orthoboulos by mule,' said Aristotle thoughtfully. 'It was the fuel-seller's beast that you used? You are, as we know, a friend of Ephippos.'

She nodded. 'He used to tease me when he came to Orthoboulos' house. Wanting to kiss me or hold my hand. Silly fellow! But he knows *nothing* – really. I paid him for the use of a mule, telling him the reason was a big cleaning-up, and he believed it.'

'And knowing how useful that fellow is, you used him later to help Kleiophon escape?'

'No. Certainly not. It wasn't *my* plan that Kleiophon should run away. Not at all. But after he had done so, I realized he would most likely have gone with the fuel-seller. The boy was always fascinated by the mules. That was a help. Ephippos sent him to me – as Lykaina – and we contrived the lad's escape, Hermia and I, with the help of Manto.'

'Hermia.' I paused in my writing to ask bluntly: 'Was it always part of your plan that Hermia should be blamed for the murder of Orthoboulos?'

'Truly, no. Oddly enough. I see now that it would have served my turn better than what I did plan. I went to quite a lot of trouble, as you can see, to have Orthoboulos killed *away* from his home. We made certain that he was killed out of the way, and then that his corpse would be found in a third place – another place entirely. I wanted everybody to think the man had taken poison while at Manto's. At least, not at Manto's, but in the house next door, the brothel extension. I know Manto well, so I am familiar with the plan of her house. I knew she had the use of the house next door but that it was empty at that time. That it was empty made it relatively easy for – for my agent – to set the body down there. Though from your account, he could have done a better job of arranging the scene. That's the trouble with trusting to an agent.'

She took another sip of her wine, and leaned back in her chair. Her arms trembled a little.

'Are you chilly now?'

'A little,' she answered, languidly, with a great yawn. I put more fuel on the fire.

'Why do you yawn?' Aristotle asked sharply. 'Do you find this tedious, recounting the story of your killings?'

'Perhaps it is fear,' she said. 'What – *what* do you think they will do to me?' Aristotle was silent.

'Tell us more,' I said. 'Make us understand. You have been guilty of a horrible murder. I want to understand *why* you did it. It was not for money, for you were left nothing in Orthoboulos' will, not even your freedom. *What* made you do it?'

She yawned once more, a big gape, and then raised her head, holding her neck erect. She looked into the lamp again, staring wistfully at its small bright flame.

'Why?' I repeated.

'Oh, gentlemen, perhaps you will not understand. For it is not mercy I am asking of you – not now – but comprehension. Imagine being a woman like me, bred in Sikilia for servitude. And sent to a strange country. And then, one day, Eros unlocked my fetters, for he gave me a free feeling. I looked at this man and was struck by the glory, the inner beauty that shone from him. *I* desired him. And he, looking at me, desired me, and when it was possible he took me into his arms, and asked me – *asked* me – if I would go into his bed. He kissed me as if he would not stop, and my arms pressed him close to me, light fire running under my skin. Our souls grew together with much kissing. And then – then he took me to his bed. It was a secret union, but he spread roses over me, and called me sweet names. Divine names.

'Imagine the glory of it – of Leda and Semele and all the women of myth who were wanted by gods! That was my feeling. He stripped naked in front of me, and stood all glorious, like shining marble washed in milk. Like flowers. Oh the beauty of a man's head when it is set just right on his neck, and the glory of his shoulders. And the pleasure of being able to run one's fingers gently along the private parts, and watch the movement at one's command. And then the pleasure of his hands running round me and between me and in me – and the wonder of receiving him within in happiness, in waves of happiness! All this have I known.'

'But – you have had conjunction with more than one man?' enquired Aristotle, though not unsympathetically. 'In your situation, several men, at least.'

'Not like this. *Nothing* like this. Not with the utter harmony, and his radiance and my own desire. The joy of sleeping entwined and waking up together. This was no brothel-contest. This was not me being wanted and pawed, or needed and forced. Nor was it merely the pleasure of being loved. I tell you – I *loved*. I gave love. I myself felt the power of loving, of perfect Eros. It is as great as the poets say. And I sum up my beloved's thousand and one attractions by saying it was "his beauty" that caused it all. I looked at him and my heart turned round. I gazed on his body and my body opened. So beautiful the gods had made him, I could not ever wish to resist!'

'The power of Beauty is very great,' Aristotle said cautiously. 'All human kind, and perhaps some animals, are much struck with it in each other. It is one of our human visions of the highest good.'

She laughed slightly. 'All human kind – yes. But there is something godlike about it. Divine manifestation! Eros will not allow one to overlook Beauty, nor to analyze it away.'

'Understandable,' I remarked, 'quite understandable, I think. When I consider who he is and how he looks, and who else has been attracted to him, I cannot wonder that you should fall in love with Philinos—'

'*Philinos!*' she almost shouted. She laughed again, a harsh sound. 'You cannot be serious! No, you cannot be serious for a moment. It was not Philinos – of course not. Philinos has been but a practical instrument. No, the man I fell in love with was Orthoboulos.'

'Orthoboulos!' It was my turn to be surprised, and Aristotle's. Who could have thought of that nice man of middle height with the pleasant smile inspiring such passion?

'Oh, yes. He was the first man I ever truly loved. And the last.'

'And therefore you killed him?'
'Oh, yes. Yes.

"By the words of a Greek man persuaded
Who, God aiding, will run into Justice for what
he has done to me."'

'Ah – Medeia. So you killed him because he married
another?'
'No – no. Not because of that. Medeia was unreasonable. We – Orthoboulos and I – we talked over the
prospect of his marriage to Epikhares' widow, and I
saw it would be to his advantage to marry again, to
have a mother for his children. And more money. We
decided perhaps it would be wrong of Orthoboulos to
let go of the chance. I believe that at that time he was
sincere in what he said. Our union could still continue
as before. It was always discreet and careful. He kept
me largely apart from his boys, so they would not be
tempted by me or ashamed of him. Thus the children
knew little of me. All except Hermia's little girl; we
were together for a very short time in the women's
quarters. Little Kharis would know me again – she's
a cute little body.'
'She's a clever little thing,' I agreed, thinking back.
'But I didn't see why Orthoboulos' marrying
should change things much. We were modest and
quiet, anyway, as I say. I would work humbly and
unobtrusively, spending much of my time on weaving. After all, I could not marry him. He could not
marry a slave. Even if he set me free, he could not
marry a foreigner! It is against Athenian law and

custom. But my beloved had sworn he would always
love me and we should always be together. So I didn't
think a new marriage would interfere with our *real*
life, our real love.'

'Yet the marriage did interfere,' prompted Aristotle.

'Yes. And how soon! Then my affection was turned
into great bitterness, for I found that to please Hermia,
his new wife, Orthoboulos was willing to sell his slaves
– *all* his slaves! The *all* to include me! As if I were no
more than an old bald butler, or some assistant to a
cook. He promised to spare me the humiliation of the
open slave-market, and agreed with Philinos to sell
me to him. That bargain was first clapped up by
Orthoboulos, and only ratified by Krito. A little later,
it came to the boy that his father had been cuckolded,
so to speak. But at the time he just thought how handy
it was, since he needed money, so he formally handed
me over and got the price. Krito sold another slave at
the same time.'

'Yes,' I agreed. 'We worked that out before,
ourselves. The Phrygian butler, Artimmes, was sold
to Philinos at that same time. Artimmes – now beyond
our reach, as Philinos has sent him well away from
any more questioning, as far as Egypt. Surely no accident. How quick Philinos was to get control of the
two slaves involved with him in the great crime.'

'But Orthoboulos—' Marylla's voice trembled with
passion, 'Orthoboulos – how could he! Orthoboulos
had disposed of me, without a second thought – like
an old table or chair when you want to get new ones!'

'So the motive of the murder was love – and
revenge?'

She nodded, slowly and stiffly. Breathing heavily from her emotion, she reached for the goblet of wine again, and slowly moved it back and forth, her arm trembling.

'Aie!' she cried softly, and then groaned. 'He took back his love and left me empty and bruised. How much better off I would be if he had been a more vulgar sort of master! He agreed cheerfully to sell me to Philinos, and my love turned to rage and jealousy. Not of Hermia – I am not like the Medeia who wished to torment and kill the new bride of Jason. Hermia was not even very real to me. I wanted to punish *him*.'

'How,' I asked, remembering our efforts at the prison, 'how and where did you get the hemlock? Did someone give you *koneion* already compounded, or did you make it yourself?'

'I made it myself. We Sikilians are very good cooks. Someone – some lover – for a joke had given Lykaina some *koneion* from Mantineia. She kept it secretly in a pot buried in the back garden. Lykaina's the kind of woman who never throws anything away! I knew about it.'

'Making the compound was a risk to you,' I remarked. 'It cannot have been pleasant. So you particularly wanted Orthoboulos to die by hemlock?'

'Orthoboulos murdered our love, so he should die as a murderer ought.'

'And to be found in a brothel?'

'I had sworn to myself and to all the gods known in Sikilia that no other woman would have him. Even if he died surrounded by females.'

'Ah,' said Aristotle. 'So it was a kind of jest.'

'Yes. And he had been in trouble in a certain brothel before – as everybody knew, because of the trial. People would *laugh* at him even after he was dead. That was my thought. He would lose honour as well as life. I was a little sorry for the children, though. And I think you will admit, my plan – to kill him here, not in his own dwelling, and have him found dead in a brothel-house – was exactly calculated *not* to throw suspicion on his wife. And it is only the spite of Krito that persecutes Hermia, not I.'

She sighed heavily, and slouched in her chair. I was aghast by what I had heard, and strained to write everything down. But the horrible tale, and the horrible smell of this house was giving me a serious headache, and as the sun went down it was harder and harder to see . . .

'Are you all right, Stephanos?' Aristotle asked.

I pulled myself up with a jerk. 'Yes. Though it is very close in here.'

'It is,' said Marylla. 'It smells, I know. The rats get in all the time now. Whoever owns this house should get a dog who likes hunting, the kind that goes down ratholes.'

'Whoever owns—? Does this place belong to one of Lykaina's men friends? Why doesn't he take better care of it?'

'Oh, some man gave it to her permanently for her use,' said Marylla. 'Of course being a woman she can't legally own it – any more than *you*, man of Stageira, can own your school or whatever it is. Lykaina thought she might come back someday, so she didn't let that man know she was heading off. But I believe Lykaina's dead. There's nobody much to mourn her – her family was from some place in Sparta – Kythera, I think. Where Aphrodite was born. You'd think Phryne would come from Aphrodite's home, but it was Lykaina, I guess.'

'How did she die? When did you learn this – how do you know she's dead?'

'Lykaina took a trip to Byzantion to find new adventures. And poor girl, she never got to Byzantion, but died on her way. Got in with the wrong crowd at a rough party in a port and didn't survive. One wild night that must have been! I was lucky enough to hear this from a sailor. You can't question him unfortunately, he sailed off to Alexander's new city in Egypt. Lykaina, a woman and a foreigner, could not own this property, so she couldn't leave it to her sister.'

'Her sister? Oh – is it Manto – is that Lykaina's sister? Both Spartans, then, daughters of a woman of Sparta, or more correctly of the *perioikoi*. From Kythera.'

'Manto is her sister. Born in Attika, and free.'

'Does Manto know her younger sister is dead?'

'No. At least, I certainly didn't tell her. She knows of course that I have been looking after Lykaina's house while she is away, and even taking her name from time to time. But Manto doesn't know the woman is dead. Why make Manto miserable to no good purpose? We cannot, after all, even be *sure* about Lykaina's death. It's not as if a funeral were needed. It seemed most convenient to keep up the pretence that Lykaina was alive, just away a good deal.'

'Surely a lot of other whores know the real Lykaina?'

'A few. Especially in Phryne's circle, but I don't mix
with them. I knew Lykaina about as well as anyone,
because of her connection to Philinos, who supported
Orthoboulos in his trial. Nobody would be surprised
to find another hetaira using the name, it's common
enough in our profession. Many of us are she-wolves.
Wolf-ladies, if you will. After all, you, O Aristotle of
the Lykeion, whose school is known by the name of
the wolf-region and wolf-god, should have some affin-
ity for the name. You too are a wolf – in your own
way.'

'You took her name because you wanted this private
dwelling for your use?'

'That wasn't the main reason. But it seemed best
not to let this property go. Of course, it was not always
in this condition, I kept it a little better once. I liked
having a place to come to, and this summer it became
easy for me to get into Lykaina's skin from time to
time. Once I went to live in Philinos' house, it was
easier still, his deme is so near Akharnai.'

'Philinos allowed you to wander about like that?' I
asked in surprise. 'Your master? After all, you are –
were – his slave.'

'Oh, Philinos. I think he liked me best when I was
playing at being Lykaina, with the black wig on –
that excites him. I would say I was a Spartan fierce
woman, uncontrollable, and had to discipline him. I
had a little whip, and the wig. I gave him orders. Even
when I heard Lykaina was dead, I never told him –
it might have put him off our amusements, and we
got very engaged in the Lykaina-play. He became
excited by me when he first met me – at the time of

the law case brought on by Ergokles. Philinos guessed that I might play games. But it was a long while before he got to play a game with me, I saw to that.'

'Oh!' I exclaimed. 'So we can see why Philinos became so infatuated – so willing to do as you wished!'

'Well.' She shrugged. 'Different men like different things. "Many forms of the divine," as the poet says. Philinos has always given me a good deal of leeway, as long as I would come back and amuse him. I told him, you see, that he would never have my *willing* favour until Orthoboulos paid for what he did. Oh, I had to make up some stories about what Orthoboulos did to me! A lot of my tales were of nasty things that actually *were* done to me – but by Ergokles, not the divine Orthoboulos. I also told him that Orthoboulos made fun of him – Philinos can't stand being made fun of. He stormed a bit about that. But with me he would often act very humble for days. Other times, he would be angry – and then penitent, and I would have to beat him and that sufficed for a time. I'll say this for Philinos, he's quite generous. If I say I have my monthly flow, for example, he gives me extra money and lets me be.'

'And I suppose Orthoboulos, once he was married to Hermia, didn't keep an eye on your whereabouts,' I suggested, as tactfully as I could. No use setting this Medeia raving.

'Once he was married to Hermia,' Marylla agreed bitterly, 'my wonderful Orthoboulos didn't much care where I was. So I could build up my life as Lykaina. By the way, when I wrote that letter to you as Lykaina, I wasn't really in this house, though Sikon came in here and fetched it and gave it to you – as instructed. Sikon is whipped and branded and looks dreadful, but he's really not a dull boy at all. Sikon, by the way, is another man from Orthoboulos' household. He was sold to somebody else after, and ran away and got the iron collar. Then Philinos bought him, cheap. Sikon does a lot of my errands. I had already designed a letter in case you came poking around. But I knew I couldn't meet you face to face as Lykaina.'

'So you had prepared to murder in the persona of Lykaina – for a long time?' I exclaimed.

'It really didn't take long to put all in readiness. Ergokles, too, was still handily in the background – if the victim had a real and obvious enemy, it seemed likely the murder charge would fall on him. The perfect opportunity. So it seemed to me.'

She reached again for the wine goblet, with both hands. 'Love and revenge. I have had both. Revenge is not sweet, but savoury. Love is sweet.'

A driblet of wine ran from the corner of her mouth. Aristotle started up with a cry.

'You are ill! You have taken poison! Marylla – you are dying while we sit here!'

'Hemlock!' I ejaculated. I ran around the table to the woman where she slumped in her chair. When I shook her, she showed no reaction. I pinched her lower leg but she did not notice.

'It's so,' said Marylla quietly. 'I shall soon not speak at all. I took extract of *koneion* in that goblet of wine, before I started to talk. So my limbs are losing all feeling. No torturers will be able to harm me, even if I still breathe.'

'How insanely stupid I was not to see this! And I a doctor, a descendant of Asklepios! And how foolish of me to come without Phokon!' Aristotle cried distractedly. 'O Stephanos, can you run for a—'

'That big slave is coming to the door,' I said, hearing before he did the sound of heavy feet. 'Suppose he attacks us? Can we fight him off?'

'Don't talk nonsense. Let him in.' And I opened the door to the heavy slave with the iron collar.

'Your mistress is very ill,' I cried distractedly. 'Please go to Akharnai town as fast as you can and fetch a doctor—'

'And a magistrate!' ordered Aristotle. 'It is urgent. As she's a small woman, the dose may act more quickly. Ask the doctor or any other citizen to fetch the magistrate. She has been poisoned. If – you may be shy of approaching such people, but here is a message—' Taking up one of our remaining tablets, he scrawled quickly upon it.

'Any respectable person of Akharnai will be able to help. But *hurry*, please!' he begged, and the slave went off. We could hear him running.

'Doctors will do no good,' sighed Marylla. 'I am going, you know.

> "To die some strange desire seizes me,
>   To gaze upon the forms of lotus banks,
>   The dew-drenched lotuses of Akheron."'

'How long have we got?' I wondered aloud.
'Not long,' said Marylla proudly.
'Some time, I think,' said Aristotle, 'and you know,

Stephanos, there is the antidote for this. You have heard Theophrastos speak of it. It may not prevent the final ill effect, but might prolong life by mitigating the effects of the *koneion*.'

'Oh, that special Indian pepper,' I said, remembering Theophrastos' lecture on plants. 'So she could still testify at a hearing.'

Marylla looked at us with pleading eyes. 'You cannot want to prolong my miserable life! Let me go, I pray you. I have told you all that you need to know.'

We sat there, in silence for a time, the two of us looking with gathering horror at the dying Marylla, who yawned and belched and then gritted her teeth as if in determination to hurry the process along without yielding any other sign of her pain or discomfort. I do not know how long we were there. Marylla could no longer sit straight, and was long past raising a cup to her lips. She slumped against the arms of her chair like a doll with cut strings.

'Better move her — let her lie down,' said Aristotle.

And with surprising gentleness he moved her, while I improvised a couch with an old cushion and the two chairs. (Neither of us mentioned the stinking mattress in the yard.) We set the portable stove next to her, so she could have a little warmth in her inexorable coldness. Her breathing was getting more irregular. The rat-foot smell was everywhere. After handling her, I gagged and threw up in a corner.

'Cold. I'm cold,' said Marylla. Aristotle moved the portable stove closer to her, and added a little more charcoal. 'I cannot feel my legs any more,' she whispered, and lay immobile, waiting.

Noises. Someone coming. At last. Feet – and light. A lantern!

'Thanks be to Asklepios – no, he's quite wrong for this occasion. But I am grateful *somebody* is coming,' said Aristotle. The door opened, to admit the burly slave and a middle-aged man, a citizen by his dress and beard.

'You need a physician?' he enquired. 'I have sent for one – he lives nearby. But your fellow here said you needed an Akharnaian and a magistrate. I am one of the officials of the deme, and I have studied medicine a little.'

'You are just what we need,' said Aristotle. 'This woman has taken poison. I have not dared to try to make her puke it out. I fear we are too late.'

'Why has she taken poison?'

'Because she has murdered Orthoboulos of Athens, and later killed Ergokles also of Athens.'

The newcomer had entered the room and taken off his cloak; seeing him ensconced, the slave Sikon slipped off into the night – I presumed to fetch the real doctor. The Akharnaian turned to the slight figure on the improvised bed. He registered complete astonishment.

'You? You – a little thing like that?'

'Yes,' came Marylla's weakened rasping voice. 'I have killed. I killed Orthoboulos. Hemlock. I helped . . . I killed . . . Ergokles. All was my own doing. Anyone else . . . was simply my agent . . . or tool. These . . . taken it all down.' She looked at us with lacklustre eyes, in which there was some shadow of rebuke.

'She should repeat this in front of more examiners, in the local gaol—'

'If only we can get some antidote!' I exclaimed. 'If you have the Indian pepper, we may prolong her time on earth, and have a public hearing.'

'No!' It ought to have been a scream from Marylla, but it came almost as a squeak. With effort, she began with one of her poor pawing hands to try to move a ring off her finger.

'Careful – the ring may have poison in it!' warned Aristotle.

I rushed over to grab the gold circlet with its one stone from her finger, and was successful. With a despairing cry, quite loud this time, and with a supreme effort, she took in her trembling hands burning charcoal, and before I could stop her triumphantly conveyed it into her own mouth. There was a horrible sizzling, a smell of burning, and smoke. The girl choked terribly, heaving as much as she was able in her paralysis, her eyes staring as if they would burst their sockets. The fire reached her lungs, smothering as well as burning. Before our eyes, Marylla triumphantly expired.

===—⬧○⬧—===

EROS AND AFTER

'Why, oh why, did I not foresee what she would do?' Aristotle said in futile self-reproach. It was morning when we were at last able to talk privately about what had happened. First there was a long dreary evening that I prefer to forget, of escorting poor Marylla's body to the local lockup in Akharnai, and giving testimony. We spoke at length in front of an arkhon, who had been hurriedly dragged out of bed. Testimony was also heard from our new acquaintance, the respectable magistrate, who most fortunately had been with us at the end. My notes had to be deciphered by others, and attested, and the whole strange statement endorsed. We were told that a messenger would be dispatched to Athens even before dawn, to arrive as the gates were opening: the Basileus would be informed as soon as it was light. Doubtless this information would put an end to the trial of Hermia.

By the end of all this ado, Athens' city gates had

long closed for the night; we put up at someone's house. I had a terrible headache and upset stomach, and spent a most wretched night. I felt better when the light came and we could mount our hired mules and ride to Athens. We went immediately to my house, where at least we could wash and have a breakfast.

'I ought to have known,' repeated Aristotle in self-reproach. 'I who have so often talked of the death of Sokrates! I should have guessed, as soon as Marylla began talking so composedly, that she had some plan. What kind of doctor can sit with someone who is dying and not notice! And all the time we were smelling the *koneion* in that house.'

'Don't mention that smell. I fear it has got into my very clothes. The smell of hemlock was apparently explained by the mattress, and likewise the dead rat. Who would expect such conduct from a mere slave! What a pity you could not use the antidote.'

'Oh, Stephanos, of course I don't believe in the antidote. It is alleged to exist, but it hasn't been properly tested. And nobody in Attika has any Indian pepper. I fear what I said about an antidote to hemlock was a bluff. A kind of threat, to make her feel less in control and induce her to say to us everything she knew. But yesterday evening – how stupid! – I didn't suspect anything – when she took that drink and began to talk.'

'And one doesn't connect a lovely girl like that with hemlock.'

'Nor a slavish mind with such decision. She was lovely. Not in Phryne's style, but beguiling – well, I dare say Kirke was very fetching when Odysseus first saw her. And Medeia.'

'But Kirke was partly a goddess and Medeia a princess. Marylla was only a slave. Yet she has brought down three men. First Orthoboulos. Second, Ergokles. And last of all, Philinos.'

'Yes. We shall have to endure the trial of Philinos, I fear. At least there are clearly no political motives in Marylla's case. And as I have the letter from Kleiophon, which I shall also submit to the Chief Arkhon and the Basileus, I hope we have the means to save Hermia from any further hearings. Perhaps, Stephanos, your future father-in-law will consent to let you marry.'

'He might not change his mind. There's still the trial of Philinos, and I shall have to be a witness in that. You, too.'

'Let us hope, however, Smikrenes will be rationally softened. Better for you to marry than run around to brothels all the time – they do not seem to be lucky places for you. But I wish we did not have to relive again the doings and death of Marylla in the trial of Philinos.'

'Philinos will say this is all Marylla's own concoction, and that he had nothing to do with any of it,' I said, feeling proud of my sagacity.

In the event, we were both wrong. For the beautiful Philinos was prudent also, and we did not realize he had been forewarned. Sikon, the slave with the iron ring and the brand, belonged to Philinos, and had taken our very first letter to "Lykaina" to his master. Philinos, sufficiently intelligent to realize that our enquiries regarding "Lykaina" might direct attention to him, was already alerted. The same slave, as soon as he saw dying Marylla speaking with the local magistrate, had straight away carried the news to his master, who took appropriate action. Philinos left his house that night and had departed from Attika before the Basileus had been made aware of Marylla's statement. Our document and its commentaries took this magistrate a long while to puzzle out. The day had passed before the Basileus (with the help of others' advice) decided not only that Philinos was guilty but also that there was no case against Hermia.

Philinos was charged with the murder of both Orthoboulos and Ergokles, and was to be tried by the court of the Areopagos for homicide. Tried in his absence – always the best way to be tried for homicide. The city officials and the relatives of both Hermia and Orthoboulos were not happy about this, however, and commissioned some men to hunt for the master and slave. Arkhias was not chosen (they knew nothing of him) but Theramenes the witness-hunter took a leading role, with his strong slave, and directed the other pursuers.

Their endeavours at tracking were successful, for they came upon the runaway and his servant in the island of Hydra. But they did not actually take Philinos – at least not alive. For when he saw the pursuers closing in, Sikon, the big slave in the iron collar, seized a dagger and plunged it briskly into Philinos. Whether it was fear of torture as a witness, or further fear that he himself would be charged with his master's crimes, that prompted Sikon's swift and unexpected course of action cannot be known. This big fellow then swiftly ran off, and actually escaped, as the pursuing party were so anxious to seize and question Philinos. The beautiful citizen, however, could not aid them, as he lay gasping his last on the ground, blood and guts spilling out slowly.

So Philinos' corpse was taken back to Athens and he was declared guilty and unworthy of any funereal memorial. The problem of the trial had vanished, like the slave Sikon himself. He had probably taken ship for Asia or Egypt, so speculation went. Such a big noticeable fellow as Sikon, who was clearly branded, would surely be apprehended, people said. But time went by and he was not caught.

The death of Philinos made an exciting story, and I noticed that the narrative became very fluid. It was not long before everyone spoke of Philinos as the major actor in all these events, assisted by a trusty slave-woman whom he had desired and who had been fascinated by his beauty. For reasons of his own (usually explained as desire for money, as well as the pursuit of a beautiful Sikilian girl), Philinos had murdered Orthoboulos, and then Ergokles. Ergokles began to grow dim, as his particular resentment of Orthoboulos became displaced onto Philinos. Marylla faded out of the story, except as a beautiful object, and a trusty tool in the murders. In some versions Marylla became a model of loyalty, killing herself rather than giving up her master Philinos to the harshness of justice.

The happy event was the liberation of Hermia, which her relatives insisted on straight away. She was released with proclamations of her innocence – though these could do nothing to repair her ears. Mediators stepped in to help arrange affairs between herself, Krito and her relatives, so she could at least get her dowry back, and salvage some of the wealth of Epikhares. Hermia and her daughter, talkative little Kharis, went to live elsewhere. Phanodemos recovered his position. Almost exactly a year later he was a member of a religious commission given special honours by Athenians.

Hermia was soon married again, to a man who was ready and able to litigate with Krito. Krito, though young, faced a future of endless lawsuits, but he had – and has – political ambitions. Debts and lawsuits do not always hamper success in the public sphere, as witness the careers of Demosthenes and Aristogeiton.

Kleiophon was heard from, but not seen. On his sea-journey he was befriended by a merchant of Naukratis, and stayed with this merchant in Egypt, becoming his assistant, and later son-in-law and partner. Strange to think of the naive Kleiophon succeeding in business as a merchant, but so it came to pass, after the years had rolled over his head.

Praxitiles produced his statue of 'Aphrodite', which has since been much celebrated. I saw it, all blooming and beautiful in new marble; most of the men who saw it at the first exhibition were physically moved by it, and I was no exception. This statue caused a scandal at the time. The people of Kos, who had commissioned an Aphrodite for their temple, rejected the piece when they saw how very naked it was. The men of Knidos, equally rich and less moral perhaps, purchased the image. It has certainly repaid them in

the number of visitors who come to Knidos just to
see it.

Praxitiles gave his lovely statue of Eros to Phryne,
as promised, with a fine verse:

Eros I am, Praxitiles portrayed
From archetype of passion in his heart,
To Phryne given as Love's price here paid.
No more throw I Love's poison with my dart
But through the eyes of lovers who have gazed
Upon Me, and acknowledged all my art.

This fine statue of Eros Phryne later gave to
Thespiai, as she had said she would. And it is to
Thespiai that lovers and lovers of beauty come to look
at Praxitiles' Eros and seek out the sweet poison power
which claims now to reside in the statue rather than
his bow and arrow. Phryne herself, the lovely hetaira,
continued to flourish for a long while.

Manto's brothel went on as usual – so I suppose. I
was careful to give it a wide berth, now I knew that
Kynara had fancied a permanent arrangement with
me. I was not willing to fall in with her plans.
Tryphaina's brothel fell on hard times for a while.

One day, I was passing through the marketplace of
Peiraieus and nearly stumbled on a bread-seller. One
of those women who make porridge and flat bread-
cakes, kneeling on the ground by their portable ovens,
and calling to the passers by 'Sition! Sition!' A hag, I
thought idly, like the rest, with shaky limbs and ugly
face. It was mere accident that I looked at this woman
more closely and saw something familiar. Her limbs

were crooked, and would hardly bear her up, some of her fingers seemed misshapen, and one tooth was missing. Yet she was not as old as the others – she was somebody I had once encountered . . .

'Thisbe?' I said tentatively. 'Thisbe of Thebes?' It was the flute-girl who had unwittingly supplied the mock *kykeion* of which Phryne had drunk. The effects of the torture had been permanent, evidently. The bread-seller shook her head at me. 'I go by another name now,' she said. 'Please, just buy some bread and go away.' She was whistling a little every time she spoke, through the gap where one of her front teeth used to be. This condition made uttering the word *sition* particularly difficult, which seemed a pity in her new profession. I tossed her an obol, but took no bread from her hands.

'It is true, what you say,' I remarked to Aristotle a little later. 'Brothels are perhaps not very lucky for me. It seems just as well that Smikrenes has consented to let me marry his daughter in Gamelion, as we arranged before. Ungrateful old boor – he should be glad for his daughter to marry such a respectable Athenian, buried as she is in the country, even working in the wet and the mud like a peasant! But he's as glad as a furze bush and as grateful as a pair of old boots.'

'You will have to put up with him,' said Aristotle. 'You always knew what he is like.'

'When Philomela comes, we won't have to bring Smikrenes with us. Meanwhile, if I want to go to a brothel I shall be puzzled which one to choose. Tryphaina's is out of the question, and I dare not go back to Manto's. I found that pathetic little bitch

Kynara has designs on me!' And I told him about the girl's fantastic plan to live in a separate abode as my concubine.

'It is not unreasonable of her, after all,' said Aristotle. 'Some men do so. Wiser whores would say it was foolish of her to tell you her wishes so frankly.'

'It is by no means my plan of life!' I exclaimed. 'And the only thing worse I now think is to live as people like Orthoboulos do, treating a slave in one's own household like a mistress. Disgusting! Contaminating the household and undermining all order.'

Aristotle, to my surprise, turned a rosy hue. 'Not all men can agree,' he said mildly. 'There is a – there may be conditions where this is most suitable. Better than consorting with unknown females promiscuously in some tawdry place of resort, and paying money. Not, I grant you, while a wife is alive, and in the house.'

'I suppose there are many ways in which people arrange their lives,' I admitted. 'I know some think having hetairai living independently and getting rich is worse. The Spartans – you and Aristogeiton both tell me – had no prostitutes in the old days. They could just jump on any helot they fancied, I suppose, and didn't need to pay for anything.'

At this point the slave Herpyllis came into Aristotle's *andron*, to take the plates away, and Aristotle quite loudly began to talk of pottery. So our conversation changed, and I was never satisfied that I had worked out what was the best way for a man – a man with natural desires – to live.